KATHARINE SUSANNAH PRICHARD

(1883–1969) was born in Fiji, the daughter of the editor of *The Fiji Times*. Her family moved when she was three and she spent her childhood in Melbourne and Launceston. In 1904, at the age of twenty-one, Katharine went to South Gippsland to become, briefly, a governess. Her father committed suicide in 1907 and the following year she began her autobiographical novel, *The Wild Oats of Han*, though this book was not published for many years. Katharine Susannah Prichard made her first visit to London in 1908 and returned in 1912, working as a journalist. In 1915 her first novel, *The Pioneers*, won the Hodder & Stoughton All Empire Novel Competition enabling her to return to Australia to devote herself to writing 'about Australia and the realities of life for the Australian people'; her second novel, *Windlestraws*, was published in 1916. In 1919 she married Hugo Throssell and moved with him to a house on the hills of Greenmount near Perth in Western Australia; their son was born three years later. Meanwhile she continued writing novels: *Black Opal* was published in 1921, followed by *Working Bullocks* (1926), *The Wild Oats of Han* (1928), *Coonardoo* (1928) – winner, with M. Barnard Eldershaw's *A House is Built*, of the *Bulletin* prize – *Haxby's Circus* (1930), *Intimate Strangers* (1937), *Moon of Desire* (1941) and the goldfields trilogy, *The Roaring Nineties* (1946), *Golden Miles* (1948) and *Winged Seeds* (1950). Her autobiography, *Child of the Hurricane*, was published in 1964, and three years later her last novel, *Subtle Flame*, appeared. Katharine Susannah Prichard's novels have been translated into many languages including Russian, Polish and Czech; she also wrote plays and poetry and her short stories were published in four collections between 1932 and 1967.

A committed communist, pacifist and founder member of the Communist Party of Australia, she visited Russia in 1933. In her absence her husband committed suicide and, returning to Australia, she threw herself further into political work. One of the founders of the Movement Against War and Fascism, she attended the National Anti-War Congress in Melbourne in 1934 and at the outbreak of the Spanish Civil War organized the Spanish Relief Committee in Western Australia. In 1943 she became a member of the Communist Party's Central Committee. Katharine Susannah Prichard was awarded the World Council's silver medallion for services to peace in 1959. On her death at the age of eighty-six, her coffin draped with the Red Flag, she was given a Communist funeral and her ashes scattered near her home on the slopes of Greenmount.

Virago also publish *The Roaring Nineties* and *Winged Seeds*.

The dreamers wait. What can the spirit urge
   Against the madness of this sorry day?
How can the timid form of Peace emerge
   Unless the marshals let the dreamers say?
And they are few and most forsaken, Lord,
   Who slaved and suffered for their human hope,
Though Thou shalt give the martyrs to the sword,
   Preserve the future from the hangman's rope!
Preserve for us, O God, the voice of those
   Who, towering o'er the tempest, speak not yet
With audibility, the battle throws
   Their protest back against their faces, wet
   With tears of helplessness and huge regret.
Preserve them for the moment when their word
   Above the ruinous carnage may be heard.

'To God from the Weary Nations'
FURNLEY MAURICE

GOLDEN MILES

KATHARINE SUSANNAH PRICHARD

WITH A NEW INTRODUCTION
BY DRUSILLA MODJESKA

To

DOON

Published by VIRAGO PRESS Limited 1984
41 William IV Street, London WC2N 4DB

First published by the Australasian Publishing Company by
arrangement with Jonathan Cape 1948

Virago edition offset from first edition

British Library Cataloguing in Publication data

Prichard, Katharine Susannah
Golden Miles
I. Title
823 [F]   PR6031.R57

ISBN 0-86068-416-4

Printed in Great Britain by The Anchor Press at Tiptree, Essex.

INTRODUCTION

In 1968, the year before she died, Katharine Susannah Prichard published an essay which her son describes as 'her literary testament'. In it she quotes Rodin that art should 'seek to understand the world and make it understood'. This, she says, was the impulse that drove her writing; it clearly underlies *Golden Miles* and the goldfields trilogy of which it is the second volume. In the same essay she describes the personal origins of the trilogy. When gold was discovered at Larkinville in Western Australia in November 1930 she and her husband, Jim Throssell, joined the 'rush'. There she glimpsed the flavour of the pioneering existence which had always attracted her but which, by 1930, existed more in Australian mythology than historical reality: 'I took a hand on the "shaker", in the morning;' she wrote, 'in the evening old miners and prospectors used to come round the camp fire and tell yarns of rushes to Coolgardie and Kalgoorlie: of the fortunes made and lost in "the roaring nineties". I was thrilled by it all. The trilogy unwound every night before I could sleep.' But it was not until she could go to the goldfields again and live with the miners long enough to understand 'every phase of a miner's life' that she could embark on the trilogy. She read newspapers and old records and took 'her Sally' to the pub: 'There she foregathered with friends, some of them famous prostitutes of the early days . . . Sometimes the memories were poured out so hilariously that the barman had to call: "Hey! Not so much noise in the Ladies!"'[1] It was almost a decade after the Larkinville rush before she began to write the trilogy.

The Roaring Nineties begins the narrative of the trilogy in the early 1890s and chronicles Sally Gough's youth, the early years of her marriage and the birth of her four children. Through her and her family it also chronicles the social history of the goldfield towns as they changed from camp sites to the large functioning towns of Boulder and Kalgoorlie. *The Roaring Nineties* integrates the narrative of the Gough

1. Katharine Susannah Prichard 'Some Perceptions and Aspirations'. Reprinted in Ric Throssell (ed.) Katharine Susannah Prichard, *Straight Left*, Sydney, Wild and Woolley, 1982, pp 206–218.

family with an analysis of the mining industry in its prospecting years, and the struggle of the miners against the incursions of capital. It is through the conflicts and concerns of the family and their community that the situation of the small-scale miners could be dramatised. *The Roaring Nineties* is usually considered the most successful volume of the trilogy. When it appeared in 1946 it was well received and was soon translated into nine languages, mostly Eastern European. *Golden Miles* appeared two years later, written during the final year of the Second World War. It takes up the story of the Gough family and the goldfields from 1914 to 1927. At the heart of that period was, of course, the First World War.

The 1914–18 War had been a formative period for Katharine Prichard. Her first novel had been published in 1915 when she was in London 'earning her laurels' as a journalist. *The Pioneers* won the Australian section of the Hodder and Stoughton All Empire Novel competition. It was 1916 and she returned to Australia with some money in her pocket, a successful novel to her name and a strong but as yet ill-defined social conscience. She hated the war 'bitterly and furiously'.[2] Her brother was killed in 1916 and in March of the year before she had visited a clearing station in Northern France and had seen the wounded within sound of the artillery. On her return to Australia she joined the campaign against conscription, which was put to the Australian people by referendum twice and both times defeated. There she met other Australian radicals and like so many of her generation was profoundly affected by the Russian Revolution. She began to read Marx and in 1920 was a foundation member of the Communist Party in Australia. For the rest of her life she remained a communist and an active party worker. Despite the time absorbed by Party work, her writing flourished. *Black Opal* was published in 1921 and by 1933 she had written several plays and five more novels, each taking a different aspect of Australian life, the timber workers in *Working Bullocks*, Aborigines and race relations in *Coonardoo*, and *Brumby Innes*, a travelling circus in *Haxby's Circus*. All were marked by strong women characters and by careful research which located the action in a recognisable and detailed historical and political context. Katharine Prichard prided herself on the thoroughness of her research and always considered her writing integral to her

2. Quoted in Ric Throssell, *Wild Weeds and Wild Flowers*, Sydney, Angus & Robertson, 1975, p.191.

political work. Marxism gave her the confidence she lacked as a younger woman.

As an Australian writer she identified herself with a radical nationalist and realist tradition of writing, which functioned as a reference point for writers of several generations. At the same time, for all the emphasis on realism and historical and political accuracy, Katharine Prichard was, like most writers of her generation, also influenced by the developments in writing which reached a peak in years immediately after World War I and which are loosely referred to as modernist. In Katharine Prichard's case it was D.H. Lawrence who had the greatest impact, and she herself said he 'had a liberating effect on the writers of his time, with regard to style, construction, the discussion of sex and thought processes. For that we are indebted to him'.[3] She did not like what Lawrence did with his writing and towards the end of her life she denied that he had influenced her work. In her later years she was vehemently against modernism, casting a retrospective light on her writing which is misleading. For one can see modernist traces in her work of the twenties and early thirties particularly in her writing about sexuality and the unconscious. By the time the trilogy appeared, this influence was less in evidence and for a combination of political and personal reasons she had moved much more wholeheartedly into the mode of socialist realism. Her output slowed down between *Intimate Strangers*, written by 1933 though not published until 1937, and *The Roaring Nineties* published in 1946. In 1933 she had visited the U.S.S.R. where she met writers and critics and discussed Soviet aesthetics, which were then approaching their most rigid phase of orthodoxy. The modernism in writing, painting and film which flourished in the early years of the Revolution had been discredited and the Comintern had ruled that socialist realism was the correct mode for writers in the international communist movement. Interacting with this were the political crises of the thirties which culminated in war. It was a period of renewed political urgency when many people felt, like Katharine Susannah Prichard, that socialism was the only way out of a terrifying spiral of depression, fascism and war. For many socialist writers, modernism came to be seen as an aspect of the decadence which was widely associated with the rise of fascism. This political dynamic was underscored for Katharine Susannah Prichard by the death of her

3. Ric Throssell (ed.), *Straight Left*, p.188.

husband. Jim Throssell committed suicide as Katharine returned from the Soviet Union in 1933. Shocked and mourning, left alone with a child on the outskirts of Perth and regarded in that conservative town as 'the red witch of Darlington', Katharine Prichard moved towards the Party for support and to fill the vacuum so abruptly created. And, of course the Party, despite its rigidities during the Stalinist period, did offer women mobility, intellectual respect and comradeship that were hard to find anywhere else in a place like Perth in 1933.

Jack Lindsay, her friend and fellow Marxist writer, sees a continuity between *The Roaring Nineties* and her earlier novels. In the first volume of the trilogy she was still able to focus on the 'triadic movement' between people, nature and work as it existed in the relatively simple economy of early prospecting and alluvial gold mining. She was in her full creative stride with *The Roaring Nineties*, the period which the radical nationalists returned to again and again, the site of a potent mythology. With *Golden Miles*, Jack Lindsay argues, she ran into problems because she was no longer writing about a simple economic situation in which political and industrial issues could be dramatised with relative ease through the personal lives of a small group of people. For Jack Lindsay, like the Marxist critic Georg Lukács, this inter-penetration between the life of individuals, dramatised in action, and a socialist understanding and elucidation of the movement of history is at the heart of socialist realism.[4]

By 1914 when *Golden Miles* opens, the mining industry was under capitalist ownership and control and an analysis of the industry involved international capital and foreign affairs as well as Australian political economy. The alluvial miners and free prospectors of the 1890s had had some degree of control over their work, and their struggles for alluvial rights could be explained by and large by local conditions. By 1914 the miners had become wage labourers with no control over the industry. The relationship between the men in the mines, the Gough boys and the individuals in the community and the mining industry were both much more complex and less immediate. The struggle for working conditions and the process of unionisation and socialist politics on the goldfields could be dramatised in narrative action as it did

4. Jack Lindsay, 'The Park and the Whole: The achievement of Georg Lukács' and 'The Novels of Katharine Susannah Prichard' in *Decay and Renewal: Critical essays on Twentieth Century Writing*, Sydney, Wild and Woolley; London, Lawrence and Wishart, 1976.

interpenetrate the lives of the characters. But the dealings of international capital and the politics of military strategy could not. *Golden Miles* gets around this problem by presenting those issues in dialogue, a technique which is frequently cumbersome.

Yet for all that it has problems, *Golden Miles* is, for me, the most interesting of the trilogy. Written by a woman in her sixties, it looks back to a period in history by which she was deeply touched. It covers the period of her own initiation into politics, the early period of her marriage, the birth of her son. It is a novel that contains the passion of her own remembering. It is also the novel in which she finally gives Sally Gough her head and allows her the emotional adventures she doggedly refused her in *The Roaring Nineties*. She goes back to explore those issues of politics and love which she had dropped in 1933 when her husband died. In *Golden Miles* we see Sally the mother of grown-up sons, watching them go, reassessing her own life and the conflicting pressures of duty, love and politics. Katharine Prichard wrote without pretence or coyness about women's sexual and emotional needs. In her play *Bid Me To Love* (c. 1927), a frank criticism of bourgeois marriage, she had her leading lady say that 'every woman of forty needs a lover to keep her self respect—and her husband's'. Such remarks were considered scandalous in Perth in 1927 and few of her plays were produced until much later. Had there been a progressive theatre company in Australia during the inter-war years she may well have had a career as a playwright. But even so there was the question of her 'outspokenness' and few of her plays were considered producable in the cultural climate of those years. In the novel she had slightly more leeway, but even so it was uncommon in the 1940s for the sexual needs of a middle-aged, working-class woman to be drawn without apology. But in a period of escalating cold war this aspect of *Golden Miles* did not attract as much attention as the radical political context in which the sexual politics of the novel were situated. Sally is not a communist but her solidarity with the working class is strong. She listens to the political debates of the men, and she understands where their arguments impinge on her life as a woman and on the community she loves. The terms of the narrative are set within a left debate and Sally's fierce independence is one of the sources of pleasure in the novel.

The theme of politics and love is also played out through Dick's wife Amy. A self-centred girl who precipitates disaster by running away with the evil capitalist Paddy Cavan, she represents an image of woman of which Katharine Prichard disapproved. She abandons her child, she is self-centred in her search for pleasure, and she marries the Goughs' arch enemy, aligning herself with goldfields' exploiters. Yet for all that Sally disapproves of her, she invites understanding, even sympathy, although one cannot exactly like her. Amy dramatises another image of sexual politics and explores the ways in which even women who align themselves with capitalism remain oppressed. We understand why she does what she does and we understand and recognise the contraditions within her position. In this she is far more successful as a character and as a focus for the dialectic of gender and class than Tom's wife Eily. Eily is a paragon: selfless, politically astute, generous, hardworking, enduring. She fades into an ideological mist.

Golden Miles, like Sally Gough's life in it, is dominated by the Great War. At its widest focus *Golden Miles* explores the politics of that bloody imperialist war. And although a lot of this is done through rather lengthy dialogue, it works precisely because the war impinges directly and painfully on the lives of Sally, her family and neighbours. At a narrower focus *Golden Miles* explores Sally's conflicting responses to war and the disillusion of a young soldier, as Lal goes to war, dashing and pleased with himself in his cavalry uniform, only to land on the bare and desperate beaches of Gallipoli. The First World War looms large in Australian mythology as the site of national blooding, the proof of Australian manhood, courage and resourcefulness: characteristics which were supposed to have come out of the pioneering experience. Yet while *The Roaring Nineties* endorsed a lot of the pioneering mythologies, *Golden Miles* is much tougher in its view of war and in that respect never slips into nostalgia. It is Katharine Prichard at her grim best. Despite her acceptance, as a communist, of the necessity to fight fascism, she was a life-long worker for peace; of the many honours she received she was particularly proud of a Jolliet-Curie medal and diploma of honour for 'notable service to the cause of peace and friendship among the peoples' which she was awarded towards the end of her life by the World Peace Council. She knew too, like so many, the pain of having a son at the front. Her own son enlisted in the Second World War while she was writing *Golden Miles* and she lived in dread of the telegram. She was one of the lucky ones; her son came home.

In his analysis of the historical novel Georg Lukács argues that it only became possible with modern war, when war became a mass experience, touching every civilian life and changing popular conceptions of history. Modern war brings home the concept of history as an 'uninter-rupted process of changes' and allows, indeed forces, an identification between the life of the individual and the movement of history which became central to democratic protest movements. This same identifi-cation also became central to the aesthetics of socialist realism. In Australia, of course, the 1914–18 War was the first war in which white Australians were affected on a mass scale. 417,000 men and women enlisted in the Australian forces, 330,000 of them serving overseas. Of these two-thirds were wounded and nearly 60,000 killed. This was the highest casualty rate of any Empire army and from a total population of less than five million, few families were unaffected. By the end of the war the country was bitterly divided by class, by religion, and it is the politics of the home front which is the focus of *Golden Miles*.

While *Golden Miles* is not without its problems, Katharine Prichard does succeed through Sally and the Gough family in dramatising 'from below' the point at which political and historical events become concrete and allow people to comprehend their existence as historically con-ditioned. She would have ascribed her success to the aesthetics of socialist realism. Like Lukács she would have argued that a critical analysis of the present is the key to an understanding of the past. But the difficulties of the novel can be attributed to the same aesthetic source, problems which are more appropriately discussed in relation to *Winged Seeds*, the third volume, where they become more pronounced. I would like to put at least part of the strength of *Golden Miles* down to Katharine Prichard's long, difficult and self-conscious experience as a writer, a woman and a socialist. While this often uncomfortable mix sometimes resulted in lapses in her writing, it also gave her the resilience and clear sightedness she recreated in Sally Gough, a woman who, like her creator, challenges the reader to confront the condition of being a woman, a sexual and political being, at the centre of the dynamic contradictions of social life.

Drusilla Modjeska, Sydney, 1984

The Roaring Nineties was set in the prospecting days of the gold-fields of Western Australia. *Golden Miles* belongs to the period when the mining industry had been established. This part of the story of Dinny Quin and Sally Gough moves from 1914 to 1927.

Every care has been taken to use fictitious names for the many characters associated with their story; and it is not intended that any individual should be identified with them.

Lal's letters are the authentic letters of a young soldier who took part in the Gallipoli campaign.

Again, I wish to express appreciation for the sources of information made available to me by old prospectors, and the records of early writers, particularly those of Sir John Kirwin, whose books contain so much valuable material on development of the goldfields.

K. S. P.

CHAPTER I

An old rattletrap, drawn by a pair of rough-haired horses, crawled over the bare flat under a dim blue sky. Red dust stirred by the horses' feet, half hid the buggy and the woman sitting on the front seat driving the horses.

Two or three times a month, she came like this on Sunday morning from that far edge of bush under haze, across the flat, and drove along the back streets among miners' shacks and houses scattered along the Boulder road. It had been a dry winter: keen and frosty in the early morning but blazing with sunshine all day.

As Mrs. Gough hung out the boys' shirts and working trousers which she always had to wash on a Sunday morning, she watched the buggy approach and disappear among the small, white-roofed wooden houses and humpies of rusty tin and bagging pressed close together and cluttering the flat.

She recognised that buggy which came in from the bush beyond the Salt Lake where Fred Cairns had a show; and knew the woman driving it was Maritana. Maritana, the half-caste, she was being called now. It was said Fred Cairns had married her. At any rate they had a swarm of youngsters, a herd of goats and a few hens running wild round their camp. Maritana was supposed to be selling eggs and plucked poultry when she drove round the Boulder on a Sunday morning. That she bought more than she sold was well known: in fact that Maritana was the gatherer and go-between for a gang which dealt in stolen gold.

Whom she worked for nobody knew, or how Fred Cairns passed on the gold Maritana collected. It was rumoured that the Big Four were behind Fred and his deals. Men who passed on a bit of ore to Maritana gained a certain amount of confidence from the idea. Nobody could name the Big Four, although it was said they were influential and respectable citizens who would, and did, protect their agents.

Since the Gold Stealing Commission had made its report more care was being exercised in transactions between those who had gold to sell and those who disposed of it. The detective staff employed by the mine owners had been increased and there had been several convictions lately. Under the new Gold Buyers Licensing Act heavy penalties could be exacted from persons found in possession of

9

gold, or gold-bearing ore, 'reasonably suspected of being stolen or unlawfully obtained'.

All this Mrs. Gough knew, and all this she was turning over in her mind when the buggy pulled up at the back gate of her boarding-house. As the mother of four sons, although only two of them were working on the mines, Sally Gough was perturbed by Maritana's visits to her place. Of course Maritana came to see Paddy Cavan. Dick and Tom had nothing to do with Paddy, or any snide business he might be carrying on, their mother was sure; but she had just realised that it was not good enough to allow Paddy to use her house for his business.

She had worked too hard: struggled for years to give Dick his chance to study geology and metallurgy. Now, when he had got a job as assistant assayer on the Boulder Reef, nothing must be allowed to interfere with his prospects. Besides, Mrs. Gough reminded herself, she and Morris had always maintained a standard of honest and decent living for their sons. She was not going to allow that to be lowered by Paddy Cavan and his traffic in stolen gold, as it would be if her house were raided—though it would be a pity to lose Paddy as a boarder at present.

Two miners, as they passed, greeted Maritana jocosely:

'Hullo, Maritana! The cops haven't got you yet?'

'The cops won't get me,' Maritana replied, with a short, husky laugh. 'Not unless they get a good many others, too.'

She got down from the buggy, opened the back gate and came into the yard carrying an empty sugar bag. Through the goat pen, and past the plots of the wilting vegetable garden, she walked slowly towards Mrs. Gough.

'Mornin', Missus Sally,' she said. 'Paddy in?'

'He is,' Mrs. Gough said dryly. 'And expecting you as usual, I suppose, Maritana.'

Maritana walked on towards the house. There was sulky defiance in the swing and stride of her spare, shabby figure.

Who would have recognised in her the wild, shy aboriginal girl she had once known, Mrs. Gough thought. Maritana had become a tall, scraggy woman, with skin like dirty brown paper, sagging on her high cheek bones. Her brown eyes had a shrewd glint, her wide mouth had become thin and hard. A sour expression lingered about it as though Maritana had tasted something vile and could not recover from the effect.

'Mind my Muscovy duck sitting there under the vine,' Sally called. 'It'd take more'n the sight of me to disturb her.'

Maritana's gurgle of amusement was cut short as Paddy opened the door of his room. Mrs. Gough could see him standing in the doorway as if he had just dragged on his shirt and trousers. His gingery mop of hair was on end and his chin unshaven. Maritana went into his room and Paddy shut the door.

Maritana was not there very long. When she walked back along the verandah and across the yard the sugar bag she was carrying had become bulkier: weighed more heavily on her shoulders.

'Good day, Missus Sally,' she remarked, with a sly, flitting smile as she passed.

'You're a fool to think you can get away with this game much longer, Maritana!' Mrs. Gough exclaimed. 'It's not worth the risk. Why doesn't your husband do his own dirty work?'

'I been a fool all my life,' Maritana said grimly. 'But this time I'm gettin' my cut. So there's no need to worry.'

She went to the gate, opened and shut it, unbuckled a strap round the buggy wheels and climbed on to her seat.

'You'd ought to see you do, too, Missus Sally,' she called, and drove off.

Mrs. Gough's blood flamed. She left the wet clothes in their box in the yard, and almost ran across the yard and along the verandah to Paddy's room.

'See here, Paddy,' she cried, furiously, walking right in on him as he sat at a table entering up figures in an account book, 'it's no business of mine how you make money, but I won't have Maritana coming here on a Sunday morning! The very dogs are barking what she's after. And she'll be caught one of these days, as sure as God made little apples.'

'Now, now, ma'am,' said Paddy, 'y'r don't have to worry about that.'

'It's all very well for you to say so,' Sally declared impatiently. 'You don't have to tell me you've got a pull with the police, Paddy Cavan. There's a good many of them in the racket with the Big Four, everybody knows. But Dinny Quin was saying, only the other day, the mine owners are sorer than ever about losses on the mines; and are talking about a big clean up. Well, my house isn't going to be in it. I won't have you bringing snide gold here and getting me raided.'

Paddy grinned.

'God, mum, you don't think I'd do that? It's ten years since I worked underground meself. If a man comes to me with a bit of stuff sometimes and asks me to help him get rid of it, well y' can't blame me, can yer?'

'Do you mean to tell me,' Sally demanded, 'that other men in this house are bringing you gold?'

'Y're not askin' me to turn informer, are ye, m'am?'

Mrs. Gough's mind skipped to the boarders who occupied the bunk-house on the far side of the yard.

'There's the two Greeks and Bill Dally and . . .'

Paddy watched her with a sly smile.

'My own two boys and Dinny Quin. If it's the Greeks, or Bill Dally who are passing stuff on to you, they've got to stop, or clear out.'

'You've forgotten Morrey.' Paddy enjoyed her consternation.

'Morris!' Mrs. Gough gasped. 'Now, look here, Paddy Cavan, if you think I don't know my own husband well enough to be sure he wouldn't get mixed up in this business, you're greatly mistaken.'

'Take it easy, missus,' Paddy chuckled. 'I didn't say Morrey was in the gold. I was merely remindin' you that Morrey's a member of this household, when y' were goin' over 'em. The master of it, in a manner of speakin', though you do wear the pants.'

'None of your cheek, Paddy Cavan!' Mrs. Gough exclaimed wrathfully. 'If you *have* made money and got on in the world—how is best known to yourself—you can't bluff me. I'm not going to have my house get a bad name, and ruin my boys' future, for you or anybody like you.'

''Course y're not, ma'am,' Paddy was all placatory guile. 'But your house isn't goin' to get a bad name through me. On the other hand, I might be able to help you—if ever the boys get into a bit of trouble.'

Mrs. Gough found herself in a whirl of anxious and bewildering conjectures.

'That's all very well, Paddy,' she said. 'I don't doubt you're in with the gang of crooks who are running this town at present. I'm not. But I want none of your protection or theirs. My boarding-house has been a decent, homely place for any man who knows how to behave himself. If you, or anybody else, wants to stow stolen gold here, you can get. That's flat and I mean it.'

'If everybody in the house who's brought me a bit of gold cleared out, y'd be lonesome, missus.'

'Do you mean to say . . .' Sally was rattled.

'I'm not sayin' anything—givin' anybody away,' Paddy replied doggedly. 'But if y' mean it, y'll have more rooms than mine to let next week. And y' know things aren't so good now, as they were a year or so ago. Kal was boomin' when I came to board here. But it looks as if we were in for another slump. There's a lot of men unemployed already, and it's goin' to be hard gettin' boarders who can pay reg'lar and on the spot.'

'I'll risk it,' Mrs. Gough assured him.

'Look here, ma'am,' Paddy argued, 'y're a sensible woman. What

in the name-er-blazes are y' carryin' on like this for? You know
the fields. You know well enough nobody blames a man workin'
underground for takin' a bit of his, now and then. Miners' privilege,
and all that. Isn't that what the mine owners themselves say? And
y' know as well as I do the prosperity of this town depends on the
money in circulation here, and that comes from the gold sold on
the spot. Not from production figures of the mines and dividends
that go overseas.'

'I know all that,' Sally said obstinately. 'All I say is, Morris and
I've never had anything to do with the snide business. My boys've
been brought up to run straight, and I won't have their chances in
life ruined for the sake of a few bob I make on your board, Paddy.'

'Meanin' Dick,' Paddy snarled.

'Meaning Dick, chiefly,' Mrs. Gough agreed. 'He's got a good
job in the assay room on the Boulder Reef, and I haven't slaved all
these years to give him a chance . . .'

'To be a little gentleman.'

Mrs. Gough's head lifted and her eyes flashed. 'All I've ever
wanted was to give Dick a chance to earn a decent living.'

'And Tom—he can slog underground, all his days?'

'Tom's different,' Mrs. Gough defended herself. 'Tom's physically
stronger for one thing, and he refuses to be anything but a miner.
Do you think I didn't want him to study and go to college, too?
But Tom had only one idea in his head. To get into the mines and
be earning a man's wages, as soon as possible.'

'Give his mother a hand keepin' the family and the old man,
to say nothing of helpin' Dick through the School of Mines and
the university. . . .'

'Tom's a good boy, Paddy,' his mother agreed. 'There was never
a better. You don't have to tell me that. But Dick's got the brains
of the family, and we've all done what we could for him.'

'Brains?' Paddy sneered. 'He's a good-looking young waster.
Tom's worth a dozen of him, if y' ask me.'

'I don't,' Mrs. Gough snapped. She wondered why she was
talking about her sons to Paddy Cavan. It was a waste of time;
but she could so easily be drawn into talking about them, her dear
boys. Her mind was always full of them, particularly Dick. Her
thoughts revolved round their doings and needs: what they said,
and how they were getting on in their work. She never ceased to
marvel at the differences of character, physique and mentality
between them.

It seemed strange that she and Morris should have children who
were so unlike themselves and each other; and yet, in each of the
boys, some trait of their parents had been repeated and intensified.

13

Sally realised this sometimes with a flicker of amusement and a twinge of anxiety. But it annoyed her to have been drawn into discussing Dick and Tom with Paddy this morning.

She had so much to do. The midday dinner must not be late. A savoury odour of meat roasting in the kitchen oven was wafted to her: her ear caught the frizzle of fat round it. She wondered whether the joint was cooking too fast. And there were wet clothes still in her basket in the yard. They must be hung out and the table set for dinner. She had no time to waste arguing with Paddy. But this matter of Paddy's deals with Maritana had to be settled; and it was a good time to settle it, before the boys came back from their swim in the new pool, and the men started to hang about for their dinner.

Mrs. Gough knew well enough why Paddy had spoken slightingly of Dick. Why there was always a surly resentment in his attitude towards Dick. He could never forgive Dick for having qualities which he himself would never possess. He was so good looking and lovable, her Dick, Mrs. Gough told herself. Irresponsible and a little selfish, perhaps in an unconscious, ingrained way; but so generous and devoted to her and his brothers, that they thought the world of him.

Sometimes Sally wondered whether she had been right to send Dick to a public school in Adelaide where the mine managers sent their sons, while Tom and Lal had grown up on the fields with nothing but a state school education, and a knowledge of the surroundings and men they would have to work among. Of course, she had hoped to send each of the boys for a few years to Prince Alfred's. Dick had thoroughly enjoyed his days at school there, and come home with the manners and confidence which made him a most presentable young man now.

And there was Amy. That, above all, was why Paddy Cavan had a grouch against Dick. Amy and Dick had gone about together since they were children. They had always been sweethearts, although as Amy grew up and Dick was still studying, or away in Sydney with Mr. de Morfé, Amy had flirted with innumerable men, young and old. She was a bright, birdlike little creature, restless and wilful, but guileless: flitted about, enjoying any sort of diversion which came her way—until Dick appeared on the scene again. Then there had been no one but Dick with whom she wanted to ride, dance or play tennis. Everybody knew it and laughed about a love affair, so naïve and destined to end in the happy marriage of the young couple. Now Dick had a job, their engagement had been announced, and they were talking of being married soon.

14

There was only one person to whom this news would not be pleasing. And that was Paddy Cavan.

Mrs. Gough could not imagine why he had ever flattered himself he had any hope of capturing Amy. Yet Paddy had done his best when Dick was away to win a place in Amy's good graces. He had sent her flowers and boxes of chocolates: given her a lovely little chestnut mare, even. That was supposed to be the basis of Amy's toleration of him. She had gobbled his chocolates, ridden his horse, made fun of and laughed at Paddy, until Paddy was beside himself with desire for her.

He had approached Laura with a proposal of marriage when Amy was only eighteen, Dick still at the School of Mines.

'Don't be a fool, Paddy,' Laura said. 'It's out of the question. You're nearly thirty, fat and going bald. Amy would never think of it.'

'I'm not much to look at, ma'am,' Paddy protested. 'But I'm well in. Amy'd have all the money she wants and we'd live in style. Up here, because y' know all about me, y' can't see the difference between Mr. Patrick Cavan and Paddy Cavan who came up on the track with the first team to Coolgardie. But in Perth I go about with all the toffs, dine with directors and their wives and daughters. There's nothing like mixing with that mob to polish up y'r manners. Amy wouldn't be ashamed of me, if . . .'

'P'raps not,' Laura admitted impatiently. 'But it's no use thinking of such a thing. Amy's in love with Dick Gough, and he is with her. It's always been understood they'll be married some day.'

Amy had laughed at the absurdity of the idea when her mother told her about it. She laughed, even more lightheartedly when Paddy attempted to make love to her. She was quite accustomed to men making love to her and wanting to marry her. Paddy's devotion was just something Amy took for granted and made use of when it suited her. . . .

'Besides,' Sally was pleased at the thought of wiping that smug complacency off Paddy's face, 'Dick and Amy have made up their minds to be married before the end of the year, so I'm not going to risk having any unpleasantness interfere with their wedding.'

'They are, are they?'

Paddy sat a moment with his lower lip thrust out, his heavy, still youthful face, sullen and brooding. This passion for Amy was the one thing which had ever caused Paddy Cavan to spend a moment's thought on anything but the achievement of his purpose. That was, as everybody knew, to be a rich and influential man, as soon as possible, and at all costs.

He had battled along from the time he was a kid on the fields, with good humour and hardihood: shrewd and unscrupulous, but likeable enough in personal relations. Now that he had made his way, held big interests in mines all over the field, people were beginning to talk of him as a coming man, respect his perspicacity in mining affairs and seek his advice. If it was hinted that his affluence owed something to the illicit traffic in gold and its ramifications throughout the mining industry, nobody cared to produce any facts which might embarrass Mr. Cavan. Paddy was well protected by the mining companies he represented and by the mine managers with whom he associated.

Mrs. Gough had been amused by his bluff and bluster, and the blarney with which he had overcome her reluctance to let him become one of her boarders. She had never been able to take Paddy at his own valuation, as a man of importance in mining affairs. To-day, for the first time she saw the power in that heavy head and stocky figure: realised the dynamic will dominating them. She thought, apprehensively, that Paddy Cavan would stop at nothing to gain his ends. But a girl's first love he could not buy up like stock on the share market. Amy's at any rate. That he would not get, Sally assured herself. Amy was in love with Dick. Romantically, hot-headedly in love with Dick. She wanted to marry him despite the fact that Dick's salary barely kept him in clothes and cigarettes, and that Dick, himself, would rather have waited until he had a better income.

His mother was dismayed at the prospect of Dick having to undertake the responsibilities of a home of his own while he was still so young and had such a small salary. But Laura, it seemed, agreed with Amy that she and Dick might as well be married, as remain engaged for a long time, or until he got a better position.

Conscious of having betrayed himself to Mrs. Gough, Paddy threw off his despondency.

'Oh, well, there's as many good fish in the sea as ever came out of it, they say,' he remarked. 'And a good fisherman knows how to catch 'em. I'd not be wishing to embarrass ye with me presence, ma'am, if y' mean what y've been sayin' about a small business transaction to oblige old mates, now and them.'

'I mean it.' Sally stuck to her guns though her heart sank. 'I won't have this sort of business transacted in my house.'

'Right!' Paddy's blue eyes were cold and hard. 'I'll vacate my room at the end of the week, by y'r leave, ma'am.'

'That'll suit me. Since Dick came home I've been wanting this room for him, anyhow,' Sally said.

She turned away, conscious of having offended Paddy, aroused his ill will and an ugly resentment by her action. Had she done right, she asked herself, anxiously. Perhaps she should have talked the matter over with Morris and Dinny before saying anything to Paddy. She intended to do so after Maritana's last visit; but had put off making up her mind about it. This morning, what with the men calling to Maritana as she drew up at the gate, and Maritana's own jibe as she drove off, the whole object of Maritana's visit had been too flagrant to ignore. Sally told herself that a presentiment of danger swept over her. She had acted on impulse, knowing how easily Tom or Dick might be implicated if attention of the gold stealing detective staff were drawn to Maritana's visits on a Sunday morning.

She rushed into the kitchen to see that the meat and pumpkin and potatoes were not burning, turned them, and moved aside the apples simmering on the stove for an apple pie. She was just going back to the yard to finish hanging out her washing when Bill Dally called:

'Heigh, missus, y'r line's flopped!'

It was the sort of thing that would happen when she was behind with everything and so worried, Sally exclaimed to herself. Everything was going wrong, this morning.

The gust of wind which had skirled through the yard in a spiral of red dust was scurrying away over the flat as she went across the yard. It had done all the damage it could, loosened the crazy prop which supported her clothes-line, and flung the wet clothes in the dust. Sally picked them up, swearing in a way that made Bill glance at her lazily as he sat on the step of the bunk-house, reading the racing news.

'It's all very well for you to sit there, grinning, Bill Dally,' Sally said crossly. 'If you'd grabbed the clothes and taken them off the line into the wash-house when you saw the dust coming, it wouldn't've hurt you.'

'For Chris-sakes, missus,' Bill demurred, 'how did I know a puff of wind and a bit of dust was going to send y'r prop flyin'?'

Sally gathered up her dust-raddled clothes. Irritated and dishevelled, she stood a moment looking towards the road where a car had drawn up in front of the house. Who on earth could be coming to see her at this hour of the morning? She made a dash for the wash-house, dropped her armful of dirty clothes into one of the troughs, and went back to the yard, trying to tidy her hair.

'Anybody at home?' a gay mocking voice called. 'We knocked and couldn't make anyone hear.'

It was Frisco who strode into the yard, debonair and well-groomed, in English tweeds and a hard hat. The girl with him was fair and golden-haired. Her white-clad figure, white gloves and

17

shoes, made Sally conscious of her bedraggled appearance, down-at-heel slippers, and dirty apron; but she stiffened to a protective dignity and her eyes met Frisco's with a challenging smile.

'Arrived last night,' Frisco explained, deriding them. 'On my honeymoon, you might say! May I introduce my wife? Sylvia, Mrs. Morris Fitz-Morris Gough.'

'How do you do, Mrs. Fitz-Morris Gough,' the girl murmured.

Sally knew Frisco's first wife had died in child-birth: she had not heard of his second marriage.

Her eyes sparkled with anger because Frisco seemed delighted to have caught her at a disadvantage; but she contrived to say in her naturally friendly and charming manner:

'I am pleased to meet you, Mrs. de Morfé. Will you come in? It's such a hot morning, and your husband knows our free and easy way on the goldfields. We usually have a cup of tea at this time.'

'No, no!' Frisco blustered, determined not to let Mrs. Gough overcome her discomfiture. 'As a matter of fact it was Paddy Cavan we came to see. A little business I have to fix up with him. Is Paddy in?'

'You'll find him in his room: first door on the verandah,' Mrs. Gough replied easily, and turned again to her washing.

She lifted the box of dust-spattered clothes at her feet and carried it over to the wash-house, while Mr. de Morfé and his bride made their way along the path to the verandah where a vine spread its green leaves in the sunshine.

CHAPTER II

Mrs. Gough could remember every detail of what happened in the months that followed her row with Paddy. And so could Dinny Quin. It was a date in their minds around which many reminiscences revolved, and from which disaster had flowed.

To begin with there was Bill Jehosaphat's visit.

That very morning, while Sally was having it out with Paddy, Dinny and Bill were tramping along the Boulder road.

'Well, there it is, the Golden Mile, the richest square mile of gold-bearin' ground in the world, they say, Bill!'

Dinny stood on the dusty road, looking back towards the Boulder ridge, and the ramshackle township stretching out from it over bare, red earth.

Bill Gerrity, the man beside him better known as Bill Jehosophat in the old days, stared at the torn back of the ridge, the high peaks of dumps round the big mines; slimes solidified into barren sierras, grey, tawny, umber and purple: the sheds and scantlings of mine buildings, batteries, treatment plants, cluttered beside them: the forest of poppet legs and sky shafts cut against blue of the sky: the tall black chimneys sending yellow fumes drifting across the township and into the distance. Nearby shacks of rusty tin and bagging were scattered between abandoned shafts and heaps of rubble, merging with the white-washed, dust-raddled houses packed as close as in a city slum, far out over the plain.

It was a foreign landscape, blasted and sinister, to Bill Gerrity who was visiting the goldfields after an absence of twelve years.

'Great jumping Jehosaphat, Dinny,' he gasped, 'I can scarcely believe me eyes. When Paddy Hannan picked up a handful of slugs over there be Maritana, and we pegged alongside of him, it was all thick bush between the camps and this end of the ridge. Now, it's bare as a desert, not a tree or skerek of scrub left.'

Dinny grinned. 'First time y've mentioned Jehosaphat since y' arrived, Bill.'

'The wife reckons it's swearin',' Bill apologised, a trifle sheepishly. 'And I'm supposed to be a reformed character. But, hell, I've been achin' for a sight of this country, Dinny, and a yarn with old mates! Sometimes, I reckon it was a mistake to've cleared out when Speck and me sold our show on the Wealth of Nations rush. Thought I was doin' the right thing goin' home to see my folks in Victoria. Got run into buyin' land and sheep, somehow—and gettin' married. But it's not all it's cracked up to be settlin' down. What with sheep and a family, a man feels as if he had the worries of the world on his shoulders. I'd give a lot to chuck it all and go off prospectin' with you, Dinny.'

'Go on, Bill,' Dinny replied, pleased all the same to hear Bill talking like that. 'A man's got to settle down sometime, and the goldfields is no place to do it. Things aren't like they used to be. Hundreds of prospectors workin' on the mines for a crust.'

Bill looked prosperous but care-worn. He had put on flesh: wore his new slop suit of grey tweed and felt hat, with some satisfaction, but had lost the zest and gay recklessness of the days when he was battling for gold. He wished he could have changed into a pair of working trousers and an old shirt to go round the mines with Dinny. But his wife was waiting for him at the hotel, and would not have approved of his doing that.

Seeing Dinny, limping beside him, in worn moles and a flannel shirt, as game and lively as he had been when they swamped along with the first team for Coolgardie in '92, made Bill feel that Dinny had had the best of things, just jogging along as he pleased, while he, Bill Jehosaphat, had tried to turn himself into a successful sheep-farmer, and the sober and respectable father of a large family. Deep lines creased the leather of Dinny's face, but there was content and a tranquil happiness in the smile of his far-sighted eyes, faded to pale blue of the summer sky, though they were, and his hair turning grey.

Dinny had got the things he valued most, here, in his life on the fields, Bill surmised. He, himself, had lost them through reaching out after something he thought he ought to have; but had not particularly wanted, except as a demonstration to himself that a man could put his money to good use, and take on obligations if he chose. He still felt he had been right to pull out of the old spendthrift, free and easy way of life, though he hankered after it. Having proved his ability to wrestle with all those other propositions: 'make good' as his parents and Phoebe had never thought he would, he was inclined now to consider himself entitled to do as he pleased. Give up the everlasting worry of sheep, sell the station, or leave Phoebe to manage it and the children; and come back to live, lousing on the dumps round the mines, or prospecting out in the back country like any old hatter. That would be happiness for him, Bill thought. Happiest years of his life had been spent chasing rushes between the limitless horizons of this sun-blasted country.

'It's the sulphur fumes from the treatment plants killed off the native vegetation.' Dinny said. 'Modest Maryanski was right when he said telluride would give the mines a new lease of life. That, and solution of the sulphide bugbear—but we got the blasted fumes. Kal was boomin' for half a dozen years after the slump in '98. Frisco—Mr. de Morfé—beggin' his pardon, and the London stock-jobbers made fortunes. The place went along like a house afire for a while. But things are lookin' bad again now. They say the big mines are played out. Don't believe it, meself.

'Look at 'em! There, in the foreground. The old Iron Duke and the Croesus, Brown Hill over yonder: behind 'em the Kalgoorlie, North and South, and Midas, the Australia and Oroya. Along the ridge the Great Boulder, Boulder Reef, Perseverance, Ivanhoe, Golden Horseshoe, Lake View.'

'Cripes, Dinny,' Bill said, 'tons of gold must've come out of 'em.'

'By 1910, the Boulder mines had turned out £ 46,000,000 worth of gold.' Dinny stoked the ashes in the bowl of his pipe and lighted up. 'Underground there's miles of workin's. A hundred and twenty miles of drives and crosscuts on ten of 'em. Y' could walk through six or eight miles on the Great Boulder when the mainshaft was down only two thousand seven hundred feet. But it's not much to look at, the Golden Mile. Precious little the people who live here've got out of all the wealth the mines've produced. The mining companies haven't spent a penny to make up for the way they've laid waste the country side. Any comforts of civilisation we've got, in Boulder City and Kalgoorlie, the people've paid for, and the mine've got the benefit of 'em: the railway, water supply and electric light. Miners're still livin' in those rotten humpies of rusty tin and bagging on Ding Bat flat. Did y'r ever see a more dreary, poverty-stricken lookin' place?'

'Can't say I ever have,' Bill admitted. 'And when W. G. Brookman, Charley de Rose and Sam Pearce pegged on the ridge, we used to call it their sheep farm. Nobody thought they'd ever get payable gold there. Remember, Dinny?'

'Do I remember?' Dinny chuckled.

'But Sam Pearce was a good prospector,' Bill went on. 'He told me himself, he tested every lease before they applied for it: got gold from all his borings in the country rock. So between 'em, he and his mates held forty acres when they struck it rich on the Great Boulder.'

'Struck it rich!' Dinny exclaimed. 'You bet they did. There was fifteen men in the syndicate backing Brookman and Pearce, in the first place, and they had a workin' capital of £150. When the shareholders met and went into liquidation, four years later, they owned nine of the biggest mines on the Golden Mile, and had a dominatin' interest in others. The capital value of their holdings was round about £30,000,000, and they cut up over £13,000,000 in cash and dividends. Can y' beat it?'

Dinny turned his back on the mines. Bill wanted to have a look at a claim he had once pegged on the far side of Cassidy's Hill, so they walked on along the Boulder road towards Kalgoorlie. It was a day of blazing sunshine and frail blue skies. The corrugated iron roofs of houses on the flat seemed to be quivering in the heat. Bill took off his coat, sweating and breathing hard. Dinny plugged along serenely. Hundreds in the shade meant nothing to him, and there was no shade on the Boulder road. When they had cut off to the right, across rising stony ground, and located Bill's claim, Bill was glad to drop down and rest for awhile on the hillside.

'It was during the last slump I went east,' he mused. 'There was talk of the oxidised ore peterin' out and Kalgoorlie becomin' as dead as the old camp. Queer how Coolgardie's never come again, and Kalgoorlie and Boulder've grown like this.'

He was gazing over the scattered encampment of the two cities, spreading for four miles over the plain under shimmering haze towards Boulder, and away for two or three miles beyond Kalgoorlie, towards the North End. Sudden puffs of dust rose and skirled on a stretch of bare, sun-baked red earth behind the most distant houses, and a dingy line of scrub still clung to the far horizon. Mt. Burgess rose above it, blue and remote.

'Comin' of the water gave the mines a new lease of life as much as anything,' Dinny said. 'With plenty of water to simplify the treatment of sulphide ore, and reduce costs, and with the railway bringin' machinery up from the coast, Kalgoorlie was on the upgrade again, in no time.'

'Must've been a great day when that "river of pure water" Sir John promised, started to flow through the fields?'

'It was a great day, all right.' Dinny's grin flickered. 'Some of us old timers was celebratin' for a week. We forgave John Forrest a lot on account of the water. And the women went near crazy with joy. Y'd've thought it was a miracle'd happened when water started to gush from the taps in their kitchens and bathrooms.'

'Nat Harper suggested the scheme at a dinner in Kanowna, the boys tell me,' Bill interrupted. 'And got laughed at for his pains.'

'It was a "fantastic dream" to think of bringin' water from the Darling Ranges to the goldfields, most of the hard heads said,' Dinny burbled happily. 'But some of us wanted the water so bad, we was willin' to dream it could be done.

'C. Y. O'Connor, the government engineer, was a great man: worked out the plans for pumpin' stations and three hundred and twenty-five miles of pipe line to bring the water from the Helena River to a reservoir on Mount Charlotte—though he never lived to see the dream come true. Was badgered to death by one of the newspapers and some of the mine managers here, who said the scheme was doomed to failure. But the water came, millions of gallons of fresh water. There it is, flowin' into the reservoir every day.

'We've got a park in Kalgoorlie planted with trees, now; and lawns where the sprinklers go for hours, keepin' the place green. And a swimmin' pool in the same street. The boys rush it on Saturdays and Sundays: packed like sardines they are, with scarcely room to splash in. It's a great place for a bath on a hot day when y' haven't got one of y'r own.'

Bill laughed lazily.

'And you've run a loop line from the main railway station out to Boulder, I see. Got trams on the roads, and suburbs of villa residences and bungalows at Mullingar and Lamington Heights: electric light in the streets and the houses. S'truth, Dinny, if I hadn't seen it with me own eyes, I wouldn't believe it.'

'Things started to move after the water came, like I told you,'

22

Dinny said. 'It was the peak year in 1906. New pubs, shops and houses goin' up everywhere. But there were rumours of another slump brewin' and some of us began to feel uneasy. The mine owners talked of payable ore givin' out—though over-capitalisation of the mines was the real trouble.

'There were more than five thousand men workin' on the mines then, and it was plain as the nose on y'r face the slump was goin' to have pretty serious consequences. More serious than when there was a good bit of alluvial gold about. The alluvial was worked out and hundreds of alluvial men were workin' on the mines for wages. But wages didn't keep pace with the big profits the mining companies had been makin', and of course a workin' miner thinks he's entitled to take up a few specimens, now and then.'

'Don't blame him,' Bill drawled, remembering he had been a working miner, himself, before the rush to Coolgardie.

'Not on the fields, we don't, 't any rate,' Dinny grinned. 'The money put into circulation by, what the law calls, "the illicit traffic in gold", helps to keep things flourishin' here. But the business life of the place depends on the mines: on the miners bein' able to pay their way. The gold-mining industry's got a strangle-hold of Kalgoorlie.

'There's been some record returns from high grade ore—like when the Lake View turned out a ton of gold a month. Six thousand four hundred tons of telluride ore made over three-quarters of a million sterling in a few months. Most of it went overseas, of course. But when the mining companies'd been tearin' the guts out of the mines for three or four years, profits began to fall. They looked round for something to make a dust up over, till they could clear themselves and unload stock. The Gold Stealing Commission was just what they wanted.'

'Must've been a bit of fun over that,' Bill surmised.

'There was a bit of fun, all right,' Dinny agreed, 'like as if you'd stirred up an ants' nest with a big stick. All the boys were scurryin' to get rid of any stuff they might have lyin' about. But it was the gold buyers and big boys in the racket got the wind up most of all.

'The fat was in the fire when a journalist named Jack Scantlebury, havin' a look round for English investors, said in an article to the newspapers that hundreds of thousands of pounds was being lost by shareholders, through gold stealin' on the mines. Detective Sergeant Kavanagh and a staff of dees were sent up to investigate. Kavanagh reported that gold stealin' was being carried on to "an enormous extent". So a royal commission was set up "to inquire into the allegations".'

Dinny laughed as he thought of it. He had a lot of yarns about gold stealing, and the tricks miners played in order to get away with a bit of rich ore.

'Before the Commission started taking evidence, The Kalgoorlie Treatment Company's plant closed over night,' he went on. 'Every man and boy who had anything to do with it disappeared. And several well-known and respectable citizens had urgent business elsewhere.

'It was well known some of the buyers had dummy mines, and plants alongside, in which they treated any gold comin' into their hands. Others were sendin' concentrates to the Eastern States for treatment. But from beginning to end of the inquiry, there wasn't a tittle of evidence to prove where the gold came from, bein' treated in these plants. Gold sold to the banks, smelted bullion, gives no indication of its origin, and if it's supposed to come from a mine that's been worked out, the bankers can't be expected to know. In some cases, monthly returns were bein' made to the mining registrar of gold from leases which didn't exist. By the way, Tassy was called to give information to the Commission, about the gold he'd been sellin' to one of the banks.'

'Tassy Regan?'

'Himself,' Dinny chortled, and went on to describe how in his own wily and witty way, Tassy had been evading a direct answer to awkward questions, all the morning, when he was forced at last to say precisely where his gold was obtained.

' "Why, haven't I been tellin' y'r Honour for the past hour," he said. "I been workin' a good patch in me mine for a year of more. Mind, I don't say she was a jeweller's shop—and she's jest about worked out now. But as I was sayin' to me mate, the other day, she was as rich a patch as I've seen in all me born days, and I've seen plenty—in the old Brown Hill, and . . ."

' "What mine was this, Mr. Regan?"

' "Why Regan's mine," said Tassy. "And as I was sayin' . . ."

' "Where is it? What is it called?"

' "To be sure now, it's called the Hard-to-Find," said Tassy, and launched into a rambling description of the whereabouts of his mine.

'A detective was deputed to go with Tassy and inspect the mine. Tassy led him by rough and round-about tracks to an abandoned shaft away out in the bush.

' "That's it," ses Tassy. "But I wouldn't advise ye to go down."

'The detective was all for doin' his duty and makin' an attempt to descend by a rotten ladder, hangin' into black depths of the shaft.

' "It's dangerous, I tell ye," Tassy assured him. "A bit of rock, or something might fall on ye."

'The detective took the hint. He didn't try to examine the

workin's of the abandoned shaft: returned and reported to the Commissioner that he'd inspected the Hard-to-Find mine, and that Mr. Regan's account of it was substantially correct. It certainly was "hard to find".'

When Bill's laughter had subsided, Dinny continued:

'The Commissioner's report did one thing. It emphasised the fact that though gold stealing was bein' carried on, on an extensive scale, "the odd specimens secured by working miners would not account for more than a small portion of it, and that the bulk of the thefts are not from underground".

'Detective Sergeant Kavanagh himself said: "I do not regard the miner as the greatest sinner. In my opinion, and I base it on very good grounds, persons in much higher positions where the facilities are greater, get away with much more and both have to depend on the receiver for their reward." Under cross examination, Kavanagh explained he referred to men in the position of—well, assayers or amalgamators, and people who deal with the gold after it comes up on top.'

'That caused a bit of a sensation, I bet,' Bill chuckled.

'Particularly when the Commissioner remarked,' Dinny added: ' "It struck me that managers of the mines of the large incorporated companies, are of the opinion that most of whatever is taken, is from below. Whereas the managers of mines where the ore is of lower grade, think most of what is stolen is taken from the treatment plant in the shape of gold amalgam and zinc slimes from the precipitation boxes." '

Dinny thought the Commission had done a good job. It had put the blame for gold stealing, on a large scale, where it belonged. There were some instances of men shipping concentrates from small privately owned treatment plants, not connected with mining leases, and netting proceeds of £ 10,000 to £ 12,000 a year.

Recommendations for tightening up the law in relation to gold stealing had been put into effect.

'Sales of gold bullion became illegal except to, or by, a licensed gold dealer on his licensed premises,' Dinny said. 'Though alluvial could still be freely bought and sold.'

But, he told Bill, there was a good deal of dissatisfaction with a clause in the Amended Police Act which stated: "Any person who is charged before a magistrate with having on his person, or on any animal, or in any cart, or other vehicle, or in his possession on any premises of which he is the tenant or occupier, any gold reasonably suspected of being stolen or unlawfully obtained, is liable to summary conviction, to a fine not exceeding £ 50, or to imprisonment with or without hard labour for any term not exceeding six months."

'This clause makes it possible for a man wantin' to work off a grudge against another to plant a bit of stolen gold on him, and arouse the dee's suspicions as to where it may be found. It's happened, two or three times, and a decent bloke has taken the knock.'

'Great jumpin' Jehosaphat,' Bill exploded, 'we'd've known what to do with a rat playin' tricks like that in the old days, Dinny.'

'That's a fact,' Dinny agreed. 'But they don't do things that way now, Bill. And there's some pretty vicious rats mixed up in the gold-stealin' business and no mistake. The Commission didn't put a stop to it. It's goin' on just the same—with ramifications which spread through the whole business life of Boulder and Kal. The Big Four are supposed to control it. Who they are, nobody knows, though some of us could make a guess. But it doesn't do to know too much. There are big and little crooks in the game. The big men can offer a dee a few hundred pounds to drop a prosecution, or keep his mouth shut.

'There was a stink about a police inspector, as a result of evidence before the Commission. He left the fields, "under a cloud" as y' might say. Another dee resigned from the force, lately, and set up in business, in a big way, down south.'

Bill laughed. And Dinny rattled on:

'It was Scantlebury, himself, said, if I remember rightly, that takin' a bit of gold was recognised as "the miner's privilege", and that mine managers admitted the miners on this field "were not surpassed anywhere for skill, industry and courage".'

'Pourin' oil on the troubled waters,' Bill murmured.

Dinny reckoned that was about it, though Scantlebury agreed the truth was, probably, that gold stealing in Kalgoorlie and Boulder had about 'the same number of sympathisers, active and tacit, as would be found in other British communities of a similar population and degree of settlement, where everybody's living is dependent on gold mining'.

'Of course, there's wheels within wheels in this gold stealin' business,' Dinny mused. 'It's true, most people who've eaten the dust of the fields for a few years, never blame a miner for helping himself, now and then. They know most of the men do it in a spirit of bravado. It's good sport beatin' the bosses, in spite of all their precautions: puttin' pimps to watch men workin' on a good patch, and havin' them searched in the change room if there's the least suspicion of a bit of ore comin' up in a crib bag, or under a man's belly band. It's all very well to talk of "miners' privilege",

26

but many a man gets three months hard, for bein' caught with telluride ore on him that isn't worth more'n a few lousy quid. It's a fact, the majority of workin' miners don't take the game seriously. If they get away with a few 'weights now and then, it's only to show they've got the guts, and are good mates, not likely to give any other man away.

'A young chap told me how he'd done some quick thinkin' once. They'd struck it so rich in the stope where he was workin' that a sheet and boards were put down to catch the fall after firin'. The shift boss, underground boss, a couple of lousers and the manager stood round to see the stuff bagged. They cleaned the boards, swept the fine gold up on the sheet and filled fifteen bags; loaded 'em on to a truck, and Jack was standin' by to push the truck along to the plat.

'Well, he figured it was tough luck for men on the drill, and the boggers, not to get a look in on that gold. He'd got to do something about it! But what could he do? Nothing, it seemed with the shift boss, the underground boss and the manager trampin' along, just behind him.

'But there was a slight bend in the track and a chow over the timber, just beyond the bend. The chow's a kind of platform on a couple of cross beams, overhead, they use now. His only chance, Jack reckoned, was to get a bit of pace on the truck round that bend, and heave a bag on to the chow. It wasn't more than the fraction of a second, he was out of sight of the bosses, round the bend. He heaved a bag on to the chow—and then let them catch up to him.

'When they got to the plat, Jacky went over to get a drink of water. The bosses counted the bags. There was one short.

' "Hell," Jack yells. "what do I know about it? Have I got it on me?"

'They searched him and went back to search the track and the stope in case the bag had fallen off.

' "We're looking for a bag missing from the truck," the shift boss says.

'The men in the stope started the fuses. They guessed Jacky had put something over.

' "Y'll be lookin' for y'r liver and lights on the wall, if y' don't get out of here, quick and lively," Tod Boyd told them. "She'll come down any minute now."

'He was a good lad, Jack Trebilcock, Young Cock, we called him. He split the sixty pounds of ore in that bag he'd stowed away in the chow, with his mates. They cleaned up a nice bit of cash on it.'

'Gosh, I reckon they earned it,' Bill laughed.

'A louser's always suspected of pimping for the boss, as you know,

Bill,' Dinny said, wound up by Bill's enjoyment of his yarns. 'And there was one of 'em on the Percy who'd been kicked out of the police force: done some dirty work snoopin' round as a divorce agent and been convicted of perjury. He tried to put two old miners away.

'When they came off shift, they were nabbed by dees, and put on a show. Gold was found in the pockets of their coats hangin' in the change room. How did it get there? They didn't know: swore they hadn't been near their clothes before goin' to the wash-house.

'Men comin' off shift stood by their mates: said they wouldn't work with a rat who'd frame a man. Not a miner would go down for the afternoon shift. The manager saw he'd have a strike on his hands, if he wasn't careful. He removed the pimp.'

'The old boys must've been pretty slick gettin' rid of what they had on them,' Bill grinned.

'They were,' Dinny assured him. 'There was a new louser on the Great Boulder bein' too energetic in the performance of his duties, too, lately. Some of the lads there are tough customers. Didn't take kindly to his snoopin' round.

'Goin' down in the cage Spud Thomas, a big, strapping machine man, says to the louser, one mornin':

' "Not too healthy, your job, Jo!"

' "What?" says the louser.

' "You got to be careful. Not overwork y'self," says Spud.

' "What d'y' mean?"

' "Mean?" Spud looks him over, gentle and thoughtful like, but a bit grim. "I don't mean nothin' except what I say. When a man's tired, he gets careless sometimes, misses his step in the dark, or a bit of rock falls on him when he's going down a ladder. Accidents like that happen in a mine."

' "Is that a threat?" says the louser.

' "Threat be blowed," Spud's as amiable as can be. "You'll find it's bloody honest to God prophecy, if you don't lay off the boys when there's anything doin'."

' "I see," says Jo.

' "Just as well," says Spud. "There was a man pimping for the boss, a while ago. Fell down a winze on the two hundred foot level. Nasty accident it was. No blame attachable." '

Bill rose and stretched.

'I could sit here yarning with you all day, Dinny,' he said. 'But I'd better be gettin' back to the hotel for dinner. The wife'll be fidgety—think I've deserted her.'

Dinny hauled himself up off the ground. It was queer to hear Bill Jehosaphat talking like that, a bit nervous and apologetic.

28

'Comin' along to Gough's this afternoon, aren't you?' Dinny asked. 'Morrey said he'd asked you to drop in. Mrs. Gough'll be real pleased to see you and your wife, Bill.'

'Missus Sally?' Bill's face brightened. 'How is she?'

'Same as ever,' Dinny's eyes had their quizzical gleam. 'Still battling along.'

'Any more of the old mob, around?'

'There's Paddy Cavan and Frisco . . .'

'Big bugs, now, I'm told?'

'In their own opinion,' Dinny snorted.

'And Sam Mullet and Plunt Pick. Sam's got his missus with him now. There's Tassy Regan and Yank Botteral, Mullocky O'Dwyer and Eli Nancarrow. . . .'

'Cripes, I'd like to see them,' Bill exclaimed.

'We'll round 'em up and make a night of it,' Dinny promised. 'That is, if Mrs. Gerrity don't object.'

'She goes to market when I get shickered,' Bill admitted. 'But if a man can't sink a few with old mates when can he, Dinny?'

'Not bein' a married man, I can't say,' Dinny replied slyly.

'But you were nearly doin' the trick once, Dinny!'

'Gord, so I was.' Dinny looked scared. 'And too full to know it! The girl got away with me cheque for £1000. When I think of the narrow escape I had, I don't begrudge her the money.'

'But there were some fine girls in the Rue, those days,' Bill mused. 'Any of them about still?'

'Some of'em married and've gone all respectable,' Dinny said. 'Better not tell you who they are now. The Japs were cleared out long ago. But Belle and Battleaxe Bertha've got a house in Brookman Street. Feel like lookin' 'em up?'

'Great jumpin'—no!' Bill was startled. 'I cut that sort of thing out long ago. What's happened to the Molloys?'

'Ted's been dead these ten years,' Dinny said. 'And Mrs. Molloy's a grandmother. Swarms of little Molloys sproutin' up all over the place.'

'And Marie—Madame Robillard? Gosh, Dinny, there was a fine woman! Don't mind tellin' you I had tickets on her once. But she never had an eye for any man but her husband.'

'Even after he died,' Dinny agreed. 'Many a man's tried his luck and got knocked back. It was the dust got Robbie. She was broken up for a while. Then she went on with her work: makin' dresses for the stores and mine managers' wives, and lookin' after the old man, Robbie's father.'

'Alf Brierly's widow married Tim McSweeney, they tell me?'

'She did,' Dinny said bitterly. 'And is as fat as a pig these days, though she still talks about Alf and cries a bit, now and then, when she runs into me.'

'And Vi O'Brien?' Bill asked eagerly. 'She was a lovely girl, Dinny? And she could sing, couldn't she?'

'Vi's got her own pub, and makin' money hand over fist,' Dinny said slowly. 'She still sings for the boys, like she used to, and keeps her family. Swears she won't marry, though there's many a man been mad about her—includin' a young priest, they say. He was sent back to Ireland a year or two ago.'

Still yarning and gossiping about old times, they came to the gate of Gough's boarding-house. A shabby green creeper with creamy blossom hid one end of the long verandah, and a bush of plumbago in fragile blue blossom sprawled beside the gate. Dinny hesitated to ask Bill in, as he pushed back the rickety gate. He knew Sally would be busy with her midday dinner, and could not spare time for a visitor.

'I won't come in now,' Bill said obligingly. 'Tell Mrs. Gough I'm looking forward to seeing her this afternoon, Dinny.'

As he turned and walked away his step was brisker than it had been all the morning. Dinny smiled to himself as he went up the garden path to the house. It was not the first time he had seen the prospect of a talk with Mrs. Gough put new life into a man. Not that Dinny suspected Bill Jehosaphat of any sentimental weakness for Sally. He had the regard for her, they all had—the men who had known her on Hannans in the early days. Big, lanky, slap-dash and kindly Bill, it was no wonder some woman had decided to make a good husband of him!

CHAPTER III

As she greeted Bill Gerrity and his wife with warm friendliness, that afternoon, no one would have recognised Mrs. Gough, as the rather work-worn and wind-dried little woman who had been doing her washing in the back-yard, between whiles of cooking the Sunday dinner and giving Paddy Cavan a piece of her mind.

To be sure, Dinny and the boys chased her out of the kitchen and washed up after the midday meal. They had bundled her off for a rest, so that when her guests arrived, Sally was looking her best in a new dress of crushed-strawberry coloured gingham. Marie had made the dress for her with a full skirt, tight bodice and a small embroidered collar. There was no doubt the colour was very becoming: cast a glow over her weathered skin and the dull rose of her mouth. She was wearing her hair in a heavy plait round her head now; and although a few silver threads showed, it still broke in a loose dark wave round her face.

Sally wished Mr. de Morfé had chosen to call that afternoon, instead of in the morning. One could never afford to appear quite unattractive to an old love. Goodness, it was disgraceful to be thinking such a thing! Sally banished the thought, though her eyes glimmered to their innate witchery, as she reflected, that even now, Frisco could not forget her.

Bill Gerrity declared that Mrs. Gough did not look a day older than when he had last seen her. Perhaps, he thought, she might be a little plumper and more serene, like a bird whose feathers have grown into the glossy pattern of its full plumage. But he could not say that, or inquire about the shadow which lurked at the back of her beautiful, brown eyes. The smile flitting in and out of them was enough for Bill, and stirred all his old homage and admiration.

'Oh, Mr. Jehosaphat, how nice to see you again!' Sally cried, eagerly. And turning to Mrs. Gerrity: 'Please don't mind our calling your husband that. You know, when I first arrived on the fields, I didn't realise he had any other name.'

'So long as I don't have to be Mrs. Jehosaphat, I can put up with it,' Mrs. Gerrity replied brusquely.

She was one of those plain, compact little women with a disapproving air, Mrs. Bill Gerrity: dressed in black, and wearing a black pudding-basin of a hat that might have been fashionable a few years ago. She looked well-to-do but as if she had no desire to be smart, or sociable. Just a country-woman, who did not like to be dragged from her own surroundings, Sally decided; and who was slightly apprehensive of meeting Bill's disreputable friends on the goldfields. It amused Morris to see Sally being so gracious and charming: playing hostess as if she were the chatelaine of a castle— which was what she might have been, if . . .

He did not allow his thoughts to wander to all the 'ifs' and 'might have beens' which no longer plagued him. He had discarded any dream of rehabilitating himself in the eyes of his family when he gave up prospecting. The sensational luck which had come to other men on the early rushes had never been his. Even Bill Gerrity had cleaned up a small fortune; but Morris decided he was born unlucky where gold was concerned, though he still dabbled in shares. Sally did not begrudge him the excitement of a flutter now and then. For the rest, he was satisfied to have got something out of life which many men never attained: a sense of not wanting more than a humdrum existence provided. And yet it was not so humdrum

31

with Sally and the boys, and the consciousness of a family happiness between them all.

There was that about Sally, Morris told himself, she still gave the spice of adventure to everyday life: could still be as fascinating a minx as when he had first known her. Dutiful wife, devoted mother, and all that she had been; but was still as self-willed and high-spirited as a brumby mare. He could not deny that she had plodded along beside him through all the years, as staunchly and sturdily as any of the bush bred horses which dragged their heavy loads along the rough tracks, out-back.

Old prospectors used to say there was nothing like a western-bred brumby for a tough journey in dry country. Morris thought their verdict might be applied to wives. At any rate, he assured himself, for grit and guts, Sally would have been hard to beat. How she contrived to keep her joyous vitality was what amazed him. Here she was now talking and laughing to Bill Jehosaphat as if they had been great friends in the old days, whereas they'd never done much more than pass the time of day when they happened to meet. But Bill was a good sort, and when he had invited Bill along for afternoon tea, Morris knew how pleased Bill would be to bring his wife to meet Sally.

Soon Mrs. Gerrity and Sally were chatting comfortably, and Morris caught Bill's eye. They went out to the verandah. Dinny followed them, and they were reminiscing to their hearts' content when Sam Mullet, Blunt Pick, Eli Nancarrow and Tassy Regan arrived. It was a great foregathering of old mates, and Bill, full of pleasure and excitement to be yarning with them again. When Marie Robillard pushed open the garden gate, he went to meet her. 'But, naturally, when Sally told me you will be here, this afternoon, I said I must come across to see you, Mr. Jehosaphat,' Marie said sweetly. 'And how goes it with you?'

'Fair to middling,' Bill stuttered, blushing like a schoolboy.

'That jumps to the eyes,' Marie cried. "'E looks marvellous, yes?' Her smiling glance went to the other men. 'So much of a world of balcony, and so prosperous!'

She went on indoors and their laughter rattled after her.

Sally was glad to see Marie. She had made polite inquiries about Mrs. Gerrity's children, and heard about the fine property Bill owned: how many sheep it ran and how well their clip had sold at the last wool sales. She had heard too about Mrs. Gerrity's anxiety on account of Bill's fits of moodiness and depression. He seemed to have no real interest in the station, she said. Was always talking about the goldfields, and wanting to get back to them: had even suggested selling out, or letting her manage the station until their

32

eldest son was old enough to take over, so that he could go prospecting again. It was all very worrying. Mrs. Gerrity confessed that she had come on this trip with Bill for fear he might never go back to the Barrabool Hills.

Marie came in then, and presently Mrs. Molloy called from the back verandah:

'Anybody at home?'

'Come in! Come in, Theresa,' Sally cried, and went to meet her.

'I just had a bit of cream to spare, and brought it for your tea, lovey,' Mrs. Molloy explained. 'Them pesky goats'll be the death of me. We're milking more nannies now than we ever did, and what with children growin' up and away at work, we don't need it so much as we used to. Y're lookin' as fresh as a flower, darlin'— But y've got company, I see. I'll be gettin' along.'

She was moving away when Sally pulled her back.

'You'll do nothing of the sort,' she said. An old friend has come to see us—Bill Jehosaphat—and brought his wife.'

'Bill Jehosaphat!' Mrs. Molloy's fat, jolly face beamed. 'Where is he, the blaigard—and his missus?'

Sally introduced Mrs. Gerrity, and in the midst of Mrs. Molloy's exclamations, Bill came in to have a word with her. It was quite a party when Sally put out the scones and the passion-fruit sponge she had ready for visitors on Sunday afternoon. She liked pouring tea from her silver teapot on special occasions such as this: and to use the flowered cups and saucers of the tea set which was a Christmas present from Dinny.

Marie talked to Mrs. Gerrity while Sally made tea. Then she called the men in from the verandah; and everybody sat round enjoying the gossip and reminiscences of old days, Bill's and Dinny's anecdotes and Mrs. Molloy's gusty comments. There was so much goodwill and cordiality in it all that Mrs. Gerrity remarked apologetically:

'He's got such good friends here, I don't wonder now why Bill's been wanting to come back.'

'These old timers,' Sally said crisply. 'They're always like that. They get all sorts of sentimental ideas about the free and easy way they used to live once, and forget about the hardships: the heat and dust and fever—scarcity of everything, never any money to pay your way. Bill was wise to get out when he could. Kalgoorlie's no place for a man with a wife and family, now.'

'D'y' mean that, ma'am?' Bill asked.

'Of course I do.' Sally liked to think she was a very common-sensical person and said what she thought. 'The struggle for existence here is as tough as it ever was, though it's different.

33

We've got more comfort nowadays: water and electric light. But they've got to be paid for, and everything depends on the mines whether you can pay for them or not.'

'That's a fact,' Sam Mullet muttered.

'I wish we could've got away when the children were little,' Sally went on. 'I wish we could have—and given them a better education. Some chance to earn a decent living. I wanted my sons to work anywhere but on the mines. But the mines've got the two eldest boys, and goodness knows whether the other two will get away. They will if I can do anything about it. There's talk of another slump now, and you know what that means: unemployment and ruin for hundreds of families. But even when there isn't a slump, the dust and miners' disease take almost every man who's worked underground for long. And, lately, there have been so many fatal accidents, a woman never knows what bad news a day will bring. It isn't easy to bring up your children properly in a place like this, either. I hope my boys will go straight, but . . .'

'Of course they'll go straight,' Dinny growled. 'Never was a finer bunch of lads.'

'That's all very well,' Sally flashed him a smile. 'But I ask myself, sometimes, how can the boys grow to be fine men here? The booze gets so many. There's nothing much for young men to do when they're not working, except booze or gamble at the two-up ring. And a man's not a man, on the mines, unless he's willing to do a bit of gold stealing, now and then. The big men, of course, run the racket; but it's the little men who are caught and get jailed, so that the gold stealing detective staff can earn their keep. No, Bill, you take my word for it, the only people who live in Kalgoorlie these days, are those who can't get away.'

'Gee, mum,' the tall handsome lad in tennis flannels who burst into the room exclaimed laughingly, 'what's wrong with Kal?'

'Dick, darling!' His mother's face lighted as she glanced at him. The girl beside Dick ran over to kiss her.

'We won our match, Missus Sally,' she cried. 'Just ran in to tell you.'

'Cheers!' Sally replied, keyed to their gay excitement. 'You must have some tea.'

She got up to go and make fresh tea, but Marie took the teapot from her, and Sally turned to introduce the young people.

'Bill, this is Amy Brierly,'' she said. 'And Dick, my eldest son. Mr. Bill Gerrity, children, and Mrs. Gerrity.'

'Better known as Bill Jehosaphat,' Bill grinned, shaking hands with Amy and Dick.

'Bill Jehosaphat!' Amy and Dick exclaimed together. They had

34

never heard of Mr. Gerrity. But Bill Jehosaphat—everybody on the fields had heard of him. Mrs. Gerrity was beginning to recognise that there was some honour attached to the name. After what Mrs. Gough had said, she was surprised to see two such attractive young people on the goldfields.

'Are they sweethearts?' she asked Marie.

Marie nodded. 'We are all very pleased. Their families were good friends in the early days.'

Amy had seated herself on the arm of Morris's chair. Her fair hair was fluffed out round a piquant, flushed face, and her brown eyes played with naïve coquetry from Dick to his father, including Bill and Dinny in their soft glance. It was easy to see that Amy liked men, and why even the old men liked Amy.

In the banter and lively din she and Dick created, nobody noticed Paddy Cavan appear in the doorway, behind Mrs. Gough, until Amy exclaimed lightly:

'Hullo, Paddy! Where did you spring from?'

Mrs. Gerrity was conscious of the awkward pause, and a vague discomfort that affected everybody as Paddy Cavan heaved himself into the room.

'Didn't know y' had company, Mrs. Gough,' he said gruffly. 'Felt like a cup er tea, if y've got one handy.'

'Certainly, Paddy.' Sally poured the tea, and overcoming her resentment of this intrusion, with easy graciousness, explained: 'You remember Paddy Cavan, don't you, Bill? I'm sure you haven't forgotten Bill Jehosaphat, have you, Paddy?'

'How d'y' do?' Bill said off-handedly.

'Fine.' Paddy assumed an aggressive assurance. 'How's y'rself, Bill?'

'Not too bad.'

They exchanged a few remarks as to when Bill had arrived, how long he was staying, what he thought of the goldfields now, although Paddy's gaze was fixed on Amy as if he were speaking to her, rather than to Bill Gerrity. Amy had no glances or smiles for him. She slipped to her feet, flipped out her skirts and grabbed her racquet.

'Come on, Dick,' she cried imperiously. 'We mustn't be late for the finals. Thanks for the tea, darling!'

As Amy and Dick swung away, calling goodbyes as they went, Bill and Dinny sent 'good lucks!' after them. Morris got up and left the room. Sam Mullet, Blunt Pick and Tassy Regan sat glowering at Paddy.

Sally had to exert herself to keep a conversation going between Bill and Paddy, Dinny having relapsed into a gloomy silence.

35

Marie chirped helpfully, and Mrs. Gerrity tried to keep her attention on what Mrs. Molloy was telling her about 'the windy toomer' that was eating out her insides. It was obvious Mrs. Gough had been disconcerted by this young man who had imposed himself on her tea-party.

Mrs. Gerrity noticed that she looked after him apprehensively, and began to clear away the tea things in a preoccupied way when he had gone.

'Like his cheek buttin' in where he's not wanted,' Mrs. Molloy breathed wrathfully. 'Paddy Cavan's getting too big for his boots, these days.'

Mrs. Gerrity thought it was time for her visit to end.

'It's been a lovely afternoon,' she said heartily to Sally. 'I feel as if I'm friends with you all now, as well as Bill. Perhaps someday, you and Mr. Gough will be able to come and visit us at Barrabool. If Bill doesn't decide to come back to the fields, of course.'

'He won't do that,' Sally said.

If Bill became reconciled to sheep, Mrs. Gerrity knew she would owe something to Sally. 'I don't believe he will. Thank you, my dear.'

When Dinny was walking back to the hotel with Bill and his wife, Bill asked:

'What the hell's he doin' there?'

'Who?'

'Paddy Cavan.'

'He's one of Mrs. Gough's boarders, at present,' Dinny said. 'That's why she has to put up with him. But he's got a nerve walkin' into her sittin'-room like that when she's got company, and Paddy knows it.'

Bill began to realise the situation. 'The Goughs've had a hard time, and no mistake. Not much luck has come Morrey's way. And Paddy Cavan, they tell me, has done well for himself. Got his iron in so many fires, he carries a lot of weight on the Boulder and in Kal, these days.'

'That's a fact,' Dinny agreed. 'But he's just the same unscrupulous skunk he was on the track.'

'Looks as if he's got tickets on Alf Brierly's daughter.'

'He has.' Dinny's laughter gurgled. 'But it won't do him any good. Amy's gone on Dick Gough.'

'Let me know when they're goin' to be spliced,' Bill laughed, 'and we'll send them a wedding present, eh, mum?'

'Oh, yes,' Mrs. Gerrity agreed, happy because Bill seemed to have made up his mind to return home with equanimity. 'Let's send it from Mr. and Mrs. Jehosaphat, Bill.'

36

CHAPTER IV

FROM the verandah in the dusk, Sally could see the last burnished rose and copper of sunset fade out of the sky. The air was oppressive for this time of the year. Perhaps it would rain before morning, she thought wearily, sitting down in her old three-legged, bag-seated chair, made from the trunk of a tree.

Frisco had presented it to her, when first she came to live with Morris on Hannans. There was something very comforting and restful about that chair. For years, Sally had brought her worries to it, and now as she lay back, she wanted to clear her mind of the uneasiness and sense of trouble brewing, which had beset her since her row with Paddy in the morning. During the afternoon she had put it away from her in order to entertain Bill Gerrity and his wife.

Her thoughts moved slowly in the sultry darkness. She could smell the musky, narcotic fragrance of blossom on the potato creeper, screening the verandah, and the faint stink of sulphurous fumes from the mines. People were singing a hymn in the little corrugated iron church nearby. The distant crash and rattle, thud and trampling of a battery still working along the Boulder ridge, droned against it.

The house behind her was quiet and dark. The boarders had dispersed after the evening meal. Morris was making arrangements for a funeral next day. Dinny had gone with him. Den was spending the week-end with Chris. She did not quite know what Lal was doing. Tom had not come in yet. Neither had Dick.

A pair of bats flittered near the verandah in the twilight. Sally's thoughts flittered with them.

She had enjoyed her afternoon: showing Mrs. Bill Gerrity that people on the goldfields knew something about the social amenities, and trying to cure Bill of a romantic hankering for the old days. It was impossible to live in the shadow of a time that had ended: could never be revived. Would he return now to his property in the green and rolling Barrabool Hills, and get over a nostalgia for the goldfields? Sally hoped so, and smiled as she thought of Mrs. Gerrity's: 'Thank you.'

What possessed Paddy Cavan to burst in on her party? He had never done such a thing before, knowing her sitting-room was not for the use of boarders. Morris insisted on that. If she would take in boarders, he said, they must understand that the bunk-house and the dining-room were their quarters. One room the family ought to be able to regard as its own; and Sally liked to assure him none of her boarders would dream of coming into the sitting-room unless they were specially invited.

That did not apply to Paddy, of course. He had impudence enough for anything. When first he had come to live with them, he tried to ingratiate himself with Morris and the boys. The boys never liked him, and it was only lately that Morris had come to tolerate Paddy's presence in the house. Now he showed a grudging respect for Mr. Cavan's advice and opinions about the share market.

Her suspicions that Morris might have been drawn into some business deal with Paddy were confirmed. There had been no time to talk to Morris yet; but she had contrived to have a few words with Dick before dinner.

'Don't worry, mum,' he said. 'If dad has done a few odd jobs for Paddy, there's nothing Paddy can fasten on him.'

And Tom? Of course, she knew how it was with Tom. He was a miner. If Tom had brought up a few specimens in his crib bag, now and then, it was to prove he had no highfaluting ideas about 'a miner's privilege': was a good mate: shared the risks of men who worked underground.

As for Dick, what was it he had said: 'Paddy didn't hint by any chance that I'm in the racket?'

'Dick!'

How scared she had been. Dick put his arms round her and kissed her. Such a dear, sensitive boy, her Dick, and sorry to have frightened her.

'I'm not,' he said, 'though I sometimes think I'm a fool not to take my cut when a shrewd trick with the slimes, or an assay, is being put over. It's the best safeguard a man's got, to be in a stunt with the others. And I'm out in the cold. Suspect because of that. But I can't suffer petty thieving. I sometimes think I'd be a better man if I'd never left the fields and could play the game according to the rules here.'

'Don't say such a thing!' Sally had protested.

'The mining game's rotten, Sal-o-my,' Dick exclaimed, bitterly. 'The only way to make your way in it, is to fight like the others. Frisco and Paddy Cavan, for example.'

'You couldn't be a crook if you tried,' Sally said sharply. 'So don't try.'

'I won't,' Dick had replied. 'Even if I never get anywhere—like Dinny and dad.'

There was anguish in the thought that this beloved son might be dogged by failure as his father had been. She had done her best to ensure it would never happen by giving Dick an education, and a chance to attain special qualifications for earning his living. But already, it seemed as if he knew more about the chicanery and corruption associated with mining than she did: how misfortune might overwhelm a man who was no more than a cog in its complicated machinery.

Her mind flickered over the struggle it had been to give Dick an education. She had been able to show Morris that she could provide for herself, and her son, in the early days on Hannans, when she began to realise Morris might never strike it rich out prospecting, or make a fortune gambling in shares. The other children had come along so quickly. For years, it seemed, there was always a baby in her arms; and yet she had managed to run a boarding-house and bring up her sons decently.

Of course, when he got over the gold fever, after that terrible rush to Mount Black, Morris had wanted to make amends for having left her to fend for herself. He shed every shred of his pride and aristocratic prejudices to become an undertaker. It was the finest thing Morris had ever done, Sally thought, and yet somehow it had broken him. With his dream of becoming a rich man, he lost the will to leave the fields. He never spoke now of any world but this of the mines and goldfields' towns.

The undertaking business had prospered for a while. Until on the crest of the boom a new firm arrived with a more showy hearse, grand plumes and comfortably upholstered mourning coaches. A few old customers had stuck to Morris, and he still carried on with his weedy horses and dilapidated funeral carriages, but the business scarcely paid its way. If it had not been for her boarders, Sally knew that she would not have been able to feed and clothe her boys so well, or give Dick a chance to go to college, the School of Mines and to study for a degree at the University of Sydney.

She told herself that she had wanted to give each of her sons the same chance. But Tom and Lal started work before Dick was through his course. Now there was only Den for whom she could do anything, and Den wouldn't hear of being a doctor or a lawyer. He wasn't studious; liked to 'muck round' with horses and cattle, as he said himself. He wanted to be a stockman. Well, even that was better than working on the mines!

Sally reproached herself that her other sons had never meant quite so much to her as Dick. It was such a joy to her when he was born. Coming of the other babies, she had taken more as a matter of course, sometimes even with bad grace. Although, she defended herself, she had given each of her children the same conscientious, motherly care. Each of her sons had his own place in her heart.

Memories of their childhood, hazy little pictures, and the sound of boyish voices surged through her mind, with a crazy cross-current of her talk to Paddy. They mingled, entwined, wove themselves together in a maze of thoughts which resolved themselves into a frantic query: 'But what could he do: How could Paddy Cavan harm me or the boys?'

Dick had never been as healthy and sturdy as Tom: he was more highly-strung and mercurial. Tom, a quiet, plodding little chap, with a pudgy, rather plain face and blue-grey eyes, she had thought inclined to be sulky at one time, and to begrudge Dick first place in her affection. But there was nothing of that sort in Tom's make-up, she knew now. He worshipped Dick, and Dick never wanted anything that Tom could not share.

When she used to ask Dick to mind the younger children—take them for a walk and see that they did not get into mischief—Tom understood he was in duty bound to look after them. Dick would start off with the best intentions in the world; but forget all about 'the nippers' to join in a scrap with other urchins, or run off to play football. Sally had been terrified of the pot holes and abandoned shafts into which Lal and Den might fall; but if Tom were with them, she knew she had nothing to fear. Larry had called himself Lal as a child, and the name stuck to him. Tom had done most of Dick's odd jobs for as long as she could remember, and often taken his punishment for not doing them. If Dick were sent to bed in disgrace, Tom always decided to go to bed early, also.

Morris had laughed at her attempts to discipline the boys. Lal and Den, too, seemed to regard it as a point of honour to stand by their elder brothers if they had been fighting, or wearing the seat out of their pants sliding on the big dump at the Golden Horseshoe. It amused Sally to remember how glum and displeased with her the younger boys had been, when Tom and Dick were in hot water for some misdeed or disobedience. It was trying at the time, but she liked to think now of the loyalty and affection her sons had for each other.

They had gone to the state school with some of the roughest and toughest urchins from the congested huts round the mines and on Ding Bat flat. Most of these youngsters fought like young roosters, tossed their pennies and gambled fiercely, swore and smoked as soon as they could pick up the fag end of a cigarette. Sally was afraid that her boys would do likewise if she were not quite stern and firm with them. She had forbidden smoking, gambling and swearing; and for a while Dick and Tom had a bad time at school. They were always coming home with torn clothes, black eyes and bleeding noses.

Sally was furious. It was not to be borne. Was she going to allow her beautiful sons to be so knocked about, perhaps maimed for life, because some beastly little bullies set on to them? No, she told Morris. She was going to complain to the schoolmaster, and if matters did not improve she would take the boys away from that school, send them to Perth, no matter what it cost. But Morris put his foot down. He said she would only make a laughing stock of the boys if she did such a thing. They must learn to stand up for themselves, use their wits to keep out of a fight, if they could not give as good a handful of five as they were likely to get.

Morris knew something of boxing, although he had never been much of a fighter himself. Enough to teach the boys how to defend themselves at any rate, he said. He remembered what his own coach at school, and in a crack English regiment, had taught him. And he took no end of trouble with his tutoring of the boys. Sent for gloves: had Dick and Tom doing exercises every morning, and shaping up to each other, in the back-yard, in the evening. Such a skinny little pair of cockchafers, they looked, prancing about in their, tiny white pants and punching gamely at each other with those big padded gloves! The physical exercise did them all the world of good; and it did Morris good too, teaching them to use their fists. Never before had he taken so much interest in the boys.

It was Dinny's idea to take Dick and Tom out with him on a prospecting trip for their school holidays. How thrilled they had been! For years, there was nothing they liked better than camping in the bush with Dinny. They had learned to handle horses and camels on these trips: how to read tracks on the earth, to find water, loam for gold, peg and work an alluvial claim. They were good prospectors and bushmen before they left school, Dinny declared.

Oh yes, Dick and Tom could look after themselves in the great mysterious country of thick scrub and stark ridges which still lay beyond the settlements of the mining towns. They liked to talk of tracks, wells and soaks on dry stretches: tell their father of 'likely country' they had seen: discuss with him the various types of gold-bearing rock, and theories about the geological formation of the Boulder mines.

That was because Dinny had taken Dr. Larcomb, the famous geologist, with him on one of his trips, and Dr. Larcomb had lent Dick a paper on 'The Pre-Cambrian Rocks of Western Australia'. Sally could hear Tom describing how Dick had shot a bush turkey, and how he had found a black and yellow-banded snake in his blankets.

Sally was sick as she thought of it, and the danger that had threatened her sons. She remembered the panic which had over-whelmed her when she had been sickening for typhoid, on the track to Lake Darlot, and one of those nightmarish reptiles slid out of

41

her blankets. Tom was very proud of having killed his snake. And how Dick had teased her about being so scared as to what might have happened if the snake had bitten one of them out there in the bush!

Was it any wonder, Sally asked herself, that Dick had become interested in geology and metallurgy? He had started to bring in bits of rock and ore from these trips with Dinny: would label them neatly and stow them away in boxes. He and Tom had built themselves a shed in the back-yard to put all their treasures in. Tom took possession of his father's dolly pot and spent hours pounding up specimens and panning off. He was much more interested in the amount of gold he got out of their samples, than Dick. Now and then Dinny brought Tom ore to dolly for him, and Tom could pan off as well as he could himself.

'There's a prospector for you,' Dinny said. 'Tom's a born prospector, if ever there was one.'

Sally was not so pleased. She did not want Tom to be a prospector. She did not want any of her sons to become prospectors, or absorbed by the mining industry. All her plans and schemes were directed towards getting the boys away from the mines, and those infectious illusions of the gold fever. It had taken a different form now, no longer depended on the unearthing of new deposits, but on the exploitation of the mines and share market.

That, perhaps, was why she was so cross when Dick and Tom built themselves a furnace and began experimenting in their shed in the back-yard. An explosion nearly blew off Tom's eyebrows. Sally put a stop then to that messing about with evil-smelling chemicals. But Dick had made up his mind to be a geologist and metallurgist.

It wasn't such a bad idea, Morris thought. There were jobs opening up on the mines for qualified men, and if Dick had the brains to study, he ought to be able to get a good job and earn a reasonable salary.

Dick had the brains, his mother was sure. And he was eager to study, though his reports from college said he was 'intellectually lazy': would only apply himself to subjects in which he was interested.

It had been a great struggle to find the money to send him to Prince Alfred College in Adelaide. Two years Dick had spent there. She was hoping to send Tom too; but Tom had started work before Dick left school; Tom, at seventeen, refused to consider being anything but a miner and lied about his age to work underground. That meant earning bigger money than he could any other way. And he had handed it over to her on every pay day. So proud to be able to, and to help paying Dick's fees at the School of Mines. The few shillings she made him keep for pocket money, Tom seemed to have little use for, although Sally noticed he was buying books and reading a good deal.

Of course, she knew Tom had a good head on his shoulders. None of her boys were fools, if it came to that. Why Dick had been selected from all the students at the School of Mines to demonstrate a new process of treating sulphide ore at the University of Sydney! It was a pity Dick had not finished his course at the university and taken his degree. She did not quite know what had happened to prevent his doing that; but anyhow, he was at home now, and had got a job on the Boulder.

Sally wished she had never let Paddy take that room next to Dinny's on the back verandah. But she needed money badly at the time to send Dick to college in Adelaide.

'I can pay for me keep now, missus—and a bit over,' Paddy had said when he came to ask for a room. 'There's a note I've been owin' you a long time for nursing me through the fever.'

'That's all right, Paddy,' Sally said dubiously. The note for five pounds was inadequate as payment for a month's board and lodging, much less for the nursing and special food she had given him.

But Paddy tendered it with such a magnificent gesture, she was taken aback: would have liked to smile and reject his spurious generosity. There was Dick's education to think of, however, and no sum of money was to be disdained if it added to her fund for that purpose. To refuse cash for a bad debt, also, was opposed to her business principles. This debt of Paddy's she had given up hope of ever collecting.

Sally apologised to herself for being so mercenary: and for deciding that she could not afford to refuse Paddy's five pounds, or his application for a room. She had three rooms vacant at the time, and would have let one to any decent man who could pay for bed and board.

She prided herself on having become a good business woman, hard and frugal, in running her boarding-house. Morris and Dinny were not pleased to know Paddy Cavan was going to be one of her boarders. They thought it would be humiliating for her to have to cook and clean up for Paddy: be his servant to all intents and purposes, but she could not allow that to interfere with her plans for Dick. She had washed and cooked for other men, and they had always treated her with respect. Sally saw that they did, even when they were drunk. Too much drinking, she would not stand, on the

43

boys' account, and the men who boarded at Mrs. Gough's were aware of that.

She would not have to put up with drunkenness from Paddy, Sally knew. He had the reputation for being a sober, hard-working young man. Too stingy to buy drinks for himself, or anybody else. Sally was not concerned about his meanness either, so long as he paid his board regularly and did not make any extra demands on her time and attention.

Let Paddy look out for himself, though, if he presumed to patronise her, or Morris, because he had money and they had not! Sally had promised herself to keep Paddy in his place as a boarder and not let him pretend to be a friend of the family. Before long, it was obvious that this was what he wanted: to share in their family life. He did his best to ingratiate himself with Morris, asking his advice on all manner of subjects, as if he attached the greatest importance to Morris's experience and judgment. And he had made clumsy attempts at a good-natured, elder brother attitude to the boys. Other boarders, she never resented calling her 'Mum', but she could never endure Paddy Cavan to assume the casual familiarity.

'What's his game?' Sally had asked herself.

Paddy did not leave her long in doubt.

'Y' gave me a lot of good advice when I was a kid, Missus Sally,' he said. 'Sure, I believe y're responsible for puttin' me where I am now. I'd be wastin' me money in booze and gamblin' but for y'r advice. I wish y'd go on from where y' left off: pull me up when I'm not sayin' things proper, or me manners is bad.'

'Are bad,' Sally corrected, smiling at having discovered the intention of this grave, uncouth lad. A sparkle of his youthful gaminerie lighted Paddy's eyes.

'Y' see after all I want to be a reputable citizen, like y' said.'

'To look like one, at least.'

'That's right,' Paddy agreed. 'Maybe, y' can't make a silk purse out of a sow's ear. I'm not wantin' to be a silk purse. But I'm after learnin' to behave so as Frisco and the mob he gets round with, won't sling off at me. Frisco, himself, was as rough as bags, once, missus. You know that. And now, he mucks round with the bloody toffs as if he was one of 'em.'

'He never says bloody in a lady's presence, Paddy.'

'Neither does a decent miner—beggin' y'r pard'n, ma'am.'

'It's no use a man pretending to be anything he is not.' Sally yielded unwillingly to the charm Paddy could exercise when he was not trying to be a shrewd and successful young business man.

'I'm not wantin' to be anything I'm not,' he said doggedly.

44

'But I am wantin' to learn how to make the most of meself and me opportunities—like Alf Brierly said. He was a great chap, Alf. It was him put me up to readin' and writin' to improve meself: taught me book-keeping and said I should go about a bit and get used to meetin' people. God, I was fond of him, missus. Who'd've thought he'd blow out his light? Who'd've thought Alf would do a thing like that?'

'A good many people think you could have prevented it, Paddy.'

'Me?' Paddy was all honest amazement. 'It's a lie. I'd've done anything for Alf, and he knew it. But things were in a bad way on the Yellow Feather, and he wouldn't take my advice. He was manager and I couldn't do anything about it. But Christ, it fair broke me up, Alf's death. I got out of the Feather because I couldn't stand seein' another man in Alf's place.'

Sally did not believe him, and saddened by the thought of Alf Brierly's death, her sympathy with Paddy and his attempts to acquire social polish had waned.

'You can't trust the little blighter,' she told herself, then as she was doing now.

But Paddy continued to occupy a room in her house, pay his board regularly and praise her cooking. He was good humoured and unobtrusive at first: took an interest in the boys' lessons, borrowed their books, exclaimed with admiration at their smartness and knowledge, learning a good deal from their explanations and arguments.

He was watching and learning all the time, Sally realised: imitating Morris's manner with men, and the way Morris treated her, with formal courtesy before strangers. Morris had always insisted on the boys showing her small attentions, opening the door for her and jumping up from her chair, if they happened to be sprawling in it when she came into the room. Soon, Paddy was standing to attention when she appeared, and bowing her out of the room as if she were a duchess. He had bought a book on etiquette, Sally knew, and practised its instruction on her. It was ludicrous to watch Paddy's efforts at polite behaviour, and to hear him stumble into the rough and ready speech of the fields when he was excited, or at a loss for a word.

He had worked as clerk for a firm of stock brokers before he set up in a small office for himself.

It puzzled Sally that Paddy never bragged about his property and investments. He was as close and close-fisted as if he had nothing to spend or boast about. She would have been easier in her mind, had he been more like the cocky, unscrupulous urchin she had known in the early days of Hannans, going his own way without giving a damn what anybody thought of him and never hiding his light under a bushel. Paddy was all bushel and no light, now-a-days. Every morning he went off to work at his office in town, and he worked hard there was no doubt: often into the small hours of the morning after a hectic day on the Stock Exchange. He looked twice his age and was completely absorbed in his job.

'You've got to take off your hat to him,' Morris said, having been won to an admiration for Paddy's pertinacity. 'He's dragged himself up, by sheer grit and . . .'

'Gold stealing.'

'Ninety per cent. of the men on the mines know something about that,' Morris objected. 'It's all right if you can get away with it, and Paddy knows the ropes.'

'Well, I won't have him doing any snide business in my house,' Sally said. Yes, she had said it long ago, she reminded herself. She had said it to Paddy himself, so no one could blame her now for insisting that her decision should be respected.

As Paddy had learned all he wanted to from Morris and the boys, he became more self-centred and bumptious. He wore decent clothes now, and carried himself with an air of importance. He had dropped the idea of becoming a polished gentleman like Frisco, and acquired a certain rugged individuality.

'Better be a rough diamond than a flash jackanapes,' Morris had told him. 'It's more your style, Paddy.'

But Paddy had never got on well with her boys, Sally reflected. He was never more than on suffrance with them. Particularly Dick —and Paddy had always been jealous of Dick. Although Paddy based a man's worth on his ability to make money, he envied Dick all those qualities which education and a careful upbringing had given him. He envied Dick, as well, his knowledge of mathematics, physics and chemistry: all the sciences which were related to the mining industry. And he envied Dick his popularity with girls.

Paddy's grudge against Dick had deepened from the time they went to a dancing class together, Sally thought. Paddy had often been snubbed by the girls with whom he wanted to dance. He was so rough and clumsy, trod on their toes, and hugged them with such gusto, that the girls scattered when Paddy approached. And Dick, slim and good-looking, all the girls wanted to dance with him. Amy Brierly had run away giggling when Paddy asked her for 'the pleasure of a dance', on one occasion.

'It's no pleasure dancing with you, Paddy,' Amy cried, and had gone off with Dick.

Paddy would never forget that, Sally imagined. He had been too busy with his schemes for being a great man to be interested in girls, until he met Amy at the dancing class. She was like a pretty butterfly that had fluttered across his path. He wanted to grab her: the impulse to chase and hold her still tormented him.

That was the worst part of her interview with Paddy this morning, Sally feared: the way she had aroused his animosity about Amy.

Her thoughts swerved to Amy.

Amy had been a wilful and spritely child when her father died. She grew pale and weedy-looking while she was at the convent in Coolgardie. After Laura married Tim McSweeney, Amy came to her mother for every week-end, and recovered her spirits.

But Laura did not like the hotel as a home for Amy. McSweeny was devoted to her and thoroughly spoilt the child. Everybody made a fuss of her, and Amy enjoyed the noisy gaiety and exuberance of hotel life. Laura had her own sitting-room and piano. Amy was supposed to practise her scales and five-finger exercises there in the morning. She never did unless Tim bribed her with promises of lollies or drives. And there was nothing Amy liked better than to drive beside him in his brand new buggy with a pair of bay horses. McSweeney boasted that it was the smartest turnout in town.

It was not good for Amy to have so much notice taken of her, Laura complained when she came to see Sally, although she had to admit that Amy was a different creature since Tim had taken her to his bosom. She glowed with health and vitality: was a warm-hearted child, needed the love and sense of security McSweeney had given her, Sally thought. He was as proud of and delighted with Amy as if she were his own daughter. Amy could twist him round her little finger, Laura said. As there seemed no prospect that she would give McSweeney any children of his own, Laura regarded it as a dispensation of providence that he should be so satisfied with Amy. Amy called Tim, dad, quite naturally and happily.

It seemed as if she had forgotten she ever had any other father. Laura, herself, could not forget Alf. Vaguely she resented Amy's acceptance of McSweeney in his place, as disloyal to Alf's memory.

She said Amy was like a kitten that purred when it was well-fed and stroked caressingly. She was grateful to McSweeney for feeding and petting Amy, for adopting her in his generous, wholesale fashion; but that Amy should respond to him with such genuine affection, alienated her mother from the child.

Laura had insisted that Amy should go back to school, and Amy remained at the convent until she was sixteen, coming home only for occasional week-ends and holidays. She had hated the dull routine and loneliness of her school life. It was in sharp contrast to the good times McSweeney gave her and the presents he lavished on her.

Amy ran in to see Sally, now and then, when she was at home for the week-end, or on holidays. She was very proud of the pony McSweeney had given her, liked to gallop madly down the dusty road, and show off her horsemanship by making the pony pig-root and prance before the boys. They were envious of her prowess: they could ride, but only rarely when Dinny was in from a prospecting trip was it possible for Dick, or Tom, to get hold of a horse and dash along the roads with Amy.

Dick and she travelled together sometimes on the train when she was going to the convent, and he was going back to school in Adelaide. There had been an attraction between them since they were children.

At seventeen, when she had left school and was living with Laura and Tim at the 'Western Star', Amy was being flattered and courted in a way that would have gone to any girl's head. Of course Amy was pretty and vivacious. Already half a dozen men had fallen in love with her and wanted to marry her. Laura said it was not good enough for Alf's daughter to be made love to by any drunken scoundrel. She decided to send Amy on a long visit to her father and mother in Victoria. Laura would not go herself. She had changed too much, she felt, to make the visit a success; but she thought it would be a good idea to send Amy to her grandparents for a while.

She had spoken to Tim about it, and he agreed that it would probably be best for Amy to go to Laura's people for a year or two —although he was miserable at the thought of losing her. Tim had been very generous, insisted on paying Amy's travelling expenses and making her an allowance.

But Amy had been away only a few months when she jumped off the morning train, and ran into the station-yard.

The first person she saw was Dinny Quin, standing beside his spring cart. He had gone up to the station to collect some cases of apples for Sally. Amy hailed and embraced him excitedly.

'I was so miserable, I couldn't stand it over there, any longer, Dinny,' she explained. 'So I just ran away, and left a note telling gran I was coming home.'

'My, you have sprung a surprise on us, Amy,' Dinny chuckled. 'Hop up and I'll drive you into town.'

As they jogged along, Amy chattered eagerly. Everybody had been very kind. But all the time she was longing to be back on the fields. Never again would she complain of the dust and heat. It was always raining in Melbourne and so cold.

'Homesick, that's what you were, Amy,' Dinny told her. 'Jest plain homesick for old friends and this dirty, ramshackle town. Queer how it gets you, isn't it? Felt like that, meself, when Mrs. Gough persuaded me to go to the coast for a holiday once.'

'How are they, Missus Sally and the boys?' Amy asked. 'Has Dick got a job, yet?'

'They're all well and Dick's still at the School of Mines,' Dinny replied. 'Me. I had a good crushing this week, and come in to celebrate.'

'How much did she go, Dinny?' Amy exclaimed. 'And where's the show?'

Dinny had told Sally all about it, and how Amy talked like an old timer, wanting to know all the news of the mines and rushes. She'd got the dust of the fields in her bones all right, he said. It was no use Laura thinking she could transplant the girl. When they reached the 'Western Star', Amy had scrambled down from Dinny's cart and run into the pub, calling: 'Daddy! Daddy!'

McSweeney met her with open arms and Amy burst into tears.

'Don't let mother send me away again,' she begged.

'Not if you don't want to go, baby,' McSweeney promised. 'But Laura won't like it, your running away like this.'

'I made up my mind all of a sudden when your last cheque came,' Amy confessed.

It was easier to explain her homesickness to Tim than to Laura. But Amy always got her own way. She persuaded Laura that she could never live with her grandmother and grandfather. They were too old-fashioned and straight-laced, always correcting her for using slang and being unladylike. If she talked to men and boys they said she was bold: and thought it a disgrace that Laura had married a publican.

'I suppose so,' Laura sighed.

Amy was soon enjoying life in her own way, rushing about to see old friends, playing tennis with bank clerks and lads from the School of Mines: going to dances and picnics with the smart set of Kalgoorlie. She tried to make herself useful to Laura: took several duties off her hand, such as checking linen for the laundry and issuing fresh supplies for tables in the dining-room, and for the bedrooms. Paper flowers were banished from the 'Western Star'. Amy arranged fresh flowers in the vases, bouquets of gum tips in big bowls for the lounge and vestibule. Tim was delighted although as likely as not, Amy might forget to dispense the linen sometimes, and to change the flowers and gum leaves when they were withered.

She had told Sally about her experiences in Melbourne, and often dropped in to see her, usually at a time when Dick was likely to be

49

coming home. Dick and Amy looked happy and self-conscious at seeing each other, and went off together on some pretext. Everybody was pleased when Amy stayed to tea, the younger boys as well as Morris and Dinny. They teased Dick about Amy: said she was 'his girl'.

But Amy fluttered light-heartedly with many other young men. Often at a dance or picnic, Dick had to hover on the outskirts of a group of admirers round Amy. She seemed to outgrow him so quickly. While Dick was still a student, Amy had become a sparkling young woman, pursued by men much older than either Dick or herself.

Dick retired to the background of her surroundings. He could not compete with men who wore dinner jackets to dances and took Amy for drives in a smart turn-out. He had no money either to spend on flowers and chocolates for her. Sometimes, Amy seemed barely to notice Dick at a party, except to preen herself before him in a pretty dress, or show off some new conquest; and sometimes, she ignored everybody to dance and flirt with Dick. Dick could not bring himself at first to forgo these small mercies. But he came home from a party, one night, white with rage. He had finished with Amy, he told Tom. She could have every other man in the town on a string if she liked, but she wasn't going to make a laughing-stock of him any more.

Dick looked wretched for a while. Wounded vanity and calf love, Sally told herself. She was vexed with Amy for hurting Dick; but glad he had sufficient strength of mind to show her she could not play fast and loose with him.

It was said soon afterwards that Amy was engaged to an American engineer; and later that she was going to marry a mining magnate, old enough to be her father. Amy denied these rumours and continued to flirt gaily with several men.

Then Dick had gone away. When one of the instructors at the School of Mines received an appointment to the University of Sydney, he offered to take Dick with him as assistant demonstrator. It was a great opportunity for Dick; and Dr. Larcomb, who had been visiting the fields, advised him to take a degree in science while he was at the university. 'The Kalgoorlie Miner' had devoted half a column to describing the brilliant career opening up before this local boy who had been chosen to demonstrate an important new process in connection with the treatment of refractory ores.

How money was to be found for Dick's preliminary expenses, Sally did not know. But found it would be, she was determined. And so was Tom, she discovered. He was as proud as she was of

Dick's achievement, and as eager for him to make the most of his opportunity.

'Don't worry, mum,' he said. 'I've been saving: got a bit in the bank. You can have it for Dick.'

She was astounded when, a few days later, he gave her fifty pounds. She wondered how on earth Tom had been able to save so much on the few shillings of his wages he kept for pocket money. She had felt, at the time, it would be better not to inquire too closely how he came to have so much money.

Dick had hated to know that Tom was earning a man's wages, and could help her, while he was still 'at school' as he said.

'Nonsense,' Sally said, when Dick objected to using Tom's savings. 'Tom's pleased to have the money to give you. He knows he couldn't do the sort of work you're doing.'

'I'm not so sure about that.' Dick was always quick to defend Tom. 'He's got a better brain than I have, as a matter of fact, mother. Slower but more tenacious. Tom'll worry over a problem like a dog with a bone, when I'll lose patience and drop it.'

Sally loved to hear the boys stand up for each other. There was a wonderful bond between the brothers.

What happened to Dick in Sydney? Sally had never quite discovered.

He was working well at the university and had passed his first exams with honours when Frisco blew along. It had been a dazzling experience for Dick, apparently, being taken up by Mr. Francisco de Morfé and introduced everywhere as: 'Mr. Richard Fitz-Morris Gough, the brilliant young metallurgist from the Golden Mile.'

Sally cursed Frisco for interfering with Dick's career. It was all very well for Frisco to be interested in Dick, and to put some work in his way which would enable Dick to earn a little extra money while he was studying; but she had dreaded the unsettling effect of Frisco's influence on her boy.

Frisco's affairs were so often on the verge of crisis, and she remembered Paddy Cavan had hinted, at the time, that Frisco was due for one of his periodic crashes. It was extraordinary how Frisco managed to weather a crash and rose again soon afterwards like a jack-in-the-box. The man was a wizard of finance, Morris said. He dominated any situation by sheer personal magnetism and financial audacity.

From little things Dick said after he returned home, Sally had gathered that Frisco persuaded Dick to drop his science course and take a job with him, boosting a group of mines which he was anxious to float into a company.

'It's waste of time for a chap like you, Dick, with practical knowledge of the fields, to bother about a degree,' Frisco had said. 'There are jobs waiting now for metallurgists on the Mile, and I reckon you've learnt more on the goldfields than you'll ever learn at a university about the problems we're up against.'

Dick agreed with him. And when Frisco offered Dick a good salary to work with him, first of all by addressing meetings of shareholders and possible investors, on the significance of the new processes for dealing with refractory ores and reducing costs of production, he accepted the proposition.

It had meant going about a good deal with Frisco, dashing to Melbourne, Brisbane and Adelaide and back to Sydney: living at the best hotels, going to race meetings and theatre parties, being invited to balls, and to suppers with ballet dancers. People seemed to think Frisco was a millionaire, Dick said. Frisco did his best to keep them thinking on those lines. He carried on in great style. It paid in the long run, he maintained: helped to inspire confidence in the mob whose money he wanted. That was all very well, Dick considered, while Mr. de Morfé was dealing with mining propositions which could become paying concerns, by the application of up-to-date methods.

But, apparently, when Dick became better acquainted with specimens from the mines for which Mr. de Morfé was making extravagant claims, he and Frisco quarrelled. Frisco had told Dick to get to hell out of his office, and Dick had got. He didn't need 'a brilliant young metallurgist from the Golden Mile' to do any more of his dirty work, was Dick's explanation, with a wry smile. Dick had come home: worked his way as steward on the boat to Fremantle, and walked in one evening with a casual: 'Hullo, Mother!'

Dick did not look like a scapegoat or a prodigal, though. He was well-dressed and had the poise of a man of the world; but he was still her dear boy, Sally assured herself. How he had hugged and kissed her, exclaiming: 'God, it's good to be home, Sal-o-my!'

Sally had read disappointment and disillusionment in Dick's eyes, and thought he was a little ashamed of having given up his course at the university to work with Frisco. Dick felt that he had failed to do what everybody expected of him, perhaps: to come home with all sorts of honours. As a Bachelor of Science, at least. But she could not reproach him on that account. She was so glad to see him and to know that whatever else had happened, Dick could still look at her with a clean, straight gaze which meant he had not been false to the standard of personal integrity she had tried to give him.

He would not hear of going back to the university. A job on the

52

mines was what he wanted immediately, he said. He had lost so much time, playing round with Frisco, and spent every penny he had earned into the bargain. Not for another day was the family going to keep him.

Dick had been lucky. He got two or three temporary jobs, before this one on the Boulder Reef was offered to him. At last, he seemed fairly settled and interested in his work.

Nothing must happen to interfere with it. Sally's forehead wrinkled again to the fret and fume of her underlying anxiety. It swirled again about Amy.

Paddy Cavan had been paying court to her while Dick was away.

Paddy and Amy could be seen riding out towards Hannan's Lake on a Sunday afternoon sometimes: Paddy bumping up and down on a raking grey and Amy racing ahead on a chestnut filly he had bought for her.

Laura would not allow Amy to accept the chestnut as a gift from Paddy; but Amy was crazy about the mare. Paddy kept her at the livery stables, nearby, so that Amy could go for a ride whenever she felt inclined.

Amy liked racing about on that high-spirited chestnut, Sally guessed. She liked cutting a dash in her tight-fitting, black riding habit and smart, little bowler hat. But that made no difference to her treatment of Paddy. Amy laughed at, and made fun of him in a way no other man would have stood, according to Laura.

'I've warned Amy that it's dangerous to trifle with Paddy,' Laura complained. 'But she doesn't pay any attention to what I say. She's a silly little thing. Quite heartless, but innocent really! So used to men being in love with her that one more or less doesn't matter. And Paddy never seems to mind how insulting she is to him. He just sits there—and gloats over her, as if he were sure to get her some day. Oh, dear, I do wish she'd get married and settle down!'

'I'd be sorry to see Amy married to Paddy Cavan,' Sally had said.

'Oh, Amy would never dream of marrying Paddy,' Laura exclaimed, startled out of her vague discontent. 'As a matter of fact, I think the only man she wants to marry is your Dick, Sally. Amy's always been fond of Dick, you know, but they had some sort of a tiff before he went to Sydney.'

'You can't wonder, can you?' Sally queried.

'I suppose not,' Laura sighed.

Sally was amused as she thought of how Amy had set about recapturing Dick.

Soon after his return, when he began to go to dances and tennis parties in Kalgoorlie, Dick and Amy had met again; but Dick, it seemed, did not want to be inveigled into their old sweethearting. The girls were crazy about him, Sally heard, and really, she could not blame them. Dick was the most personable young man in town. He danced and flirted with any girl, except Amy: took Poppy Dowsett or Leila Melleson to parties and picnics, and sometimes for a drive on Sunday afternoon when he could hire a sulky at the livery stables.

Amy came to wail to his mother about the way Dick was treating her.

'It's as if he hates me, Missus Sally,' she said. 'And I can't bear it. I can't really! To see Dick going about with that stuck-up Poppy Dowsett makes me so miserable I don't know what to do.'

'Serves her right,' Tom growled, when Sally told him about Amy's visit.

He could not forgive Amy for the way she had gone riding with Paddy Cavan; and philandered with other men, even before Dick went to the Eastern States.

'But I think Dick cares for Amy,' his mother ventured. 'He's still got a snapshot of her, when she was a schoolgirl, in a wallet he carries about in his breast pocket.'

Tom smiled.

'I reckon he does,' he said slowly. 'Dick's just giving Amy a taste of what she gave him.'

'Laura says it's breaking her heart,' Sally told him. 'She says Amy's really in love with Dick, and crying her eyes out at night because Dick doesn't like her any more.'

'You'd better tip him the wink, mum,' Tom advised.

Sally did not know whether to take Amy's love-sickness seriously; but she thought she might as well tell Dick that Amy had come to see her, and wept because he was being so unkind. Dick seemed quite pleased at the news. He went about whistling and smiling to himself for a day or two. Then he had gone to see Amy.

Dick had told Amy she was the only girl in the world for him, Sally understood, and that he wanted to marry her. Amy was radiantly happy. Dick gave her a little ring, made from a slug he had found when they were both children, set with three little Australian diamonds. Amy was delighted with it, and she and Dick went about everywhere together, as an engaged couple, very pleased with and enamoured of each other.

That was all very well while it lasted. But before long Amy was talking about their wedding. It was no earthly use to say she and Dick were too young for holy matrimony. They were lovers and

54

young people matured early on the goldfields: sometimes had to be married in a hurry. Laura did not want that to happen, neither did she, Sally told herself.

She thought Amy and Dick should have a home of their own as soon as possible. She had said so to Dick. He was taking a glass or two of beer now, as every young man of his age did; and sometimes, when he came in from spending an evening with Amy at McSweeney's, Sally was afraid he had been drinking too much.

But it was Laura who appeared most anxious not to delay the wedding. She was so pleased Amy wanted to marry Dick; and terrified that she might change her mind, or something come between them. Dick seemed a rather easy-going and restrained lover, quite satisfied to wait until he was earning a better salary before marrying. Amy had been hurt by his reluctance to make definite arrangements for their wedding. He wanted to help his mother with Den's education, before undertaking family responsibilities himself, Dick tried to explain. Amy could not understand that. She said his mother and brothers meant more to Dick than she did; and that he could not love her very much if he was willing to wait months, perhaps years, before they could be together.

Dick laughed at her jealousy, but Amy had broken down his resistance. She would be the most tempestuous and seductive sweetheart, Sally was sure: wanted Dick all to herself and quite soon. It did not matter where they lived, or how poor they were, Amy protested; but Tim had promised to build them a nice little bungalow at Mullingar, and her mother wanted to buy the furniture for it. She had already given Amy all her household linen, and Amy and she were sewing busily for her trousseau. So why should they wait?

Why, indeed, Sally asked herself.

It was sweet to think Dick wanted to help her and that he would have liked to do something for Den; but after all, there was no necessity for him to make any contribution to the family funds, just now. And it was important for Dick to establish himself. He was young, of course, to be undertaking the responsibility of a home of his own; but if Amy meant what she said, and was willing to manage on Dick's salary, they ought to be all right and quite happy. It was fortunate that Tim McSweeney and Laura could afford to give them a house and help them to start housekeeping.

If Laura survived McSweeney she would be a rich woman, and Amy inherit all she possessed. In any case, McSweeney would not forget Amy in his will. Sally smiled to think of herself ruminating in such a worldly wise way, and regarding this as quite a good

55

marriage for Dick, promising him some financial security and a comfortable old age.

Yes, she had been quite right to take a firm stand with Paddy Cavan, Sally assured herself. She could not allow anything to interfere with Dick's prospects now.

CHAPTER V

TOM was the first to come in. He looked tired and thoughtful, a big, solid lad, in his loose white shirt and best trousers. He had had a good day, he said: been to a union meeting in the morning, and ridden over to the Kurrawang on his bicycle to do a bit of organising among the foreign workers. Charley O'Reilly had taken him home to tea. He had ridden back with Eily in the evening and they had gone to Marie's. A few people always dropped in there on a Sunday night to yarn with old Robbie.

Sally liked Tom to tell her what he had been doing, and to know he liked to sit talking to her for a while before he went to bed. But to-night there were several things she wanted to say to him.

She told Tom about her row with Paddy; and what Paddy had said about him and his father.

'Paddy's got nothing on me, mum,' Tom said gravely. 'I've never had any dealings with him, though I have brought up a few 'weights now and again. But I cut it out long ago. The game's not good enough as you say.'

'Don't think I don't understand why you did it, Tom,' Sally said. 'I know the men are justified, and you've had to show you're good mates with them. Besides—we don't need money so badly now.'

That was just to indicate she knew where those 'savings' had come from when she needed money for Dick to go to Sydney. She could see the surge of blood to Tom's quiet face; but his eyes did not falter. He would not admit that she had been a guilty partner in that affair, Sally guessed.

'It's been a tough struggle to bring up all you boys, decently,' she tried to explain. 'I haven't wanted much for you, just that you should be honest, clean-living men, and have some education for earning your living. But the way things are in this town now, it seems that men like Paddy Cavan can get away with anything, and men who do just little things against the law have to pay the penalty for the big crooks as well as themselves. I feel we must be extra careful: not let them bring any disgrace on us.'

56

'Don't you worry, mum,' Tom said gently, as he was leaving her, 'Paddy can't hurt us.'

Sally was not so sure of that. He was a good boy, her Tom, she told herself, so staunch and reliable, but not as quick-witted in his judgments as Dick.

Morris was not so easy to handle when he came in from a wake he had been hauled off to attend unexpectedly. He was in anything but a good humour because he saw no chance of being paid for the coffin, or funeral expenses. The widow had wept on his shoulder, he told Sally, and exclaimed before the assembled company:

'Surre, it's a grand coffin ye've made for father, Mr. Gough! And I'm mighty obliged to yer for the loving kindness. Me old man always said, ses he: "Maggie when I breathe me last, see to it me old friend, Morrey Gough, has the puttin' away of me. He'd not bother ye about the price of a few boards to cover me old bones, or the turnin' out of his hearse and mourning carriages to take an old mate to the cemetery." Wisher-wisher, God bless us, it's fine the sintiments ye old timers have for each other, and I'm not denyin' I'd be hard put to it to find the money to bury father, if I'd had to depend on one of these money-grubbin' firms makes their profit out of the tears of heart-broken widders and orphans, Mr. Gough.'

It was quite useless for Morris to explain to the half-drunken old woman and the derelicts boozing at her expense, that Mat Waddleton had never been a mate of his, or come foot-slogging into Coolgardie with the first team.

Sally had to laugh and try to console Morris for one of those losses to which his business was liable. She made him a cup of tea, and when he had recovered from his chagrin at having to bear the cost of old Waddleton's funeral, told him about her interview with Paddy.

'I made it quite clear to Paddy,' Sally said, 'that I wouldn't have him using this house as a dump for stolen gold.'

'Nonsense!' Morris exclaimed testily. 'He doesn't do that. If he does bring a bit of gold here, it doesn't stay very long. Maritana takes it out to the plant. And Paddy's responsible for it, not you, if it's found in his possession.'

'That's not the point,' Sally declared. 'I don't want my house raided. I'm not going to take any chances from now on. I'd like you to understand that, Morris—and not have anything to do with Paddy's transactions.'

Morris had taken a few drinks at the wake, perhaps to console himself for getting nothing else out of it, Sally thought. The blood was heavy in his face.

'Not so much of the stand-over, Sally,' he said irritably.

'If you have been doing any odd jobs for Paddy,' Sally continued, more mildly, 'it must stop. We've got the boys to think of, Morris, and you can't afford to get into an awkward position on their account. Dinny says there's a new man on the gold stealing detective staff who's sworn to clean things up—and he's getting busy. Warned the Big Four he's going to stop the racket, and Dinny told me to tell you to stand clear.'

That was making it easy for him, she decided. Dinny had not said so; but she was sure he would have, had he thought she needed that message for Morris. She had been able to have only a few words with Dinny while she was serving the midday meal; and he was only too pleased to hear she was sending Paddy Cavan away, 'with a flea in his ear', as Dinny put it.

'I suppose Dinny knows what he's talking about,' Morris conceded. 'But there's no need to get the wind up about me. I've had mighty little to do with gold for Paddy. If a chap's been in a jam, and asked me to stow away a parcel for him now and again, I've done it, and brought it along to Paddy later. That's all.'

'It's enough to send you to jail,' Sally said angrily.

'God,' Morris groaned, 'a man has to show he's got the guts to take risks, even if he isn't in the game. Business in this town depends on it, and customers have got to be considered. The Big Four see to it that he hasn't many if he gets in their way.'

'Well, I'm not having anything to do with it,' Sally said flatly, 'and Paddy's packing at the end of the week.'

'He won't forgive you for turning him out,' Morris said.

'Forgive me?' Sally's temper flared. 'I like that. What has Paddy Cavan to forgive me? Do you think I'm going to change my way of life to suit Paddy Cavan, Morris? Do you think I'm going to let my house get a bad name, and have the police turning the place upside down to please Paddy Cavan? What's come over you? You talk as if Paddy were the little tin god he thinks he is. And he's just the same as he always was, all bluff and impudence.'

'Mr. Patrick Cavan's not the same proposition as Paddy Cavan, Sally,' Morris reminded her dourly. 'He's a wealthy man, now, and carries more weight in this town than we do. And he's as unscrupulous as ever. I'll be glad not to see his ugly mug around the place—but I'd rather have him as a friend than an enemy.'

Sally thought she should make amends to Morris for having bullied him into support of what she had done, whether he approved of it or not.

'Oh well, we can do without him, either way,' she said. 'But you were quite right, Morris. I should never have allowed Paddy to come into our house as a boarder. He's been unbearable lately, ordering me about as if he owned the place.'

'To hell with him,' Morris growled.

'That's what I say.' Sally's laughter rippled. 'Come on, darling, you look tired. Let's go to bed.'

CHAPTER VI

DINNY went along to Tom's room, that Sunday night when he heard Morris and Sally talking in the kitchen. He had finished off a bit of carpentering for Morris and locked up the shop. There were several matters he wanted to discuss with Tom; and he had found a cutting from an old newspaper that he thought Tom would like to have a look at.

He saw Tom under the shower as he passed the bathroom, and sat down on a chair under the window to wait for him.

There were some things about Tom his mother never realised, Dinny thought. First of all, that he was not physically as strong as she liked to think. In his working clothes, he looked a fine, hulking chap; but if you saw him under the shower, the immaturity of the big boy's body doing a man's work underground, hurt somehow. It needed flesh and brawn, and the skin was too white where the sunburn on the neck and the legs ceased, although Tom took a lot of trouble to brown off during the week-end: kept out in the sun as much as possible, and went about without a hat.

Then, too, Tom had always been a great reader, educated himself in ways that most people knew nothing about. Dick may have learnt a lot at college and the School of Mines; but Tom kept up with him, reading all Dick's books and a darned sight more. You had only to look at the shelves he had rigged for himself in his bedroom to know that.

The shelves were made out of the red karri shingles used for fruit cases; but Dinny wished he had got inside his head half the stuff Tom had learnt from those books of his. Some of them he had read, and given Tom: *The Martyrdom of Man*, Bellamy's *Looking Backward*, Koropotkin's *Fields, Factories and Workshops*, Tom Paine's *Rights of Man*.

There were other books Chris Crowe and Monty Miller, or old Robbie, had lent Tom, which Dinny found too tough for him: Haeckel's *Riddle of the Universe*, Darwin's *Origin of Species*, Carlyle's *French Revolution*, Dietzgen's *Positive Outcome of Philo-*

59

sophy. Books by Emerson, Huxley and those chaps Chris was always talking about Edward Carpenter and Frederick Engels, as well as books of poetry, mining reports, paper-covered booklets and pamphlets on every subject under the sun, were neatly arranged on Tom's shelves. Tom always had a few newspapers lying round, too, which Dinny liked to borrow and browse over.

He was looking through some of them when Tom came in, his hair still wet and in his pyjamas.

'Hullo, Dinny,' he said.

"Lo, Tom,' Dinny said, watching Tom pick up a book and throw himself on the bed to read.

Dinny knew how it was. Tom had very little spare time and every moment was precious. Dinny pretended to be reading the *Worker*; but his thoughts were preoccupied with Tom, and the yarn he would like to have had with the lad.

Sunday was a great day for Tom: a day when he could walk about in the sunshine, enjoying the blue sky overhead and the bare, hard earth spread out all round. Dinny knew how Tom felt about it. He knew how Tom loathed working in the foul darkness underground: slogging away doggedly as he shovelled dirt, the sweat pouring off him. And he knew why Tom was working as a miner: had no idea of being anything but a miner all his days.

Dinny had a great affection for the boy: loved the latent strength in his grave quiet face and grey eyes. But there was little an old man like himself could do for Tom Gough. Tom must go his own way, and Tom would discover the right way to go, Dinny decided.

He was proud of Tom: had no fear for Tom, as he had for Sally's other boys. None of them was as sure of himself, as Tom, or as able to stand up to anything the future held. They were all as dear to him as if they had been his own sons, Dick and Lal and Den, as well as Tom. Particularly Den, the young rascal. He was out at the camp with Chris this week-end, because he wanted to ride a good-looking horse Dinny had got hold of, and his mother was a bit nervous when Den was riding Moppingarra.

For the last year or two, Tom had been reading those books which dealt with the causes of life and the history of human society. Dinny thought that Tom, like himself, had been born with a query in his brains. He wanted to know the why and wherefore of things, and was groping for the answers.

Dinny remembered having taken Tom to his first political meeting. It was during an election campaign when Wallace Nelson was standing for Hannans. A little man like a gnome with a big, bald head and a rorty sense of humour, 'Wee Wally' was also an orator who had got his training in the Old Country. Miners and prospectors flocked to his meetings. They were proud of him, and of the punch he put into his addresses. In parliament no one cared to bait 'Wee Wally'. His wit and ability to discomfort an opponent with adroit repartee had been demonstrated too often.

And Wally was in his best form that night when he spoke on 'The History of the Great Labour Movement'. Dinny and Tom had gone early to get a good seat. Dinny could still see Tom sitting beside him and listening to Wallace Nelson, his boyish face tense and pale, his eyes glowing.

Tom had grown up in an atmosphere of discussion about the rights of working men and the social system under which they lived and worked. Being a thoughtful lad, when he became a miner himself, he wanted to know more about ownership of the mines, work in the mines, the whole legal, financial and political scheme of things woven around him. He had set out to get all the information, which would enable him to see clearly and steer his own course, so that he could serve what Wally Nelson had described as 'those high ideals of the Labour Movement'.

In one way Tom had been more fortunate than Dick, Dinny thought. He had been reared in the university of Kalgoorlie. 'It didn't give a man diplomas and degrees. But it did give a man a knowledge of how people lived and worked: what forces made for the welfare of the working people, and what kept them in poverty, ignorance and fear of helping themselves. In this university Tom had found good professors, men like Chris Crowe, Monty Miller and old Robbie, who had no end of book-learning and who had been thinking deeply for years on the subjects which concerned Tom. He had heard them arguing, butted in with questions, tried to unravel the differences of their points of view, and come to some conclusions on his own account.

That was evident, Dinny considered, because before long Tom was taking an active part in union affairs. He had the common sense which recognised the need to do small, practical things in order to reach a distant objective; but as well, his mind had been free to study the problems of existence, as Dick's had never been. Dick had been pot-bound by his special studies and lost sight of the broader issues; but Tom, plugging away at his books at night, and working in the mines by day, had acquired a scientific and philosophical knowledge which gave him a sound basis of thinking about the purpose of life and work.

Tom did not talk much about what he knew or thought. He was a reserved chap, and yet popular with his mates. He had made his way by working among them, standing solidly to them in any dispute with the mine managers. 'Tom Gough's a good miner and a good mate.' That's what the men said, Dinny knew, and it was the highest tribute they could pay a man.

But Tom had been seeing a good deal of Charley O'Reilly, lately. Charley had a wife and a large family: worked wherever he could get a job. He had tried several on the mines, but they never lasted long. Slogging underground drove Charley to savage desperation. Sooner or later, he was sure to let a foreman, or underground boss, have such an outburst of fury that there was nothing for it but the sack. Charley was black-listed of course. It was impossible for him before long to get work anywhere except on the woodline. That was hard and ill-paid toil: falling and hauling timber in the bush and loading it on trucks to keep furnaces on the mines going. But at least it enabled him to retain his health and feed his wife and children. Charley was fond of his wife and children: would not allow them to starve, even if he was a wobbly, he said.

Monty Miller was another man associated with the I.W.W. Monty and his two sons had been out prospecting when one of them died of typhoid. Dinny's was the nearest camp at the time, and he had got to know Monty then.

Spare, energetic, and as straight as a gun barrel—'a grand type of the intellectual working man'—that was how a visiting journalist had described Monty Miller. But Dinny had not been seeing eye to eye with Monty recently, though Monty quoted yards from Emerson to prove that political action would never aid human progress. Monty had brought Chris out of his shell more than anybody had ever done: started him talking about 'The International Association of Working Men', and the scientific socialism expounded by his old friend, Frederick Engels.

His own mate, Chris, and Nadya Owen, were the only two people Dinny had heard put up a sound argument against the I.W.W. scheme for a new form of social organisation, based on industrial unionism. The wobblies raged and raved at Chris and Nadya. Nadya called them anarchists and syndicalists, but managed to hold her own in an argument.

Dinny wondered how Tom was faring in this conflict of ideas: what he was making of it.

Tom thought a lot of Charley O'Reilly, Dinny knew. He rode out to the Kurrawang often on a Sunday afternoon to see Charley. Dinny wondered whether Eily, Charley's eldest daughter, had anything to do with that. A slip of a girl with rough dark hair and shy eyes, Eily was working at a restaurant in Boulder now; and Dinny had seen Tom dancing with her at socials in the Workers' Hall.

But Tom had been very friendly with Mrs. Owen lately. People were beginning to talk about seeing Tom walking along the road at night with Mrs. Owen, and making visits to her house.

The gossip of a few malicious women was to blame, Dinny guessed. They could not understand that a young man might be interested in a woman for any reason except philandering. And Nadya Owen was a foreigner. Foreign women were supposed, as a matter of course, to be loose and immoral.

It did not matter that Mrs. Owen did not look in the least like 'a fast woman'. She was rather plain and dumpy, with high cheek bones, a sallow skin and hair the colour of dried grass, drawn straight back from her forehead and twisted into a knob at the back of her head. As for her clothes, they were always drab and shabby. She never seemed to care what she wore, or tried to please anybody. And yet there was a queer magnetism about the woman. Even when she was sitting dumb and apathetic, while Claude talked about his broad humanitarianism and tolerance of 'the other fellow's point of view', people stared at Nadya, wondering what she was thinking: what was going on behind her moody silence.

Claude Owen looked much older than his wife; but they got on well together. A dapper little man, with a bumpy forehead and short-sighted eyes which smiled blandly from behind gold-rimmed spectacles, Claude was 'a benevolent idiot', Charley O'Reilly said. His smug, patronising air irritated everybody, but he wasn't a bad sort: devoted to his wife. He had mentioned to several people, as a profound secret, that Nadya's father had been shot, leading a demonstration of workers in Russia. She, herself, had been smuggled abroad to escape from the Tzarist police.

An Englishman, himself, after they were married and came to Australia, Claude had vague, optimistic ideas of making his living as a writer. He had been glad to do any sort of work when he found there was no opening for his talents in Perth: drifted to the goldfields as agent for a life insurance company. Nadya's second child was born soon after he lost that job. He had been unemployed for months. Marie took the family under her wing, paid their rent and fed them until Claude was taken on as a clerk at the Perseverance.

Marie liked Nadya, and the Owens were often at her house. It was there Tom had met them. And Dinny. He, too, sometimes dropped in on a Sunday night to yarn with 'the old communard', as the I.W.W. boys called Marie's father-in-law.

Dinny thought he understood Nadya's attraction for Tom. She was an intelligent woman: could argue forcefully with Charley O'Reilly and Monty Miller, although as often as not she sat as if she were not paying any attention to what was going on round her.

It was only when she was drawn into heated discussion that her face became beautiful with the intensity of a spiritual fire burning within her.

Charley O'Reilly and some of the younger men thought they could learn a lot from Nadya, and asked her to join a discussion circle they had formed. They did not invite Claude to the circle. He was expected to stay at home and mind the children on the night the circle met, once a fortnight. That was the excuse. But as a matter of fact nobody wanted to listen to lengthy expositions of Claude's views on pacificism or theosophy; and they did want to hear from Nadya something about what was happening in Russia. Tom had seen a good deal of Mrs. Owen at this discussion circle. She had lent him books: he had lent her books, and usually he walked home with her after a meeting.

There was no more in their friendship than that, Dinny was sure. Claude was quite benign and approving about it: believed in the 'equality of the sexes', he said; and Nadya was as free as he, himself, to make friends and study economics if she wished. He knew he had her safely anchored, Dinny had heard Marie say. Nadya was consumptive and had two children.

Mrs. Owen would not play any female tricks on young Tom, Dinny thought. But he was disturbed about her influence on him. Had Tom become obsessed with the revolutionary ideas she expressed? To Dinny they were foreign and dangerous. Perhaps he was an old fool, he told himself; but he still thought the Australian working class had done pretty well in the past and could build a new law and order from gradual transformation of the capitalist system, or on Charley O'Reilly's plan for reorganisation of the trade unions.

Dinny wanted to thrash the whole matter out with Tom, and find out where he was getting in this ferment of ideas. But Tom was so deep in his reading, it did not seem fair to disturb him. Soon, Dinny knew, the lad would have to close his book and get some sleep. He had to be up early in the morning and start work with the first shift.

Dinny's paper fell as he glanced at Tom. From Tom his glance flew through the window.

It framed a clutter of white roofs and a fragment of starry sky, with the dark heave of the ridge running down from the Boulder to the great pyramid of the Horseshoe dump. Lights were twinkling among the mine buildings, and a feathery, white vapour drifting across the stars poisoned the air. The rattle and crash of batteries still working reminded Dinny of the ceaseless toil, the powerful machinery of the mining industry, grinding so many lives to dust.

64

He felt uneasy and depressed as he listened, and looked at Tom, knowing that to-morrow, soon after sunrise, his young body would be swallowed up by the mines. With thousands of other men, swarming ant-like along the tracks to the change rooms and cages, Tom would be shut away during all the bright hours of day, toiling there in the stinking bowels of the earth. And for what?

Dinny cursed. Tom looked up with a fleeting smile.

'What's on your mind, Dinny?' he asked.

'Nothing. Nothing more than usual, lad,' Dinny said. 'Here's a cutting from an old newspaper I thought you'd like to see.'

'Thanks, Dinny.' Tom took the cutting.

'Y'r mother tells me she had a row with Paddy this morning and he's gettin' a move on,' Dinny said. 'A good thing too, I reckon.'

'I reckon,' Tom replied, his eyes returning to his book. 'Going back to camp to-morrow?'

'Eh-erm.'

Dinny limped towards the door. He stopped as if the idea had just struck him:

'Gosh, Tom,' he said. 'I wish y'd come out prospectin' with Chris and me. Never set foot in the bloody mines again.'

Tom's reply was what he might have expected, Dinny told himself.

'I'm a miner, Dinny. My job's in the mining industry.'

CHAPTER VII

WHEN Dick stumbled into the room which he and Tom shared, Tom was still reading.

The brothers' eyes met on their usual glance of greeting; but Tom divined immediately that something unusual had happened to Dick.

Dick walked to his bed and sat there bemused. His mind was still full of moonlight and the fragrance of paper daisies. Early in the evening, after a day of strenuous tennis, and foregathering with young friends, Amy had pursuaded him to take her for a drive.

They had driven out to a stretch of open country where they often picnicked in the spring time, and made love to their hearts' content. Bushes along the road, fleeced with pale mauve blossom, threw off a faint, tangy smell of turpentine. Parakeelia spread its magenta silken floss over the red earth: pink everlastings and the dark, purple-blue of dampiera grew in vivid patches Along a dıy creek bed the wild cassia, laden with tiny golden cups, shed a perfume so subtle and exquisite that it stirred the brain like a strain of music. But over and above all, when the first hot days began, the air was filled with the dry musky fragrance of the paper daisies, lying in a white coverlet on the ground and spreading far away into the distance.

Sunset cast a rosy and golden glamour over this wilderness which flowered for only a few weeks in the year. The stars came out with a tinselly glow. So wide and shallow, the bowl of the sky over the flat land, it seemed you could almost touch the evening star as it glittered in the sky darkening quickly to blue-purple. All the aboriginal spirit fires were lighted in the Milky Way. Later, when the moon rose, they could scarcely be seen in the purity of its light.

'Let's go out to Nanjamiah, Dick!' Amy had begged, which was what she liked to call the place. The native word meant 'our own place'.

Dick hired a sulky and horse at the livery stables, and soon they were on their way to that spot where young lovers could lie in each other's arms without any fear of a guffaw, or prying eyes to disturb them.

Amy spread a rug on a drift of paper daisies while Dick tethered his horse in a clump of scrub. The moon was full and they lay for a while, relaxed and happy to have escaped from the hot, dusty town and other people.

Usually, it was enough to enjoy the tumult of their senses, the pleasure of long kisses, the yielding and withdrawing of their bodies in the overtures of youthful passion. At first they had been guileless and innocent in their fumbling caresses: afraid of dangerous rapids in their love-making. But it had grown in intensity until that night its magic swept them resistlessly to a joyous abandonment.

It was Dick who recovered first, and sat up with a startled exclamation.

'Cripes, Amy, what have we done?'

'Don't be silly,' Amy murmured drowsily. 'We're engaged, aren't we—going to be married?'

'But that's why . . . we should have waited,' Dick gasped. 'Your mother . . . dad and mum . . . they'd never forgive me if they knew. I seem to have let them down.'

'Nonsense, darling!' Amy twined her arms round him. 'I wanted it—just couldn't bear waiting any longer. Why should we, after all?'

Yes, why shouldn't they have taken the fulfilment of their love when they wanted it, Dick asked himself. There was never a more beautiful night to beguile young lovers into forgetfulness of the conventions, malicious gossip and their obligations to parents. It wasn't the earth he and Amy were living on at all, out there in the moonlight among the paper daisies, but an enchanted place filled with silver radiance, a faint musky fragrance, and the thrilling joyousness of their love.

No wonder they had been so drunk with each other, and so thoughtless of consequences! But what did it matter, as Amy said. They were engaged and going to be married! Nothing could come between them now.

Amy had clung to him with shining eyes as they went back to Kalgoorlie. Dick, filled with awe and a protective tenderness, drove with one arm round her.

'I'm so happy, darling,' Amy whispered, when they were saying good-night. 'We'll have to be married before long, now.'

'Do you think so?' Dick asked anxiously. 'Do you think . . .'

Amy laughed softly. 'The sooner the better. Then there won't by any talk, bye and bye.'

She kissed him with moist, clinging lips and disappeared into 'The Western Star'. It seemed a dark, sordid barn to hold her on such a night.

Dazed and dazzled, but with a feeling that was like a weight on his shoulders, Dick made his way home.

As he sat on his bed, Tom was aware of the vague smile playing at the corners of Dick's mouth, and a frown on his forehead, as if there were some snag in his pleasant reflections.

'What's it all about?' Tom ventured, guessing that Dick wanted to tell him.

'Amy, and a drive out beyond the Lake.'

Tom got the measure of Dick's elation and disturbance.

'Maybe we'll be getting married sooner than I expected, Tommy,' Dick went on slowly. 'And it's got me rattled, this business of getting married. Of course, we're in love and I want to marry Amy, but . . .'

'Amy's keen on getting married?' Tom asked.

'The sooner the better, she says.'

'Well, what's wrong? It's something to have a girl so willing.'

Dick's smile flashed. It was always a help to talk things over with Tom.

'But I know what it is to be hard up, don't forget,' he said. 'Stony, motherless broke, like I was in Sydney. I slept in the park and scrounged bits of bread from a rubbish tin. And there were plenty of blokes doing the same. Makes me sweat to think of it. A job—having enough money to pay your way—seems the most important thing in the world, now. And what's worrying me, is how on earth I'm going to keep a wife and family on the screw I earn.'

'Being a bit previous aren't you?' Tom laughed. 'But at any rate, this isn't Sydney, old man, and with mum and me around, you'll be all right. 'Tany rate aren't you "the young metallurgist with a brilliant career opening up before him on the Golden Mile"?'

Dick laughed, his spirits rising.

'I'd forgotten that. Hope you're right, Tommy.'

He yawned and stretched, beginning to undress.

'Sally tell you about her row with Paddy?'

Tom's eyes had fallen again to the book he was reading.

'She's right, I reckon.'

'I suppose so.' Dick didn't sound too sure.

Tom glanced at him.

'There's going to be a clean up,' he said. 'Men on the mines are saying the new inspector on the gold stealing detective staff means business. They reckon the mugs'll get it in the neck if they don't look out. But Kane's after the big boys.'

'He could make things awkward for Paddy.'

'You bet he could.'

'And Paddy could make things awkward for a good many others.'

'What are you driving at, Dick?' Tom twisted on the bed to face his brother. 'You haven't had any dealings with Paddy—have you?'

'Lord, no!' Dick was emphatic about that. 'He put a proposition up to me the other day, but I turned it down flat. And was he mad? That's not what I'm getting at. He tried to tell Sally she couldn't put him out because you and dad were in the gold.'

'I told her it was a damned lie,' Tom said.

'You've never done much in that line, Tommy?'

'I've brought up a few specimens,' Tom said. 'But not lately. Not for a long time as a matter of fact.'

'Oh well, everybody on the mines has had a crack at the game, some time or another.' Dick brushed Tom's admission aside. 'From managers to nightmen. Dinny was telling me, the other day, Dunnycan Bob made a fortune out of what he brought up in the pans: cleared out and has bought himself a farm in the south-west. The only thing that's worrying me is, if Paddy turns nasty, can he fix anything on you, or dad?'

'Not on me!' Tom said quickly. 'I've never been able to suffer Paddy, or sold him any gold. Asked mum to shunt him years ago. But dad's done a few odd jobs for Paddy. I reckon he'd make the most of that.'

'Get on to him not to touch another parcel,' Dick spoke quickly, decisively. 'Dad'll take it better from you than from me, Tom.'

'Right.' Tom rolled himself a cigarette, and pushed the makings towards Dick. 'But I heard mum having a bit of an argument with dad a while ago. It went hot and strong, at first. Then they trotted off to bed, chatting and laughing, so I guess mum got her own way and made him promise to toe the line.'

'You bet she did,' Dick smiled, smoking thoughtfully. 'Sally always gets her own way. I don't see how Mr. Cavan can do us much harm, even if he tried. And surely he wouldn't try, seeing he's lived here so long, and mother's been so good to him.'

'I wouldn't put anything past Paddy Cavan,' Tom said. 'There's nothing he wouldn't do to get what he wants, Dinny says. And I reckon he's about right. But Paddy doesn't want to be implicated in the gold-stealing racket, so he can't very well do anything to implicate anybody else.'

Dick inhaled, and blew out his smoke, thoughtfully.

'He's got tickets on Amy,' he said. 'He'd get even with me if he could.'

'You bet,' Tom agreed. His glance strayed again to his reading. Dick lay back, as if his anxieties had been assuaged by this yarn with Tom.

'You're quite a spruiker in the miners' union, they tell me, Tommy,' he said. 'You ought to go in for politics.'

'Nothing doing,' Tom laughed. 'My job is to build the union and get a better deal for miners on this field.'

'That's all right.' Dick turned over to go to sleep. 'But you might as well be member for the district some day, sonny. Think how pleased Sally'd be!'

'But Dick . . .' Tom was ready for an argument.

Dick did not want to argue. He was beginning to feel drowsy. 'Not to-night, Tommy,' he protested. 'By the way,' he added, 'we'll have to get on to young Lal. He spends most of Sunday at the sway.'

'What?'

'Lal's spending a darned side too much time playing two-up,' Dick said.

'Thought as much.' Tom jerked himself out of his preoccupation with those reasons of his for not being a politician.

'Sally'd have a fit if she knew,' Dick murmured. 'Just as well Lal's going into camp this week. Dead keen on his military training.'

'I'll have a word with him,' Tom promised.

'Right.' Dick was almost asleep. Tom went on reading. He was still reading with an expression of insatiable hunger when Dick muttered in his sleep:

'Cripes, Amy, what have we done?'

Tom smiled as he looked at his elder brother, lying there on the bed where he had slept since they were youngsters. His devotion to Dick was implicit and inalienable. It seemed to him that everybody must love Dick. It would have been extraordinary if they did not. He was so good-looking and lovable, Dick: had the same charm of manner as his mother, and her lively, generous disposition. No wonder Amy was so much in love with him! Only Paddy Cavan, probably, had a grouch against Dick.

Tom's thoughts surged to a hatred of Paddy Cavan and the men of his kind, greedy, unscrupulous egoists who gained some sinister power over the lives of others by their lust for money and authority. He was afraid that Dick would always have to reckon with Paddy's hostility, not only on Amy's account, but because they were types which would never have anything in common.

All the same, Tom could not believe that Paddy would have sufficient influence to damage Dick professionally. After all, Dick was a scientific worker and would make his way in branches of the mining industry which Paddy Cavan did not control. It was a comforting conclusion to arrive at, and Tom slept on it with some satisfaction.

CHAPTER VIII

'WHISTLE'S gone, son!'

Tom was sleeping like a log. As she stood beside his bed with a cup of hot tea, Sally wished she need not waken him.

'Gee, thanks, mum!' Tom dragged himself from the depths of sleep drugged consciousness. He knew his mother had already been up an hour or more, cutting cribs and getting the breakfast ready. She had made herself an early cup of tea, and brought one along to him, in order to arouse him easily. There was no need for Dick to bestir himself yet, so she slipped out of the room quietly, not to waken him.

As he went off to the shower, Tom could hear mine whistles shrilling in the distance, one after another, and men in the bunkhouse, groaning and yawning, coughing and spluttering-out sleepy curses. Getting to work on Monday morning was always harder than on any other day. Memory of the previous morning's sleep-in had to be overcome, or maybe the hang-over after a booze-up over the week-end.

Sally was busy serving breakfast when Tom went into the kitchen.

Usually Lal and Den gave her a hand with it, but Dinny was there this morning, trotting into the dining-room with plates of porridge that the men called 'burgoo', and thick white cups of tea. Sally had big pans of steak and eggs sizzling on the stove and slapped the steak and eggs on hot plates with a dollop of fried potato and cabbage known as 'bubble and squeak'. Dinny took a tray of them into the dining-room and shoved a loaded plate beside each boarder. It was always a busy, noisy half-hour, with the men in a rush to get to their jobs, scuffling for a glance at the *Miner*, commenting on the news between mouthfuls, chiacking each other on their week-end diversions, guffawing over a joke; and growling, with resigned good humour, as they stuffed the lunches Sally had cut into their crib bags of black fracture cloth, and went off 'to keep things goin'' for the boss', as they said.

Paddy Cavan used to eat with the men until lately; but now, he waited until the first rush was over, and had his breakfast in lonely state, or with Morris and Dick, Lal and Den.

Tom ate with the men, and disappeared with them: rode his bicycle along the track to the mines, or hopped on a tram if his bicycle were out of order. This morning it was, and he had no time to overhaul it and patch the punctures it had sprung the day before, so he boarded the rattle-trap of a tram, crammed with miners and mine workers, which clattered along the Boulder road to the leases, every few minutes, at this hour.

It was a sombre crowd of men which filled the trams. Old men and young had the same tense, driven look on their faces. In their dark, shabby working clothes, every man carrying his black crib bag, they seemed to be just what the wobblies called them, wage-slaves: an army of men, condemned to hard labour for life, or as long as they had the spirit and strength to carry on with the heavy and dangerous work by which they earned a living. Haggard and hopeless, the faces of the middle-aged and older men were. Dull and apathetic, coughing and spitting, holding themselves together with a sort of desperate jocularity, they allowed themselves to be transported to the hell of their daily work in the mines, always with a secret fear that they might not come out of it alive, certain that at best they were going to swallow dust and fumes which would eat out their lungs and destroy them before their time, knowing that the wages they received were a paltry fraction of what they earned for the boss: no more than enough to pay the rent, buy food and clothing, and a few pots of beer to keep a man from worrying about being a man and a miner.

The younger men took their submission to the yoke of the mining industry more easily and recklessly, though they understood what it meant. They only had to look at men who had been working in the mines for several years to do that. These men were coughing and spitting, the 'grave-yarders' among them too numerous not to give a lad a quirk of dismay, and quicken his resolve to make the going good if he had a chance to get away with a bit of gold and quit the blasted mines before they got him.

The trams disgorged their swarming hordes at the Boulder Block, and the men streaked away following dim trails to the shafts in which they were working.

In the dark interior of change rooms near the shafts, there was a welter of naked bodies, fat and thin, mostly thin, as the men, chiacking each other and cursing, stripped off their surface clothes and thrust themselves into the clammy, filthy flannel shirts and old trousers used for working underground. Most of the family men had taken their working clothes home for a wash over the week-end; but there were many whose working clothes were still rank with the sweat and underground mud that had soaked through them.

In the winter, if the steam was off, the clothes were still damp when the men put them on, and in summer they dried like a board. A man had to fight his way to his pegs, hang up his decent clothes, and get into his underground outfit, heavy boots and all, pick up his crib bag, 'spider' and candle: dash over to the store for more candle.

Then he had to go to the office for his plod—the card on which he filled in particulars of the work he was doing, its position in the mine, and the hours he was working. A machine miner applied for his steel, fracteur, and any gear required for the job.

'Come on, get a bloody move on,' the shift boss called from the brace.

To the mustered truckers and boggers, machinemen, timber-men and samplers, he yelled his orders.

'The fourteen hundred, Scotty, boggin' in crosscut!'

'Christ, that hot bastard agin,' Scotty growled.

'Go on the chute at the thousand two hundred, Pete!'

That wasn't a bad job, and boggers standing round Pete eyed him off, muttering:

'Eggs must be good!'

'He's ridin' the goat!'

'Been boggin' seven years on this mine, and these bastards of foreigners, just started, get all the best pozies!'

To a trucker the shift boss ordered:

'Go to the six hundred, number four "chinaman", Snowy, and pull till Bill tells yer to stop.'

To Tom's mate, he remarked:

'Your mate fired last night, Ted. Two misses, so keep off the west wall. Y're breakin' too much bloody mullock. Better do a bit of risin'.'

He was still talking when the whistle blew, and the bracemen bawled the level where Tom and his mate were working. They crossed over to the cage, and jammed in it with other boggers, machine miners and truckers. The first draught of foul, damp air struck them as the cage slobbered against wet walls of the shaft, dropping to the thousand six hundred and fifty feet level.

On the plat there, the men hung up their crib bags, trying to sling them out of reach of the cockroaches that swarmed everywhere and would finish a man's tucker before he got to it, if he wasn't careful. Then everybody squatted on the crib board for a few minutes, to get their eyes used to the dark: tied bowyangs round the legs of their trousers, filled pipes, or rolled a cigarette exchanging a few words on the football and races, or any sensational news in the morning *Miner*.

Grabbing a truck, a man would mooch off along the drive from the walls of which water was dripping, and the rest of the cage load followed, drifting away in twos and threes to squelch along the muddy track, shovels and picks over their shoulders, until the twinkling of their lights was lost in the humid darkness of the long tunnel.

Presently the crash and rumble of falling ore vibrated through the guts of the mine, the drills set up a chattering roar in distant drives, the grinding clatter and howl of the day's labour took its accustomed course, with only the shrilling of the plat bells and occasional muffled shouts from truckers and boggers to break the dreary monotony.

The crosscut in which Tom and Ted Lee were working was as narrow as a grave, seven feet high by four at its widest, with a blind end. Ted barred down, inspected the rough walls and overhanging roof for loose rock, cleared away any treacherous looking fragments, giving the west wall a careful investigation. The fuses which had failed to fire charges in the holes bored by his cross-mate at midnight, were a danger no experienced miner could take lightly. A man never knew how far a faulty fuse might have smouldered, and cause an explosion and fall of rock which would finish him.

Ted was satisfied to keep off the west wall that morning, in accordance with the shift boss's instructions. Tom gave him a hand rigging his machine, water and air hoses, saw that the ventura, for pumping a bit of fresh air was working, and then got on to shovelling away mullock the last firing had brought down.

It was back-breaking work, and as he slung his shovel loads of

73

heavy broken rock, the drill with a screech and deafening racket was boring into a massive wall of stone, filling the small cave in which he and Ted were working with a fog of dust and the exhaust from the machine: a mixture of foetid oil, compressed air and water.

Tom had to fill his trucks and shove them out to the plat. He held an 'unofficial' plod, because he was bogging for a machine man; but that did not mean he would escape being 'chatted' by the shift boss if his number of trucks for the day was not high. He had to keep up his tally and clear away the mullock Ted and his cross-mate brought down. Most of the boggers rushed their plod before crib, sweating and cursing as they pushed the truck loads of from fourteen to twenty hundredweights along the dimly-lit, narrow gauge lines to the plat. Draught horses could do no better, or as well, Tom thought bitterly. Dobbins the boys called the big heavy trucks.

He was better off than some of the men bogging for a machine miner. Ted was always good for a 'sling back' on pay-day, if he had been getting good cuts, and Tom busting himself to truck off for him.

'There's some hungry bastards,' the men said, 'making big money on their ore, and never give the poor bugger boggin' for 'em a sling back.' The sling back might be ten bob on pay-day, or no more than a few pots of beer, but was always appreciated.

Firing began at eleven-forty-five. And when the knocker line signal was given for firing, from every drive and crosscut, men crawled to the stopes, and along to the plat for crib. Trousers and shirts, wringing wet, were squeezed, noses cleared with an expert blast and swipe of the fist, sweat rags wrenched from belts to mop faces heavy with grit and dust, hands washed and mouths rinsed at the tap. Gurgling, coughing, spitting and sweating, many of them exhausted by the first spurt of their morning's toil, men squatted on the crib board, thrown down on the plat floor.

The artillery of the explosions went on behind them as the men ate their thick sandwiches, pasties, or hunks of pale home-made cake, and swigged a mouthful of tea from their billies. Only the machine men did not touch their crib until they had counted the number of explosions on their job. Then they could eat with an easy mind, or cursing the rotten fuse the company was handing out these days.

Munch, munch, munch, and the rustle of cockroaches chasing a tasty morsel! Nobody bothered to talk much until he had had a feed. Some of the men who had been on the beer over the week-end might have the spews as soon as they began to eat, and start retching nearby. The stench mingled with rank body odours, sweat of the

74

men and their steaming clothing in the pervading dank atmosphere of the mine.

Presently, tobacco smoke from pipes and cigarettes, rolled from the makings, was arising like incense; and the men leaned against the board at their backs for the desultory conversation which filled the last moments of crib time.

Somebody started off with a grouse about his job.

'Christ, she's hard borin'!'

'No bloody steel agen!'

'Bastards laid no sollars—and it's tough goin' shiftin' that ore without the boards is laid under it before firin'.'

'Strike, can't you chaps keep off the blarsted job!'

'Spun five 'eads Sundee,' a two-up fiend piped up, and the sports got into a wrangle about Sunday's football match.

'Tigers is the best bloody team and no umpire can beat 'em!'

'She's not a bad sorter tart,' Smiler McRae could be heard confiding to his mates. 'But her old woman's a fair cow. "No y'r don't, Smiler," she ses, "y'r not walkin' out with my Ruby. A girl never knows when she'll be bringin' home a joey if she goes with you." But Ruby managed to give her the slip Saturdee night, 'n we had a good time all right. Joey or no joey, the old woman can't blame me if Rube's willin'.'

'Lot er youse bastards not in the union yet,' Ted remarked in his casual way. 'How about it?'

'Wot's the bloody good of the bloody union?' Lenny Low growled. He was a louser, known as Lenny the Louse, and suspected of being a pimp for the management.

'The only bloody chance we got er gettin' anything out of the bloody bosses is through the union,' Ted replied, calmly. 'Some of youse bastards are always belly-achin'. But, Christ, when it's a question of nuttin' out what yer can do about it, ye just sling off, and keep on lickin' the bosses' boots. You'd oughter join up, and go to union meetings.'

'The emancipation of the working class depends on unity of the trade union movement,' Jo Halliday, a gaunt, dusted miner sprawling beside Ted, said.

'Swallowed a dictionary, Jo?' A squat, square-headed bogger with blood-shot eyes jeered.

'No. Jo hasn't swallowed a dictionary, and if youse bastards don't know what emancipation of the working class means, it's time you did,' Ted said. 'It means, the workers ownin' the mines and the land and the factories, and runnin' things to suit themselves, through a workers' government. It'd give every man, woman and child in the country a fair deal. That's right, isn't it, Tom?'

'That's about it, Ted,' Tom said slowly.

' 'E's a bloody red-ragger,' the Louse spluttered.

'Well, if that's red-raggin', suits me,' Andy Spark, one of the older machine men, butted in.

'Too bloody right, it'd suit any workin' miner, a set-up like that,' Jock McLean, his mate, agreed.

'But what chance've yer got of gettin' it? Buckley's—and the black alley for tryin'.' Vic Uren, the Louse's offsider, tried a sickly grin.

The argument went hot and strong for a while, and petered out when one of the sports declared: 'Kittiwake ought to win the hurdle, Saturdee.'

'Hasn't got a bloody dog's chance!'

'Not if Maneroo's tryin'.'

'Garn, wot are yer givin' us? Daisy Bell's home and dried on the pig's back.'

The men turned with relief to a topic which stirred some immediate interest and excitement.

It wasn't until they were shying scraps from their crib bags into the rubbish bin, knocking out their pipes, relighting their candles, and taking off their coats, preparatory to getting back to work, that a short, thick-set timberman with a swivel eye came up to Ted.

'Eh, Ted,' he said, 'what d'yer make of the way things are shapin' in the old Dart?'

'Looks like the shindy between Austria and Serbia'll work up into a war—and we'll be dragged into it, I reckon,' Ted said gravely.

Tom was thinking about that, and what Nadya had been saying, the night before, about this war that was brewing, as he began to work again and his back and arms swung to the heavy lift and fling of every shovelful of mullock.

Fatigue was setting in and he worked slowly, mechanically, after a couple of hours, sickened by the poisonous fumes released by the mullock as he shifted it, depressed by the men's reaction to Ted's plea for a stronger union. Ignorance and apathy dogged every attempt to make many realise their rights and power, and the need for co-operative effort to ensure improvement of their conditions.

Through Tom's mind the glorious promise of what he had been reading the night before flickered and shone like the grail of humanity's quest: a future of peace and prosperity for all mankind. But how to achieve it? How to arouse decent men, workworn and drugged by their deadly toil, to the need for thought and action which would bring them nearer the great objective. That was what tore at and tormented him as he shovelled and flung the heavy, broken rock, sweating and straining with every stoop, lift and swing, through the leaden hours of afternoon.

Could men like the Louse and Vic Uren have any influence on the majority of hard-headed miners and mine workers? Tom assured himself they could not. They could only queer a man's pitch with the mine manager, when they carried tales of a bit of gold walking, or of a red-ragger talking too much. The men, he knew, had a sneaking fear of these snoopers, but could 'square' them, as often as not, when a big stunt with gold was on; and they dare not try any dirty tricks to tramp men like Ted Lee and Joe Halliday, who had a reputation for being honest and reliable workers, respected by the management as such, and by the men as good mates.

There was comfort in the thought, and that although men like the Louse and Vic Uren might be with the dark forces threatening to plunge the world into war, the armies of the workers of the world would some day unite and ensure peace and a future of freedom and happiness for all men. Nadya had made him believe that this was not just a dream. It would surely happen. But when and how to bring it about? That was what a man had to decide and help to achieve.

When he stopped for a moment, gasping for breath, and swept the sweat from his eyes, Tom could see Ted standing beside his drill, in the sweltering fog of the small, enclosed space where they were working. It still reeked of the fumes from the morning's firing and they could not hear themselves speak above the shattering din of the drill.

Ted worked stripped to the waist, as Tom was, and cursed the ventura which was out of order; but he was pleased with the rock he had brought down. He was striking the lode and bored for his second firing. His job though exacting was less laborious than a bogger's. Every shovelful weighed a ton as Tom loaded his last truck for the day.

'Thats' the dobbin' y've been lookin' for, eh, Tom?' Ted called. He had dismantled the drill and set his fuses. They tramped off to the plat together.

A queer silence had suddenly fallen on the level. From every drive and crosscut came the men who had downed tools. A long shuddering sigh was wafted from the empty workings.

The men plodded along, dragging their feet, shoulders sagging, nothing left of the labour power they had brought to the mine that morning. The machine miners who had fired, waited listening for their charges to go off. Usually they were on contract. Parties of four working on each job, and the two machine men, the gun men, were responsible for the fuses. They lit from twenty to twenty-four

77

fuses, and had to report how many of the bores charged were heard to explode, so that the next shift taking over could be told of any lurking danger from unexploded charges.

On the plat, bowyangs removed, lamps emptied, boots loosened, honking the dust and phlegm from noses and throats, coughing, and cursing with a grim gladness and impatience, men bustled round the shaft to be up in the first cage.

'No shovin' and rushin'!' the platman yelled, as it clanked in to take them to the surface.

The men packed in, jamming themselves together like sardines, lamps jabbed into gizzards and faces. Four rings and she climbed, Smiler commenting blithely: 'She's holdin' by three strands!' The men's eyes turned upwards watching for the dim light above.

Blinking in the sunlight, they stumbled out of the cage. Haggard and exhausted, with the foul smell of the mine still clinging to their damp and filthy clothing, some of them slumped on the ground near the shaft before they slouched across to the change room, though a few of the younger men could still raise a derisive yell to the after-noon shift.

'By Christ, what shift you workin', mates?'

'You'd oughter be comin' off!'

'How'd yer like to be workin' day shift?'

In the change room, with the rush of getting out of their wet working clothes and fighting for the showers, came renewed energy. The fresh air had revived most of the men, and the thought of beer at the nearest pub stimulated sluggish pulses. Only the 'week-enders' whose weekly bath even was doubted, ignored the showers, satisfying public opinion with a swipe of arms and faces under the tap.

In the blaze of the late afternoon sun, the ant-like trail of hundreds of miners and mine workers was presently going back across the bare red earth to the tram stop, surging round the Fimis-ton pub there, or on trams and bicycles, streaking homewards.

CHAPTER IX

TOM worked day shift that week, and every day was the same as another, underground, for himself and round about four thousand men working on the mines. Except that some days were worse than others. Days, when there was a fatal accident: miners had to be dug out from hundreds of tons of fallen rock and rubble, and shattered, blood-soaked bodies carried by their mates on a stretcher out of the stope, along the manway and drives to the plat. Scarcely a day passed without a minor accident on one of the mines. The number reached thousands every year. When a well-known figure was missing from his usual place at crib time, as the result of a fatal accident, there was no throwing off the gloom which enveloped his mates.

More accidents occurred on the night shift than in the day time, and every man working night shift knew he had to watch his step, particularly in the early hours of the morning when his vitality was at its lowest ebb. Towards six o'clock, he could feel a return of energy, and look forward to the moment of reprieve, slinging tools to the ground and making for the top. So the days went, piling into weeks, months, years: year after year, for a working miner.

Tom hated night shift, not only because work was more arduous and dangerous in the small hours: but because it shut him off from his evening meetings, and he found it difficult to sleep during the day.

Not many men in a small worker's home slept well during the day-time, with the noise of children, and women doing their household chores, going on round them all the time; and there was the temptation to sit about and yarn, rather than try to sleep when the heat and flies and noise nearly drove you crazy.

A miner on night shift was always more fagged when he went below, than a man who could take his eight hours' rest through the night in the quiet and cooler air. Tom was made that way. Often he could not get the noise of the drills and the smell of the mine out of his head. He felt like a rat coming from some underground sewer into the light of day. His sleep during the day was always shallow and broken by vibrations of what was happening about him. Although Sally tried to keep the house quiet, he could hear dogs barking, fowls cackling, a girl singing in a house nearby, Den and Lal skylarking in the yard when they came in to lunch. He might lie for hours in a twilight of semi-consciousness, falling only for a brief period into the deep oblivion which restored his natural vigour.

Tom took the disadvantages of his calling with the stoicism which was part of his make-up as a miner. There were worse jobs in the mine than bogging for a machine man, he told his mother. The machine man had the worst of it when he was working in a rise. Tom had seen Ted drilling in a rise, only a few feet from the roof overhead: standing on a great hummock of ore, and hauling up his steel: having to bar down up there, after firing, and work in the hot, foul air that always rises. Sometimes you couldn't see the light of

79

his lamp for the fog. Ted boasted that he had done four hundred feet of rising in the last three years.

But he didn't like winzing.

'I don't like anybody workin' over me head,' he said. 'No, I don't like it. Winzing's the worst job on the mine, I reckon. Winzing, anything can happen to a man. Y'r mate might drop a tool on you, or miss somethin' crook with the staging, though I'm not slingin' any mud at you, Tom. It's just the feelin' I got. If I'm workin' on a winze, I put up me own brace and I know where I am, bar down and see to me own air and water.'

Winzing consisted of putting down a shaft in the mine to a lower level. One man on top worked a hoist, lowering the machinery for boring to his mate. Any defective hoisting, or fall of loose rock was likely to kill the man below. When he had bored, and charged for firing, he was drawn up again. After crib, his mate went down to clear up the dirt, and every bucket had to be carefully loaded to prevent the rock shifting. Fumes and dust were worse in that narrow hole than anywhere. There was supposed to be a ladder against the wall of the shaft.

But Ted could never forget how his brother had been trapped in a winze when the hoisting gear broke down, and the ladder was not long enough to reach the bottom of the shaft. His mate had lost his head, dashed about frantically, but didn't throw down an air pipe. Ted's brother had tried to stop the fuses burning to the fracture, but one got him.

'It's hard to tell how these accidents happen,' Ted said. 'As a rule, there's only one man can tell you, and he's dead.'

Tom had worked with Ted rising and winzing: learnt more from him about every phase of these hazardous jobs underground than he would have learnt in a lifetime from many another man.

He remembered one bad scare they had got, bench stoping to a lower level, when hundreds of feet were between them and the upper drive, with only a bit of timber and 'laggings' across it, for safety. They had heard the crack of an explosion and heavy fall of earth, grabbed their lamps and come through the manway, shinned down the chain ladder that looked as if a fly couldn't cling to it, and scrambled through a drive in which there had been a big fall. Stumbling along it another explosion and fall had extinguished their lamps. God, that panic-stricken rush with other men along the stope to the shaft! Tom hoped he would never have to live through anything like it again. With every crack and rumble, it seemed as if the whole mine were falling in; and men waited, mad with fear, for the cage to take workers from lower levels to the surface, wondering whether it would be wrecked and they be entombed before it returned for them. But that time, it was only a creep that had occurred in old workings, and no lives were lost.

On several occasions he had seen acts of extraordinary heroism, men facing death without a moment's hesitation to save mates from a ghastly end, as when Red Miller found a lad on the plat looking white about the gills.

'Firing's begun,' he gasped, 'and Jack's not out.'

Red dashed back to the crosscut. Between concussions of the charges going off, he made his way to where Jack Gordon had been working: found him lying on his back, a little off from the face. A premature explosion had knocked him unconscious and blinded him. One hand was gone and the other smashed to pulp, but Jack was still alive.

As Red dragged him away from the face, a ton of ore came down on the spot. One flying fragment caught Red on the head; but dazed and the blood pouring from that gash in his head, he had managed to stagger on, dragging Jack until he reached the drive, where other men ready to go after Red were waiting.

And there was Mick Lalich who had stood with his back to the sliding ore in an ore pass to prevent it showering down on a spalder who had lost his footing and fallen down the pass. In the fraction of a second Mick and his mate would have been annihilated by that cataract of broken rock behind him. He had held it back, just long enough for his mate to be hauled to safety, and to be swung out of danger himself. Mick had injured his back badly and got a medal for that deed. There were almost as many incidents of matter of fact gallantry as accidents in the mines. Very few of them earned more than a passing, sober tribute from his mates who knew a man's worth from that moment.

It was a different world underground. The lousers might pimp for the shift boss, underground foreman, or the underground manager; but they were a breed apart. Supposed to be trustworthy men who picked the gold from rich ore and put it in a bag to go straight to the gold room, they had been known all the same to work with a hollow pick handle and become rich on the proceeds. Lenny Low was suspected of making a good thing out of his job. He had a pull somewhere, men on the Reef agreed: either he'd 'got something on one of the bosses', or was 'cutting-up' with one of them.

The shift boss was responsible for seeing that the specifications for work were carried out. He said himself sometimes that he 'got all the manager's dirt and passed it on to the men'.

And, of course, there were rackets. The manager would grant a rich block to a tributer for half, or a quarter share of the gold. The tributer hired his steel from the company: would send up his bits to be sharpened, and couldn't get it back from the blacksmith.

'Y' didn't send back twenty bits,' the blacksmith would say. Or: 'We haven't got y'r steel. Not enough steel on the mine to keep you bastards going'. Got no steel for yer.'

Palm oil was indicated. A man would get his bits. But it would be the same next week. Another tributer would have been greasing the blacksmith's hand and get the first man's bits.

Some of the boggers too had to be fixed. They'd load up a skip: put three hundredweights to a skip.

'Here, what's up,' the tributer would object, 'loadin' like that?' His money was in the number of skips of ore he produced.

'I got orders to load up the skips,' the bogger, who was on wages, would reply. 'You chaps can't have it all y'r own way. I got to make me livin' same as you. If the boss says load up the skips, I got to load 'em.'

A tributer could lose two or three pounds on a loaded skip. He'd shell out to the bogger, and the skips would go back to normal.

Then the ore going through the cracker had to pass over a grid and into a bin for sampling. A manager on the Boulder Reef got his own men to do the sampling. They'd take three samples, one for the boss, one for the tributer and one for the umpire. If a tributer was splitting with the manager, it would be all right; but if he wasn't and struck a rich patch, the samples would be swapped. A man on a two-ounce crushing might find himself landed with half an ounce. Or the samples would be mixed, and two men be given a one-ounce bag.

The stunt had to be cleverly worked, because a tributer usually knew round about how much his ore was going. A lot of that sort of swindling had been going on until recently. But Big George, a Queensland miner, forced a showdown, and queered the pitch for a manager and his crew.

Sling backs to the shift boss got some men their jobs. Dings and dagoes were accused of making a regular practice of getting a job by this means. But most self-respecting miners swore they 'wouldn't crawl to any man for a job'. Contractors who knew their shift boss suffered from an itchy palm, might be forced to come to terms with him in order to get a good position to work in. Their pay depended on the number of trucks of ore they could claim.

'How many trucks did y'r send up?' they might ask a bogger.

'Ten and a couple of windys,' was a reply which would incline a machine miner to be generously disposed towards that bogger: a windy being a truck which was not over-filled.

A miner also had to keep sweet with the tooley, who brought him his steel, and took away the blunt bits to be sharpened. There was a good deal of this scheming to add a few shillings or pounds to a man's pay. No one objected to a wages man getting a few bob extra from a machine man making big money. It was only when a boss slugged the men the sling back galled.

But these tricks were of little consequence compared to those that were worked, up above, in the treatment plant, and in the gold room, in the offices of the company, at directors' meetings when complicated deals were put through to boost or depress shares, 'passing the buck' to the public, so that the interests of mining magnates might be protected, no matter what the effect on small shareholders, or a working community.

Every working miner could be depended on to stand by and help another if he needed help. Up above, he might be as mean as they make 'em, and about as popular as a bad smell, but underground if he saw a trucker in difficulty, he would just bog in and give a hand: not wait to be asked. Everybody, underground, knew the danger. Even in stopes supposed to be safe, you could see the roof sagging under rotten timber. 'She's liable to come down any moment,' the men would remark casually.

Sometimes an underground manager might be aroused about a spot like that: blow up the shift boss and get the place repaired; but as often as not it would remain untouched for months.

If you asked them, the men would say they were not afraid: not exactly, though they were always conscious of the danger. They might seem to become careless: monkey about in the cage, burn each other with their lamps, take unnecessary risks, but it was with a sort of bravado that carried them along. All the time, underground, the sense of that danger held men together, as if doomed and damned though they were to earn the right to live by labour in the mines, they could still draw from each other the strength and satisfaction of an instinctive, inexplicable bond.

This feeling among the men reconciled Tom to his work as a miner. It was not what he had wanted: not what at first he had intended devoting his brains and energy to. A mine had always been to him a miracle of human ingenuity. He had thought, before he left school, that he would study engineering: become a mining engineer, a master of all the knowledge which enabled men to design underground workings, plan the levels of a mine like a gigantic honeycomb, devise new methods of production and transport, ventilation and treatment.

There was nothing Tom liked better than to pore over the maps of a mine. He knew the workings of the Boulder Reef like the palm of his hand. But the dream of being a mining engineer he had put from him when he had been working underground for a year or so. Not only because his mother needed the money he could give her, but because he realised the toll heavy labour took of his strength, and that it would be almost impossible for him to work and study sufficiently to reach his goal, particularly after he became interested in union and political matters.

It seemed more important now to fit himself for the struggle of the workers against the whole system of ideas which used and abused them so flagrantly, than to equip himself for a position which would be much better than theirs. A stubborn loyalty to the men he worked with had become fixed in him. He could not separate himself from them, and from the struggle of the working class for a better way of life. Always on the horizon of his consciousness, like a mirage, glimmered that vision of a better way of life.

CHAPTER X

DALLY was drunk. His eyes gleamed, fishy and phosphorescent, and his thin, withered face creased to an uneasy grin as he lurched across the back-yard at Gough's, clutching a bottle of beer.

'Have a drink, missus?' he queried gently, genially, standing in the kitchen doorway.

'Get out!' Sally replied. She was too busy cooking sausages for the evening meal, the hot fat spluttering and flicking her face, to be bothered with Dally when he had been drinking. He knew she was annoyed when he came home, drunk like this, so early in the week. At the week-end, particularly after pay-day, she did not make a fuss if he were a bit above himself. But she had no patience with a man working underground who did not keep off the liquor, or at least limit himself to a few pots during his working week. Most of them did, knowing how their stomachs behaved when they went below with a hang-over.

Dally had been with Mrs. Gough a long time: was a quiet, unobtrusive man and a good boarder when he was sober: paid regularly and kept his room in the bunk-house as clean as a ship's cabin. He did his own washing and mending, too, and now and again liked to cook a meal. Dally had been a sailor. He was always talking about getting away from the mines and going back to sea.

But not to work for wages. To buy a boat of his own, was what Dally dreamed of, and to live on it: go cruising up the coast and do a bit of fishing, or carry cargo for the small coastal towns. He had read a good deal and liked to talk about what he thought of things in general. Nobody, however,. attached much importance to what Dally thought. Occasionally, Sally was interested to hear about his experiences and the books he had read; but he was a nuisance when he was drunk.

'You cross with me, missus?' Dally queried, screwing his neck sideways like an inquisitive rooster. 'You think I'm shickered. And you don't like a man to be shickered. Not on Monday. Not on a Monday afternoon.'

'Clear off, Dally,' Sally replied impatiently. 'I've got no time to be bothered with you, just now.'

'Preju-dice,' Dally crowed, 'damned burgyose prejudice, not wantin' a man to get drunk in the boss's time. You got to get rid of these burgyose prejudices, missus. Tom says I'm a muddle-headed id-id-jut, missus. That's what he says. "Y're a muddle-headed idjut, Dally." But:

"The colonel said before he died,
And I don't think the old sod lied."

What did he say, missus? What did the colonel say? Can't remember, for the life of me.'

'Listen, Dally, I've just about had enough of you,' Sally cried, unable to restrain her exasperation. 'If you don't clear off, I'll call Tom.'

'Ssh! Ssh!' Dally waved his arms deprecatingly. 'This emotional stuff! Most un-nesh-essary. Just what I said to Mrs. Baldy Mack, the other day, when I took her old man home. We were pretty full. Pretty full, I got to admit, missus. But, God, she's a tartar, that woman. Did I say tartar? Tiger, I mean. Though hip-hippo-potamus might better describe the—the lady's sample—no, ample proportions. God, if she fell on a man it'd be the end of him. And she near fell on me for leadin' Baldy into mischief. It was touch and go, missus. Did she snort when she saw me leadin' Baldy home? Yoicks! Give me the works, vitriol and T.N.T., donner and blitzen, hell's bells and all the muck on the G.M. A cyclonic disturbance of the first magnitude, it was. I assure you, Missus Gough. Fair took me breath away to hear that woman curse!

'Baldy passed out at the first blast: lay in a swoon. Y're humble servant, Francis Ed. Dally, held himself together, very dignified, always the gentleman. Falsely accused, con-con-fronting irate female: "Madame," says he, "this conversation is closed." And passed out at her feet.'

85

Sally's smile was what he had been playing for. Dally congratulated himself on having exorcised her irritation.

He was an ingenuous, likeable enough chap when he was sober, and quite amusing when he wasn't too drunk, Sally admitted to herself. His inhibitions peered through a pleasant garrulity, illustrated by anecdotes of amazing variety; but if he had been 'bending the elbow' too freely, he was liable to slump into unconsciousness at any moment, and have to be carried off to bed. After sleeping heavily for an hour or two, he might wake with a crying jag, and slink off for a bottle to cure the complaint.

A skinful of booze helped a man to forget the drudgery of his work underground, Dally said: gave him the only sort of heaven he was ever likely to know. A place where he could be happy and generous, a fine fellow without any highfaluting ideas about fighting for the rights of the working class, and without the consciousness of his own defeat in life gnawing at his vitals. It was all very well for Tom to argue that a man should be struggling to improve the lot of the workers: no use to let booze make them satisfied to keep slogging for the sake of a week-end spree. That suited the boss all right. Of course booze was the best weapon the bosses had to keep the workers making profits for them. A man was a mug to be put off his fair share of those profits for a few pots of beer.

But there it was. A man had to have his beer and keep on working to get more beer. If the miners didn't get their beer, where would the mining industry be? The bosses saw to it there was plenty of beer, even if it was only the poor, chemically doctored stuff served nowadays. Oh yes, the breweries were gold mines which the boss class used to extract from the working miner most of what had been paid to him in wages. Beer was the dope the bosses sold to keep a man from worrying about being a miner, and a wage-slave at that. What could you do about it, when a man was too dog weary and thick in the head to care what happened, so long as he could put new life into himself swigging beer, 'glorious beer'?

Of course Dally was a socialist. He liked to expatiate on what socialism would do for the workers. Drunk or sober, he would hold forth on the beauties of socialism: liberty, equality and fraternity for all men.

'But how are you going to get it?' Tom would demand.

'The mob'll get it when they wake up,' Dally replied complacently. 'No use bustin' y'rself to wake 'em up till they're ready.'

'Nothing will ever be done without organisation and discipline,' Tom maintained. 'It's men like you, with your rotten go-as-you-please ideas, are holding the workers back. All you care about is boozing. Trying to kid yourself nothing can be done till a miracle

86

happens, and you know that sort of miracle won't happen unless we make it. There's a job to be done, and a tough one. You and your sort are lying down on it, Dally. You're too damned lazy and stupid to go to the union meetings even: give us your vote when it's needed. Turn out on Sunday morning? Hell, a man's got a hang-over, wants to sleep in, stow away a few pots before dinner! You're a damned disgrace to the working-class movement.'

'That's right, son,' Dally would agree equably. 'But it won't make any difference if I don't go to union meetin's, or if a coupler hundred old boozers like me don't go to union meetin's, if you young blokes go on the way y're doin'. We'll be there when the whips are crackin'.'

'Not you,' Tom said bitterly. 'You'll be playing the boss's game, same as you are now.'

If she called Tom to remove him, Dally would start that argument, Sally knew. He always did when he was on the defensive and Tom might be goaded into handling him too roughly. She had seen Tom come in looking tired after his day's work, and preoccupied. He had to go to a union meeting later, and probably had some report to prepare so she didn't want to bother him to get rid of Dally.

Dally, taking advantage of her more good-humoured attitude, opened his bottle of beer.

'How about a little drink?' he wheedled.

The beer spurted over the kitchen floor, and Sally seized the bottle.

'Come on,' she said firmly. 'You can finish it in your room if you want to; but I'm not going to have my kitchen messed up with the stuff.'

She marched across the yard to the row of rooms in which most of her boarders slept, and Dally followed her, swaying unsteadily.

'This emotional stuff . . . these damned burgyose prejudices,' he muttered dejectedly. 'We got to get rid of 'em, missus. We got to get rid of 'em.'

"As the colonel said before he died,
And I don't think the old sod lied."

Oh yes, missus, and he was talkin' of beer, I reckon. He was talkin' of beer when he said, "Hic est gloria mundi".'

In the morning, Dally looked sick and ashamed, apologised for having made a nuisance of himself. He promised Mrs. Gough that such a thing would not happen again. He said solemnly that he would not start 'bending the elbow' so early in the week, knowing very well that he would; and that she knew he would, although he did not very often anticipate the blissful period of his week-end booze-up.

Her boarders were all on day shift that week, so there was no need to rush round preparing a second breakfast, as she had to when the men who had been working night shift came in for a meal. Her day was broken by meals at all hours when the men were working different shifts; but this morning she could take things easily: do her ironing and get on with the mending of socks, shirts and working trousers which piled up in the clothes basket, after the freshly laundered clothing had been stowed away in cupboards and chests of drawers.

It was just about knock-off time, in the late afternoon, when a mine whistle shrieked wildly, and she ran to the garden gate. The wives and mothers of miners on the goldfields knew that shrill blast too well to panic when they heard it. They knew on which mine a serious accident had occurred from the sound of the whistle. Each mine had its own, and almost every day, from one or the other, could be heard that long urgent wail, warning of disaster and death. Although it struck terror to the hearts of the women: made their 'insides turn over', as they said, and they waited, sick with apprehension, to see whether their man's mate or some stranger would come to the house, they had learned to nerve themselves to the sound of the accident signal, and to assure themselves that the bad news was not for them until it arrived at their door.

All the time, many of them were at their gates watching anxiously as the ambulance passed. More than one ambulance indicated a serious accident and several men injured. Sally had never got over the shock of that afternoon when the ambulance halted at her door, and Morris had been carried out of it, in a state of collapse. And now Tom was working underground, she always had a pang of fear that the whistle might be for him, if not to-day, some day. A sickening grief and anxiety possessed her whenever she heard it. That shrill, eerie whistle always meant pain and suffering for somebody.

The ambulance passed in a cloud of dust, and women called to each other over their garden gates, looking down the road and across back-yard fences, to see whether men from the mines were visiting any of the neighbours. It wasn't until Dally came home that Sally heard what had happened.

He was sober: looked ghastly, sick and shaken. Sally knew what was the matter as soon as she saw him. She had seen that look in a man's eyes too often not to know the shock and misery which went

with a mate's death. A bogger working near Dally on the Perseverance had been killed by a fall of earth.

'The poor silly cow,' he said tremulously, leaning against the
kitchen door. 'It was jest about knock-off time. We'd all left the
stope: were gettin' ready to be pulled-up, but he wanted to fill
another truck. Kept goin', and down she came. Jest a bit of luck
Toffer Green forgot his lamp and went back for it, and there was
the poor sod lyin' with a couple of ton of dirt on him. A few minutes
before there'd been four of us workin' alongside of him. The two
machine men and him and me.'

'Was he a married man?' Sally asked.

'Too right, he was,' Dally said bitterly. 'That's what was the
matter with him. Cliffy didn't give a damn about anything till he
married Rosy Drysdale, Old Dry's youngest daughter. Since then
he's been bustin' himself to make a bit more money. Was always
talkin' of the house he was buyin', and the furniture, and the missus
—and the kid comin'. Reckoned a bloke had to knock up a fair
pay if he was a married man.'

'He'd no right to be working by himself,' Sally said.

'It's agenst the minin' reg'lation,' Dally jeered. 'Agenst the
minin' reg'lations for a man to be workin' in a place that hasn't
been properly barred down before we go into it. But the way things
are on the Percy, jest now, a man's in a hurry to make the most he
can out of his job.

'The machine man says he barred down after firin', and the
ground was O.K., as far as he could see. But the fact of the matter
is a gunman doesn't get paid for barrin' down, only for the amount
of ore he can get trucked. It's tonnage that counts with him, and
some bastards are so hungry for money, they can't think of anything
else. I'm not blamin' 'em. It's all part of the system. The blasted
pressure forces men to work like that. A gunman's got to keep up
his average like everybody else. He can't afford to spend too much
time messin' about barrin' down. And if he can, his mate can't.
So there you are, missus! We all know it, and take our chances.
Hungry, measurement hungry, money hungry, we all are, and that's
the truth of it.'

Dally had consumed a few pots of beer on the way home, Mrs.
Gough did not doubt; but they could not dispel the effect of seeing
a man he had been working with a few moments before, lying a
bloody pulp of broken bones and bleeding flesh. She knew the
shock and horror would haunt him for days. If she had had a few
bottles of beer handy, she would have given them to Dally and let
him get dead drunk. It was what most women on the fields who
understood how a man was feeling in circumstances like these, would

have done. Most of them were reconciled to boozing at the week-end, and loss of pay at the two-up ring, though they took it with some hearty grousing, perhaps.

'You can't blame a man,' they said, 'for getting a bit of pleasure out of anything when he's been workin' underground all the week.'

Many of them took a few pots themselves when they went shopping on Saturday afternoon after pay-day, and had a flutter on the races. There was a marvellous sense of relief in knowing that for a night and a day at least their men were out of the mines.

Cliff Benton's funeral took place next day, and men on the Perseverance stopped work to attend it. Dally shaved and dressed in his shabby best suit. He never wore a hat except at a funeral; but every miner wore a hat for a funeral, so Dally put on his dilapidated felt hat, and went off to walk with his mates behind the hearse and mourning coaches to the cemetery.

The long procession of men, similarly dressed, trudged drearily along the dusty road below the ridge with its clutter of mine buildings, sky shafts and smoking chimney stacks, through the Boulder township to the bare, desolate patch of open ground where hundreds of white headstones marked the cemetery. Most of the men had marched like that behind the remains of many another mate, and the thought in almost every man's mind was: 'You never know whose turn it may be next.' He could see the same crowd at his own funeral: wondered whether the boys would look as grave-eyed, stiff-lipped and really mourning for him, as they were for Cliff Benton who had been a fine lad, hearty and vigorous, 'as full of fight as a butcher's dog', the day before.

At the graveside, there were some who like Dally thought of 'snatching it': turning down their job in a mine where creepy ground had been responsible for several falls and fatal accidents recently. They tried to persuade themselves that they would find some easier, less dangerous means of earning a living. But the priest gabbled over the service for the dead: the gravel was soon being shovelled over Cliff Benton's coffin, and the crowd of grim-visaged men disintegrated, drifted away through the cemetery and along the hot dusty road in the glare of the afternoon sun, to the nearest pub.

There they drank thirstily, desperately, to blot out the recollection of Cliff Benton, his crushed body, and his wife sobbing by the graveside, and that they must start work in the mine again next morning.

Soon the depression and lurking fear which had oppressed them, lifted. The grim bravado characteristic of a mining fraternity, began to reassert itself. Miners would not admit that death and a funeral could intimidate them. There was a challenge to their courage, and hardihood, the risks they were facing every day and standing up to, in the ceremony they had just been through. Jocose banter and some good-natured contempt were levelled at any weakling who got the wind up because of a fatal accident: talked of pulling out of the mines and chasing another job. It was a reflection on the guts and spirit of men who worked underground, tended to undermine a man's confidence in himself, and the illusion every miner needed to foster that no more risks were attached to working underground than on the surface, if a man took reasonable precautions for his safety, and saw that the mine owners did likewise.

But no man deceived himself as to why he was a miner. He was quite cynical about his reasons for hanging on to his job: better wages than he could earn in almost any other and a chance of making a bit extra on the gold. That meant slinging it when he had got enough money together for a good home, to give his missus a bit of comfort and the kids a decent education: have some sort of security in his old age. There was always resentment of a man who got scared about the risks of the game, and dropped out before there was anything to boast of for his pains.

'Same old story,' Dally mumbled when he came back to Gough's boarding-house, drunk and garrulous, 'all men are mortal, except me. Nothing can happen to me. It's always the other feller. I got a bellyful of the hocus-pocus at the graveside, missus. A big, fat priest in fancy dress, gabblin' Latin, and Cliff's missus cryin' her eyes out. Y'r could hear her sobbin' all through the damned service.

' "Hic est corpus," the priest says. That's where they get the words hocus-pocus from, I reckon. It's hocus-pocus they put over the mob at a burial service, all right. A strapping lad like Cliffy Benton to be smashed up and put out of his life, and all the parsons can do about it, is stuff religion down y'r throat, and try to make y' believe Cliffy's gone to glory: "God knows best."

'Fat lot of good it'd do Cliffy, gettin' round with the angels, when all he wanted was to go home to his missus, or have a pot and a wongie with his mates. It's a crime. That's what it is—for a man to be cut off in his prime like that. A black, dastardly crime, and no amount of religion smarming over the truth, and tryin' to make y'r believe in the glorious resurrection of the dead—is goin' to get over it. But all the priests do is keep on tellin' a poor bugger—beggin' y'r pard'n, missus—no matter what sort of a raw deal he gets here, it'll be all right in heaven. Makes a man feel like joinin' the wobblies tomorrer.'

'Or doing what Tom says,' Sally said sharply. 'Get better

organisation and discipline into the unions so that you can force
the mine owners to improve conditions in the mines.'

Dally went off singing dolefully:

> *You'll eat . . . bye and bye-ee*
> *In that glorious land above the sky-ee,*
> *Work and pray . . . live on hay,*
> *There'll be pie in the sky,*
> *When you die-ee.*

CHAPTER XI

THAT morning was like any other when Tom went below with the
first shift. Except that it was Wednesday and men working with
the mechanical doggedness of the middle of the week. Jollifications
of the last week-end had lost their power to dispel gloom, and the
next were still too far away to arouse any exhilaration. Wednesday
was a hard, dull day, and yet Ted Lee, Tom's mate, barred down and
rigged his drill with more cheery vigour than usual. The ore he
had been bringing down was showing better values.

'Looks all right!' he commented briskly, glancing over the ore
cluttering the entrance to the end in which he and Tom were
working. 'Get a move on clearin' up, Tommy, and I'll make it
worth your while.'

'Right!' Tom bogged into shovelling off the ore.

He guessed that Ted was hoping for even better results from his
next firing. So was Abel Morgan, the shift boss, apparently. He
had come along to inspect the stope soon after Ted started work.

Through the country greenstone, forming the walls the lode ran
sparkling in the candlelight, although no gold was visible. A fault
breaking the lode and pushing it aside, appeared in a dark band
of greasy graphite.

The lode had a way of vanishing mysteriously in this mine; and
as the gold bearing stone was petering out, Ted had been afraid
he would be up against the problem which had baffled solution on
the Barrier Reef before.

As a matter of fact the old manager, after spending a lot of
money on exploratory work, had given it up in despair. He considered the mine was done, with the petering out of its richest ore
body. A new manager taking over, had the luck to strike the lode
again, two hundred feet from his predecessor's workings, and
Barrier Reef stock recovered on the strength of it.

But Tom did not like the look of that greasy graphite on the west wall. He pointed it out to the shift boss.

'Christ, I'll get a couple of "toms" for her, Ted,' Abel exclaimed affably. 'Now y're showin' values she's worth shorin'-up.'

'Get em, right away, or I'll be snatchin' me time,' Ted replied. 'Values or no values, this place is a death trap without a bit of timberin'.'

Through the dust and din of the morning's work, Tom caught a glimpse of him now and then, a sturdy intrepid figure up there on his precarious staging. When the deafening chatter of the drill was silent a moment. Ted could be heard cursing blunt bits and called:

'Hand's up another steel, Tom! Some of this stuff's got as much bite as an old Moll at a christenin'.'

He had a word about it to the shift boss when he came along again with the underground foreman to discuss timbering bad ground in the stope. Tom realised, as he shovelled assiduously under the eye of the bosses, that he had not been as fully aware of the danger in that ground as Ted; and guessed Ted knew nothing would be done about it until the ore was more promising. Money would not be wasted timbering a place that might soon be abandoned. His life and Ted's were of less value than the ore they handled. But now that it was richer, the positional importance of the stope had to be considered.

All that made no difference to him as a wages man, Tom reflected. He could break his back shifting the blasted ore, and get no more for his pains than the few bob extra Ted would sling him for loading his trucks.

It was quite right what the men said, 'a bogger's a miner with his brains bashed out'. His lot was hard labour for life, unless he graduated to the status of a machine man; and that was what he was after, Tom reminded himself, a job with an experienced miner like Ted on a machine: being a gun man in his own right. He was young and inexperienced for the responsibility yet, perhaps; but he wondered whether Ted would give him a chance if the ore kept on improving and he wanted another machine man to work alongside him. A party of four, two machine men and two boggers, might take on the development of this stope.

When they knocked off for crib, he had made up his mind to broach the subject with Ted. It was two men's work really, firing fuses in the sort of place where they were working. Ted had to move quickly to get his last fuse lit before the first had travelled far. There was always the danger of a running fuse, and premature explosion. Ted said he had heard of a running fuse, but never seen one.

'If y'd seen it, y'r would'n be here to tell the tale, Ted,' Andy Spark told him, one day.

'That's a fact,' the men agreed. Fear of a running fuse, a defective fuse along which a thread of fire leapt swiftly and ignited the charge before a miner could escape from the explosion it brought about, haunted the minds of all the older men. But a damp fuse, which might smoulder sulkily and cause a delayed explosion, was more dreaded these days.

Ted waited to check off the number of his shots before opening up his crib. Then, having heard the explosions and got a full count, he settled down on the board, a pleased grin on his face. When he had taken a swig of cold tea from his billy, and polished off the substantial pasty and sandwiches his wife had put up for him, he was ready to yarn and crack a joke with the boys.

'What's struck Abel?' Jo Halliday asked. 'He's stickin' to you like a bad smell to-day, Ted.'

'Search me,' Ted replied. 'Thinks I may be puttin' something over him, p'raps. Suits me all right. I'm gettin' Oregon toms out of him for a bit of bad ground.'

The men's laughter gurgled and died away.

'He's not a bad stick, Abel!' Smiler conceded. 'Better than some of these American shift bosses, go down with the first cage, crib with the boys and never take their eyes off of them. They've got a new man on the Lake View, Chook Deane was tellin' me. He's great on e-fficiency.'

'E-fficiency!' Lenny Low spluttered. 'What the hell's that, Smiler?'

'That's what this here bloke was explainin',' Smiler continued, squinting past Lenny and his mate. 'Seems some of the truckers was shovin' these big, new trucks along to the bins when he came along, about knock-off time.

' "Sit down, boys," he says. "Have a smoke? That's right!" he pipes up when the boys squatted, cursin' him for keepin' them back. "We're goin' to get along fine. Always like to have a talk to the men when I'm on a job like this. E-fficiency, boys, that's what we're after. E-fficiency, it's a great thing, boys! Got me where I am. What's it mean? Well, if you been pushin' twelve trucks, it means gettin' thirteen away."

'Nobody cracks a word, so he goes on:

' "Me, I was a trucker, once: did a bit more than the best man: was made shift boss. Got better results out of the men. That's e-fficiency, boys."

'The boys were all sittin', starin' at him as if he was makin' a great impression on them, so the Yank goes on:

94

' "I guess you boys don't want to be truckers all yer days. You don't want to do nothin' but shove trucks around the mine, do yer?" No answer. "And even if y' get to be shift boss, what's that? Bein' shift boss isn't good enough for a man with ambition. And y've got to have ambition and e-fficiency, haven't y'r? What's *your* ambition?"

'He turns to the man nearest him, who looks as if he was deaf and dumb.

' "Come arn, boys, speak up?" says the Yank, beginnin' to get a bit rattled. "Every man's got a right to his ambition, and it's e-fficiency'll take him where he wants to go. Get me? What's y'r ambition, buddy?"

'This time he hits on Blue Ryan and Bluey lets him have it.

' "My ambition," Blue says, drawlin' it out, "is to be hung for rape when I'm ninety-nine." '

Smiler's yarn started others: but the sports were getting busy with one of their cockroach races. Smiler went off to bring his pet cockroach from the tin matchbox in which he kept it.

'Somebody's done the dirty on me, and let Carbine out of his stable,' he howled presently. 'Look, it's empty.'

He stood gazing sadly at the empty box in his hands.

'And him, the best racin' cockroach on the Golden Mile,' Smiler lamented.

The men chiacked him good-humouredly. 'He wasn't no racin' cockroach, Smiler.'

'Too big and fat!'

'Mick Doherty's Red Legs had him beat anyhow!'

'Mick was showing off his cockroach with legs painted red. He kept it in a cigarette tin, and was backing it to beat the field.

Vic Uren was crying the odds:

'I'll lay three to one Red Legs!'

'Three to one Red Legs and Battleaxe Bertha!'

'Five bob on Bertha? Right y'r are, Ted.'

'What y'r givin' us on Stinker?'

The men made their bets with noisy jocularity and watched the sports heat a piece of tin for the cockroaches to race across.

'Look at 'im shiverin' like a dog to get started,' an owner commented proudly.

Or: 'See he's sharpenin' his razors to go like greased lightnin'!'

When the starters were put down, and began to scramble across the hot tin, there was as much excitement and barracking for the favourite, as if these clumsy insects were whippets or two-year-olds. Curses and guffaws burst forth, as the cockroaches shot off sideways, or turned back on their tracks.

There was always a good laugh to be got out of the cockroach races: the bets gave them a gambling interest; but nobody cared which cockroach won, so long as a bit of fun could be got out of the foolery.

Making their way back along the level to the drives and crosscuts or winzes in which they were working, most of the men were still chuckling at the way Mick Doherty had carried on when his Red Legs played up at the post and a little black devil Stew McIntyre had picked out of his crib, sprinted gamely across the hot tin.

From the plat as they disappeared in the narrow, dimly lit cylinder of the drive, the dark, seeping walls of the mine seemed to close in on the men. The noise of their boots squelching on the mucky tracks, staccato exclamations and hoarse laughter were lost in the great underground quiet, heavy, humid and menacing.

Then the rattle of ore down the ore passes began again and the shrilling of plat bells, a distant whirring and buzz of drills, the clatter of skips running on narrow rails from the drives, and being switched off to be shot down to a lower level where they were taken on by a horse-drawn tram to the shaft and hauled up to the cracker. No sound of voices rose above the rumble of grim dumb labour, the groan of mechanised industry, muffled and fixed, in the hollow darkness.

But from the face where Ted Lee was still barring down, prizing off any loose rock and scrutinising the wall from which his firing had brought down a couple of tons of ore, Tom heard a shout which brought him, Lenny Low and Abel Morgan to the foot of the dump on which Ted was standing. The dust and acrid fumes of firing hung heavily about them; but Ted was beside himself with excitement, his face ablaze through the sweat and grime which covered it.

'Get an eyeful of that,' he shouted as Lenny and the shift boss scrambled up to him, and Tom followed them.

On the broken face of the lode, he saw the sort of shoot of gold he had heard about but never seen. Gold was glittering in streaks and solid clots in a schisty matrix. It was lying exposed on the ore the firing had brought down. Tom stared at it in the same state of crazy excitement as the others.

'Ker-i-st-a'mighty!' Lenny gasped.

'She's rich, all right, Ted!' Noah swore breathlessly. 'Reg'lar jeweller's shop.'

'Last day or two, I reckoned I was on to something good,' Ted exulted.

'The samples was promisin'.' Abel chuckled. 'We been keepin' an eye on what you was doin'. That you, Bob?' he yelled, as the underground foreman hove in sight. 'She's here. all right! Was jest goin' to send for you to have a squiz at her.'

Big Bob climbed the heap of ore and stood gaping at the rich shoot. Things had been in a bad way on the mine, Tom gathered as Bob and Abel talked. There had been a chance of the Boulder Reef having to close down. But if this shoot opened up like it promised, she would have a new lease of life.

'Maybe we've struck the old Brown Hill lead again!' Bob exclaimed.

He and Abel knocked off lumps of ore, examined and pocketed them. Lenny Low lost no time doing likewise. Ted and Tom watched rich specimens disappearing into his bag and baggy trousers. Their eyes met: but Ted signalled a warning.

'P'raps we're mugs not to help ourselves, too, Tom,' he growled, when Tom had gone back to his job; and Ted, scrambling down for another pinch bar, managed to get a word with him. 'But we couldn't get away with anything. They'll keep us skinned, watchin' from now on. But jeeze, why did I get so excited and yell before we'd got a bit stowed away.'

Tom was conscious of feeling that he and Ted were mugs. Few men on the mine would have missed this opportunity to pick up a few specimens and stow them away to dispose of later. Not many of their mates would believe that they had nothing hoarded somewhere, under a chow or behind old timber. Ted and he would be almost ashamed to admit they had let such a chance slip. The most maddening part of it all was to know that the shift boss, Big Bob and the Louse would get away with a fair bit, while Ted and he had to stew in the juice of their own stupidity. Though, of course, the louser, Abel and Big Bob could argue that they were acting on behalf of the company by removing a few samples to indicate the richness of the shoot.

Tom had gone back to shovelling the mullock piled up near the entrance, overcome by a sense of not being 'a miner's bootlace', and having been let down by those highfaluting ideas which were all right for a man working above ground, but had no place in the code of a working miner. It was not the honesty or dishonesty of grabbing a bit of gold that worried Ted, only the risk of being caught.

The Louse volunteered to go up and pass the good news on to the underground manager.

'No, you don't,' Big Bob said curtly. 'I'll go meself. You stay here with Abel, Lenny, until I get back. And you men,' he turned to Ted, 'better watch your step. There's goin' to be trouble if this gold starts walkin'.'

'No need to watch my step, or Tom Gough's,' Ted said.

The underground manager when he came down, did not allow himself to be dazzled by what he saw. He brought along a couple of boggers to bag the rich ore, and gave his instructions for the bags to be counted and shepherded to the treatment plant. The ground was to be cleared, and a new plan of operations worked out.

'Can y'r beat it?' Ted growled when he and Tom had been subjected to a pretty thorough inspection, passing from the change room to the showers in their underpants.

A gold stealing detective could run his hands through a man's hair, poke his finger under his tongue, peer into ears, turn out his pockets and crib bag, or billy. But 'the law protected his balls' as the men said. It was not permitted to uncover a man completely, and some old hard-doers, to rile the dees were suspected of having devised a means of hiding a scrap of gold where it could not be found.

Ted was sore and wrathful at being subjected to the ignominy of this search. Tom took it more equably; but with a surge of indignation at the injustice done to miners by such a procedure, while officials of the mine went scot free.

It was infuriating to think of Lenny Low cashing in on Ted's toil, and of the shift boss, foreman and perhaps underground manager, having their cut by mutual agreement. It was no wonder men, placed as Ted and he were, felt justified in helping themselves. There was no end of satisfaction in feeling they could outwit the bosses, if they set their minds to it.

The risk of being caught in possession of gold 'reasonably suspected of having been stolen', and going to jail for a few months, did not carry any stigma in a mining community: nobody attached much importance to it except a few people like his mother and Ted's wife. To them it would be a calamity and a disgrace for anybody belonging to them to be arrested and sent to jail for gold stealing.

Ted, naturally cautious, and earning good money as an experienced machine miner, had been satisfied hitherto not to give the dees any cause to make trouble for him. Tom knew that Ted had not even been tempted to get away with any gold until he saw the Louse and the shift boss helping themselves. That was the way Tom, himself, felt. He had not wanted the blasted stuff until he saw those others making so free with it. Then a madness to grab some had come over him. He realised Ted had been right to warn him off.

There was no doubt they would be closely watched while they were working on the shoot; and after all, it was good to think he need not worry about the dees searching and trailing him.

Tom could not endure the thought of the shame and grief his mother would suffer, if he were caught in any gold-stealing stunt. She had held her head high and battled along gamely for years, and he knew how she felt about this business. He was glad that he could go home with an easy mind: tell her the whole story of the rich shoot Ted had struck, without bringing a shadow of anxiety to her eyes.

He had told Sally about it, and got the quick fear of her first glance. It was almost as if she had said: 'I hope you didn't do anything foolish?'

'No, I didn't!' Tom's clear, candid gaze assured her.

His mother laughed happily.

'Let them keep all their gold,' she said, kissing him. 'We've got some things money can't buy, son.'

What did she mean by that, Tom wondered, as he went off to his room. Probably, the knowledge of a personal rectitude nothing could tarnish, and the pride and peace of knowing contentment within the circle of her own home.

But life was not so simple as that, Tom reflected. There were those sinister forces outside Sally, her home and her sons, always threatening the security of the small fort she had built for herself. No one lived alone in a world where war, disease and the ruthless struggle for wealth and power, swept thousands of little people like her into the maelstrom of economic and national crises.

CHAPTER XII

DEN and Lal were scuffling in the back-yard. Sally could hear them slang-banging each other one moment and grappling the next with gusts of laughter. Then Den was crying: 'Le'go! Le'go, you big punce!' And Lal demanding: 'Well, are you going to sling off at me again?'

'No, Lal! No!' Den promised, and making his escape, yelled from across the yard: 'But you can't ride for nuts, and I'm not going to give you Moppin to take to the war.'

Sally's heart floundered. Rumours that there was going to be a war in Europe had been drifting about the goldfields for months;

but she could not believe that they had anything to do with her. She had heard the men discussing the rumours at meals: talking about 'another blood bath' before the year was out, and she shuddered at the thought of it.

Several Austrians and Germans had disappeared from Kalgoorlie and Boulder. Serbs, Bulgarians, Italians and Greeks, who worked on the mines, were gathering in excited groups and jabbering, in their own language, over the latest news. The Dings, as the northern peoples were called, and the Dagoes, which included the southern European races, had never fraternised very much, and now the boys were saying:

'The Dings and the Dagoes are ready to fly at each other's throats.'

That was all very well for foreigners, Sally thought. It was quite natural they should be concerned about the possibility of a war in their own countries. But that it could reach this remote Australian town, and her, personally, she had never imagined.

Lal was a senior cadet, of course. He had been drilling and spending his holidays in camp for the last year or two, because of compulsory clauses in a recent Defence Act which required all youths to do military training for a few weeks every year. Den, too, was in a cadet corps at school. But this military training, everybody believed, was merely a precautionary measure to provide for national defence. Fear of the rising power of Japan had reconciled most people to legislation for the defence of Australia.

Sally remembered the Boer War, and that Australian troops had been sent to support the British fighting forces. She remembered how anybody who spoke against the war had been regarded as a 'traitor', and hounded out of the town, although later, it was recognised that those 'traitors' were right. As Dinny said, there was every reason for being ashamed that Australian miners had given their support to a war brought about by British financiers to control the gold mines of the Rand.

Was it possible that if Great Britain were involved in this European war, Australian troops would be sent overseas? And that her own boys might be called upon to fight with them? Sally was panic-stricken at the idea.

His horse was Den's dearest possession. If he had not been a born horseman, Sally would have been scared for him to ride the spirited, half-broken brute. But Den handled him so well, she felt she need not worry when Den was riding Moppingarra.

Lal had nothing like the same horse-sense. Lal had ridden Moppin in some military sports recently and he had played up badly. Den yelled advice to Lal from the crowd, not to saw the horses's head off, and the crowd had joined in, laughing and jeering at poor Lal when Moppin bolted and threw him. Until recently, when he went off to drill, Lal had ridden one of the horses Morris used for the hearses. But they were poor-spirited, broken-down old mokes, and now Lal was borrowing Moppin, paying for his feed, wanting to buy him from Den. Because he thought, evidently, that if there were a war, mounted troops would be needed as they were in the Boer war.

Sally felt sick with fear when Lal came in for his dinner that night before going to his weekly drill. He was wearing his uniform and felt hat: his boots were shining. He looked very spic and span, and so proud of the stripe on his sleeve: walked like a soldier, straight-backed, with a swing of the shoulders and jaunty stride. Sally saw him for the first time as a soldier. But what did her boy know about this terrible business of war, she asked herself miserably.

After dinner, when the washing up had been done, she went into the sitting-room, and sat there sewing while Den did his homework. He sprawled over the table, grunting and groaning about it, ruffling his thick gingery hair, and glancing at her, now and again, for a word of encouragement.

He was rather like a brumby himself, Den, Sally told herself, though he did try to take an interest in his lessons to please her. All his instincts were to fling up his heels and race off into the bush. And she had hoped he would want to study: go to an agricultural college, and have some sort of training for work on the land which he had set his heart on. That was not to be, apparently.

Den cared for nothing except horses, hanging round a cattle camp, yarning with stockmen and drovers, and giving them a hand whenever he got a chance. He was just like any other goldfields youngster to look at, as sun-dried and skinny, with gingery-golden hair like Morris's and bright brown eyes full of an urchinish joy of life; but he had this passion for horses and cattle. It was curious, Sally thought; almost as if her father and her own upbringing had something to do with Den's ambition to be a stockman.

'Tell me about when you were a girl, mum,' he would say, when he was quite a little chap.

Den was never tired of hearing about his grandfather who had been a pioneer of the south-west; and Warrinup, with the homestead and stockyards looking over the river flats, and flanked by virgin forests of karri and marri. How many cattle did it run? How many horses were there on the station? Who was managing it now? Den was full of questions about the old place.

'Gee, I wish I could go there, mum!' So many times he had said that, Sally herself began to feel homesick for a sight of the forest country of her youth.

'Some day, we'll go to Warrinup for a holiday,' she had promised him.

'Haven't you ever been back since you came to the fields?' Den asked.

'No, darling,' Sally told him. 'You see my father and mother were angry with me because dad and I ran away to be married. They didn't want me to go home again.'

'Gee, that's tough!'

Sally smiled to herself thinking that to Den it was as if she had been banished from the garden of Eden.

'I bet they're sorry, and want to see you, now,' he exclaimed hopefully.

'Your grandfather and grandmother are dead,' Sally had told him. 'But I daresay Bob—that's your Uncle Bob—owns Warrinup now. He'd be glad if we could visit him.'

She was ashamed to confess that she did not know what had happened on Warrinup for many years. Whether her brother was still there. Who was in charge now. Since the death of her father and mother she had not heard from her sisters. Cecily and Grace were married she knew; but what had happened to Fanny and Phyllis, she had no idea. She had become so absorbed in her own life on the goldfields, nothing else mattered for a long time, Sally excused herself. When the children were little, she could think of nothing but her daily work and providing for them. The years had fled so quickly.

It was difficult to believe her boys were all grown up now, and able to fend for themselves—except Den. And how to give him a start in the work he wanted to do was her next problem. It was no use trying to get him to pass examinations if Den had made up his mind that he was going to be a stockman and drover.

Sally sighed, looking at the boy's sturdy, adolescent body bowed over his lesson book. He was a good boy, Den, she told herself: doing his best to stuff his head with a lot of English history and poetry in which he wasn't interested. 'A spoilt brat!' Dick said, because Den usually got his own way with her; and it was a fact, she admitted. Den knew how to manage her better than any of his brothers. That was because he was the youngest, and there wasn't the same need to be firm with him, that there had been when the boys were all little together, and no time could be wasted arguing with them about what they should and should not do.

She had been rather strict then, Sally thought: she had expected and insisted on too much obedience, perhaps. Dick and Tom, and

Lal rarely broke the rules of their home life, even now. Den, on the other hand, contrived to ignore them guilelessly. And yet, there was a very close sympathy between her and her youngest son. It was as if they understood something the others could not share when they talked about Warrinup. It enhanced her prestige with Den that she had been brought up on a cattle station: knew all about mustering in the wild southern hills: could ride and break-in horses. He was very proud of that, and respected her as an authority on the handling of horses and cattle.

Den wanted to leave school at the end of the year, and Sally had begun to realise that it was no use to keep him there, or to send him to college for a year or two, if he were going to be miserable about it. She must try to give him the sort of life he wanted. At least fulfil that old promise to him about going on a visit to Warrinup some day.

It could have been done quite easily, if Paddy Cavan had not upset her plans. Loss of the money he paid her for board would mean that she had less to put by for any extra expenses. But then, she had been saving for some time to provide for Den's going to Dookie Agricultural College.

If the money was not going to be needed for school fees, she might as well use it to let Den have the holiday he had dreamed of for so long. It would be wonderful for them to go to Warrinup together. How delighted her father would have been with the boy. A boy who would love Warrinup as Bob, his only son, had not done. Bob had always hoped to could get away from the place. From the time he came home from school, her brother had girded at being stuck away there in the bush. He would have been glad of the chance Den had now to study and go to the university: but he had been forced to help his father, and carry on for the girls' sake and his mother's, after his father's death.

Poor old Bob, what queer tricks life played with people! Sally hoped Den would never have to endure being tied to a job for which he was not suited. Perhaps he would be able to help Bob. Perhaps Bob would be glad to have Den on Warrinup. Sally had a sudden, dazzling vision of Den taking over the management of Warrinup, in the distant future. It left her breathless, and as excited as if it might happen.

'Den, darling,' she said, presently, making her voice sound quite even and casual. 'I'm going to write to your Aunt Fanny, and tell her we'd like to pay them a visit on Warrinup during the school holidays.'

The light danced in Den's eyes.

'Do you mean it? Do you really mean it, mum?' he gasped.

'Don't get too excited,' Sally cautioned. 'They haven't said they can have us yet. And we'll have to wait until after Dick's wedding. Then too, if there's a war, Den . . .'

Den nodded.

'We couldn't be away if Lal . . .'

'Will he be going?' Sally asked, her voice trembling.

' 'Course, he will mum,' Den replied cheerfully. 'I'd be going meself, if I was a bit older.'

'Don't say such a thing!' Sally cried. 'Do you realise what war means, Den? Hundreds of boys like Lal killing each other, getting wounded, lying in the most terrible pain on battlefields, in hospitals . . .'

'Gee, mum, I didn't think of that,' Den's expression sobered. 'But Colonel de Morfé says . . .'

'Oh, he's a colonel now, is he?' Sally kept her eyes on her work. 'He wouldn't lose any time getting a front-seat for himself.'

'He's been in the militia for years, Lal says, and turned up in camp, a couple of weeks ago, as a colonel. Been recruiting men for a mounted regiment.'

'Well, what does Frisco say?' Sally asked impatiently.

'He says,' Den replied, pleased to show off his information, 'that Germany is backing Austria, and Britain will have to wallop Germany or lose her colonies. P'raps Australia.'

'I don't believe it.' Sally said. 'And anyway, how on earth do you know what he says?'

Den grinned.

'His motor car was stuck in a soft patch on the road, just when school was let out, and some of the kids started to sling off at him.

' "What price the bone-shaker?"

'And: "How about goin' for Old Shack and his horse to pull you out, mister?" '

Old Shack was the town drunk and had a horse and cart which he drove along the back streets collecting all sorts of rubbish when he was sober.

Sally smiled to think of Frisco in the brand new motor car of which he was so proud, being subjected to such an insult.

Den went on:

'But Nipper and I thought we might cadge a ride. So we went up to him, and Nipper says:

' "Anything we can do, sir?"

' "My oath!" says Colonel de Morfé. "You can all get behind and shove." So we got all the kids to shove behind, and shoved for all we were worth, and the engine started again right enough.

' "Hop in!" yells Colonel de Morfé. The whole mob of us scrambled on board and he drove us all round town, mum.'

Of course, Sally told herself, it was just like Frisco to fill up his car with children like that and make a display of his good-heartedness. Still, most of the youngsters had never been in a motor car before, so it was a great adventure for them.

'I managed to snaffle the seat beside him,' Den went on. 'And he said to me:

' "What's your name, son?"

' "Denis Gough," I told him.

' "Oh it is, is it?" he says, laughing. "Give my respects to your mother, and tell her I hope she'll come to my next New Year's Eve party." '

Sally blushed and her eyes sparkled.

'Like his impudence,' she exclaimed heatedly.

'Why, mum?'

His mother's eyes fell before Den's bland, curious gaze.

'Mr. de Morfé used to be a friend of ours in the early days of Hannans,' she said lamely. 'But I haven't forgiven him yet for the way he treated Dick in Sydney.'

'Did he treat Dick badly?' Den asked.

'He did,' Sally said fiercely. 'He sacked Dick, at a moment's notice. Oh, well, perhaps Dick sacked himself. But Frisco knew he had no money, and Dick had a hard time before he got home.'

'Gee, I didn't know that. I didn't know he'd treated Dick badly,' Den muttered. 'I wouldn't've got into his blasted car, if I'd known, mum.'

'What else did Mr. de Morfé say?' Sally asked, overcoming her agitation.

'He said he'd have to sell the car when war is declared,' Den said. 'That was why he had been made a colonel. Because he was going to the war. He had been a soldier in Mexico, he said, and knew all about fighting.'

'God help us if there is a war, and men like Frisco are going to run it!' Sally exclaimed.

When Morris came in she made him a cup of tea, and asked what he thought about the possibility of war everybody was talking about. Did he think there would be a war?

Morris said he was afraid so, and that Great Britain would be drawn into it—and Australia. Morris was very perturbed by the situation. For the first time in many years, he talked like an Englishman: remembered he had been a soldier. Even the boys

105

did not know that. Morris had never told them about his home or people, any of his associations with the Old Country. But now, Sally felt, many memories had taken hold of him.

When they went to bed, Morris said that, of course, he was too old for active service. And anyhow he had been kicked out of the regiment. For the first time, he mentioned to her the reason for his having come to Australia. He had lost money at cards, it seemed, and taken funds of the regimental sporting club to pay a gambling debt. He had been sent to the colonies in disgrace, but with some expectation that he would redeem himself and return home, some day.

After his father's death, Morris had lost all contact with his brothers and sisters. He did not want to revive it. There would be no welcome for him in England now. But it was hard to realise a man could do nothing to defend his country if war broke out. That seemed to be the only consideration troubling Morris.

'Lal will want to go if it happens,' Sally cried despairingly. 'Oh, Morris, what are we going to do if Lal is mixed up in the fighting?'

She wept quietly against his shoulder until Morris fell asleep. For a long time she could not sleep herself. Her mind was haunted by the distant mutterings of that murderous chaos threatening to overwhelm the world. All next day as she worked about the house, it overshadowed her thoughts, making her forget minor worries about Tom and this new rich shoot where he was working, and about Paddy Cavan and his insufferable behaviour.

Paddy had intimated that as he was vacating his room on Saturday, he wanted his washing and mending done for the week. And he had complained about the way she washed his socks.

Paddy had bad feet and his socks smelt atrociously. Sally would never put them into a tub with the boys' and Morris's socks. It had been one of her trials for years to wash Paddy's socks. The stench from the tub they were in made her feel sick, and it had required an effort of will to plunge her hands into the stinking water, and rub and rinse those socks.

'I'm not going to do your washing this week, Paddy,' Sally told him calmly. 'You can send it to the laundry.'

'You've been paid to do it,' Paddy snarled. 'I reckon it's up to you to do it, or hand me back five bob of what I gave you for board.'

'You can have the five bob,' Sally said, giving him the money. 'But you've never paid for half of what I've done for you, Paddy.'

'Putting the hard word on me for a bit more cash, are y'?' Paddy jeered.

'Get out of my kitchen,' Sally commanded. 'I've had enough of

you and your meanness, Paddy Cavan. I don't want to see you, or
have anything to do with you again.'

Paddy had slouched off saying sulkily:

'Maybe y'll change y'r mind about that, Mrs. Gough.'

CHAPTER XIII

OUTSIDE the pubs, at every street corner, in Kalgoorlie and Boulder,
crowds of men and youths collected to hear the racing results, and
pass on the news of the fields. on a Saturday afternoon. After the
fortnightly pay, the pubs were full of men, and the shops of women
and children with money to spend.

So busy and gay the sprawling townships were, the main streets
swarming with men, women and children dressed up in their best!
Buggies, sulkies and spring carts lined the wide thoroughfares,
with here and there horses hitched to a post, and a few motor cars
to indicate that prosperous citizens were keeping abreast of the
times. But during those critical months of 1914, the rumours of
war were almost as much discussed round the pubs as the racing
news. Lazily, casually, except in the vicinity of the foreign restaurants and wine shops where Greeks, Italians, Serbs, Bulgarians and
Macedonians gathered in agitated groups.

Sally and Marie liked to do their shopping together on this gala
afternoon after pay on the mines. It was quite exciting to join the
throng in the streets, and inspect goods in the shops, put out at
bargain prices to tempt women with money burning a hole in their
pockets. They did not join 'the pub crawl' which was a recognised
feature of Saturday afternoon among miners and their wives, who
strolled along the streets, taking a drink at one pub and then
another, in order to meet their friends and forgather for a little
conviviality in beer parlours, but usually dropped into a pub near
Paddy Hannan's old reward claim, for a glass of beer after their
shopping.

It was a rather disreputable looking place, though clean and quiet;
and in a back parlour which was called the 'Ladies' Room', they
often met old acquaintances of early days on the fields. It was
pleasant to dump their parcels and rest there for a while before
starting to walk home. Besides, that glass, or two, of beer gave a
certain fillip to their jaunt; and if Dinny or Morris happened to see
them and tease them about 'drinking at the Reward' on a Saturday
afternoon, they had a good excuse. Theresa Molloy's daughter,

107

Adelaide, had married the licensee, Bill Feathers, and Theresa herself, was cooking for Adey at the pub.

Adey, who brought drinks along to the 'Ladies' Room', and helped her husband in the bar, was always pleased to see such old friends as Mrs. Gough and Mme. Robbillard.

She fussed about them happily.

'There's one thing,' Adey said, 'you can always be sure of your glasses being clean here. A man comes in for a drink, sometimes, has got the most awful cancer on his mouth. But I keep a special pot for him and wash it in phenyle. They're not so particular in some places.'

'Oh, la-la, Adey,' Marie cried. 'We will always have our little drink with you!'

'God save us, if it's not Mrs. Gough!' a tall gaunt woman, sitting at a table by herself in the corner, remarked when Adey had trotted off to bring Sally's and Marie's beer.

'Oh, it's you, Mrs. Gallagher,' Sally said, recognising a sturdy old whaler who was known in the early days as 'God-Save-Us-Sarah'. 'I haven't seen you for ages. How are you?'

'I'm fine,' Mrs. Gallagher said slowly, 'when I get a few pots into me, though me rheumatics is bad, and I miss me old man.'

'You were great mates, weren't you?' Sally queried. 'Went about on all the rushes together.'

'It's the truth,' the old woman agreed. 'God save us, but where would Sandy've been without me? I knew more about gettin' about the country and prospectin' than he did. He was a good man, Sandy. Left me a nice wad in the bank, and I'd've been sittin' pretty to-day if I hadn't taken up with that blaigard, Charley Quartermaine.'

'Not Buck Quartz?'

'The same,' Mrs. Gallagher agreed grimly. 'Never you take another husband, dearie. Never you go to bed with a strange man and let him get hold of y'r money.'

'I won't,' Sally promised.

'Oh, well, he leaves me alone, now, Mr. Buck Quartz,' God-Save-Us-Sarah chuckled. 'He called me for everything because I wouldn't tell him where I had a bit of gold stowed away.

' "You bloody old bitch," he says.

' "I can stand that I ses. That's good Australian, but if you call me a dirty, greasy old gin again, I'll knock yer blasted head off." He did—and I let him have it. Split his head open with a mother's cauliflower, and there was him, bleedin' like a pig, and bits of broken china all over the floor, when the neighbours rushed in and carted him away in the ambulance.'

'*Mon Dieu*, did 'e die?' Marie asked breathlessly, wondering whether she and Sally were talking to a murderess.

'Die? Not him—not Buck,' God-Save-Us-Sarah exclaimed wrathfully. 'He's gettin' round again now, as large as life—but he leaves me alone.'

She lifted her big glass pot. It was empty, and she gazed at it mournfully.

'Have this one with me,' Sally said, as she expected to.

'Don't mind if I do,' Mrs. Gallagher replied graciously.

'The same, all round again, Adey,' Sally said, when Adey appeared with the drinks Marie had ordered. Adey gathered up Mrs. Gallagher's empty glass and whirled away briskly.

'She's a good girl, Adey,' God-Save-Us-Sarah murmured as if talking to herself. 'Not like some of these flash barmaids don't know how to treat an old timer. There was another girl used to be real good to Sandy and me. We'd always go to the Sun Inn for a booze-up because she was there. She'd got the most g-glorious head of ches'nut hair. When she washed it, it'd hang round her like a cloak. and she'd wash it, just for us to see. "Wakeful" the boys called her, after a racehorse won the Melbourne Cup. They reckoned that girl was a winner, and she was too.'

'Hullo, ma, how's things?' Two other women came into the parlour and seated themselves at a table near Mrs. Gallagher.

'I don't know whom you are,' God-Save-Us-Sarah said with befuddled dignity, 'but I do know I'm not your ma.'

The newcomers, Mrs. Plush, a small. spry woman, and Mrs. Green, a fat, jolly derelict, laughed good-humouredly.

'That's all right, we know you, Mrs. Gallagher!'

Rosy Ann Plush and Amelia Green were well-known identities, who figured in the police court occasionally for being 'under the influence' and obstructing the police in the execution of their duties. Marie and Sally recognised them with a friendly nod. Women who had seen each other about the goldfields for a good many years needed no introduction.

Mrs. Plush and Mrs. Green went on with the conversation which had been in full spate when they entered.

' "I've always kept meself respectable, 't any rate," I ses to her,' Mrs. Plush said.

' "Respectable?" she ses, "What's that?"

' "What's respectable?" I ses. "Well, it's workin' hard, bloody hard, like I've done, and payin' your way, and never carin' what anybody says about who y'r drinkin' or sleepin' with. That's what I call respectable,' I ses.'

'Quite right, too,' Mrs. Green agreed. 'Her sort don't know what work means.'

Adey returned with the drinks. She set them down at the various tables, and God-Save-Us-Sarah gulped at her foaming beer greedily.

'I do love to see a lady get behind a good pot,' Mrs. Plush tittered. She lifted her own glass.

'Blow the crown off of her and sink the shaft—as the boys say!'

'Skin off y'r nose!' Mrs. Green replied.

Marie and Sally clinked their glasses.

'Skin off y'r nose, dear,' Sally murmured to Marie.

'But no, Sally, I could not bear it,' Marie laughed. 'Do not wish such a misfortune to befall me.'

They were still laughing and gathering up their parcels to go, a little enlivened by two beers, when they looked up to see Colonel de Morfé in the doorway.

'Hull-lo!' he cried delightedly, and came towards them. 'What on earth are you two doing here? God, what luck! I just dropped in to see Bill Feathers on a bit of business and Adey told me she had distinguished visitors. Sit down! Sit down! You must have a drink with me.'

'But we were just going,' Marie protested.

'Nonsense!' Frisco blustered. 'Old friends can't run away from each other like that.'

He was looking very dashing and gallant in his new uniform. 'Besides I've got some interesting news for you.'

His glance had wavered to Sally's troubled face, as if he feared she should not wait to talk to him.

'Very well,' she said. 'We'll sit down again for a few moments. But I don't want another drink.'

'She won't drink with me!' Frisco exclaimed with mock indignation to Marie. 'But you will Madame Robbie?'

'No, thank you,' Marie replied sweetly. 'I have already drunken too much.'

'So have I.' Frisco declared. 'But I want another whisky! Heigh, Adey! Adey!' he called.

Adey came running at the sound of his voice and Frisco ordered his whisky.

He threw himself in a chair and leaned across the table gazing at Sally.

'Well, what's your news?' she asked impatiently.

'News? Oh, my news!' Frisco laughed. He had used the idea of having some interesting news as a pretext to detain them, and wondered now what he could say.

'Is it about the war?' Sally queried anxiously. "Will we be drawn into it'

'We will, my dear,' Frisco said gravely. And then laughed as a fragment of news occurred to him. 'But that wasn't what I was going to tell you. An old—shall we say—acquaintance of yours is back in Kalgoorlie. Lili!'

Sally had suspected his subterfuge. She recognised that glint in his eyes and the derisive note in his laughter.

'Mme Malon?' Marie inquired.

'But she isn't Mme Malon any longer,' Frisco explained. 'She's just Lili, and is working with Belle again.'

'*Comment?*' Marie cried in distress. 'What 'as 'appen to her, *ce pauvre Lili?*'

'It's poor Lili, all right,' Frisco agreed. 'She's had a rough spin. Before he died, it seems, her Paul got into deep water with his speculations. His brothers came to the rescue and managed to get control of his assets. They did Lili out of every penny she might have had—and so she went back to her old life. But, of course, she isn't as young as she was, and it wasn't so easy to get along. I believe she wrote and told Belle her troubles, and Belle sent her the money to come back here. Belle's got her own establishment, now, you know, and Lili says she is " 'appy! oh, so 'appy, to be together with friends again!"'

Marie and Frisco slipped into talking French, and Sally sat listening, not able to follow what they said, but understanding that Marie did not like the way Frisco had told his story. It was to embarrass them, Marie imagined, perhaps. Frisco appeared to be protesting that nothing was further from his intentions. He had poured himself two or three stiff whiskies from the bottle which stood on the tray beside him.

'I adore Sally. You know I adore Sally, Mme Robillard. Always have I adored her!' he said, suddenly in plain English. 'Not for worlds would I do anything to hurt her feelings.'

Sally stared at him transfixed. The reckless passion that at one time had surged between them, swept over her again, like a dust storm out of the distance, obliterating everything but consciousness of their two selves.

'My God, she's more beautiful than ever, isn't she?'

Marie was terrified to hear Frisco talking like that, and to see Sally looking at him with wide open eyes, as if she were almost as demented as he.

'I can't get you out of my mind, Sally. No matter what I do.' Frisco's voice was thick and hoarse. 'I've been married—twice married, and we're getting old now. But still I'm mad about you.

Aren't we ever going to be together? Aren't we ever going to be lovers before we die?'

'Shut up,' Marie whispered furiously. 'Everybody is listening.'

She glanced at the other women in the room, apparently absorbed in their own conversation; but with ears cocked in the direction of Colonel de Morfé.

'What do I care?' Frisco almost shouted. 'The whole world can know as far as I'm concerned.

As if the spell he had put over her were broken, Sally gathered her parcels and stood up.

'Colonel de Morfé's drunk,' she said quietly. 'We had better go, Marie.'

As she moved to the door, Frisco swung to his feet, and stood before her.

'I can't let you leave me like this, Sally,' he cried. 'You must answer my question.'

'Don't touch me!' Sally's eyes blazed. 'It's the same as it's always been.'

She walked away, her skirts brushing quickly out of the room. Frisco turned to Marie with a despairing gesture.

'For God's sake, make her understand I didn't intend to annoy her.' He slumped into his chair beside the table. 'I was just so glad to see her and couldn't resist trying again.'

Marie was almost hysterical when she caught up to Sally, walking along the track towards Maritana Hill, where a few dilapidated tents and dumps still marked the site of the old camp. The late afternoon sunshine threw a garish light over the torn, red sides of the ridge. The sky above, and away to the far horizon, had the frail, clear blue of a wild bird's egg.

Sally was no longer angry. She stood brooding over memories the place conjured up as Marie rejoined her. Marie was trying to restrain an impulse to laugh and cry over that crazy scene in the pub. But Sally's first words were more of a surprise than anything Frisco had said.

'He's a devil, and I hate him,' she cried stormily. 'But I wish we had been lovers, years ago, Marie.'

CHAPTER XIV

WHEN Sally got home that afternoon, Paddy Cavan's room was empty. Paddy had removed his belongings in a spring cart, just after he came in from Kamballie, Dinny said. The house was empty and Dinny had wondered what all the hammering and banging was about. He found Paddy nailing up a box, and in a great hurry to be off.

'It was all I could do not to yell "good riddance to bad rubbish" after him, like a kid,' Dinny explained, with his little gurgling laugh. 'But I didn't, missus, I jest said: "So long, Paddy."'

'And he said: "So long, Dinny!" And Old Shack drove off with Paddy sitting alongside of him in his cart.'

'I'm not shedding any tears to see the last of him,' Sally admitted, bustling about to get tea.

Dinny had lit the fire for her and the kettle was boiling. Her preparations for the evening meal were always made before she went out on Saturday. Soup was on the hob, vegetables ready for the pot, chops and steak handy to slap on the grill at a moment's notice.

'Some people give this town a bad name,' Dinny burbled. 'But I reckon there isn't many places y' could go out of an afternoon and leave all the doors and windows open.'

'I suppose not,' Sally said.

'I was talkin' to Mr. Toombs at the Fimiston post office, on me way in,' Dinny went on. 'He says you can't beat the miners and workin' men of Boulder for honesty when it comes to dealin' with each other, or a man like himself has a wife and six kids to look after. It's only the big crooks, they might feel like takin' down for a bit of gold now and then.'

'He ought to know,' Sally commented absent-mindedly. She was still disturbed by her encounter with Frisco, and wondering how soon it would be common gossip.

'He does, since he near lost a swag of notes this summer.' Dinny was not to be done out of his yarn. 'He was tellin' me, after pay, there's hundreds of men come in and send money orders from the post office to their wives and mothers, and he's always got a lot of money to take to the bank.'

Sally forced herself to listen to what Dinny was saying, although half the time she was thinking: 'What would the boys say if they knew? How would Morris take it if he got wind of the gossip?'

'Well, there was a ragin' dust storm, the afternoon Toomsby started off to go to the bank with £ 350, in notes, in his little Gladstone bag,' Dinny went on. 'And just as he was steppin' on to the tram, it gave a lurch and he dropped his bag. It flew open, and there was notes blowin' everywhere before he could stop the tram and sprint back to collect 'em. Just before he got back and picked up his bag, he saw a man on a bicycle stop, grab a few and ride off.

'There wasn't much Toomsby could do but search round and gather up all the notes he could find. He only found about twenty pounds worth: was near out of his mind with worry when he went back to the post office. He didn't have a hope of bein' able to replace the money, and it looked like the sack for him all right. The wind would have blown the notes all over the auction, and anybody who picked one up would reckon they were a gift from heaven. But men who'd seen the accident, sent word around, and all that afternoon and night, miners and kids were knocking up Mr. and Mrs. Toombs to give them bundles of notes. One old bloke brought £40 he'd found caught in the wire netting of his fowl-yard. In the end, Toomsby got £330 back. He reckoned that shyster on the bicycle lit out with the £20. And he wasn't a goldfields man! Men on the mines round about put in to square up what was missin', anyhow.'

'Nobody like them when you're in trouble,' Sally smiled at Dinny with the firelight glittering in her eyes.

She rang a cow bell and the boarders trooped into the dining-room. Dinny helped her to serve them. They were almost finished when the boys came in from a swim at the pool, and Morris soon afterwards.

They would have to wait until she was ready to feed them, Sally said, but she was quite pleased that the family could sit down to a meal together.

Of course, Morris would talk about the 'war clouds gathering over Europe', and Dinny wanted to know about 'the jeweller's shop' Tom and Ted Lee had opened up on the Boulder Reef. The gold-stealing detective staff was working overtime to see men working in the stope didn't get away with anything, Tom told him. Dick and Lal and Den all had items of interest to swop with Dinny. They cheered when they heard Paddy had taken his departure.

Sally felt that shameful episode with Frisco in the pub could no longer disturb her, as she sat in the midst of her family and heard the happy, care-free voices of her sons chiacking each other and Dinny; and Dinny giving them back as good as they gave, with an anecdote or two and a gurgle of laughter.

'Father Ryan's been payin' us a visit at Kamballie,' Dinny said. 'And some of the kids are as wild as goats there: never seen one of their riverences before. A woman whose husband works on the Perseverence has half a dozen of 'em. She's got a shack near the main track and was entertainin' the priest when one of the kids comes in.

' "So y're nine years old, ye little haythin, are ye?" says the priest.

114

' "Yes, mister," says the kid.
' "Ye mustn't call me mister," says the priest. "Ye must call me father."
' "Yes, mister," says the kid.
' "Ye must call him father, Jimmy," says the mother.
' "But he's not me father," says the kid. "Me father's a little bloke works on the Percy" !'

Only Morris looked glum and preoccupied in the clatter of the boys' laughter and the rattle of their voices. He asked if Paddy had left any message for him. No, Dinny said, Paddy had not left any message. Morris seemed put out that Sally was not at home when Paddy had gone away.

'What did you expect me to do, Morris?' she asked brusquely. 'Wish him god speed?'

'Hardly.' Morris did not smile. 'But it might have been as well to part good friends.'

When the meal was finished, Dinny and Tom went off to a meeting in the Workers' Hall. Dick was taking Amy to a dance, and Den and Lal going for their usual stroll round the town on a Saturday night. Morris settled down to read his newspapers.

After she had washed up and put the dishes away, Sally got out her knitting, and sat near him in the parlour. Morris usually read and took forty winks over his newspaper before going to bed.

But to-night, he did not nod over his newspaper: was worried about something, Sally thought. Morris was looking old and very weary. His face had an unhealthy pallor, his cheeks hung in flabby jowls, and the gingery and grey tuft of hair on the top of his head which usually stood on end, drooped dejectedly.

Sally wondered if the undertaking business was getting too much for Morris, and whether he would not have to give it up soon. If there was a war and Lal went away, Morris could not carry on by himself. What would he do? Sell up, or try to find someone to work with? She was not going to allow Den to take Lal's place. That was certain. Was this what was worrying Morris, or had he something on his mind in connection with the business he had been doing for Paddy? She was going to ask him, when his face lit up and he exclaimed excitedly:

Just listen to this, Sally. "By the end of 1907—that's seven ago, mind—"The Great Boulder had paid £ 2,644,300 in dividends, the Golden Horseshoe £ 2,520,000, The Oroya-Brownhill £ 2,058,000" . . .'

It was amazing Sally thought that Morris could find such satisfaction in these figures of mine performances. He identified himself with them and was as proud of the mines as if he owned them:

would gaze at the poppet legs and plants scarring blue of the sky above the ridge, and gloat over the wealth they had produced, although it had not been for him, nor for the people who lived and worked in the country to which they belonged.

'What's it got to do with us?' Sally's needles clicked to her impatience. 'If we'd got some of that money I'd be better pleased.'

'We might have,' Morris said slowly, 'if some swine had not got down on those shares I held in the Great Boulder.'

A flush crept over Sally's face, and her eyes flashed.

'You still reproach me with that, Morris?' she asked.

'I wasn't reproaching you,' Morris grumbled, putting aside his vague intention of reminding her that she had been responsible for the loss of the shares. It was the one grievance he held against her: had loomed all through the years of their married life as the golden opportunity of which he had been deprived.

'It was bad luck,' he continued reluctantly. 'No one to blame but myself. You didn't understand the importance of a wad of shares, anyhow.'

He could see Sally as she had been when she arrived on Hannans: tired and a little dismayed by the sight of Ma Buggins's brushwood shed; but cheery and very attractive with her neat figure, red lips and beautiful brown eyes. The dregs of his passion stirred. He remembered how hungry he had been for her after their long separation, and how brutally he had taken her in that shed, with the moonlight pouring down on them, and half the camp wandering nearby.

Morris was ashamed to remember it now, and the row with Ma Buggins which had followed next morning when he found he had lost his wallet. Those shares were in it. He had thrown the wallet down on their baggage when he went out to water the horses, thinking Sally would look after it, and in the morning it was gone.

No trace of the wallet or shares had ever been found. Shares were legal tender in those days: changed hands so frequently, it was impossible to check up on how any man came into possession of his scrip. The man who held his Boulder shares had handled them shrewdly, Morris was sure, and no doubt made a fortune out of them.

Sally followed his thought and understood the way the loss of those shares had rankled with Morris. She could never feel that she was to blame for their disappearance; but if it was any comfort to Morris to believe she, and not he, had been careless of that damned wallet, she would let him believe it. Sally had come to this decision long ago.

'My poor Morris,' she thought, 'he hasn't had much luck!'

And he was thinking, as he watched her work-worn hands ply grey wool over the knitting needles to make socks for one of the boys or him:

'My poor Sally, she's had a tough spin with me.'

But Sally's mind would not lie in the doldrums. She abhorred regrets and recriminations.

'After all, Morris,' she said, with the smile which could always woo and win him from any dejection, 'we're fairly comfortable and happy now, aren't we? We've got nothing to complain of. The boys are fit and well, and . . .'

'My God, Sally,' Morris looked at her with a gleam of his old ardour, 'at least I gave you your sons!'

'Thanks awfully, dear.' Sally's laughing eyes banished his dejection. 'I can never thank you sufficiently.'

Morris rose and stretched.

'Let's go to bed,' he said, yawning. 'I don't envy any man in the world while I've got you, Sally. Never did. Though there hasn't been much else in my life to boast about.'

Sunday had come and gone with only a small, unpleasant surprise to mar the restful quiet and happiness of the day. Three men who used to sleep in the bunk-house had disappeared over night, taking their clothes and trunks. Their board was paid up to date; but it was unusual to clear out like that without a week's notice or any explanation. Dally told Dinny that he thought Paddy was at the bottom of the other boarders' moonlight flit. Paddy had offered Dally a good job on a new mine he was opening up, out Laverton way, if he reported for work on Monday morning. There was nothing doing as far as he was concerned, Dally said. He knew when he was well off, if other blokes didn't.

What did it mean? Sally was perplexed and dismayed. Did Paddy think it would annoy her to lose these boarders? Was this the beginning of his attempt to get even with her for turning him out of the house? It seemed to be; but she refused to be intimidated or worried by Paddy Cavan and his petty spite.

Dick wanted to move his books and clothes into the empty room that morning. Sally had a curious reluctance to let him.

'I'll scrub it out and air it to-morrow, darling,' she promised. 'I couldn't bear you to sleep there with the smell of Paddy still in the room.'

Dick teased her about her fussiness: but he too was perturbed about the mean trick Paddy had played her in arranging for other boarders to leave when he did. Dick was sure Dally was right and Paddy had something to do with their going.

'What does it matter,' Sally said cheerfully. 'I'll soon let the bunks again. Paddy Cavan can't put me out of business.'

Tom and Dick tried to persuade her not to take any more boarders: give herself a rest from so much cooking and washing for a while.

'Nonsense,' Sally cried, rejoicing in their concern for her, but unwilling to give way, 'I like to be independent, and have a little money of my own. We won't let a room in the house to anyone again, though.'

It had been a good day, with the boys all at home, skylarking in the yard, washing up for her, and yarning with Morris and Dinny after dinner.

CHAPTER XV

EVERYBODY had a feeling of relief that Sunday because Paddy was not there to butt in on a conversation, or sling off at Den and Lal fooling with each other. The boys hung round the verandah after dinner, listening to Morris and Dinny argue about British foreign policy and to what extent an Australian Labour government would be bound to support it, in the event of war.

From some heated differences of opinion, Dinny turned the discussion to a Miners' Relief Bill before parliament, which was concerning everybody on the goldfields at the moment.

'I reckon there's more accidents on the mines and more men going out to miners' complaint, now, than there was in the old days,' he said.

'Nine men killed, four hundred and thirty-seven serious accidents, last year.' Tom could always give facts and figures.

'But there are more men working on the mines,' Morris demurred. 'Over five thousand, not including tributers, who make the total up to nearly twice as many.'

'That's a fact,' Dinny agreed, 'but the job's become more dangerous, what with the creeps in old workin's and the depth they're sinkin' at now.'

'All mine owners thought of, in the early days, was tearing the guts out of the mines,' Dick butted in. 'They have got some science into the game now.'

'Y're right there, Dick,' Dinny agreed dubiously, 'but it doesn't seem to've done the mine workers much good. I was talkin' to Bob

Gillespie the other day. He's underground foreman on the Golden Horseshoe: can read the stones like a book, the boys say.

' "The geologists, Dinny," he says, "they can tell y' the name of a stone when y' show it to 'em. They can't tell y' where the gold is. These mines have got 'em beat. They've never found gold. The old miners and prospectors have found all the gold. Look on me map here," he says, "It's wandering around like pink sea-weed." '

'How about the diamond drills?' Dick laughed. 'And beating the "sulphide bug-bear"? Didn't science have something to do with them, and giving Kal a new lease of life?'

' 'Course it did,' Dinny chuckled. 'And they gave the bosses a stranglehold on the mining industry, too. But what's it done for the workers, that's what I want to know? Where the hammer and drill men'd use a pound of fracteur, they're usin' cases now, and the machine drills has worsened the dust "enormously". That's what the union secretary told the commission.'

'There's no doubt about it,' Morris smoked over what he had to say. 'The fumes and dust are bad enough and this back-filling with cyanide sands has poisoned the air underground more than ever. But is the bill going to make for better conditions, better timbering and ventilation, or is it only going to deal with effects: give men suffering from silicosis and miners' phthisis some compensation?'

'That's the point, dad,' Tom said. 'Jack Dodd, the union secretary, has been trying to make the politicians see the bill doesn't go far enough. Owing to the increase of dust and fumes, we've got to have additional ventilation, a real dust preventive and a workers' inspector to watch the miners' interests in bad ground. Dusted miners were cut out of the Workers' Compensation Act, and we've got to fight for them. We say an industrial disease is as much an accident as a broken neck.'

'Just a question of whether you get a bit of rock in your lung, or on your head, Tommy?'

'Exactly.' Tom's eyes went to Dick with a smile. 'But the mine owners are scared. They say "the industry can't stand any more burdens". There are so many "dusted" and T.B. miners. Thirty-three per cent. of the men working underground are suffering from miners' fibrosis, Dr. Cumpston told the commission two or three years ago, and twenty-seven per cent. of the men working in the treatment plants. The average life of a machine miner, he reckoned, is forty-two years.'

'For goodness' sake, Tom,' Sally cried, distressed at the thought of such a fate for him, 'get another job! I can't bear to think of you working underground any longer.'

'Don't worry, mother,' Dick flew to her rescue. 'Tom'll be member for the district before he's that age.'

'Sure, he will!' Dinny warbled. 'But Tom's quite right. The mining companies'll fight tooth and nail to prevent any clauses in the bill interferin' with their profits. What do a few hundred lives matter? Miners' lives? All the mine owners care about is dividends. They don't mind the government makin' a grant of £ 10,000 from the charity vote for the relief of stricken miners, dolin' out twenty-five bob a week to doomed men, and spendin' a few thousand on a sanatorium at Wooroloo, for him to die in. That comes out of the pockets of the workers. But catch the mine owners doin' anything about it, unless they're forced to.'

'The mining industry ought to be made to bear the burden of the men rendered incapable by it,' Tom said.

'Hear! Hear!' Dick interjected.

But Tom was too much in earnest to notice the raillery in his brother's applause. 'Dividends paid by the gold mines of Western Australia have amounted to £ 22,838,420 over the last twenty years,' he said. 'And what has been done with those millions? Have the mine owners used a fraction of them to give workers on the gold-fields a better life? Is there one public service they have provided? Have they made any attempt to assist disabled miners? Is there one public institution they have given us?'

'There's the drinking fountain in the Square,' Den piped up.

Everybody laughed.

'I forgot the drinking fountain, Den.' Tom's slow smile reassured Den. 'But in South Africa the mine owners spent £ 50,000 on building a sanatorium and they pay £ 5000 a year for its upkeep. Here, where the mining companies've got bigger dividends out of the mines than in any other part of the world, the mine owners've done nothing for the workers. Charley O'Reilly says the Golden Mile is the dreariest, damned desert of a place he's ever seen, and it's time the mining industry was run to serve the interests of the people.'

'Quite a good speech, my boy,' Morris remarked dryly.

Tom understood that his father thought he had been talking like a mob orator.

'I didn't mean to make a speech, dad,' he said. 'Those are the facts. And that's the way I feel about them.'

'Always say what you think and feel, and you'll be all right, Tommy,' Dinny said warmly.

'We're proud, dad and I, you can put your ideas together so well, son,' Sally chimed in, eager to defend Tom, and rebuke Morris for sarcasm at his expense. 'It's the every-day heroism of the miners

I can never get over. And now, you're one of them, anything that hurts them, hurts me.'

'Takes guts to be a miner and no mistake,' Dinny exclaimed, and launched into a yarn to restore everybody's good humour. 'Bob Gillespie was tellin' me one of their directors wanted to inspect the mine recently. So he was showin' Mr. Philpotts around. Scared? He was like an autumn leaf, Mr. Philpotts, tremblin' and holdin' on to himself for all he was worth.

' "Put y'r left foot in the bucket, mister," Bob says to him when he was goin' down a winze.'

' "I c-can't," ses Philpotts.'

'And when he did, the bucket topples over and he clutched at Bob. So Bob put a safety belt on him and lowered him carefully. But y' never saw anything so pitiful as the way he looked up at him, Bob ses. Like a ewe when y'r goin' to cut its throat.

' "It's all right," Bob yells down to him. "She's a good winze, mister!"

'When he got to the bottom, the bucket was goin' round like a merry-go-round, the boys said, and Philpotts was jest about all in.

'He told Bob he never wanted to inspect a mine, agen.'

Dinny got his laugh, and Morris, by way of making amends for having snubbed Tom, observed, ruefully:

'I don't blame him. Felt that way myself the first time I went down the shaft we sank on Coolgardie. Remember, Dinny?'

'Do I remember?' Dinny chortled. 'You were white around the gills, and no mistake, Morrey. But that didn't stop y' goin' down every mornin' we were workin' in the shaft. That's what I call guts. There's some blokes though don't know the meanin' of fear. They do things that are jest plumb crazy. You got to admit that, Tom!'

'Too right, I admit it,' Tom said. 'Some of the contract men are measurement hungry: would rather feed air to their machines than themselves. But that's mostly because they want to make big money, while they can, and get out of the mines as soon as possible.'

'And there's some old fools, carry on the way ther've been used to,' Dinny added. 'Won't have anything to do with safety fuses for example. Bob was tellin' me, awhile ago, he was workin' on a winze with Paddy Flynn and his mate, Fat Dahill. Paddy's half-blind. Can't see to fire his charges, and he'll go back into the smoke ten minutes after they've gone off, if he's let. Bob says he had a bad spin with him. One day, Paddy'd fired eighteen holes.

' "There was me," Bob ses, "waitin' on the winze to pull him up: waitin' for him to knock, or pull on the rope. Had everything ready, put on the brake. Waitin' . . . waitin' . . . Me legs began to tremble. It's a hell of a time, you put in, waitin' like that. Then Paddy knocks, and I yank him up. The first shot goes off as he lands on the brace."

'But three of Paddy's shots didn't go off, and he was bustin' to go down and see what was wrong with 'em. The winze was full of smoke. But Paddy ses: "She ought to be all right."

' "Y're not goin' down yet," Bob ses.

'And when he did go, y'r couldn't see him for smoke. His candle was showin' red through it.

'It wasn't long before he pulls on the rope that time. Bob could feel the rope tremblin', and Paddy jest flopped out of the bucket, lookin' like death, and all wet and draggled. He'd got his rods and come over dizzy, managed to get to the water and pour it over himself. That saved him. It was all he could do to reach the bucket and pull the rope.'

'Old flathead!' Tom muttered.

'And his mate jest as bad,' Dinny went on, 'though he's younger than Paddy, and oughter have more nouse. But it was touch and go with Fatty Dahill too, and Bob pulled him up a few days later.

' "I could feel the rope shiverin' in me hand," Bob said. "I hoisted steady, and not too quick, to give him a chance, and four feet from the top he fell back.

' "Here, hang on to the hoist," Bob ses to Paddy, grabbed a rope, and went down the ladder to where Fatty was hangin'. Bob put a slip knot over him.

' "Jesus, it'd've cut him in two, if he'd slipped to the bottom of the shaft," Bob ses.

'But there was Fatty hangin' over the bucket, one leg caught in it, his head and body in mid air. They got him up all right and he come to.

'And Paddy started yellin' and howlin' at him. "What did ye do that for ye bloody fool? Did ye want to do the rope trick or something, hangin' there be y'r bloody calves? God A'mighty if ye must do acrobatics, try another spot next time. Haven't ye got a bit of sense, lettin' go the rope, an' openin' y'r mouth like a great gawk, as if that'd help ye? Here's me, all of sixty, and never carried on like that in all me born days."

' "Shut up, Paddy," Bob ses to him. "Can't y'r see the man's unconscious?"

' "Jesus-God," ses Paddy, "if he must be havin' fits, the winze is no place for 'em." '

Dinny got his laugh, but rattled on:

'Well, Paddy reckoned he'd try the safety cartridges after that.

' "Are they all right?" he asks Bob.

' "Sure, they're good," Bob ses, and got some for him, showed him how to use them.

'Paddy took the cartridges down with him when he went to work. When he and Fatty came up for crib, Bob sat down with 'em, waitin' for the charges to go off. They waited and waited.

' "You did'n forget to fire 'em, Paddy?" ses Bob.

' "No, I didn't forget to fire 'em," ses Paddy.

'After a bit there was three bangs. They waited, but no more went off.

' "Better go down and see what's happened," ses Paddy.

' "Not yet. Not it I know it," ses Bob.

' "It's all right, half an hour after y've set 'em," ses Paddy.

' "Y're waitin' more'n half an hour on this lot," ses Bob.

'When he did go down, Paddy found the three shots round the king fuse had gone off and nothing else. Bob went down himself to see what was wrong: set all the cartridges again and went up. They waited, but not another one went off. Paddy'd got the cartridges damp or something. Bob told him a mate of his had used 'em for two years and only got two dead'uns in that time, but nothing'll persuade the old fool to use safety cartridges now.'

'A lunatic asylum's the place for him, not the mines,' Morris said.

'Bob took a risk going down the shaft when Dahill was hung up like that,' Dick said, paying the tribute everybody felt was due to Bob Gillespie.

'He did,' Dinny agreed. 'The chances were he'd've been thrown to the bottom and smashed up with Fatty.'

'It's one of those fine things men do on the mines every day,' Sally exclaimed. 'But it's not often you hear of a miner being called a hero.'

'He was in the Bonnie Vale disaster,' Dinny remembered.

'What was the strong of that, Dinny?' Lal asked. 'I was a kid when it happened.'

'It was in 1907,' Dinny said. 'There'd been a bobby-dazzler of a rain storm. Cloud burst, or something. The Westralia and the Eastern Extension at Bonnie Vale got flooded. The Vale of Coolgardie too was full of water. Storm water rushed from the surface and broke into the tunnel shaft and swept on to the main shaft. It rose from the number ten to the number nine level. Skips were blocked, and the men comin' off shift had a tough time gettin' away from the flood waters. They had to wait two hours before the shaft could be cleared and they were landed on the surface. But one man was missing, an I-talian, name of Varischetti, Modesto Varischetti. He'd been workin' on the number ten level, in a twenty foot rise. And the water was up to the number nine by then.

There must've been a hundred feet of water over him, and he was drowned, most of the boys reckoned, unless he'd escaped by another pass. They searched every level.'

'Did you think he'd got away, Dinny?' Den asked eagerly.

'Some of us old miners thought, if he'd stayed in the rise there was just a chance he was still alive,' Dinny replied cautiously. 'We reckoned the water as it rose would force air into the rise, and the compressed air keep the water back. I remembered when a miner was caught in a flooded mine at Bendigo, he was saved because of that.

'I knew Varischetti, and knew he was tough. A decent sort of bloke round about thirty-three and the father of five children. His wife had died a few months ago, other dagoes on the Westralia said. Varischetti was very popular among them, and Jo Marengoni, his mate, was sure Modesto wouldn't lose his block, if he'd found himself trapped. He'd been caught twice before in a mining disaster. Once at Clunes in Victoria, he'd been entombed in a mine for two days.

'Well, at eleven o'clock that night, men keepin' watch for a signal on the number nine level, heard Varischetti knockin', and everybody went mad tryin' to get pumps and work out how they could rescue him. Would y' believe it, there wasn't a pump on the mine, or in Kal? The Great Boulder had one, but it was dismantled for recastin'. They started baling out with skips, but that only reduced the water a few inches. The mine managers said even with pumps installed, it would take a fortnight at least to get the water out of the mine.

'On Wednesday, Varischetti was still knocking and his brothers and Jo Marengoni goin' round weepin' and cursin' to think of Modesto caught like a rat in its hole. His machine pipe was givin' him some air, but with the terrific weight of water in the stopes, it seemed there wasn't much hope for him.

'Then the manager of the brick works in Coolgardie brought along a pump, which started to throw five thousand gallons an hour, and Inspector Crabb of the police force wired the Minister of Mines for divers. But before they arrived, Frank Hughes, who was a miner on the South Kalgurli, offered his services as a diver. Seems he'd been diving for the Queensland Government once, and knew the business, but had no gear.

'Four divers arrived by special train from Perth, with their gear, next day. But none of them knew anything about mining, so it was Frank Hughes put on the diver's dress and went down to see if he could find Varischetti. He'd studied a plan of the mine, and worked out how he could reach him. And, my God, if there was ever a heroic thing done, it was when Frank Hughes went through the flooded drives of that mine. You know what it'd be like, Morrey —and you, Tom—gropin' through the dark and dirty water, and the whole rotten caboose likely to cave in on you any moment! It was ten o'clock when Frank went down, and Diver Hearne with him to look after the diving gear, and there was a great crowd on top waitin' for news. Mostly miners who knew what Frank was doin'. And I tell y'r, Morrey, me heart was in me boots when twelve o'clock come, and there was no signal from him. I was more scared for Frank than for Varischetti.

'At one o'clock, he got back to the plat on number nine, where Hearne was waitin' for him, just about exhausted. But he'd found Varischetti in the rise, and said he looked in good nick. You should've heard the cheers go up, when Frank came on top for a breather. He went down again at four o'clock, takin' compressed food in a tin and a message to Varischetti. But still the problem of gettin' him out had to be solved.

'At first, we thought they could bring him out in a diving suit, but he hadn't had a meal for four days then, and Frank was afraid he was too weak and unnerved to stand the struggle through the water. Another pump was installed, and the water was fallin', but so damned slowly.

'Don't forget the number ten level was flooded and Varischetti cooped up in the rise three hundred and fifty feet along it. Frank had nutted it out that their best way to reach Varischetti was from the number nine level: get him up a pass, sixty-two feet south from where he and Tom Hearne were workin'. The pass went twenty feet up into the stopes, and they planned to lay an inclined shoot of boards, make a "chair" and haul Varischetti up that way to the number nine level.

'But they had to wait until the pumps reduced the water in number ten, sufficient to get Varischetti through the water along the drive to the pass. That was goin' to be "perilous", as Frank said. But it was their only chance of gettin' him out alive, and while Varischetti seemed to be keepin' fairly well, it was the best thing to do.'

'I remember the awful suspense, waiting for news,' Sally exclaimed. 'Was Varischetti alive? Had he been rescued? Nobody could talk of anything else. As day after day went by, we could think of nothing but him, hanging there between life and death, with the dark water below and the mine closing in on him. It seemed that only a miracle could save him.'

'It was the miracle of one man's grit and brains, chiefly, that did save him,' Morris said.

'That's a fact, Morrey,' Dinny went on. 'It was nine days before Frank got Varischetti out, but every day he went down that pass in the diving suit and along the dangerous drive to see how Varischetti was holdin' out, take food and messages in a sealed tin, and cheer him up by lettin' him know they were planning to bring him out in a couple of days. Varischetti couldn't speak much English, but he wrote messages to his mate, and Jo read them out to the crowd that was always hanging round the shaft. In one, I remember Varischetti said something about wonderin' if he'd ever see "the light of heaven" again. He was gettin' "very tired", he wrote, and his strength was "vanishing".

'Frank made up his mind he had to get Varischetti out that day. When he made his first trip below, he thought he could wade along the drive with just his head above the water, so decided it would give Varischetti more confidence if he didn't wear the diving dress. He started off to bring him back in ordinary working clothes. Found the water was up to his eyes in one place: had to dive through it, and go back. Made a third attempt later and got through.

'He smoked a couple of cigarettes with Varischetti, explaining to him what he had to do.

'Varischetti came down from his perch and Frank fastened the life-line round him, and held on to him round the middle. They hadn't gone very far, and the water was up to Varischetti's armpits when he collapsed. Frank hoisted him on to his back and carried him the rest of the way to the pass.

' "Tom Hearne was there," Frank said, "and did his work like a Briton. I put Varischetti up the shoot and Tom pulled him through. Dr. Mitchell was on the spot to look after him then. He said Varischetti was suffering from exhaustion and immersion but his pulse was all right."

'Hundreds of us were collected round about the mine on the dumps and on every shed. There were flags flyin' from the poppet heads, and when the signal came up from below: "Both skips on", we thought Varischetti and Frank were arrivin'. But first of all two of the miners who'd been helpin' below, hopped out. Then Frank Hughes landed and the crowd went crazy with joy, cheerin' and huggin' him. We'd been warned to be silent at first when Varischetti came up, as any shock was likely to be bad for him.

'The sight of him, ghastly and doubled up, wearin' green glasses and wool stuffed in his ears was enough to sober any man. It was like as if he'd returned from the dead.

'But Varischetti wouldn't go to hospital, so the manager put him in a cab and took him off to his house to lay up for a few days. And every dago in sight, wild with joy, mobbed Frank.

' "If you're satisfied, so am I," Frank ses with a grin and walked off.'

'Thanks, Dinny,' Lal said, choked by his admiration for the matter-of-fact gallantry of that miner. 'If a man could do something like that in his life, it would be worth while.'

'It wasn't only going down the pass and along the flooded drive once, but every day, and two or three times a day to cheer Varischetti up,' Tom muttered.

'Cripes, Dinny, he was a hero!' Den cried excitedly. 'Did they give him a medal?'

'Oh yes. One from the King of Italy and one from the Royal Humane Society. Frank Hughes was one hero of the mines everybody delighted to honour,' Sally admitted. 'The newspapers were full of him and the wires of congratulations he received.'

'Hughes himself always tried to share any credit with Hearne,' Morris reminded her. 'His life, he said, had depended on the way Diver Hearne assisted him and looked after his gear. Then too, he never forgot a good word for Inspector Crabb, and the men who manned the pumps night and day.'

'All the same, he worked the miracle of saving Varischetti,' Dick mused. 'I wish I had the same sort of guts.'

'There's nothing wrong with your sort of guts, son,' Sally said quickly.

'Isn't there?' Dick's eyes were laughing at her instinctive partisanship. 'I hope you're right, mother.'

Sally often talked of that afternoon, because it was the last the family spent, yarning together in a care-free, desultory way. Never again did they all meet to argue, gossip and laugh with Dinny over his yarns.

CHAPTER XVI

THERE was a thunderstorm during the night, and heavy rain fell. Sally could never explain the presentiment with which she waked next morning. It was as if there were some trouble lying in wait for her: something she must do to ward it off. The thunderstorm, and all the talk of war, she thought, had given her that queer sense of apprehension.

Although there were not so many cribs to cut and breakfasts to cook, she was up at dawn as usual, remembering that she had a busy day before her. The copper fire had to be lit for her big weekly washing, and then she intended to clean out Paddy's room, and cubicles in the bunk-house her other boarders had vacated.

In the rush of putting her first copperful of clothes on to boil, giving Tom and Dally their breakfast, hustling Dick and Den, Lal, Morris and Dinny, along for theirs, and getting them all off to work, she had not much time to think of anything except what her hands were doing, and what Morris and the boys were shouting:

'Got a clean pair of socks for me, mum?'

'What in the name of blazes have you done with my grey sweater, Sally?'

'Anybody seen my bike pump knocking about?'

But when her men folk were all gone, that vague uneasiness assailed Sally again. What was it she was fretting about, she wondered? Why had she become so nervy? It was as if an alarmed instinct were urging her to do something. But what? She could not discover.

She had tidied up the kitchen, and was going over to the wash-house to get on with her washing, when a dark figure, squatted near the vine growing across the back verandah, rose to meet her.

It was Kalgoorla, very dirty and wet, from having been out in the rain all night: some prospector's old felt hat dragged down over her head, and a man's coat wrapped over the bedraggled skirt clinging to her thin bare legs.

'Him feller sit tight,' she muttered, with a little laugh, squinting at the duck under the vine. 'T'under not mak'm walk about.'

'My, you gave me quite a fright, Kalgoorla!' Sally exclaimed. 'It's ages since I last saw you. Where have you been all this long time?'

'Bin walk-about,' Kalgoorla said, her sombre face brightening because Missus Sally was pleased to see her.

'But I thought you were camped out near Maritana's place,' Sally said. 'What's happened? Don't you look after the goats for Maritana, now?'

Kalgoorla's face clouded.

'Wiah,' she said flatly.

Sally knew her well enough to guess something was wrong and not to ask questions. Kalgoorla would tell her perhaps later on. She had suddenly realised Kalgoorla was a godsend: could help her that day.

'Come along,' she said, briskly. 'We make cuppa tea. You hungry feller, I bet, Kalgoorla! And by-m-by, you give me a hand, with washing, eh?'

The glint of a smile lighted Kalgoorla's eyes.

'Eh-erm,' she said, as she shambled after Sally towards the house.

Kalgoorla was so dirty that Sally hesitated to take her into the kitchen. But she could never forget what she owed this old gin: how Kalgoorla had looked after her when she might have died of typhoid in the bush; and how stoically Kalgoorla had worked for her when she opened her first dining-room on Hannans. Kalgoorla knew what Missus Sally was thinking and stopped to wash her feet under a tap in the yard, drying them on her skirt, before going into the kitchen.

'There now,' Sally said, when Kalgoorla was seated before an enamelled mug of tea, a hunk of meat, and two or three slices of bread spread with golden syrup, 'tear that into you, while I root out some clothes.'

Kalgoorla made short work of her meal, and when Sally brought her one of Morris's shirts and an old print dress, she went off to the wash-house to scrub off some surface grime before putting them on. From washing herself, she started lifting clothes from the boiler and washing them, as she had done often before for Missus Sally.

Seeing her at work over the wash tubs, Sally went back to the house. Kalgoorla knew that job. She could leave her to it, she told herself; and she, herself, would set about cleaning out Paddy Cavan's room.

Instantly, she knew the cause of her uneasiness that morning. The fact that Paddy had left the room, and nobody had gone into it to see everything was all right, struck her forcibly. How could she have been so careless? She had just glanced in to see Paddy had not removed any of the bedding or furniture on Saturday, and shut the door. And all day, on Sunday, the family had been enjoying the pleasant sensation of knowing he wasn't there. They had the house to themselves, and could be free and easy together without that great, stupid oaf wanting to be on the same terms with everybody. But Sally had been conscious of that room as a source of danger in her house. What sort of danger, she had not considered. It was as if it had been occupied by a diseased person, and she was disturbed by the idea of Dick moving in, until it had been thoroughly cleaned and disinfected.

Paddy's smell still clung to it, as Sally went into the room: a smell of bad feet and of a young man who wet the bed at night, and had to be provided with a waterproof sheet for his mattress. As she threw the bedding out into the sun and went through papers left in the wardrobe and chest of drawers, she found her latent fear of some menace lurking in the room growing on her. Why hadn't she investigated it before, she asked herself. Why hadn't Morris or Dinny suggested that it would be as well to look around and see Paddy hadn't left behind any stuff which could incriminate Dick in his illegal business? Paddy knew Dick was going to have this room. He knew Dick would be moving into it as soon as he left.

It was absurd to be so suspicious, she argued with herself. Absurd to think—mean and vindictive though he might be—Paddy would be guilty of a really dirty trick to make trouble for her. But you never knew! Sally destroyed every scrap of paper lying about. An appalling thought struck her. Suppose Paddy had left some gold which Dick might be held responsible for, in the room!

No, no, Sally told herself, he would not do that! It was ridiculous to imagine such a thing. Of course, it had happened! Men had been framed by having stolen gold planted on them when somebody wanted to work off a grudge. But she could not believe Paddy would stoop to that. He was a money-grubber and ambitious; but he had some good points. She and Paddy had been good enough friends, until recently, when she let him know plainly that she was not going to allow her house to be a centre for the gold-stealing racket.

Paddy laughed at the idea, tried to bluff her out of suspecting he had anything much to do with it. And he had always pretended to be grateful for what she did for him, in the early days, when he was a half-starved urchin, scavenging for a living. Hadn't she given him many a feed, mended his pants, nursed him when he was sick, and tried to make a decent man of him?

Oh yes, he had played on her vanity, and she had tolerated his business deals to a certain extent. Until their final bust up! Even that did not destroy a lingering confidence Paddy would never forget their old association.

But Sally was taking no chances on such a supposition. She scrutinised every corner and cupboard in which ore or concentrates might have been secreted: pummelled and thumped the mattress: up-ended the table and chairs: moved the bed in order to examine the floor-boards beneath it. Stolen gold was often stowed away under the floor. The detectives never failed to look for it there.

One of the floor-boards looked as if it had been moved recently. Sally stared at it, sick with fright. She remembered what Dinny had said about having heard Paddy hammering when he came in from Kamballie.

She ran for a claw hammer. It was a good thing she was handy with tools, she thought, as she prized out the nails in that board. She had had to be in the early days. Morris was no earthly use with a hammer and nails, and he had been away on the rush to Lake Darlot when she needed help most, fixing up her bush dining-room, and making her camp comfortable. But that morning her hands were trembling, and she worked frantically, fearing that at any moment detectives from the Gold Stealing Detection Staff might be walking in on her.

She was scarcely surprised when she found three small black balls in a box under the floor. She had known something was there from the moment her eye lighted on the loose floor-board.

The black balls were covered with a piece of bagging and weighed heavily in her hands. She knew what they were immediately. Gold amalgam, from one of the treatment processes on a mine. What to do? She was panic stricken: realised that Paddy had done this for a purpose. Where could she hide the amalgam, so that if the house were raided, it would not be found? That was what she had to decide, and quickly. Few places escaped the keen eyes of the gold-stealing detectives. They made a thorough search, and were used to the shifts miners' wives and mothers resorted to, in order to hide bits of telluride, or tell-tale rich stuff like concentrates and amalgam.

Sally wrapped the balls in a newspaper Paddy had left lying on the floor. She intended to put them in her own wardrobe until she had nailed up the boards. But, on the verandah, she paused looking across the yard, hoping for an inspiration.

Kalgoorla was hanging sheets on the line and under the vine Sally could see the Muscovy duck sitting on her eggs. What was it Kalgoorla had said? 'Him feller sit tight! T'under not make'm walk about.'

The duck's round glazed eyes blinked at her. That was it, Sally decided. The duck would sit on the gold for her.

She waited until Kalgoorla had gone back into the wash-house. Then went over to the duck, and stooping beside her, stowed the three black balls under her broad breast. The duck snapped viciously at her hands, wriggled over the new eggs in her nest, and settled down comfortably.

Sally ran back to the bedroom: could not finish her work there quickly enough. She had to nail the board back into position, scrub the floor and stain it so that the place where it had been moved, would not show. She felt easier in her mind when that was done, warned herself she must not get rattled: that she must be quite natural and self-possessed when the detectives arrived.

What Paddy's plan had been she could not imagine. But sooner or later she felt sure, now, detectives of the Gold Stealing Detection Staff would pay her a visit.

Sally hoped it would not be until to-morrow. If she could only tell Morris and the boys what had happened, they would advise her. They would know what to do.

Had Paddy left any more of his ill-gotten goods about? She

could not rest until she had crawled under the house to have a look round. She was afraid the detectives might find her there: decided to tell them that she had been setting a rat trap, and set one to prove her story. Kalgoorla's eyes widened to a stare of amazement when Missus Sally emerged, very dusty and dishevelled from under the house. But Sally could afford to laugh at her then, and say gaily:

'All right! Set'm rat trap, Kalgoorla.'

'Wiah!' Kalgoorla was not taken in by that as a reason for Missus Sally to make herself look as dirty as a gin. But what Kalgoorla thought didn't matter, Sally consoled herself, and hoped the rat trap would snap on any prowling hands.

She washed, changed her dress and tidied her hair before going across to open up and clear out the bunk-house. But there was nothing to fear from the men who had left those rooms! They did not know who would be going to occupy them, and Paddy knew Dick was to have his room. He had aimed at fixing things so that Dick would be found in 'possession of gold reasonably suspected of having been stolen, or unlawfully obtained'. Sally was sure of that. Kalgoorla could scrub out the bunk-house, she decided, and went back to the kitchen.

There were still beds to make, sweeping and washing up to do, and it was midday before she could sit down on the back verandah, and feel that her house was in order. Paddy's room smelt of the disinfectant she had used on the floor, but it looked clean and tidy, with Dick's own mattress and pillows, fresh sheets and a blue and white counterpane on the bed. She glanced at the white duck sitting there serenely under the vine. Thank God for maternal instinct, Sally exclaimed to herself. Nothing would move that duck until her eggs were hatched, she knew, and they were not due to crack for another week.

Kalgoorla went off early in the afternoon, with some food and her old clothes under her arm. Sally gathered that Fred Cairns had chased her away from his camp; but Kalgoorla was making back there because she was afraid he was 'badgee', cross feller, with Maritana.

'That feller Fred Cairns, him no good,' she said, her face heavy and scowling.

Kalgoorla was right about that, Sally knew. Fred Cairns had a bad reputation for flying into mad rages. He was supposed to have a couple of men working for him on a show near his camp: but it was an open secret that a treatment plant near the show kept them busy.

The afternoon dragged away slowly. Sally brought in dry

clothes from the line, folded and damped down those that would have to be ironed. She was sitting on the verandah in the sunshine, altering the black silk dress she was going to wear to Dick's wedding, and trying to persuade herself there was nothing to fear now—Tom would be home soon, and Morris and Dick—when two men walked round the corner of the house. So quietly, they had approached, Sally did not know they were there until they blocked out the sunshine.

'Detective-Sergeant Kane and Detective Smattery of the Gold Stealing Detection Staff,' Kane said. 'Sorry, Mrs. Gough, but we have a warrant to search the house.'

Sally knew them by sight. The tall thin man with pale cold eyes who had come to the goldfields recently, and promised 'to clean up the gold-stealing racket'; and Smattery, the tough, rat-faced runt who was the most hated man in the force. The men said that Kane 'wasn't a bad sort' and out to get the big crooks as well as the small fry in the traffic.

He had drawn attention to the fact that two well-known men had been selling gold to their banks as coming from certain leases, but made no returns to the Department concerning production on those leases; and that neither the Department nor the police had taken any action in this matter. He had exposed the possibility of corruption in the force, also, by giving evidence in a recent case of having been offered £200 as a bribe to drop a prosecution. Kane incurred the displeasure of some of his employers even, it was rumoured, by being too zealous in the performance of his duties. The goldfields would become too hot for him, he had been warned, if he pursued the line of investigation on which he had started. So he had been concentrating lately on tracing leakages from the big mines. That was a job which Smattery had been doing for some time. He had pimps on every level and in every surface plant; and a reputation for being well in with the big crooks. His activities never embarrassed them, at any rate; but more than one man who had become dangerous to their interests, swore he had been trapped by information which Smattery could only have obtained from an agent of the Big Four.

All this gossip of the town whirled through Sally's mind as she faced the detectives, summoning her courage and common sense to meet the ordeal before her.

'What?' she exclaimed, the words rushing from her instinctively. 'Search my house? In all the years I've lived on the fields . . .'

'We have our orders,' Smattery interrupted roughly.

'Carry out your orders by all means.' Sally sank back into her chair. Despite good intentions, her limbs were shaking. 'But you will understand, Detective-Sergeant Kane, my surprise that such orders should have been considered necessary. There is nobody in this house who would have given any cause for them. I am convinced there is some mistake.'

'One of your sons is a miner on the Boulder Reef, and the other works as an assayer, has the run of the sump house and processing of gold,' Smattery sneered. 'A nice combination.'

'Our information cannot be disregarded,' Kane said coldly. 'It was thought advisable to make the search before your sons come home to avoid unnecessary unpleasantness. Proceed, Smattery.'

'We have nothing to hide,' Sally said quietly, picking up her sewing. 'Search as much as you wish.'

The detectives tramped past her along the verandah. The set of their shoulders, the queer, scenting expression of their faces, the purposeful way they took off their coats to begin a thorough overhaul of every room in the house, touched Sally's sense of humour. She was tempted to laugh. An hysterical, irresponsible laughter bubbled within her; but almost as if it had uttered a warning, the duck blinked at her.

'You do your part,' it seemed to say, 'and I'll do mine.'

Sally scolded herself for having lost sight, for a second even, of the need for being calm and self-possessed. She knew that she should have accompanied the detectives and watched them while they went through the rooms; but it would be more than she could bear, she thought, to see them going through the boys' and Dinny's cupboards and drawers, throwing their books and clothes on the floor, turning mattresses upside down and leaving everything in disorder behind them.

It was in the room vacated by Paddy Cavan that they worked most strenuously. Sally could hear them moving the furniture, ripping open the mattress on the bed, and then tearing up the floorboards. Smattery went crawling under the house while Kane stalked indoors to inspect the sitting-room, her own and Morris's room, and the kitchen. All the time she went on stitching, with a smile at the Muscovy duck now and then, to assure her everything was going on as well as could be expected.

'Who occupies this room?' Smattery demanded standing in the doorway behind her. He was red-faced, dusty and savage after his crawl under the house, and failure to discover what he had expected.

'No one at present,' Sally replied sweetly. 'It was occupied by Mr. Patrick Cavan until recently.'

'That's a lie,' Smattery snarled. 'It's your son, Dick Gough's room.'

'Who told you that?' Sally queried, resenting the way the man spoke to her: as if she were a criminal. She had heard of his bullying tactics and how he tried to intimidate miners' wives when he raided their homes like this. But she ignored his insult to strike where her dart would have most effect.

'Never you mind who told me,' Smattery blustered. 'It's my business to know.'

'Oh well, you've been misinformed, this time,' Sally said lightly. 'None of my sons has ever occupied that room.'

Kane had returned from his investigation indoors.

'We know Mr. Patrick Cavan was living here until a few days ago, Mrs. Gough,' he said, covering Sally with a keen suspicious stare. 'But the room has been nicely cleaned out and tidied up since Mr. Cavan left.'

'And look at it now!' Sally cried indignantly. 'You've wrecked the whole house: made it look like a bear garden. It will take me hours to put it to rights again.'

'Too bad,' Kane replied cynically. 'You'd better complain to Mr. Cavan. He's an influential man in this town, I believe.'

'Oh, is Mr. Cavan a friend of yours, too?' Sally inquired guilelessly. 'I know he's a friend of Detective Smattery's. You used to come to see Paddy here, didn't you, Detective Smattery? I wondered where I'd seen your face before.'

'What's that?' Kane's voice rasped.

'Th-the woman's lying,' Smattery stuttered, aware of an awkward situation arising from what Sally had said, although it was true enough. He had on two or three occasions conferred with Mr. Cavan in his room. But he could not afford to have Kane inquiring into his associations with Paddy Cavan. 'I've never spoken to Mr. Cavan except on official business, and never on these premises,' he declared. 'Looking as outraged by the truth as only a dishonest man can,' Sally explained, afterwards.

'Come on,' Kane said curtly. 'We'd better inspect the yard and the bunk-house while we're about it.'

Smattery strutted past him and out into the yard. Sally saw him go into the shed Dick and Tom had built for themselves years ago. It had been used so long for storing wood and dumping all sorts of rubbish in that she had almost forgotten their old furnace still stood in it. Smattery called Kane and they had quite a busy time throwing out the wood, empty bags, a broken chair of two, and a pile of fruit cases.

When they came back to the house they were covered with dust, but looked satisfied with the result of their exertions.

135

'Nice little treatment plant you've got there in the back-yard, Mrs. Gough,' Smattery said, with a smirk.

Sally realised that the construction which might be put on the boys' old furnace was no laughing matter; but she could not resist a fleeting smile at the hot, begrimed faces of the detectives.

'You do work hard, don't you?' she said. 'And it seems such a pity to have wasted your time. The boys built that shed when they were schoolboys and trying all sort of chemical experiments. It hasn't been used for anything but storing wood and odds and ends of rubbish, for years.'

'That doesn't mean the furnace and tools couldn't be used again if occasion arose,' Kane said sharply.

'Do you think so? Do you really think so, Detective-Sergeant Kane?' Sally queried with blithe irony. 'If occasion arose, you are aware, no doubt, that there are treatment plants better equipped, these days.'

'I am aware of it,' Kane retorted, as he turned away. He paused on the edge of the verandah to glance back at her.

'Good afternoon, ma'am,' he said with a glint in his keen, pale eyes, as if admitting she had won for the time being. 'Sorry to have bothered you. But I am inclined to think we haven't altogether wasted our time.'

CHAPTER XVII

'PADDY thought he'd got everything fixed all right, mum,' Tom said when he came in and heard Sally's news. 'That's why the dees came before Dick and I got home. Reckoned it'd be easier to handle if they had only you to deal with.'

'That's about it,' Sally agreed. She was busy with her evening meal, the kitchen full of a nice, cabbagy smell, and the savour of a hot-pot she had hurriedly put in the oven. Tom was hungry and tired: would have liked to sit down to his dinner at once; but he could not detach his mind from Paddy Cavan's attempt to frame Dick.

'What are we going to do now, Tom?' his mother asked anxiously. 'That's what's worrying me. Are we going to expose Paddy? Or just hold our tongues about the whole business? It might have been better to let the dees find the blasted stuff where Paddy left it, since Dick had never been into the room.'

'No, mum,' Tom answered her, 'you did quite right. They'd have found some way of proving possession. But Kane's not a bad sort. He would have smelt a rat about Smattery's information, and guess Paddy had something to do with it.'

'I hope you're right, Tom,' Sally said, still dubious.

Then Dick came in, and they told him what had happened.

'So that's Paddy's game,' he said thoughtfully. 'The rotten dog! I've been expecting he'd try to get even with me for queering his pitch in the sump house. There's a lad been getting away with a fair bit, passing it on to his father, who sells to Paddy. I warned young Syles it'd got to stop. Now inquiries are being made about a difference between the output of slimes and the assay. I daresay Paddy's got hold of some samples that would've made it awkward for me, if they'd been found in my possession.'

'You bet they would've,' Tom agreed. 'Paddy only missed ·the bus because you didn't move into that room as soon as he thought you would, or because the dees were too quick off the mark, acting on their "information".'

'And because mum had her wits about her,' Dick remembered. 'Gee, darl, you and your old Muscovy beat Paddy and the dees anyhow.'

'I'm not so sure of that,' Sally's smile glimmered. 'That's what Kane said,' she added. 'This was Paddy's first round, but what will he do now?'

When Lal and Den got home they were told the house had been raided; but not about the gold Paddy had planted and what had been done with it.

Then Morris came in, carrying the worn Gladstone bag in which he brought home his papers and accounts. Book-keeping had always been difficult for him to cope with, and recently Dick had been helping him to put the accounts of 'the coffin shop' as he called it, in order. But Morris was later than usual; and started to explain with slightly aggressive exuberance that he had had a busy day. Some of the boys warming up after a funeral had dragged him into a pub for a few pots on his way out of town.

'Shut up, dad,' Tom said. 'There's been a raid on the house and mum's worried.'

'What?' The news had a sobering effect on Morris.

'Scram!' Tom jerked his head at his younger brothers. 'We've got to talk this over with dad.'

Sally gave Morris an account of what had happened, and he slumped into a chair beside the table.

'Do you mean to say, you think Paddy put up a thing like that? Stowed the gold and gave information to the police, in order to work off a grouch against us—against Dick?'

'There's no other explanation of why the dees came here,' Sally said.

Morris swore in a way the boys had never heard him swear before their mother. He called Paddy Cavan all the names he could lay his tongue to, and vowed he would show him up for the lying, low-down crook he was.

'It's no use talking like that, Morris,' Sally said sharply. 'We've got to decide what's to be done. Paddy will guess I've found the gold and removed it.'

'I'm to blame, mum,' Dick said quickly. 'Let me handle it. I've brought all this trouble on you by queering Paddy's pitch on the mine, an—if I weren't going to marry Amy, Paddy wouldn't be cutting up so rusty.'

'God Almighty!' Morris stared at him aghast. 'Is that what's at the bottom of it?'

There was something so conscience-stricken and wretched in his eyes that Sally cried:

'You haven't forgotten your promise? You haven't had any more dealings with Paddy, Morris?'

'No,' Morris said. 'But a chap brought me some stuff on Saturday. And when I got home Paddy had gone. I've been chasing the damned town to find out where he's staying. Shack says he dumped Paddy's baggage at the railway station and he doesn't know where Paddy went after that. They say in his office, "Mr. Cavan's out of town", and they don't know his whereabouts.'

'What have you done with the gold, dad?' Tom demanded.

'It's in that bag,' Morris said miserably. 'I've been yanking it about all day, looking for Paddy. We'd better dig a hole in the garden and get rid of it.'

Tom grabbed at the bag, and took out the parcel of ore wrapped in hessian and newspaper.

'Give it to me, Tom,' Sally demanded, thinking she would sit on it until they decided what to do with the parcel.

But Kane and Smattery walked through the open doorway.

'Thanks, I'll take charge of that,' Kane said, confronting Tom, while Smattery stood behind covering him, a hand in his revolver pocket.

Tom's first impulse was to knock him down and make a dash for the door, but he knew that nothing was to be gained by resistance. The implications of the whole bizarre scene which had arisen so suddenly forced themselves upon him. It was almost unbearable to see his mother transfixed with horror, his father and Dick standing helpless beside her. Tom knew what he must do. He was almost

138

relieved that he could shoulder responsibility and divert attention from them.

'Our information wasn't so far out after all!' Smattery could not resist to crow over Kane. 'I guessed if we watched the house, and hung around when the old man and the boys came home, we'd have something to go on.'

'What's your name?' Kane asked Tom.

'Tom Gough.'

'And how did you come by this parcel of ore?'

'That's my business,' Tom said steadily

'You're a miner on the Boulder Reef?'

'I am.'

'Mate to Ted Lee who's just opened up a rich shoot on the one thousand eight hundred level,' Smattery jeered.

'Are you Lee's mate?' Kane demanded.

'I'm bogging for him,' Tom said.

He was ready then for Kane's official phrases, intimating that he was arrested for 'being in possession of gold, or gold-bearing ore reasonably suspected of being stolen, or obtained by unlawful means'.

Morris could not stand that. His shabby, portly figure assumed a dignity he had not worn for a long time.

'You're making a mistake, Kane,' he said. 'My son's got nothing to do with this. I'm the man you want.'

'Don't worry, Mr. Gough,' Kane replied blandly. 'We know you're in this too. A warrant will be made out for your arrest and you'll be charged with having assisted to commit an offence.'

'It's an outrage,' Sally stormed. 'The most dastardly frame-up that's ever been worked on the fields.'

'We've heard that old story before,' Smattery sniggered.

'Your son will have an opportunity to prove his innocence in court, ma'am,' Kane said stiffly. 'We have to do our duty.'

'It's all right, mum.' Tom seemed quite unruffled. 'Everything will be all right. Don't get upset.'

His smile went to Sally's heart. She understood well enough that Tom was prepared to be the scapegoat in this disaster which had befallen his family.

'Oh, Tom,' she wailed, 'I can't bear it!'

Dick put his arm round her, and Morris thrust himself forward.

'I'm going to the police station with you, Tom,' he said. 'I have a statement to make.'

'Say nothing, now, Dad,' Tom begged. 'It won't do any good.'

'Get goin',' Smattery said roughly. 'We can't stop here all night.

Y' can be charged together. Save us the trouble of havin' another warrant made out, and comin' back.'

The figures of the detectives loomed huge and sinister to Sally, as they closed round Tom, and then blurred to a formless mass. She was aware that Morris had gone out after them, as she dropped into a chair beside the table and a storm of weeping broke over her. Lal and Den coming in were stunned by the sight of her grief. They had never seen their mother in tears before; but they knew why she was crying. They had seen Tom and their father being taken away by Kane and Smattery.

Detectives of the Gold Stealing Detection Staff were known to every urchin in the township, and often before Den and Lal had seen a miner being escorted to the police station by those solid plain-clothes men whose very backs announced their jobs. That Tom had been arrested was no more than a minor excitement; but their mother's distress gave the matter a very different aspect.

'Did they get anything, Dick?' Lal asked.

'Enough to make things look bad,' Dick said shortly.

He leaned over his mother: his voice affected her like a restorative.

'Listen, darling,' he said, 'you must pull yourself together. I'll have to get a lawyer and arrange about bail.'

'Oh yes.' Sally raised a tear-drenched face. 'I'll come with you, Dick.'

'No,' Dick said firmly. 'This is my job, mum. You explain to Den. Lal can come with me.'

CHAPTER XVIII

MEMORY of those days in the dingy, crowded court house clung to Sally. She never got over what she had been through during that time.

George Sloan, the lawyer Dick engaged to defend Tom and Morris, was the best man available, Tim McSweeney considered. He was a new-comer, and not yet familiar with conditions in which the law was administered in Kalgoorlie, but an honest and conscientious young man. The prosecuting attorney, Mr. Ezra Joblin, an old man with the face of a white rat, had won too many cases for the Chamber of Mines not to know how to handle this one, and George Sloan, Dinny was afraid.

'Most unfortunate,' Mr. Sloan remarked sympathetically, when Sally interviewed him to give her account of finding the hidden amalgam, and how the detectives came to arrest Tom. 'The worst of it is that on this charge, the onus of proving that he came by he gold lawfully, falls on the defendant. And you see, Mrs. Gough —although there's no doubt in my mind Mr. Cavan was playing to get your family into trouble—the facts we must deal with have nothing to do with those which you disclose. It would complicate matters, in my opinion, if we divulged any of this information in connection with the amalgam you found in that room. This information could have been useful if your son, Dick, had been charged. But the charges refer to the parcel of gold found in Tom's possession, and to your husband's statement in connection with it. Therefore, reference to this other incident cannot serve any useful purpose —unless evidence crops up to make it necessary. I am inclined to think that even an attempt to prove malicious intention would not affect the case, as far as the law stands with regard to your husband and Tom, and it might involve your other son in further inquiries.'

'I see that,' Sally said, reluctant to forgo an exposure of Paddy Cavan, and yet anxious to protect Dick. She could not bring herself, however, to withhold any information which would clear Tom.

'You think it would not help Tom to mention this matter?' she asked.

'It might even be used to complicate the situation,' Mr. Sloan told her, 'if a suggestion arose that the brothers were working together to defraud the mining companies. Kane would make the most of that old furnace and the various tools for treating gold, found in the wood shed.'

'But they haven't been used since the boys were at school!' Sally cried distractedly. 'Even the detectives would have to admit those things were covered with dust, just lying with any old rubbish. We'd forgotten all about them.'

'The prosecution might argue that they could be used when the opportunity presented itself,' Sloan pointed out.

'My God,' Sally wailed, 'it's almost as if they wanted to make out we're criminals.'

'They do,' Sloan assured her.

'What's the use of trying to live honestly and decently if all this can be stacked against you?' Sally's anger blazed. 'I'm beginning to understand why people up here say: "If you're not in the gold, everybody'll think you are, so you may as well be in, and have some fun for your money, as out of it, and pay just the same".'

'Your husband supplied evidence for the prosecution,' Sloan reminded her.

'Oh yes,' Sally admitted, with a sinking heart, 'but I can't altogether blame Morris You've got to understand life up here, to realise it's a point of honour to oblige a man when he's in difficulties with a parcel like that: says the dees are after him. Morris thought it would be quite safe for him to give the parcel to Paddy when he came home. Of course, he had received some small sums as commission before; but on this occasion, I'm sure, he didn't want to touch the stuff. He had promised me not to let any more men leave parcels at the shop for Paddy. He had already told one man that he wasn't going to take charge of anything for Paddy in future. And then a miner came along: said he had to get rid of the gold and persuaded Morris that the dees would never think of looking for it in one of his coffins. But Morris was so uneasy about it that he tried to find Paddy. . . .'

'Yes, yes, I know all that,' Mr. Sloan interrupted a little impatiently. 'It looks as if Low and Cavan came to some understanding in the matter. No doubt Cavan resented Mr. Gough having refused to accept the other parcel. But your husband's statement to the police makes his case very difficult to handle, Mrs. Gough.'

'I suppose so,' Sally agreed listlessly.

'Never mind, we'll do our best to get both Mr. Gough and your son acquitted,' Mr. Sloan promised, to cheer her. 'There's a technicality the detectives overlooked we might work on. After all a bird in the hand doesn't prove possession of that bird.'

That was why, Sally explained, Tom and Morris had been advised not to refer to those balls of amalgam Paddy had planted to injure Dick; and she, herself, when she had to go into the witness box, did not speak of them. Her evidence had consisted simply of telling what happened when Morris came home that night. He suspected, when he could not find Mr. Cavan, that the gold had been left with him, for a malicious purpose, she contrived to say. That was why her husband was telling her and her sons about it.

Miners, prospectors and old friends filled the court and Sally was aware of their murmur of sympathy. It did not affect her shame and misery at having to appear before them, like that. She had always held her head high and prided herself on a reputation for uncompromising honesty and independence. Most goldfields folk would not regard the charges against Morris and Tom as seriously as she did, she knew well enough. Most people would be concerned chiefly about the rotten luck Tom and Morris had struck to be caught as they were. She could endure the prospect of Morris having to bear the penalty of breaking the law. He had been playing with fire, knew the risks he was taking, and had got burnt; but that Tom should have to share his guilt filled her with an overwhelming bitterness.

142

Who could blame her if she had lost control of her feelings and told everybody in the court just what was at the bottom of this case, Sally used to ask, when she talked about it? But even then, she knew it would be a mistake. Once Tom must have guessed how seething with fury she was. He had caught her eye and smiled as if saying: 'Keep cool, mum. Don't do anything foolish!'

In spite of everything, she had never been so proud of Tom, as when he stood on that wooden platform, with a rail round it, listening to the evidence of perjured witnesses against him. He looked what he was, Sally told herself, a fine type of young man, straight and fearless. She had never thought Tom good-looking before, or realised how dear he was to her. His rather heavy features seemed to have firmed and hardened over night, his thoughtful eyes to have gained a clearer light. His character stood clear-cut from among the people about him.

It was infuriating to see Paddy Cavan sitting with the crowd in court, a grin on his smug, fat face. Just as well Dick had accompanied her, Sally said afterwards, and that Amy was with him, Dinny and Marie alongside her. There was a moment when it seemed the wild rush of her anger would defy all the rules of police-court procedure. She had been tempted to stand up and denounce Mr. Patrick Cavan as the biggest gold thief and swindling, treacherous crook on the Boulder.

Of course, it would have done no good. She would have been bustled out of the court: made an exhibition of herself to no purpose. Sally was glad she had got the better of that tempestuous impulse, although it was as much as she could do to overcome her frenzy at the time. Seeing Tom in the dock treated like a criminal, Morris looking so broken and appalled by the position in which his folly had placed them; and knowing that Paddy Cavan was responsible for the whole situation, had driven her almost demented.

The prosecution was trying to prove that the gold in that parcel found in Tom's possession was identical with gold being picked out of the rich shoot on the one thousand eight hundred level of the Boulder Reef. The underground foreman and the shift boss testified to the fact that Tom Gough had been employed in that section of the mine: but old Joblin could not induce them to say anything detrimental to Tom's character. It was Mr. Leonard Low, louser for the company, who stated that on the day the rich shoot had been uncovered, he had been suspicious of the behaviour of the accused, and had warned him that a strict look-out was going to be kept for any gold walking from the shoot.

'It's a lie!' The words burst from Tom. It was the only time his composure was broken.

The magistrate had reproved him: told him that he must not address the witness, and would have an opportunity, later, to make any statement he wished.

Experts had been brought in to examine specimens found in the possession of the defendant, and although, usually, it was impossible to identify gold as having come from any particular mine or lode of the Golden Mile, there was a peculiar scale associated with the gold in this shoot of the Boulder Reef, which enabled them to say that the ore found in Tom Gough's possession was identical with that being mined in the number three lode, south stope, of the Boulder Reef, one thousand eight hundred feet level. With this opinion, Mr. Low professed himself in agreement.

Another witness, Victor Uren, who everybody knew was Lenny Low's mate, testified that he had heard the previous witness warn the defendant: and that on the day in question he had heard Tom Gough boast in the change room that he: 'had got his cut out of the new chute but the bloody dees would never get anything on him.'

The muttering and restive movement of scores of miners at this information, which would only be given by a police pimp, aroused the magistrate's ire. He threatened to clear the court if there was a repetition of any such demonstration to intimidate a witness.

In the witness box, Tom had taken the bullying cross-examination of Ezra Joblin, coolly, and with several straight lefts which disconcerted even that wily, old campaigner.

Sally thought nobody could believe Tom had stolen that wretched gold when the prosecuting attorney finished with him. People in the court did not believe it, Dinny assured her. And the *Miner* next morning, announcing the verdict, commented on 'the contrast between the honest and straightforward bearing of the young miner, who was the defendant, and the obvious bluster and nervous agitation of some of the witnesses giving evidence against him'.

The case had aroused considerable interest, it was stated, because Mr. and Mrs. Morris Gough were old and respected members of the goldfields community.

Morris had not shaped so well in the witness box. He looked ghastly and unnerved; but pulled himself together and spoke with quiet dignity.

He had fought to exonerate Tom: was prepared to go any lengths to do so. Tom had not 'squealed', or given information that the police could use against any other man, even Lenny Low, although he denied that Low had ever had occasion to warn him, or had done so. The underground foreman had warned him and his mate, Tom stated. The remark in the change room ascribed to him by Vic Uren, Tom declared, was sheer invention.

Morris could not allow himself to be bound by the miners' code which condemned 'squealing' under any circumstances. He was determined not to allow Paddy Cavan and Lenny Low to get away with this day's work, if he could help it. He hoped to destroy the case for the prosecution against Tom by discrediting the chief witnesses; and was ready to bear the consequences of an admission that he had passed on gold to Paddy, so long as he exposed Mr. Patrick Cavan's responsibility in those transactions.

The sensational part of his evidence was when he named Mr. Patrick Cavan as a receiver of stolen gold, and when he said that he had taken the parcel of gold from Lenny Low for Cavan when Low persuaded him that he was in difficulties, and Cavan would take charge of it immediately.

Morris did not deny receiving parcels before for Mr. Cavan, or receiving a small commission for them. But he accused Paddy of having set a trap for him, and left this parcel on his hands, in order to work off a grudge, he, Paddy Cavan, had against the Gough family.

Mr. Cavan's counsel rose to protest at the first mention of Paddy's name.

'My client is here in court, Your Worship,' he declared. 'And is prepared to go into the witness box and deny the preposterous allegation that he was ever a party to such transactions as the witness has described.'

When Mr. Patrick Cavan went on to the witness stand, he swore 'to tell the truth, the whole truth, and nothing but the truth, so help me God!' After which he declared that there was no truth whatsoever in the statement of the previous witness that he had ever accepted from him parcels of gold, knowing them to have been stolen, or unlawfully obtained. He demanded that the witness produce evidence of his having done so, or of his having any connection with the traffic in stolen gold.

'Good God!' Dinny groaned.

As a director of the Boulder Reef and Associated Mines, Mr. Cavan said he was emphatically opposed to the illegal traffic in gold, and determined to see that this racket which was injuring the fair name of Boulder and Kalgoorlie in the eyes of overseas investors, was stamped out. It was his business to protect the interests of shareholders, and owing to serious leakages on the mines recently, he had offered the police any assistance in his power to pursue their investigations.

Far from bearing his old friend, Morrey Gough, any grudge,

Paddy protested, it was Mr. Gough who was making false and malicious accusations in order to protect himself and his son. On the face of it, the allegations that he, Patrick Gavan, was concerned in buying gold stolen from a mine, in which he was one of the largest shareholders was preposterous.

'Preposterous!' Paddy exploded the big word a second time with tremendous indignation. He had just learnt it from his lawyer, Sally guessed, and was impressed by the sound of it.

There was no doubt Paddy had bluffed his way out of an awkward situation. Almost everybody in the court knew he was lying, and although many men had gasped and grinned at his effrontery, was there one of them, Sally wondered, who would accept Paddy's challenge, and admit he had sold stolen gold to Mr. Cavan? Paddy would have seen to it that Morris had no proof of other deals with him, Sally realised.

It was too much to expect any man would blow Mr. Cavan's bluff sky high. Too much to expect that any man would incriminate himself by admitting that he had sold Paddy stolen gold. Colonel de Morfé, Sally suspected, could have produced sufficient evidence to ensure for Paddy the longest term of imprisonment provided for by the Gold Buyers' Act. But could he afford to have his business connection with Mr. Cavan made public?

Sally had seen Colonel de Morfé in court that first day. And Maritana, looking at her with mournful, troubled eyes, as if she knew what part she had played in this sordid drama. Frisco had avoided Sally's challenging glance after Paddy's statement: would have liked her believe that he was powerless to refute it, Sally thought cynically; and that he resented the circumstances which had thrust these humiliating proceedings upon her.

The prosecuting attorney, summing up, paid a suave tribute to the paternal sentiment animating the witness, Morris Gough. His attempt to defend his son without any consideration of the cost to himself was very laudable, no doubt. But Mr. Joblin asserted viciously: 'These sentiments have nothing whatever to do with the facts of the case. Moreover, the contemptible attempt of the father of the accused to discredit witnesses for the prosecution and a well-known, highly respected citizen . . .'

A loud boisterous laugh drowned the rest of what old Joblin had to say, and muffled laughter rocked the crowd in the court.

'Silence!'

'Order in the court!'

The bellow of the constable on duty suppressed this unseemly mirth, and Mr. Attorney Joblin snapped his peroration to a conclusion, somewhat out of countenance, and realising that no oration of his could whitewash Paddy Cavan as far as a goldfields crowd was concerned.

He got his verdict, however. Tom was sentenced to six months' hard labour before the court adjourned.

The charge against Morris could not be heard until next day.

CHAPTER XIX

PEOPLE were muttering and exclaiming in agitated groups round the court house next morning. 'Did y'r hear . . .' 'They say . . .'

Dinny had got wind of the rumour that some sensational evidence was to be produced in support of Morris's statement about Paddy Cavan's connection with the traffic in stolen gold. Everybody knew that he was 'in the gold'. But who was going to be game enough to produce evidence to prove it, and give himself away? Perhaps others as well.

Dinny went about among the men to find out what was at the bottom of the rumour. He heard that people sitting behind Maritana had said she was very excited—'had gone off like a packet of crackers' when Tom Gough was convicted. She had told a couple of miners near her that she wasn't going to let Paddy Cavan make trouble for the Goughs and do nothing about it. Missus Sally had been a good friend to her in the early days; and, Maritana said, when she came to the court house next day, she was going to tell the police what she knew about Paddy Cavan.

He thought he could treat people like dirt, the lying bastard! But she'd show him. She'd show Paddy he couldn't tell Fred she was no use to him, and make Fred send her and her kids back to Bardoc's camp. Bardoc had been Maritana's aboriginal husband before she lived with Fred Cairns everybody knew. Paddy had got the wind up about letting Maritana do any more collecting for him it seemed. He wanted to cover his tracks: had sent word that Fred was to get rid of Maritana and clean up the place. Maritana was being done out of 'a cut' she had been expecting, apparently; and she was seething with rage against Paddy, more on her own account than the Goughs', it turned out. But she saw a chance to strike back and her aboriginal blood boiled over at the thought of taking it.

The men to whom she had been talking tried to dissuade her from opening her mouth, but she went crook on them, they said: reckoned she'd rather go to jail than live like a gin in a black's camp. again. And the government would have to look after her kids if she was taken away from them. She cleared off, swearing she'd be in the court next morning and get square with Paddy Cavan, no matter what happened.

Dinny said those chaps had talked over Maritana's outburst with their mates. Some of them were perturbed that she might do as she said, and be forced to name miners she had collected gold from to hand on to Paddy. Others thought she had just gone snake-headed for a moment, like aborigines do when they lose their temper; and that she would cool off and realise she had better keep her mouth shut. Even if Maritana was a half-caste, and you could never be quite sure when she would act like an aborigine, she had a lot of common sense. She was too deep in the racket herself not to know she would be jailed if she talked about the gold she had collected for Paddy, and she was very fond of her kids. Besides Fred Cairns would see to it that she did not bring the dees round his camp.

Morris was charged with 'aiding the commission of an offence'; but by his own statement to the police, he had laid himself open to a more serious charge, under the Gold Buyers' Act, of receiving gold, 'knowing the same to have been obtained by a crime'. This was an indictable offence, and the offender liable to imprisonment for fourteen years, although no goldfields jury was likely to agree on a finding which would penalise a man to that extent.

Sloan said that Kane was keen this charge should be proceeded with, because it would enable him to pursue a line of investigations which might unmask some of the big men in the gold racket. Old Joblin, however, had scouted the idea that 'the Gough case justified further action', and pressure had been brought to bear on Detective-Sergeant Kane to drop his pursuit of the matter. Dinny remembered a boast of Paddy's that he knew enough about men in the mining world to run a good many of them out of the town before they 'put the boots into' him.

For the time being, whatever the reasons for leniency on the part of the Gold Stealing Detection Staff, and the police, Dinny was satisfied that Morris would not have to face further prosecution.

Tom's conviction had taken all the fight out of Morris. He went through the procedure in court again as if unable to throw off the despondency which had laid hold of him, stubbornly refusing, however, to withdraw or qualify the statement he had made to the police, or his evidence in the witness box the previous day.

Convicting him with a fine of £50, or six months' hard labour, the magistrate remarked, with some acerbity, that the accused clearly saw a chance to make money by handling illicit gold, and was fortunate not to have been charged under the Gold Buyers' Act. He did not appear to be 'a man of the dangerous receiver type', or to have prospered very much out of this or any other gold he may have dealt with, but it would be impossible to say to what extent he had been unlawfully dealing with gold. In the interests of justice, therefore . . .

Sally sat stunned and mortified, listening to the magistrate utter those caustic and humiliating words about Morris. She stared at his square, wooden face, wondering how any man who had an inkling of what lay behind this prosecution, as he would not fail to have, could permit himself so to kick a fellow citizen, taking the count, after all, for no more than criminal stupidity.

For a few moments, Sally could not move. She should not take Morris's conviction so hardly, she knew. Perhaps there was something to be thankful for, in that he did not have to face the more serious charge; but for him to have been addressed by the magistrate like that—for Morris to have to go to jail for six months, 'took all the stuffing out of her', as Dinny said.

Convictions for gold stealing did not greatly disturb people of the fields, Sally knew. They were part of the gamble of their lives, and stirred more neighbourly goodwill than any other misfortune. Women had to be philosophical about risks their sons and husbands took every day, and this one of getting away with a bit of gold was more of a joke than anything else. Sometimes it came off, and a new coat, an armchair, or a decorative kitchen dresser, the desire of every housewife's heart, was added to the family possessions. It was just bad luck, if a man got a few months at Fremantle because the dees happened to find telluride of gold on him, or stowed away somewhere about the house he occupied. A secret satisfaction remained that the mining companies who kept men working underground and made coughing wrecks of them before they were middle-aged, could not have everything their own way.

There were always a few men who enjoyed the spice of adventure in defying the mine owners, and giving the dees of the Gold Stealing Detection Staff a run for their money. The Chamber of Mines spent thousands of pounds a year to maintain this special force of its own detectives. That was another grievance which rankled with the miners. The mine owners were authorised by the government to maintain their own police force which harassed workers in their homes. Moreover, a principle of British justice had been subverted in order to facilitate convictions for gold stealing.

It was all very well for the Chamber of Mines to talk about the difficulty of proving a case and getting a conviction where gold was concerned; but Mickey Troy, when he was Minister for Mines, had pointed out that 'the law relating to gold stealing is much more severe than the law applying to the theft of any other property except pearls. In cases of ordinary theft, the guilt of the person charged has to be proved by the prosecution, but in the case of gold, the actual possession of gold-bearing ore by any person is prima facie evidence of guilt. Having been found in possession of ore, he is required to prove his innocence.'

Sally admitted that she felt as if she had been badly bashed by life on the fields, as she tried to adjust herself to the blow of Morris's conviction. She was seething with a sense of the hardships and injustices most of the workers who came before this court had to endure in their everyday lives. Their conflict was hers. Her back straightened as she thought of it, though she was so miserable and depressed on Tom's and Morris's account.

No one was surprised when Maritana did not turn up at the court house that morning as she had promised. The rumour which had caused so much suppressed excitement—that she was going to throw a stick of dynamite into the evidence—fell flat and fizzled out. There was a feeling, almost of relief, when no incident occurred during the normal course of proceedings, which might have brought trouble to many homes.

It was thought old Joblin had been particularly vicious in his summing up. He had tried to make out the evidence indicated that Morris Gough had been concerned not only in an isolated incident of gold stealing; but that in a series of incidents over a long period, he and his son had systematically been engaged in attempts to defraud the mining companies.

When the magistrate rapped out his sentence, a murmur of protest droned through the crowded court. Everybody knew, Dinny said, that Tom and Morris had been framed; and the sentences passed on them were regarded as pretty stiff under the circumstances. But this magistrate had been handing out sentences which were tougher than usual in minor gold-stealing cases. Three or four months, hard, with or without the option of a fine, could be expected as a rule; but latterly sentences had been more severe.

A mysterious explosion in the vicinity of the magistrate's house had intimated the unpopularity of some of his decisions but made no appreciable differences to the uncompromising manner in which he exercised his power in the interests of the mine owners. For months, under his jurisdiction, there had not been an acquittal on a gold-stealing charge: sentences ranged about the maximum he could impose.

But Mr. Cavan had given people something to gasp and guffaw about when the Gough case ended. Before the court adjourned, his lawyer had risen to announce that Mr. Cavan was willing to pay the fine imposed on his 'old friend, Morrey Gough'. This was referred to as 'a magnanimous gesture' by Mr. Cavan's legal adviser; and appealed to the sporting instincts of some of the men who had uneasy consciences about their relations with Paddy. They said Paddy 'wasn't such a bad sort after all'.

Mr. Cavan's business associates saw it as a shrewd move to stave off further investigation; and regain some of the ground he had lost in public esteem as the result of allegations made during the case. Only the miners laughed and swore at the rotten joke Paddy had put over them. Morris declined emphatically to allow Mr. Cavan to pay his fine.

He refused also to allow Sally to pay the fine, or to appeal against the magistrate's decision. That would involve further legal expenses, he said: and if Tom was going to jail he would go with him. Sally understood Morris felt morally responsible for Tom's sentence, and that he must share it.

Amy had come to the court, and sat with Dick each morning. She was so much in love with Dick, she wanted everybody to know it, Sally thought, and that she was with the Goughs in this as one of the familly already. Gossip had been busy with Paddy Cavan's attentions to Amy Brierly for a long time, and many whispers and hints were woven into the suggestion that Paddy's animosity towards the Goughs had something to do with Amy. The presence of the young lovers in the court sent grins and curious glances in their direction. People exclaimed to each other that Paddy looked as if he were suffering from a stomach-ache when he saw them sitting close together and smiling into each other's eyes.

As she walked out of the court that morning, Amy said impulsively:

'If it'd been you, and not Tom and your father, it wouldn't've made any difference to me, Dick.'

'It was me Paddy was gunning for,' Dick said bitterly. 'But his plans didn't work out quite as he expected. I've got an idea he didn't mean things to happen this way: but they more or less got out of hand when the dees took charge. He's let himself in for more than he intended, it seems to me.'

All kindness, and eager to express their goodwill and sympathy, men and women crowded round Sally.

'Cheer up, Mrs. Gough, Tom and Morrey'll soon be back agen!'

'You don't have to fret about a little thing like this!'

'It's all in the game!'

'Makes no difference to their mates and old friends!'

'Rotten luck—but it might've been worse!'

So many voices chimed about her, with their hearty good-natured exclamations and advice, that the tears she had been trying to restrain welled in Sally's eyes.

'I know. I know,' she said brokenly. 'But it's hard to bear all the same.'

'Don't be downhearted, darlin',' Theresa Molloy clutched hold of her to say. 'Everybody knows Paddy Cavan's at the bottom of this. Hell won't be full till he's there.'

Colonel de Morfé was standing by his car, at the edge of the footpath when Sally made her way into the street with Marie and Dinny beside her, Dick and Amy following. He pushed his way through the crowd to say:

'May I drive you home, Mrs. Gough, you and Dinny?'

'No thank you, Colonel de Morfé,' Sally said stiffly. 'Paddy Cavan's friends are no friends of mine, from now on.'

'God, Sally,' Frisco protested, falling into step beside her as she walked away. 'I pulled more strings than you'll ever know of, to keep the prosecution from going any further.'

'Thanks,' Sally said tartly. 'It wouldn't've suited Paddy for the prosecution to go any further. Or you, for that matter. Not with Kane on your tracks.'

'Kane?' Frisco laughed. 'He'll be shifted before long.'

He lifted his hat with the flamboyant grace of Frisco Jo Murphy. reminding her of what he had said long ago, as he murmured derisively:

'Y'r humble servant, ma'am! If ever I can be of any service . . .'

'If ever you could have been, it was now, and you weren't,' Sally said.

She was glad Marie and Dinny were with her and that she could walk on with them, knowing that they would need no explanation of her anger with Frisco.

'Colonel de Morfé!' Dinny chuckled. 'Y' can't beat Frisco. Bein' a colonel racin' round in his own car, he fancies he puts it all over Paddy Cavan! If there's goin' to be a war, Frisco means to come out on top. He's not gettin' round in uniform for nothing.'

Her troubles of the moment obscured Sally's anxiety about the war. She could think only of Tom and Morris. They would have to spend the night in the Kalgoorlie lock-up and be sent away to the jail at Fremantle by train next day.

It pleased her to hear that the morning shift on the Boulder Reef had refused to go below with Lenny Low and Vic Uren. A deputation had waited on the mine manager and informed him that owing to the unsavoury reputation of the two men, and that it was believed they had given false evidence against Tom Gough, Tom's mates would not work with them. There would be a strike on the mine if they were not immediately removed. Low and Uren were paid off, and the shift started work, congratulating itself on having made a stand for their mate, and rid themselves of such vermin.

Prisoners Morris and Tom might be, but they had quite a send-off at the railway station. Dick could not get away from work, but Lal and Den went with their mother and Dinny to say good-bye to Tom and Morris. Friends and neighbours had mustered in force to shake hands with them and cheer them up. Sally never appreciated the loyalty and community spirit of goldfields people so much. They took the sting out of Morris and Tom's departure in charge of a constable, by treating it as no more than an ordinary trip to the coast for a holiday.

But for days afterwards Sally felt half-dead: went about her house work with a drugging lassitude. She could think of nothing but the jail at Fremantle: Tom and Morris within its grey stone walls, wearing convict's clothes, herded with all sorts of criminals to some ignominious toil, eating the poor, tasteless prison food, shut into dark, airless cells for the night.

Dick said she was exhausted physically and mentally by the strain and worry of the past few days. He and Dinny urged her to take a holiday: make that visit to Warrinup she had been talking of for so long. Her sister Fanny had written to say that Bob had died several years ago and that she and Phyllis had been managing Warrinup ever since. They were alone in the old home now, although sometimes Cecily or Grace and their children came for a holiday. It would be a great pleasure if Sally and her boy could spend a few weeks with them. They would look forward to seeing their dear little sister, soon.

Sally would not hear of going to Warrinup, now. Goldfields folk might attach no importance to convictions for gold stealing; but she could not endure the idea of explaining to her sisters that Morris and Tom were in jail.

She would not go away, just yet, Sally said. By and by when Morris and Tom were allowed to have a visitor, she would go down to Fremantle to see them.

It was not until she saw the duck in the yard with several blobs of yellow fluff beside her, that Sally remembered those balls of amalgam on which the Muscovy duck had been sitting. Her melancholy abstraction cleared in an instant and she ran to find them. They were no longer there in the duck's nest. It was cluttered with broken shells and two or three eggs which had not hatched.

Sally's wail of consternation brought Dinny hurrying towards her. He had been in his room, and explained immediately what had become of the gold.

'It's all right! Don't distress y'rself now, ma'am,' he said soothingly. 'I looked after Paddy's nest eggs. And they're far away now where neither he, nor Kane, will ever find 'em.'

'Oh, Dinny,' Sally wept, 'why didn't you tell me? However could I have forgotten the wretched things for so long.'

'Best to forget 'em now,' Dinny told her. 'It's not like Paddy to take the loss of a bit of gold easy, once he's had his hands on it. I reckoned he'd think you knew what happened to that amalgam, and might come pokin' around, makin' a nuisance of himself. So I decided to get rid of it, and hang around for a while—jest in case Mr. Cavan paid us a visit, and I could deal with him. I told Dick I would, and that made him easier in his mind about bein' away at work when y' might need him.'

'Oh, Dinny, how good you are to us!' Sally blew her nose and squeezed back her tears. 'But you don't think Paddy'll try any more of his dirty tricks, do you?'

'Hell won't be full till he's there, as Mrs. Molloy says,' Dinny replied. 'And I wouldn't put anything past Paddy Cavan. But the boys tell me he's playing mighty safe jest now. Won't buy a bit of gold. Morrey gave him a scare all right, and Paddy's got the wind up about the way this bloke Kane's nosin' around. That doesn't mean, all the same, he mightn't come along and try makin' things uncomfortable for us.'

'Let him try,' Sally said, her eyes alight with the resurge of her fighting spirit. 'Though I feel as if I could murder him—so it's just as well you're here, perhaps, Dinny!'

But Paddy did not come near her, and presently everybody was gasping at the news that: 'Mr. Patrick Cavan has been summoned to a meeting of his directors in London. He left by the *Orontes* and expects to be away from Kalgoorlie for several months.'

CHAPTER XX

NEARLY a month later, Kalgoorla shambled into the back-yard late one afternoon. She looked such a scarecrow, so gaunt and weary, in her bedraggled gina-gina and the old hat dragged down over her head, that Sally exclaimed:

'Why, Kalgoorla, what's the matter? You sick feller?'

'Wiah,' Kalgoorla mumbled. 'Bin walk-about, walk-about. See Meeri? Any feller about see Meeri?'

From beneath the dilapidated hat brim, her bloodshot eyes, matted with dirt and pus, peered eagerly. Her voice had a sharp, wild note.

'Meeri? Maritana? No, I haven't seen her,' Sally said. 'Not since one day in the police court. We heard she'd gone bush because she was afraid after all to give evidence about the gold stealing.'

Kalgoorla muttered to herself.

'What is it?' Sally asked. 'Can't you find Meeri?'

Kalgoorla's voice rose to a wailing scream. 'Find'm Meeri? Wiah! Walk-about, walk-about, no find'm track, no find'm Meeri. Fred Cairns say: "Get the hell out of this, you bloody old bitch. Maritana gone bush." Wiah. Meeri no go bush.'

Kalgoorla squatted on the verandah. She tried to explain why she was worried about Maritana, though she called her always by her aboriginal name, Meeri. Sally gathered that when she did not see Maritana moving about Fred Cairns's camp as usual, Kalgoorla had gone to him and asked him where her daughter was. Fred Cairns said Maritana had gone bush because the police were after her. Kalgoorla had searched for her tracks in the bush. She had looked for them at every gnamma hole where Maritana might have camped. She had found the camp fires of her own people, and sent messengers to the tribe of Meeri's aboriginal husband; but no native had seen Meeri, or her tracks in the bush.

Then Kalgoorla had come back to the scrub near Fred Cairns's camp. She hid there, waiting and watching to catch a glimpse of Maritana, thinking she might have gone off somewhere in her buggy, or Fred Cairns might have driven her far away, far away, in his car. Perhaps that was why she had not picked up Meeri's tracks, Kalgoorla thought. Meeri would not stay away very long from her children, Kalgoorla was sure. When she did not come back to the camp, Kalgoorla had gone again to Fred Cairns and asked him: 'Where Meeri? Which way Meeri bin go bush?' But he had put the dogs on to her, and threatened to break every bone in her body if he saw her hanging round the camp again.

Sally understood the fear that lurked in Kalgoorla's heavy eyes. She felt sick with fear and horror herself. There was no need to say what they were both thinking: that Fred Cairns was trying to cover up something in connection with Maritana's disappearance. But what? Fred and Maritana had been living together for years. They had got along well enough: reared 'a mob of kids' as Fred boasted. He had seemed proud of them, and of Maritana: the way she stuck to him, ran the camp and helped him with his business. Fred had always been rather a pariah: never been known to have a mate. Now and then a couple of toughs worked for him on the mine not far from his camp; but everybody knew that was merely a blind for the treatment plant stowed away further out in the bush. Sometimes Fred had come into a pub for a booze-up; and Fred

Cairns was like 'a shark in heat' when he'd been drinking, the men said. Morris had said that once, Sally remembered. Fred's reputation for flying into crazy rages made even old dead-beats, cadging drinks, steer clear of him when he was drunk. Fred had been known to walk out of a bar and cut a dog's throat when its barking annoyed him.

With growing consternation, Sally recollected Maritana's outburst in the court. She suspected Fred would have been angry with Maritana about that.

Kalgoorla, reading her face, guessed Missus Sally was disturbed about Maritana's disappearance and had discovered a reason for it.

Sally knew it would be difficult to make Kalgoorla understand that the police should be informed. Kalgoorla feared and hated the 'pol'eece' who were responsible for making so many of her people suffer the penalties of the white man's strange justice. Her instinct, Sally realised, would be to let the tribes deal with the matter in their own way, which would only bring retribution upon them. Broken and disintegrated though they were, the aborigines were aroused, now and then, to take summary vengeance for an outrage committed against one of their women.

She must not let that happen, Sally decided. There were all the other issues involved, and their bearing on the gold-stealing racket.

'I don't know what we should do, Kalgoorla,' she said, overwhelmed by her fear and troubled thinking. 'Maybe we send for Dinny Quin. He help us. He tell us what to do.'

'Eh-erm,' Kalgoorla agreed.

'You stay here with me,' Sally went on. 'Make a little fire in the yard, or sleep in bunk-house, to-night?'

'Eh-erm,' Kalgoorla muttered listlessly.

'Come along, then.' Sally moved off to the kitchen. 'We make cuppa tea and get some tucker.'

Kalgoorla ate silently, ravenously, and drank two or three mugs of tea. Then Sally sent her over to the wash-house, while she rooted out a dress and warm jacket to replace the dirty rags and remnants of an old coat in which Kalgoorla had wrapped her scraggy body.

'Wash'm all over. Make'm clean feller, Kalgoorla,' Sally warned, feeling at the same time that it was brutal to bother a native woman about washing herself and dressing up when she was so distraught: her mind plunged in an unfathomable rage and grief.

But Kalgoorla would do as she was told with dumb courtesy, Sally knew, because this business of washing and wearing clean clothes was the rule of living with white people. It would have been impossible to let her come into the house unless she cleaned up.

And it was necessary to keep Kalgoorla until Dinny arrived, not only because of what she could tell him, and the police, but for her own sake. There was no knowing what might happen to Kalgoorla if she went prowling round Fred Cairns's camp again, now that her suspicions were aroused, and she might be expected to pass on those suspicions to other natives, and even the police.

Besides, Sally always insisted, she had a deep affection for Kalgoorla. Morris resented her tenderness for this dirty, sore-eyed old gin. Maybe because she reminded him of something he would rather forget. Sally thought: how Kalgoorla had saved her life when she was so ill on the track to Lake Darlot, and Morris himself had gone on to the rush. But Dick and Tom and Lal always made a fuss of Kalgoorla, laughing and joking with her as if they were glad to see her whenever she paid Sally a visit. And well they might be grateful to Kalgoorla, Sally told them. Kalgoorla had been a godsend to her often enough when they were little and she had so much to do, cooking for boarders, looking after them, and trying to make ends meet. But that day, she could only think of Kalgoorla as a mother in an abyss of misery and anxiety about her daughter.

As soon as Den came in from school she got him to ride over to Kamballie with a message for Dinny. She waited anxiously for Dinny to return with Den: could not throw off a suffocating sense of something fatal and sinister having happened to Maritana; and of the responsibility she and Dinny would have to share in starting investigations into the cause of Maritana's disappearance.

Kalgoorla made herself a little fire in the yard and slept beside it. When Sally heard her, wailing in the dawn, she knew that Kalgoorla felt, as she did, that Maritana was dead.

CHAPTER XXI

There was nothing for it, but to inform the police, Dinny said when he heard Kalgoorla's story. He explained that to Kalgoorla. Sunk in her sombre brooding Kalgoorla muttered apathetically.

'You must tell pol-eece all you know, Kalgoorla,' Dinny said. 'Help'm find Maritana.'

'Eh-erm,' Kalgoorla agreed.

'Don't let her out of your sight,' Dinny warned Sally. 'If there's been any dirty work, it mightn't be safe for her to go wandering about until this business is cleared up.'

'Fat chance I've got of keeping her if she wants to go,' Sally said.

But Kalgoorla understood more than she had given her credit for, Sally thought, when a police sergeant came back with Dinny to question her. Kalgoorla had stood up to his bluff, good-natured hectoring with grave stolidity, and convinced him there was cause enough for her anxiety on Maritana's account.

He and a mounted constable rode out to Fred Cairns's place and found it deserted, except for a few hens scratching in the dust, and a horde of goats. A baby's wailing led the troopers to where the children were hiding. They had run off at the first sight of those formidable figures on horseback. 'Scared and half-starved looking, they were, the whole pack of 'em,' Sergeant Dogherty said. But he had at last induced the eldest girl, who was carrying the baby, to talk. She said her mother went bush a few weeks ago, and their father had gone off to look for her. The baby was sick and snivelling all the time. Sergeant Dogherty thought it was going to die; but that kid would not leave the other children to bring it into hospital with him.

Dogherty had questioned two men working on Fred Cairns's mine. They said the kids had had a tough time since Maritana went bush; and Fred had gone out to try to find her and bring her back home. Maritana had a son before she took up with Fred Cairns. He got round with a tribe which hung round the Ninety Mile. Sometimes Maritana took the kids and went walk about with this son and the abos he knocked about with. But this time Maritana hadn't taken the kids with her, and that was what Fred was sore about: leaving him with a baby not a year old on his hands.

Fred had taken his car, these men told the detectives, and gone out towards the Ninety Mile. The troopers found his car in the bush a day or two later. The country was scoured for his tracks, or any clue to his whereabouts. But Fred Cairns had vanished as mysteriously as Maritana, leaving all those youngsters in the shack at Celebration to fend for themselves.

Of course there were the goats and fowls, half a bag of flour and some tins of jam in the hut, and the youngsters could have fed themselves for a while. But after a week or two, what would have become of them? Kalgoorla went out to look after the children. The baby was dead when she got there. There was an inquiry over the tiny body, and the police took charge of the rest of the Cairns kids. They were sent to orphanages and homes for neglected children in various parts of the State.

All sorts of theories as to the reasons for Maritana's desertion of her family were discussed. Most of them hinged on the idea that she had got the wind up about the police being on her tracks, or that the Big Four had scared her into taking cover until her threat to give evidence at Morris' trial was forgotten. 'Nasty accidents' had happened, but murder was almost unknown on the goldfields. Few people imagined there was anything sinister about Maritana's disappearance.

'Hear Maritana's done a moonlight flit,' men remarked casually to each other.

'And Fred Cairns is out lookin' for her—with a gun.'

'Bloody shame, leavin' a man with a swag of kids like that!'

'How about a man leaving a swag of kids on their own in the bush?'

After a week or so when the police had made no further progress with their investigations, interest in the affair died out.

It was almost forgotten when the news burst that Germany had declared war on Russia, general mobilisation had been ordered in France, British naval reserves were being called up, the fleet coaling and taking on provisions and munitions. The stock exchanges of the world closed. There were prayers for peace. Like a thunderbolt the announcement struck the goldfields: 'We are at war!'

People who had asked: 'What's a war in Europe got to do with Australia?' looked aghast. Sally knew some of the answers. She had heard them often enough; and yet it was difficult to realise that the causes of this war in Europe, which seemed so remote from Australia, were going to involve even men of these outback towns in the barbarous business of slaughter and death. 'I don't want my boys to kill any other mother's boys,' she said.

'Oh, God,' she cried desperately to herself, and to the other women who came running from houses along the street to talk to her, 'aren't there other ways than war to settle the differences between nations? Can't the politicians and statesmen of the big powers, if they've got any brains, do something better than send men out to murder each other in a quarrel between nations?'

'Damn them, I say! Damn and blast the whole lot of them!' Theresa Molloy cried. 'There's three of my lads gone up to the drill hall, already.'

'And my old man's cleaning the gun he got in the Boer War. If he can't have a crack at the Germans, he says, he can put up a fight for Australia if the Japs come here.'

Soon the flags were flying, bands playing 'Rule Britannia', and 'God Save the King'. Leading citizens made stirring speeches. Men of the 84th Infantry Goldfields Regiment, who turned out in uniform, were mobbed and cheered. Patriotic fervour rose in a tumultuous wave, sweeping excited crowds into a frenzy from which national passion and an heroic exultation drove all normal thinking. The windows of German smallgoods shops were broken, and any German or Austrian who had not yet been interned was hustled off to the police station, or to the military authorities. Sensational stories of spies and plans for sabotage of the reservoir and railway ran like wild fire through the town. Rumours of mysterious lights, and signalling from high buildings came up from the coast.

Lal went into camp, proud and happy to be regarding himself already as a soldier. Den gave him Moppingara, so that Lal could volunteer for overseas service with the Light Horse.

What was to be done about his father's business which he had been managing since Morris's arrest? Lal scarcely gave it a thought. He left it in charge of an old carpenter Morris had employed for years.

'It's all right, mum,' he said, impatiently. 'It'll be all right. Barney Allen can carry on.'

Sally could not blame Lal for thinking the war of more importance than the undertaking business. He was glad to get out of it anyway: had always wanted to be a soldier, and now his chance had come. Lal thought of the war as nothing but an opportunity for heroic deeds: something in which honour and glory were to be won. He had taken to military training, parades and camp routine like a duck to water, even during his days as a cadet in the citizen forces. They had been a pleasant change from the depressing business of measuring the dead and organising funerals. And, what a different person Lal was when he came home on leave for a few days—every inch the swashbuckling young warrior, in his smart uniform, striding about with spurs jingling, and emu feathers in his felt hat.

But Lal was satisfied he was doing what every able-bodied man ought to be doing, Sally told herself. He believed that the might of the German Empire had to be broken, and that Great Britain had to be supported in her resistance to a German bid for world domination.

Perhaps he was right, Sally conceded. If the defence of Australia depended on breaking the strength of the German navy and army overseas, then Australians were morally bound to fight with the British forces. But Australia must retain sufficient men to defend her own shores and inhabitants, people were soon saying. What had Australia to do with the death of an Austrian Archduke, and the plots of Serb patriots, the intrigues of German and Russian diplomacy?

There was more to it than that, Charley O'Reilly declared.

'The causes of war are economic, a struggle for markets and spheres of influence. The armament firms sool the nations on to blast hell out of each other in that struggle. War's their business. They make colossal profits out of it: are the bulwark of the capitalist system. The workers of Britain and Germany are just mugs to slaughter each other for the profit of the armament manufacturers —and the boss class.'

Sally was shocked when Dinny agreed with him. She could not bring herself to consider abstract theories about war, this war in particular.

The war for her was a crude fact, menacing the lives of her sons. She felt helpless to save them from it and yet, all the time, her mind was revolving in an anguish round ways and means of preventing them from being driven 'like sheep to the shambles', as Charley O'Reilly said.

To be sure, enlistments on the goldfields for the first expeditionary forces to be sent overseas were not as high as was expected. The Federal Government had promised twenty thousand trained men for this force, and volunteers were in camp. But few miners had signed up. Men on the Boulder were saying:

'What about Australia?'

It was all very well for Andy Fisher, the Prime Minister, to pledge 'the last man and the last shilling' for defence of the Empire. But all sorts of people were beginning to express an uneasy feeling that Australia might be left in the lurch, if a policy of denuding the country for overseas service were given free rein. After all Australia was a part of the Empire, local business men protested, and it was no secret that her defences were totally inadequate: equipment and man-power far short of what was required for effective resistance to enemy attack.

There were too many foreigners and working-class agitators on the goldfields, the recruiting officers complained. But Hughie Mahon, member for Kalgoorlie, had uttered a word of warning against war fever.

'War may be a fine game for princes and such like,' he said, 'But it is a poor one for the working class and the masses who fight.'

'Every old scoundrel on the Golden Mile is making the most of the war to blow his bags,' Dinny declared. 'They're gettin' a great kick out of talkin' about how they would be layin' down their lives for King and Country—if only they were a few years younger.'

'But they won't be layin' down their profits,' Bill Dally mumbled. 'It's all right soolin' the workers on to die for 'em. But nothin' doin' when it's a question of sharin' profits on the war with the men goin' to fight.'

'There was a meeting of unemployed at the Workers' Hall the night before war was declared.' Charley O'Reilly exclaimed. 'Did the patriots do anything about it? Not on your life. We could starve as far as they were concerned. But, now, they say: "There's a job for the unemployed." Let'm feed the guns. Let'm be bloody heroes and die for us.'

'Like hell, we will,' Barney Riordan muttered.

But the invasion of Belgium, and the cabled news of German atrocities, aroused deeper feeling in support of the war. Stories of the brutal massacre of unarmed villages, of a woman found bayoneted as she sat beside her sewing machine, and of an old man hanging from the rafters of his cottage, with a fire lighted beneath him, brought realisation of what a German victory might mean in any part of the world.

'A man can't sit back and let these bastards rule the roost,' men said to each other: men who didn't want to fight: who didn't want to surrender their personal rights to go into the army.

They walked off to the recruiting depots under an indefinable compulsion, obeying some instinct to take a stand against aggression and cruelty. There was a sober gallantry about these men. It was one of the bright threads in the stuff of which humanity was made that, at times of crises, men and women could show this spark of the divine, Sally thought. And a crime to misuse or abuse it.

Was it true, as Charley O'Reilly said, that they were poor fools being doped and bluffed by a well-known ruse to boost recruiting? Every nation, he maintained, would spread stories of barbarities and atrocities against the other. War, in itself, was a barbarity which was responsible for the German campaign of frightfulness. But scarcely anybody would listen to Charley by then. He and some of the I.W.W. boys were rough-handled and run out of town when they talked like that.

All the forts and military outposts on the Australian coast had been manned up to war strength. It was said that fifty thousand trained men were ready for home defence. But what did that amount to as a force capable of defending a country, the size of all the British islands and most of Europe, with a coastline of over twelve thousand two hundred miles?

Had the menace of Japan been forgotten? There's a treaty between Japan and Great Britain, hecklers at public meetings were told, and 'it is forbidden to mention Japan as a potential enemy'. Her treaty obligation would prevent Japan attacking Australia when Great Britain was at war. Treaty obligations? Had they prevented the Germans from invading Belgium? The 'scrap of paper' view of treaty obligations was becoming generally accepted.

'We've always been told the British navy's Australia's only protection against invasion,' Dinny growled. 'But with the British navy tied up in the North Sea, what are we going to do?'

'The battle for Australia is being fought in the North Sea—and in France and Belgium,' Lal exclaimed full of indignation and military bluster.

'Hope you're right, lad,' Dinny replied, smoking thoughtfully. 'But don't be bluffed into thinking it will end there.'

It was almost a comfort to Sally that Tom and Morris were safe from this war hysteria. She could not have imagined that she would ever regard their imprisonment as 'a blessing in disguise'.

It was hardly that, even now. But, at least, she reflected bitterly, Morris could not rush off and offer his services for defence of the Empire. Although, for so many years, he had lived on the fields and no longer dreamed of leaving them, he did not forget that he was an Englishman. His pride of race and loyalty to the Old Country might be taken for granted. During the Boer War, he could never endure any criticism of British policy, and although he was an old man now, Sally did not doubt he would be eager to serve in any capacity that might assist Great Britain to defeat her enemies.

Morris would expect his sons to feel as he did, she feared. Not only Lal. And military service had no attraction for Dick and Tom and Den. They would hate the war and every moment spent in training to take part in it. If it were necessary, they would go into the army, as a matter of duty, she thought. But she was terrified at the prospect of all her sons being caught up and swept away by the horrible business of war.

She had to remind herself continually, that Den was still at school and in no danger at present, and that Dick was going to be married in a few weeks. She hoped that his love for Amy and the responsibility of a home would weigh more heavily with Dick, than the appeals of recruiting sergeants, the everlasting incitement of the military bands, and those stories of disaster and atrocities with which the daily newspapers were full.

'Oh God,' she prayed, 'keep Dick out of this war.'

CHAPTER XXII

DURING those first months of the war, Sally felt as if she were living in a nightmare. She could not endure the military airs the town band used to play on marches through the streets. They were being used to stir up patriotic emotion and stimulate recruiting. Sally could only feel they were playing men to their death. Beneath the blare, and lively rhythm of the brassy music, she could hear the cries of the wounded and dying men on distant battlefields: the thunder of guns and the whine and crash of falling shells.

But with Lal in uniform, Sally found herself behaving like any other mother of a soldier. She had to believe that Lal was fighting in a good cause: that there would be no peace on earth until Germany was defeated, and Great Britain and France could make 'the world safe for democracy'. This was a war to end war, the newspapers were saying. Never again would the German war machine be permitted to disturb the peace of Europe. But now, when the Kaiser was making his bid for world power, the war must be fought until victory—and peace—were assured.

Sally worked for the Red Cross, joined a committee to send comforts to the troops and knitted khaki socks in every spare moment. Marie was knitting too. She confessed that her father did not believe the war was being fought for the reasons the governments of Great Britain and France and Russia had announced. But she was sorry for the poor boys who would be fighting through the terrible winter of Northern France. She could not rest unless she did something to relieve their suffering. After all, it was little enough one could do: to knit a few socks, give a few shillings. Maybe, it was a weakness in her character to support the war in any way, if she did not believe it was being fought for the reasons Great Britain and Russia put forward; but Marie admitted that she could not think clearly when the *sales* boches were over-running France.

Amy was all rapturous excitement about preparations for her wedding. Sally was glad of it, because she thought it would keep Dick's mind off the war and any claim it might have on him.

The bungalow at Mullingar was finished and furnished. Dick had been spending every evening and week-end up there, helping Amy to hang curtains, lay linoleum and install all their belongings. He was almost as delighted as she with the new cleanliness of everything, and the bright, pleasant homeliness of the place. They were going to be married in the Anglican Cathedral, much to Tim's disappointment, and a crowd of guests had been invited for a wedding breakfast, reception and dance at the 'Western Star'.

Amy dropped in to see Sally, now and then, on her way to Marie's for a dress fitting. Marie was making her wedding-dress and several new dresses for the trousseau.

'Tim wanted me to get my wedding dress up from Perth,' Amy

explained blithely. 'But I wouldn't hear of it. The managers' wives all say Mme Robbie's the best dressmaker they know. Her dresses are always smart and in good taste I think, don't you, Aunt Sally? She's made me the most adorable evening dress in ivory marquisette with a silver stripe, over eau de nil silk, and my going-away dress is to be blue-grey, sort of haze colour, and I've got the duckiest little hat with a blue and green cockade, to go with it.'

Amy chattered happily about the dresses Marie was making for her, the plain linens for everyday wear, and the afternoon frocks and evening dresses: the shoes and hats she must have to match, the gloves and handbags.

Amy was much more concerned about what her bridesmaids were to wear, than the war news which was extraordinarily depressing just then. Sally felt uneasy and conscience stricken about abetting Amy in all the lavish expenditure for her wedding, when every day the misery and suffering caused by the war were pressing more heavily on one's mind; warning of the grip they would presently take on conditions nearer home. But Amy must have bouquets of rosebuds and forget-me-nots for her bridesmaids sent up from Perth, with her bridal bouquet, in ice. Dick had ordered them, and a gold necklace and pendant for each bridesmaid. There were to be three of them, and Lal was to be best man if he could get away. If not Den would substitute for him.

'You must come and see my glory box,' she told Sally. 'It's full of the loveliest undies and household linen.'

To please her, Sally had gone to Amy's room at the 'Western Star', and exclaimed admiringly as Amy spread out innumerable embroidered traycloths, d'oyleys and hand towels, sheets and cushion covers, as well as the dainty undergarments she had collected to delight Dick's eyes.

Sally wished that Amy had not wanted such a big wedding. Dick too was disturbed when he heard Tim's plans for the reception, wedding breakfast and dance at the 'Western Star'. It was going to be a slap-up affair, Tim boasted. 'Nothing too good for his little girl!'

'Must we have so much fuss?' Dick asked ruefully.

'Oh, darling, we'll only be married once, and there's always a fuss about a wedding,' Amy replied, winding soft arms round his neck. 'I'm enjoying every minute of it, and so happy, I don't know whether I'm standing on my head or my heels.'

Dick seemed reconciled to the whirl of preparations for the wedding after that. At least he was taking part in them with good grace, until a white feather fluttered out of a letter Sally had brought him from the post box.

'I don't wonder,' Dick said slowly, looking at the feather.

'You're not going to let the crazy Janes who do that sort of thing upset you, are you?' Sally exclaimed.

'No,' Dick said. 'But if it wasn't up to me to marry Amy . . .'

'Dick!' Sally shied away from realising that what she dreaded was happening: the war was reaching out after Dick. 'What's the matter? Don't you love Amy? Don't you want to marry her?'

'Of course, I love Amy,' Dick said. 'But I'd rather not be getting married, just now.'

'Then, why . . .'

'Don't ask me, Sal-o-my.'

'Oh dear!' Sally paused to be sure that her chagrin did not distress him. 'If that's so, I wish Amy hadn't wanted such a flash wedding.'

'So did I,' Dick smiled ruefully. 'But as she wants it this way, I've just got to go through with it.'

Sally was not surprised that Dick and Amy had yielded to the imperious instinct of youth in their love-making. Of course, being well-brought-up young people, they should have waited indefinitely, until they were married, for the satisfaction of those instincts. But Sally doubted whether many young people did. Boys and girls matured early in the hot, dry climate: and, she suspected, experimented with those first thrills of sexual experience, quite naturally and carelessly. It was a mercy there were so few disasters. Now and then one heard of a girl 'in trouble', or a young couple 'beating the barrier'. But who cared, so long as the young couple concerned were prepared 'to do the right thing' by each other? Tim and Laura, of course, might accuse Dick of betraying their confidence where Amy was concerned. 'But,' Sally reflected, 'Laura at least knows her Amy.' She remembered that Laura had suggested what might happen if Dick and Amy were not married, quite soon, although such an idea had not entered Sally's head until then.

'Never mind, darling!' Sally was concerned only to reassure Dick. 'There's nothing to worry about, really. If people talk, by and by, what does it matter? You're both very young to be undertaking the responsibility of married life—that's all I'm bothered about. Although, after all, Amy's not any younger than I was when I ran away with your father.'

'That's a good omen.' Dick bent over to kiss her. 'Amy and I are going to settle down and be as happy as Larry—if only I can make enough dough to keep the family.'

'Of course you will,' Sally smiled to chase the last dubious shadow from his eyes. 'You've had a lot of expense, lately, what with fixing up the bungalow, presents, bouquets and booking rooms at the coast for your honeymoon. My cheque will help with that.'

'Your what?' Dick demanded.

'Father and mother of the bridegroom, cheque for £ 100,' Sally replied lightly.

She stood up and took a bank slip from an envelope on the mantelpiece.

Dick's hand trembled as he held it

'Oh, no you don't,' he cried, and tore the cheque in half.

Sally sat down in her chair.

'Very well,' she said. 'If that's the way you feel about it, I'll send it to Amy.'

'Sal-o-my!' He was on his knees beside her. 'How can I let you give me so much money? Every shilling toiled for and saved until it's like gold. And I've never done anything for you. Never helped you with Den, or given you the good time I meant to.'

'My precious,' Sally folded the dear, dark head in her arms. 'You have been the joy of my life. To make things a little easier for you is the greatest happiness I could have.'

Next day, she took out the dress she was going to wear at Dick's wedding. What a long time ago, it seemed, since she had started to make some alterations in it. That very afternoon the detectives had called. All the trouble and misery of Morris's and Tom's arrest followed. She had bundled the dress away then and forgotten about it. Now, it was only a few days before the wedding, and she almost wept when she saw the little jagged holes silverfish had nibbled in the stiff black silk.

'Never mind,' Sally told herself, 'people only look at the bride at a wedding. Nobody'll notice me.'

She was happier about Dick. He looked happier and more settled in his mind. His marriage, she thought, would bring out all Dick's finest qualities: his tenderness and that protectiveness which as an elder brother he had always shown to the younger boys. Sally was sure Dick would not lightly let anything interfere with his obligations to Amy.

Her thoughts flew away rejoicing at the prospect of Dick's happiness, as she sat darning the holes in her dress to wear at his wedding. But over those thoughts swarmed sad and bitter ones, grieving that Morris and Tom could not be there: fearful and troubled thoughts for Lal, who had sent word that he would not be present either. Soon he would be going overseas into the very midst of battles and bombardments—the hellish chaos of war. Sally trembled, trying not to let her mind dwell on it.

Her fingers went on stitching. Den would have to be Dick's best man instead of Lal. She had ordered a new suit for him, a white shirt, patent leather dancing pumps. Den had been learning to dance and was in a stew already about whether he would remember all the things a best man ought to do for Dick.

Tom's first letter from jail, Sally reminded herself, had asked her to buy a wedding present for Dick and Amy from him. The dear lad, he had left several signed cheques on his Savings Bank account for her to fill in and use if she needed them!

Tom and Morris were permitted to write only one letter a month from jail; and a short one at that. Morris's letter had been very formal and constrained, telling her nothing except that he was 'as well as could be expected under the circumstances' and not to worry on his account. He hated writing letters, Sally knew. She had received only one or two from him in all her married life; and they were all just the same, stark brief communications of which the best part was the signature: 'your loving husband, Morris'. She smiled as she thought of it. Morris had never wished her to forget that he was her husband and that he loved her.

Tom's letter was written obviously with the intention of cheering her. He was 'fit and full of beans', he said: 'quite enjoying his sojourn by the seaside'. He was sunburnt and had put on weight. Hard labour in the open air was a picnic after working underground. The hardest thing to get used to, being locked up in a cell, after the day's work, and lights out at nine o'clock. If only he could find something worth reading in the library, 'stone walls would not a prison make, nor iron bars a cage'.

A black and white butterfly fluttered across the courtyard, one evening. Tom had watched it sail away over the prison wall, his thoughts flying with it, right back home to hover beside her.

But Tom was thinking of someone else too. She must be a good deal in his mind, Sally reflected, and wondered how much, because Tom had written:

'I wish you'd go to see Nadya Owen, some day, before you come down for your visit next month, mum. She's ill, was to go to the sanatorium, and I'd like to know how she is.'

And then there was a message for other friends: 'Give Charley and Eily all of the best from me, and Barney Riordan, Peter Lalich and any of the boys you come across. I'm O.K., mum,' Tom wound up. 'Don't worry about me. But I'll be glad to see dad out of this place. It's harder for him than for me. I wish something could be done to make things easier for him.'

Sally had seen Mr. Sloan, but he seemed to have lost interest in the case, and could only advise her to obtain medical evidence that

Morris was unfit for laborious work. She had done this and written to the member for the district asking him to arrange for any possible concessions to be made by the prison authorities on Morris's behalf. She intended going down to Fremantle, to visit Morris and Tom after Dick's wedding.

When Dinny read Tom's letter, Sally had asked him to tell any of Tom's friends that he was well and in good heart. But why should Tom have asked her to go to see Mrs. Owen? It was going to be a little awkward, Sally thought. Was she to assume that Tom was in love with this woman? She had heard the gossip, but did not attach any importance to it. Clearly, though, Nadya Owen was on Tom's mind and a matter of tender concern to him.

Of course, she must go to see Nadya, Sally told herself. But she had delayed going until she could feel less perturbed at the idea of Tom having an attachment for a married woman. Perhaps it was no more than an idealistic devotion he gave this strange, foreign woman. She was so much older than he, and how a could a woman with a husband and children ever bring Tom any real happiness?

What would she say to Nadya? How would Nadya receive her visit? As condonation of the understanding between her and Tom? Sally resolved that she must try not to give that impression. And yet she did not wish to interfere. It would be unfair to take advantage of Tom's imprisonment to interfere in his personal affairs.

So hot, it was, that afternoon, Sally put aside her sewing to make a cup of tea. There was a knock on the door and she opened it to see Nadya Owen standing there in the glittering, white light.

Nadya was a short, rather thick-set woman, with brilliant hazel eyes and lank, fair hair. But Sally realised the charm of her unusual personality as soon as her eyes lighted to a smile and she said, brusquely, but with beguiling candour:

'Mr. Quin has told me that you were coming to see me before you go to Fremantle, Mrs. Gough. I thought it might save you some trouble if I came to you.'

Nadya's voice was husky. She looked ill. Her face was the colour of greasy paper.

'It was good of you,' Sally said, a little defensively. 'Tom was anxious to know how you are. I'm afraid you're not well enough to have walked over here in the heat.'

In the sitting-room Nadya sank into an armchair.

'I'm all right,' she replied, struggling for breath. 'At least, right enough to do that.'

'Mrs. Owen,' Sally said impetuously. 'What is there between you and Tom?'

Nadya was lying back in the chair with her eyes closed.

'Oh, please,' she said wearily, 'do not ask that? It is not necessary. How could it be?'

After a moment, she continued: 'I do not understand, myself, what there is between Tom and me. But it is not as you think. A great idea gives us much sympathy and understanding. Me, I am what you call a fanatic about socialism. And Tom is young and strong. A good man for the working class.'

A thin irritating cough caught and strangled the slow hoarse voice.

'You see,' Nadya whispered, 'you have nothing to fear from me. If Tom thinks he loves me, it will pass. I am not young, or beautiful —and doomed.'

'I'm sorry.' Sally glimpsed the tragic necessity that had brought Nadya to her. 'I didn't mean . . .'

'Don't be sorry.' Nadya's voice was grave, although it had an inflection of irony, as if she were amused by Sally's attempt to say that she did not believe there had been anything 'wrong' between Tom and herself. 'I feel just as you do about anything that could hurt Tom. His life will be of more value than mine. I have had the happiness of showing him how to make good use of it. That is enough. Tell him I said so, some day, will you?'

'But, surely . . .' Sally faltered. 'Why not tell him yourself?' she wanted to say, but the words would not come.

Nadya understood why.

'I do not deceive myself,' she said quietly. 'The day after to-morrow I go to the sanatorium. If I did not know it would be less painful for Claude and the children this way, I would not go. Most likely, I will not see them again, or Tom—unless there.'

Sally could not make any of the usual foolish optimistic remarks when a woman was facing her end with such matter-of-fact simplicity. As if to spare her too acute an awareness of that shadow of death, Nadya went on, forcing her voice to a casual lightness:

'It is a vile disease, this phthisis of the throat; but let's not talk of it any more. There is something else I want to speak to you about.'

Sally made tea, and while they were drinking it from the best cups which Sally had produced as evidence to herself that she was being very nice to Mrs. Owen for Tom's sake, Nadya said, with her queer, brilliant smile:

'I wish we had met long ago.'

'So do I.' Sally was at her ease now and curious to discover how this woman's mind worked. 'I've wanted to know more about your ideas.'

'My ideas?' Nadya replied, with good-humoured irony. 'About

the working-class movement and socialism? They're not so much *my* ideas, as Dinny and Tom would tell you. But simple enough. I believe that the land and anything in it or on it, belongs to the people. It's as much theirs as the air and sunshine; but it has been stolen from them, by all sorts of tricks, through the ages. Now that we know this, we must organise to make the masses of the people, the workers, strong enough to claim what belongs to them, and build a new economic system, based on their ownership. That will mean a few men cannot hold property and wealth, and use everybody else to serve their interests. The people will own and administer the affairs of their own countries, in the interests of the many, not of the few.'

'But must there be a revolution to bring it about?' Sally asked anxiously.

'Revolution means change—fundamental change in our way of life,' Nadya said gravely. 'At every stage of history when a new social order has begun there have been forces opposed to it. I don't believe that reforms we get under the capitalist system make much difference to all the injustice and deprivations the working people suffer. Our economic system has to be changed from the basis of capitalism to the basis of socialism before there can be any hope for men and women to enjoy their full rights as human beings: live at peace with each other and other nations. Can it be done without a bitter struggle?'

'Perhaps not,' Sally admitted. 'But I can't believe this ideal state of things will ever happen.'

Nadya's eyes flamed.

'The historic role of the working class is to make it happen,' she said.

Her faith in the accomplishment of this colossal, almost super-human task, appalled Sally.

'What about the war?' she said weakly. 'Hasn't it put back the hopes of socialists for a century? The workers of France, Germany, Russia, Austria—and Australia, are all slaughtering each other. For what? To defend their national systems of government—capitalist systems.'

'I don't know.' Nadya's face became heavy and dull, as she thought. 'At first, I felt it was like the end of the world, this war. I was in despair. It seemed to have swept all our efforts to ensure solidarity for the workers—a sense of international brotherhood—into the chaos of the past. But,' and her face changed as if a light were glowing behind it, 'now, I feel sure, in Russia at least, there will be an attempt to overthrow the Tsarism and bring about a new social order. After the war with Japan, my father and I were work-

ing for it. He was killed, and some friends arranged for my escape
. . . I was supposed to be "a dangerous revolutionary". A girl of
eighteen. Hard to believe, isn't it? And now I'm just a piece of
driftwood—out of the revolutionary movement and of no use at all.'

'Oh dear,' Sally exclaimed. 'I can't understand your wanting
to be in it.'

'What's the use of living,' Nadya cried passionately, 'if you
can't any longer serve the greatest cause on earth? If you can't
work to free humanity from injustice and degradation?'

A fit of coughing exhausted her, and she slumped back in her
chair.

'You mustn't excite yourself like that,' Sally said, giving her a
glass of water. 'I shouldn't have let you talk so much.'

Presently Nadya was smiling. 'It's nothing,' she said huskily.
'I wanted to ask you—do you know Eily O'Reilly?'

'When she was a child,' Sally remembered. 'Tom brought her
home, with a pet kid he'd rescued from a Slav barbecue.'

'She is a fine girl, and very fond of him,' Nadya said. 'She
would like to come to see you, I know.'

'I'd like her to come,' Sally said, reproaching herself for not
having been more interested in Tom's friends.

'I will tell her,' Nadya promised. 'We have worked a lot together
and I hope that so good a young comrade and Tom will find happiness with each other, some day.'

'You're very brave, my dear!' Sally could not help saying.

'I? No!' Nadya's face was thoughtful and serene. 'I love them
both. That is all.'

She looked satisfied that her mission, whatever it was, in coming
to Sally had been accomplished. Perhaps, Sally thought, Nadya
had wanted to clear away any misunderstanding which gossip about
her friendship with Tom might have caused. She had done so.
Their emotion for each other had remained something powerful and
obscure which must not be allowed to affect their individual lives,
Sally imagined. The selflessness and gallantry of Nadya's devotion
to the working-class movement was responsible for that, no doubt;
but Sally could still only think that Nadya was obsessed by a wild,
hopeless dream.

'Do you feel well enough to go home alone? she asked anxiously
when Nadya was leaving. 'Shall I come with you?'

'No, no.' Nadya moved away, as if she could no longer endure
the pity and vague hostility of Sally's glance. 'I feel better for
the rest—and our talk.'

She had gone then with a fleeting smile and quiet 'Good-bye.'

CHAPTER XXIII

EILY came next Saturday afternoon, looking fresh and pretty in a blue frock that matched her eyes: a straw hat blown awry on a tumble of dark hair. She had ridden over from Boulder on her bicycle and lost some hairpins on the way.

'Oh, Mrs. Gough,' she explained shyly, 'Nadya said that you would like me to come, and I did want to, because . . .'

'Of course, Tom's friends want to hear how he is,' Sally said, liking the girl immediately, her simplicity, and directness. 'Come in and I'll show you his letter. I've only had one, and he can't tell us much; but I'm sure he'd like you to see it.'

Eily murmured a flustered 'thank you': snatched off her hat and made a futile attempt to tidy her hair. Sally took her to the back verandah where she was plucking a big, white drake for dinner next day. She gave Tom's letter to Eily, and went on pulling feathers out of the bird. He was a great-grandfather, she explained apologetically, and bound to be as tough as old boots if she did not put him on to simmer for a long time. Besides there were too many flies about to leave the job half done.

When Eily had finished reading Tom's letter, she looked at it as if it were a holy relic, exclaiming:

'He's wonderful, Tom, isn't he?'

Sally was taken aback: a little amused by this hero-worship of Tom. She had never thought of a girl feeling like that about her dear, good, stolid Tom. Even Amy, although she was so much in love with Dick, did not speak of him with such bated breath, such pride, and a curiously impersonal admiration.

Nadya had spoken of Tom in the same way. What was it made Tom's friends so devoted to him? These two women both loved him. Each in her own fashion, and yet with something between them which inspired their affection for Tom: his for them. Was it because they regarded him as a champion of the things they believed in? 'A grand young battler for the working class,' as Dinny said.

To her, Tom was just a good son, Sally reflected. She remembered the quick-witted and practical way Tom had acted to get that gold out of sight before Morris could be arrested, and had been forced into the position of bearing a burden and blame he should not have had to carry. She knew in doing that he had been thinking most of her: saving her worry and distress. Always she had been able to rely on Tom in domestic emergencies: had accepted his services as a matter of course. Never quite realising them for what they

173

were, perhaps: an indication of a noble nature, capable of great things. Nadya and Eily honoured Tom for just those qualities his mother had not sufficiently appreciated. Sally reproached herself for it.

She was grateful to Eily for loving Tom with such youthful ardour: making no attempt to keep it out of her eyes.

'Yes, Tom is wonderful,' Sally said. 'I'm glad you think so, Eily.'

Eily blushed. Yes, it really was a naïve girlish blush that crept under her tough, sun-tanned skin, Sally perceived.

'I didn't mean . . .' Eily tried to explain. 'I've got no right to let you think Tom and I are sweethearts, Mrs. Gough—or ever were, as some people imagine. Tom doesn't feel like that about me at all, or care for anybody just for themselves. The working-class movement is all he cares about, really. I love him for that as much as anything. So does Nadya.'

'It sounds rather complicated,' Sally said dryly.

Eily had begun to pluck the duck, as if it were quite natural for her to share in any work that was being done.

'But it isn't,' Eily looked up in surprise. 'Nadya and I are comrades. She knows I love Tom, and I know—he thinks the world of her. But that doesn't matter, because we're all working for the same thing. I don't wonder everybody, who knows her, adores Nadya. Dad says her mind is like a pure flame burning in her body—though they don't agree politically in lots of ways.'

'Don't they?' Sally replied lightly. 'That's a pity.'

Eily could not allow a matter of such importance to be treated with sly jesting.

'You see, dad's an old member of the I.W.W. and doesn't believe in political action,' she said seriously. 'And Nadya says the workers must be organised politically and industrially before they can assume power.'

'It's beyond me.' Sally brushed away a fly that had settled on her perspiring forehead, as if she were brushing away the whole subject. 'I've never had time to do anything but run a boarding-house, and look after my husband and children. Maybe, some day, I'll be able to study politics and economics, like you and Mrs. Owen. At present, I can only think of Morris and Tom in jail, and Lal in the army, and wonder what's going to become of Dick and Den.'

Eily's blue eyes darkened to her sympathy.

'I know. It's been dreadful for you, lately,' she said. 'But soon Tom will be home again—and things won't seem so difficult.'

Tom. It was all Tom, as far as this girl was concerned, Sally thought, and smiled at Eily's confidence in Tom's ability to dispose

174

of all one's troubles. But there had been something very moving in Eily's warm and generous response to her rather grumpy excuse for not wishing to discuss matters about which Eily was better informed than she was, Sally recognised. She chided herself and her smile delighted Eily.

'That's right,' she said briskly. 'I've got nothing to growl about, really. The war and this heat have got on my nerves, that's all. Did you ever see a duck with so many feathers?'

'I'll finish it,' Eily said eagerly. 'Do sit back and rest a bit.'

Sally sat back and watched the girl's slim brown fingers pull out the tiresome fluff and tough tail feathers until the old drake lay clean and naked between them.

'I'm going to finish him,' Eily declared.

'Oh no, it's a nasty job,' Sally protested.

But Eily picked up a newspaper and knife. Kneeling beside the tank, she quickly yanked out the entrails, washed the bird, and took it back to Sally in triumph.

'There,' she said happily, 'I am quite a good slushy, aren't I?'

Sally had cleared away the feathers and got afternoon tea ready while Eily was busy with the duck. They sat talking over their tea, about the restaurant where Eily worked, her family and Tom. Always the conversation came round to Tom: what he had said and done on various occasions, mostly industrial and political, or in connection with the Workers' Rights Committee and the secretarial work Eily was doing for him.

'Come again, dear,' Sally said, when Eily jumped up in a hurry, saying she must not be late for a meeting. 'I'll be glad to see you.'

'Oh, I will,' Eily promised and ran off as if this visit had been all excitement and pleasure for her.

Sally wished she had made it pleasanter: not let it be mixed up with the duck which had spattered Eily's clean, blue dress with gore. But she guessed that Eily had been happy just to talk about Tom, and find his mother amiably disposed towards her.

'She's a good girl, Eily,' Dinny said, when they were talking about Eily's visit. 'I reckon Tom could do worse.'

'So do I,' Sally agreed. 'And she's quite good looking, Dinny. I liked her blue eyes, untidy hair and guilelessness—though she thinks she knows such a lot.'

'She does, too!' From Dinny's little chuckle you would have fancied it was rather a joke. 'Eily's read every book her father's got he says, and can give him points in an argument.'

'It's a shame for a young girl to be so wrapped up in politics— all that stuff.' Sally sounded quite indignant.

'Better than being a flibbertigibbet.' Dinny's glance was shrewd

175

and quizzical. 'When did you start thinking it was a mistake for a girl to learn all she could and use her brains, missus?'

'I don't know. It's this war, I suppose,' Sally cried, disconcerted by Dinny shooting such a question at her. 'It's got me all worked up and muddled, Dinny. With Lal in it, I am too—and I just can't endure people putting on superior airs and making out the war's a bloody farce. As far as I can see, we've got to go through with it.'

'But you don't want Den and Dick to join up.'

'No,' Sally admitted miserably.

In those days before Dick's wedding the war news was bad. The British armies in Northern France had met with disaster after disaster, and the first Australian troops had sailed for active service abroad. Sally was in a ferment for fear Lal might be sent away before she could go down to the coast to say good-bye to him. As soon as the wedding was over, she promised herself that she would go down to Fremantle to see Morris and Tom, and this would be an opportunity for spending a few days with Lal.

Through the whirl of preparations for Dick's wedding, and her anxieties for Lal, she thought a good deal about Eily and Mrs. Owen: the new interests they had given her and the insight into Tom's character which she owed to them. But she had almost forgotten Maritana, and Kalgoorla's search for her, until Kalgoorla stalked into the yard. Then it all came back, the suffocating sense of something horrible and fatal behind Maritana's disappearance and desertion of her children.

Kalgoorla's eyes were bloodshot and smouldering: her heavy, dark face working under a passion of rage and grief.

'Find'm Meeri,' she muttered brokenly. 'Bin find'm bones and dress, down shaft longa Goongarrie track.'

CHAPTER XXIV

As she dressed for Dick's wedding Sally could not get Maritana out of her mind. Kalgoorla was wailing in the yard, and odds and ends of the talk that she had been hearing all day kept rattling through her brain.

That very morning, the *Miner* described how Kalgoorla had led the police to an abandoned shaft on the track to Goongarrie. She had been prowling round every old shaft for miles around, it was stated, fearing that her daughter who had mysteriously disappeared three months ago, had been the victim of foul play. When she found an old shoe, and the shreds of a green dress among prickly bushes which had grown up beside deserted workings of the Santa Lucia mine, the police were informed. An experienced miner, lowered into the shaft, discovered the body of a native woman under a heap of loose earth which had been dislodged from the surface. The body was in a horrible state of decomposition; but a green dress still clung to the skeleton, and a necklace of coloured beads hung round the neck. Although the face had rotted away, Kalgoorla and several other natives identified the body as that of an aboriginal woman, known as Maritana. Sergeant Dogherty, who had charge of the case, was conducting further investigations.

The town was agog with the news: everybody talking about it. Most people believed that Maritana's death was linked up with the racket in stolen gold. There was no doubt she had been connected with it: perhaps knew too much. All sorts of mutterings could be heard about the reasons for her disappearance. Maritana's outburst after the first day of Morris's trial had not been forgotten. That it had probably got her into hot water with certain rough customers who handled stuff for the big buyers was the general opinion.

Sally knew the feeling of most people on the fields about gold stealing. She knew all the undercurrents which would be stirred and contending against each other in the business of finding a scapegoat.

The miners who managed to bring up a few 'weights or ounces, now and then, did not regard themselves as criminals. They said that what they lifted was a flea-bite compared with what men in more responsible positions grabbed; and, the miners argued, they were entitled to get back on the mining companies because of the way a working man was exploited to produce profits. Every miner knew the mining companies resorted to all manner of illegal tricks to filch the time, labour and rights of men dependent on them for a living. This amounted to robbery on a large scale; but for the most part went unchallenged.

Nevertheless the traffic in stolen gold had grown to such proportions, that business men in the town declared it played an important part in local prosperity: kept money on the fields and paying bills. So operations of the Big Four had come to be regarded as a subsidiary of the industry. Where the illicit trade began and ended no one could say, except the Four perhaps; and their identity was unknown. But it was generally believed that some mining men with big reputations had also a stake in the illicit trade. For that reason, while prosecutions against miners for stealing small amounts of gold were common enough, a threat to expose important figures in the mining world created consternation. Anything likely to shake the confidence of shareholders and precipitate a fall in mining securities, struck at the stability of everyday life in Kalgoorlie and Boulder; and must be avoided at any cost.

Maritana's disappearance had been a relief to many business men in both townships. They understood well enough why it was advisable to suppress her evidence. Of course, Paddy Cavan had saved the situation for himself and his associates by ensuring that no more was heard of Maritana's attack on him; but other interests were served as well. Nobody held a brief for Paddy himself, and most people realised a personal grouch was responsible for the charges laid against Morris and Tom. It was tough luck they had been caught napping, men said casually, attaching no importance to the matter. But several stout citizens, mine managers and shop-keepers, breathed more freely when the Gough case was disposed of.

You had to hand it to Mr. Cavan, Morris's lawyer had remarked. The man had his head screwed on all right. His ingenuity, or low-cunning, whichever you liked to call it, had the quality of genius. He had made an extraordinary position for himself in mining affairs, obviously: would go far. There was nothing to stop him, now that he had a controlling interest in an important group of mines.

It was considered a shrewd move on Paddy's part to leave the goldfields immediately after Morris and Tom had gone to jail, although everybody was astounded when his agent announced that Mr. Cavan had been called to London to confer with his directors on important business.

Paddy was well out of the way before any suggestion arose that Maritana had not just gone bush rather than appear in the police court again. But when Maritana's body was found, people were shocked and horrified into wondering what he had to do with the crime.

'Paddy knew what had happened, and skipped before he could be blamed,' men were saying round the mines and the pubs.

'That's what it amounts to, I reckon,' Bill Dally declared. 'Paddy gave his orders, Maritana's mouth was to be shut—and it was shut all right.'

A good many men who were 'in the know', he told Sally, and had sold a bit of gold to Maritana, occasionally, 'wouldn't have it on their minds' that there was any put-up job to get rid of her. They said Fred Cairns and Maritana might have had a bust up. He had laid her out 'accidental-like', then got scared and tried to dispose of the body.

But if any man could give information which would lead to the arrest of Fred Cairns, or throw any light on the cause of Maritana's death, he was dumb. An uneasy feeling was being experienced, however, that the racket was getting too hot for the comfort of a working miner. This new Inspector on the Gold Stealing Detection Staff looked as if he meant what he said about cleaning up the whole business, and the big boys were getting windy. The stink about Maritana's death had caused two or three treatment plants in the bush to pack up and vanish.

'There's no harm in gettin' away with a bit of gold,' Bill Dally growled. 'But it's over the fence, if blokes in the game'll come at murder to cover their tracks.'

'The dogs on the Boulder are barking what's behind it all,' Dinny said. 'But nobody's telling the police. . . .'

Den and Dinny were in a great state of excitement as they, too, dressed for Dick's wedding. They kept coming to Sally for assist-ance with their studs and white bow ties. Barbered and shaved, in his brand new turn-out, Dinny looked almost as spic and span as Den, with his well-oiled head and ruddy face held stiffly over the hard, white shirt and high, peaked collar he was wearing for the first time. Den was very pleased with his appearance: looked years older in his new navy suit, a white carnation in the buttonhole: struggled frantically into the white gloves he was supposed to wear as Dick's best man.

Dick himself was not so excited, or feeling so important, although he had been singing the Yeoman's Wedding Song, and shouting light-heartedly to Dinny and Den all the time he was dressing, warning them not to forget this and that, or to run away with the bride if he were late for the ceremony. But Dick, too, had to be helped with his tie, and a shoe-lace had broken at the last minute. Sally hunted desperately for another, and finally took one from a pair of her own shoes.

At last they were all ready. And surely no bridegroom ever looked happier or more handsome than Dick in his dress suit and shining white shirt! Sally laughed at the sartorial elegance of her escort: she had never felt such an insignificant little wren, she said. But Dick said: 'You look marvellous, Sal-o-my!' So nothing else mattered.

And indeed, Sally flattered herself, that old black silk dress with its full skirts, and the bertha of ecru lace, Marie lent her to wear, was still becoming. The spray of red roses Dick had given her made it quite picturesque. They had come up from Perth with his bouquet for Amy and the bridesmaids' posies. The sweetness of his thought drifted about her like the fragrance of the roses.

In the crowded church, neighbours and friends—all the people of Kalgoorlie and Boulder who had known Amy and Dick since they were children—craned their necks and buzzed with excitement, waiting for the bride to appear. They dearly loved a wedding, and Amy Brierly's wedding to Dick Gough promised to be a social event nobody wanted to miss.

The guests could be recognised by their party clothes, and were a target for criticism before the bridal party arrived. Sally guessed her own old dress and Dinny's new suit would not escape comment.

'You'd've thought she'd sport a new dress for her son's wedding!' she heard somebody whisper. And: 'Cripes, look at Dinny Quin dressed up like a sore finger!'

But Dick had won the women's hearts as he stood waiting for Amy.

'Looks the part, doesn't he?' a fat, middle-aged woman gurgled. 'Wouldn't mind marryin' Dick Gough, meself.'

Then Amy's procession from the church door to 'The Voice that Breathed o'er Eden', wheezed out by an organ which had suffered from years of heat and dust, provided the spectacle everybody was anticipating. Amy looked demure and lovely in her white satin gown, mists of tulle floating about her; and each bridesmaid in her big hat and flounced frock of pale blue organdie clutched a posy of pink rosebuds with suitable agitation, while Tim McSweeney, bursting with pride to be acting father to the bride, and uneasy in his conscience about setting foot in the Anglican cathedral, the groomsmen all red in the face and looking as if they would choke in their stiff white collars, rocked the whole congregation with a desire to chuckle and chiack.

It was hot and stuffy in the church. Sally was glad when, after the ceremony, she and Dinny and Marie could walk along to the 'Western Star' together.

Receiving their guests in the lounge at the hotel, Dick and Amy were as radiant a young couple as you would wish to see. That was what everybody said. Young, good-looking and in love! What luck they had to be setting out on their trot in double harness with so much in their favour! People chattered and exclaimed about marriage in general: their own marriages in particular. Few men and women had any illusions about their own experience. But a wedding was a good excuse to make merry at somebody else's expense.

Tim McSweeney was in his element dispensing a lavish hospitality; and delighted to number notabilities of the city among the guests guzzling his champagne and partaking of an excellent dinner.

'Tim's doing his step-daughter well,' a raucous voice struck Sally through noisy chatter after the toasts.

Bob Dowsett was talking to Mrs. Archie Malleson sitting beside him.

Mr. Dowsett had become manager of one of Paddy Cavan's mines. He was bald and paunchy now. Mrs. Malleson's yellow, buck teeth made her smile more formidable than ever.

'He adores her, of course,' Mrs. Archie replied brightly, as if Tim's idiosyncrasy were rather a joke. 'They say he'll leave Amy all his money.'

'Dick Gough's doin' pretty well for himself, all right,' Mr. Dowsett gurgled jocosely. 'She's a pretty, little thing, Amy. Hot stuff some of the boys say.'

Sally stared at the speakers, stiff-backed and indignant.

'My God, Mrs. Gough must have overheard us,' Ada Malleson drawled to her partner.

There were other mine managers, as well as municipal councillors, bank managers, prosperous shopkeepers and their wives, seated at the long tables, and a host of young people who were Dick's and Amy's friends. Sally saw Marie and Dinny and Mrs. Molloy at the far end of a table near the door; Theresa resplendent in purple satin, and Marie, aloof and elegant in a dove-grey evening gown she had worn on many other occasions. These three were the only representatives of the old prospecting fraternity who might have expected to be invited to the wedding of Alf Brierly's daughter and Morrey Gough's son.

Sally realised that most of the guests were strangers to her, although she had a slight acquaintance with some. She contrived to keep a polite conversation with the clergyman who sat beside her; and with all the important personages Tim presented to her in the lounge, before he bustled away to see that the tables were cleared and the dining-room transformed into a ballroom.

It was necessary for her to be Mrs. Morris Fitz-Morris Gough, and carry herself with serene dignity, Sally told herself. She could not allow these people at Dick's wedding to imagine his family was suffering any humiliation by Morris's absence, to-night. So she smiled and replied amiably to every banal remark about 'the young couple', wondering why people uttered the same common-places over and over again.

A sharp pain bit and gnawed at her heart with the strain of it all. She knew that men in the mining world, with whom she talked politely, could make or break Dick as suited their purposes; and that all their seemingly good-natured banter and toasting of 'health, wealth and happiness, good luck and good hunting', to the newly married pair, would mean actually nothing, if ever the need arose for helping Dick to earn a decent living.

Sally tried to throw off the bitter thoughts seething in her brain, and an insidious depression invading her participation in the gaiety about her.

'You are tired, chérie,' Marie murmured, coming to sit beside her when the dancing was at its height. 'I know how it is with you. But we must not spoil Dick's happiness.'

'I'm trying not to think of anything else,' Sally told her. 'But if only Morris and Tom were here, and Lal. . . .'

'They would want you to be glad for Dick,' Marie said.

'Oh I am,' Sally cried. 'Dick has always loved Amy, and it's good to think all this just means their happiness together. In the sorrow and trouble of the world to-day, at least they will have had to-night, Marie. But I hate having to look pleasant and talk to men like Bob Dowsett and Mr. Archibald Malleson. They are working hand in glove with Paddy Cavan these days, everybody knows.'

Marie's little laugh fluttered. 'It was so droll—Dinny and I watched them speaking to you. They were very uncomfortable, darr-ling.'

Laura trundled across the room and sat down beside them. Marie moved away, aware that Laura would prefer to have these few moments to herself with Sally.

She was fat, and tightly corseted into her blue brocaded satin gown: still handsome, though her faded eyes looked out from a flabby, unhappy face.

'Don't blame me for this mob, Sally,' Laura said petulantly. 'Tim and Amy thought it would be good for Dick to have influential men at his wedding. They might be useful to him some day.'

'I hope he won't ever have to depend on their good graces,' Sally said.

Laura's dreamy gaze went back over the years. 'They weren't much use to Alf, were they?'

It was then Colonel de Morfé joined them. He had arrived too late for dinner; just come up from camp on business, he said, and rushed in to wish the youngsters good luck and a good innings.

'They'll be delighted, I'm sure,' Laura said coldly. She rose, glancing back at Sally. 'Excuse me, dear, I must send Amy off to change her dress.'

'Laura's never forgiven me for queering Alf's pitch on the Midas,' Frisco remarked cynically.

'Neither have I,' Sally told him.

'All's fair in love and gold,' Frisco laughed. 'You've got to fight ruthlessly, or go under, Sally. Haven't you realised that yet? Won't you ever realise it.'

'It's better to go under than flourish on such a rotten code,' Sally replied.

'Game to the last,' Frisco mocked. 'But where's your sense of humour, Mrs. Gough? You should have observed that fighting according to the rules of big business isn't always a flourishing proposition. Take me, for example! I've fought and lost that way. But am still gambling on a come-back through this war, Oh, playing the hero, of course, fighting for King and Country!'

'You wouldn't lose sight of that,' Sally said.

'I'm a blackguard. You were quite right, Sally. Remember you told me once: "You're a blackguard. You'll always be a blackguard, Frisco."'

The derisive familiarity of his manner was infuriating.

'I don't wish to speak to you, Colonel de Morfé,' Sally said.

'But I wish to speak to you, my dear.' Frisco drew a sardonic satisfaction from the blaze of her eyes and heightened colour. 'In fact, my only reason for coming to-night was to see you, Sally.'

Sally could not forgive him for having failed to help Morris and Tom; but her heart quailed at the thought that he was going into the midst of the war and its dangers.

'Confidentially, and strictly between ourselves,' Frisco said, 'the Australian Expeditionary Forces have got their marching orders.'

'Lal will be going, too?' Sally cried.

'I suppose so.' Frisco sobered to her distress. 'You're such a damned maternal little creature, Sally. But still the most fascinating woman in the world to me.'

'Damned maternal! Is that what I am?'

'And my beautiful bitch of a wife refuses to have children.'

'You have a son you've never acknowledged,' Sally reminded him.

'God, yes,' Frisco brooded.

As if his brooding had conjured it out of the past, through the music and noise of laughter, chatter and shuffle of dancing feet, they could hear somebody singing: 'Oh Maritana, wild wood flower.' It was only an old drunk in the bar, Sally realised. The men had been talking about Maritana, no doubt, and somebody remembered that song Frisco used to sing when she was a wild young thing, as shy and graceful as a rock wallaby.

Frisco's lean features were wrung as though by the same memory. He averted his eyes from Sally's.

'You don't think I had anything to do with that horrible business, Sally,' he asked harshly.

'Not directly.'

183

'Sally, I swear . . .' Frisco tried to detain her as she moved away, 'that I didn't know Maritana was in any danger. Fred was fond of her. She was happy enough with him. Who could have believed she would go off the handle like that, and threaten to blow the gaff on the gold buying?'

'No,' Sally said slowly. 'I couldn't have imagined a native girl would have more guts than any of the white men who knew more than she did. But they've punished her—and you're as much responsible as anyone, Colonel de Morfé, if you knew she was to be scared into keeping her mouth shut, to protect the criminals who rigged that case against Tom and Morris.'

She left him then, with his head in his hands, muttering: 'Don't say it, Sally! For God's sake don't say that!'

Sally walked across to where Theresa and Dinny were sitting.

Dinny's collar was limp and his tie had twisted awry. Theresa looked as if she would burst if she sat there, trussed up in her purple grandeur much longer.

'I had a dance with Dick, the dear lad,' she told Sally eagerly. 'And he says I'm as light as a feather on me feet. But Dinny's tryin' to make out his dancin' days are done.'

'It's got my goat, this party,' Dinny confessed. 'I can't help thinkin' of Morrey and Alf. . . .'

'We don't belong, here. That's what's the matter,' Sally told him. 'Let's go as soon as we can.'

'Say the word, and I'm ready.' Dinny bounced to his feet.

But they had to wait until the bride and bridegroom went off on their honeymoon. Dick and Amy had left the ballroom to get ready for their journey, and Sally sat down beside Marie and Theresa.

'Gosh,' Dinny exclaimed, making an effort to entertain the ladies, 'I've been to some grand weddings in me day! Remember when Sam McGullicuddy married his girl Maureen to Mick O'Malley. . . .'

Sally knew that yarn and so did Marie, but Theresa begged obligingly: 'Go on, Dinny.'

And Dinny went on:

'Sam had a shanty a bit out from Kookynie. He was a sick man: jest about all in, and he wanted to see his daughter married before he passed out. She was in the family way, and wouldn't tell him who it was she ought to be marryin'. So he made up his mind it was Mick O'Malley and he'd got to do the right thing by Maureen. Sam arranged for the wedding to be at his place and a whole mob of us was invited out to celebrate. There wasn't any parson handy in those days, so Sam decided he'd say a few words that'd put the fear of God into Mick, to make the thing bindin' when the warden came out and could fix up the papers. There was to be a big spread and plenty of booze. Sam was a good hand with his 'cordion and going to play for the singin' and dancin' himself. But when the boys tramped out to Sam's place from miles round about, Sam was dead. He'd had a heart attack that morning, and passed out all of a sudden, his missus said. And there was the bride to be, six months gone and weepin' her eyes out. She didn't want to marry Mick, she said. But her mother wouldn't hear of that.

' "The weddin's goin' on," she said. And, strike, if she hadn't roped in the Member for the District to do the trick. He'd blown into the bar the night before. The Member for the District was an old bloke named Clem Hyde who'd gone a bit barmy about standin' for parliament. He'd cruise round the camps in an old buggy with a couple of horses at election time, and do anything for a bottle of whisky and a chance to make a speech.

'Well, he made a pretty good job of marryin' Maureen to Mick O'Malley, threw in a bit of latin and talked about her bein' a good wife to Mick till death did them part.

' "Sure, 'twas a deadly sin ye committed goin' to bed with Mick O'Malley before ye were wed, Maureen," he said. "But I don't blame ye, nor him neither, seein' the flesh is weak, and he's gettin' a nice little pub into the bargain. But I'm after tellin' ye to cherish her, Mick, and vote for Clem Hyde at the next elections, or I'll put a curse on ye and ye'll come to a bad end."

' "Say: 'So help me God,' Mick," says Clem.

' "So help me God," says Mick.

' "Say: 'So help me God,' Maureen," says Clem.

' "So help me God," sobs Maureen.

' "Where's the ring?" says Clem.

' "Christ A'mighty, where'd y' think I'd get a ring up here?" says Mick.

' "Ye can't be married without a ring," says Clem.

' "Hold on," says Mick, "till I make one out of a bit of copper wire I have fixin' me bridle."

' "I don't want to be married with a bit of copper wire,' cried Maureen. "I want a proper wedding ring."

' "Whist now," says her mother, "I'll give ye me own wedding ring. I'll not be needin' it now, with me poor Sam, stone-cold in the room, beyond."

'So Clem sticks the ring on Maureen's finger and says: "That's the lot! Y're Mrs. O'Malley, now, Maureen," and Mick kissed her, and we all go off to the bar to down a few before starting on the big spread Sam's missus had laid out.

'It was then the lad from the Six Mile, Syd Cox, blew in, and ses: "Hey! What's doin' here?" And we told him, and he ses: "Maureen!" as if he was shot. But we filled him up with Sam's beer and he was soon as lively as the rest of us.

'Mick was the only one who could play the 'cordion though, and after we'd had a good feed, things were pretty willin', with everybody wantin' to sing and dance, and Sam's missus and Maureen, bein' the only women present, hoppin' round with each one of the boys in turn. But I noticed Syd Cox gettin' more than his turn with Maureen, and givin' her a good hug into the bargain. There was a bit of a brawl when Mick caught Syd kissing Maureen. But we carted them off to the bar for another round of drinks, and there was more singin' and dancin'. Every now and then Sam's missus would cry out: "You're a nice lot of blokes not to show more respect to the dead!"

'So we'd drink up and shout: "Here's to Sam McGullicuddy, God rest his soul!"

'And Clem Hyde'd start addressin' the meeting: "Friends, citizens and fellow workers of the goldfields. Politics is a dirty bizness and I'd not be dirtying me hands with it. But ye need an honest man to represent ye in Parliament. What I say is . . ."

' "Vote for Clem Hyde!" we yelled.

' "That's it, boys, vote for Clem Hyde!"

'And there was more drinks, and more singin' and dancin' until we were all dead to the world.

'When we woke up round about noon, next day, some of us couldn't remember whether it was a wake, or a wedding, or a political meetin' we'd been at. There was poor Sam, stone-cold in a back room, sure enough. And the Member for the district snorin' on the verandah. But Maureen—she'd cleared out with the lad from the Six Mile. Left a note for her mother to say we'd married her to the wrong man; but Syd said it didn't matter because it wasn't a proper marriage anyhow. They'd taken Mr. Hyde's buggy and were going to get a real parson in Kalgoorlie to fix them up, so as Mick wouldn't make out he had any claim to the baby, and Syd could come back and help in the bar.'

'Oh, Dinny,' Sally laughed. 'I'm glad there wasn't any mix up like that to-night.'

'You bet there wasn't,' Dinny said, pleased to see her look brighter.

Amy appeared then, in her smart blue travelling suit. Dick came in and stood beside her, wearing the light tweeds he had bought for the occasion. They were pelted with rice and confetti, and ran out to the car in which they were driving to Coolgardie on the first stage of their trip to the coast. The car moved off to shouts of 'Good Luck!' 'All of the Best!' and a rowdy singing of 'For they are Jolly Good Fellows.' From the rear of the car, several old boots and shoes were dangling, and a roar of laughter resounded, as if it were a relief to ridicule this idyll of love and marriage.

CHAPTER XXV

Lal wrote that the regiment was to march through Perth on December 18th. There would be a parade and military sports on the showground next day, and it was rumoured that the troops would be embarking soon afterwards.

'Gee, mum, I've just got to see Moppin', Den exclaimed. 'Lal says he's in great nick, jumping out of his skin. All groomed up and I wouldn't know him.'

Sally wanted to take Den with her but was worried about the expense.

'The lad's breaking his neck to see Lal as much as Moppingara,' Dinny said. 'I'll shout him the trip.'

That was Dinny all over, Sally used to say, always ready to help her over any difficulty. She could not refuse to let him give Den this opportunity to see his brother again—and his horse. Nobody knew better what it had cost Den to part with Moppingara. The war seemed to be nearer and more appalling now that Lal was going into the thick of it.

Mrs. Molloy had promised to come and look after the house and boarders when Sally and Den made their long-promised visit to the coast. But Perth Molloy was in the Light Horse; and when Theresa knew about the parade, and the probability of embarkation soon afterwards, she decided to go down to see her boy off, too.

'It can't be helped,' Sally told the men in the bunk-house. 'You'll have to do for yourselves for a few days.'

'That's all right, missus,' they agreed. 'Don't you worry. We can manage.'

Dinny said he and Chris would come in from Kamballie and be camp cooks. But Marie would not hear of that.

'But of course, chérie,' she said eagerly, 'it is my job. Let us not speak of it any more. It will be something I can do for you, and for Lal.'

'Oh, Marie!' was all Sally could say: all that Marie would let her say to express her gratitude. However good-natured the boarders might be, she was afraid of losing them, if she had to be away for some time.

Marie knew, as well, that she could not afford to lose the money her boarders brought in, Sally guessed. The legal expenses in connection with Morris's and Tom's trial, and that gift to Dick, which was duly mentioned among the wedding presents, had left her funds at a low ebb. Despite Dinny's offer, this trip to the coast would cost a pretty penny, and soon Morris and Tom would be coming home. Tom might be out of a job and Morris unable to work for a while. So it was a relief to feel she would still have a means of providing for them; and Marie declared that she would be glad to get away from her sewing for a while. She could bring her father-in-law over to live at Gough's, and he would be 'so 'appy to yarn with Dinny and Chris'.

Three days before Sally and Den were due to leave, a letter arrived from the south-west, which threw an extra bustle into their preparations for going away. It was from Sally's sister, Fanny. She wrote to say that she and Phyll were looking forward to Sally and Den spending the summer holidays with them. But Phyll had been ill and Fanny was having a hard time to keep things going on Warrinup just now. She had only an old man to help her. Their young stockman had enlisted, and it was impossible to get another, owing to all the men in the district going to the war.

If Den was a good horseman, and wanted to learn to work stock, could he come down as soon as possible? Phyll was almost crippled with rheumatism, and Fanny did not know what she was going to do, if she could not get some assistance. The cows would have to be sold, and a lot of young cattle and horses disposed of, and it would be a pity if she had to sell at a loss.

Fortunately they had good neighbours. Fanny did not know how she would have managed if Charlie Wells had not brought in the cows and helped with the milking lately. 'But, of course, it was not fair to depend too much on one's neighbours, who all had their hands full just now. . . .'

Den was beside himself with excitement. So delighted and excited at the prospect of working among cattle and horses on Warrinup, that for a few moments he forgot about seeing Lal and Moppingara. He sobered down soon, however, to ask anxiously:

'I'll be able to see the parade first, won't I, mum? I'll be able to have a word with Lal, and say good-bye to Moppin?'

'We'll wire Aunt Fanny, and say we'll be in Perth this week, and you'll go to them, as soon as Lal sails,' Sally said.

She had a busy time getting Den's clothes ready, so many more than the best ones he would have needed for a few days in Perth.

188

There were socks and jumpers to darn, shirts and trousers to mend, an extra pair of pyjamas to run up on the machine.

It was out of the question for her to think of going with Den to Warrinup, Sally decided. Next year, perhaps, she might make a flying visit to see how he was getting on. She was afraid life on Warrinup might not be all that Den imagined, now that Phyll and Fanny had turned the old place into a dairy-farm.

Would two old maiden aunts be able to make allowances for a youngster brought up on the goldfields like Den? He might irritate and upset them in a thousand ways. Did they realise he was so young? Would they expect too much from him? Was Den going to feel lonely and miserable away from home for the first time, and shut off from the lively go-as-you-please companionship of boys and girls of his own age? The dreary, monotonous toil of a dairy-farm was not what he expected, although it would be quite a good breaking-in, if he intended to settle on the land.

Anyway, he would be out of the grip of the war. Safe, for a while, at least, Sally told herself—although from what Fanny said, young men in the south-west were volunteering, and the farms and stations being left to struggle along as best they could. But the troops had to be fed, Fanny had said, and Den would be doing his bit on Warrinup as much as anywhere else.

If only he were willing to stay there! If only he got the satisfaction out of working on the land, he thought he was going to get! Sally prayed that he would, and that a least one of her sons would escape the blight of the goldfields and the mining industry.

Lal had escaped. But to what?

Den—it was only Den for whom she had any hope. He had always been straining away from the fields. His mind had been filled with dreams of green paddocks, great forests and broad shining rivers since he was a child. Memories of her own old home, no doubt, were responsible for that. Unconsciously, Sally realised, she had been conditioning Den for this way of escape. If only his hunger for an adventurous life among cattle and horses could be satisfied. If only Den would be content to work on Warrinup and get the fatal air of the fields out of his system! That fine dry air, betraying to fantastic mirages lying always on the horizon. Perhaps this was just a mirage, Sally fretted: that Den would not be caught and wasted by the mining industry, or the war.

For the time being, anyhow, Den was thrilled by the prospect of going away.

On the railway station, just before the train started, Sally heard him talking to some of the boys he had been to school with, played football and got into scrapes with, since he was a kid.

'I'm leaving Kal for good,' Den said. 'Going to see Lal and Moppin in camp first, and then going down to be a stockman on my aunt's place in the south-west. Bye and bye, I reckon, I'll have a look round and take up land there, meself.'

Den would have liked to be swanking round with spurs on his boots and a stockwhip over his arm, Sally had no doubt. He looked too much of a 'towney,' for his own liking, in the new suit he had worn to Dick's wedding and a potty felt hat on his head. But his freckles danced with gleeful anticipation, the sweat poured down his hot face, and his ginger hair stood on end, when he raked it back, having got rid of the hat to which he objected strongly when Sally bought it for him. Not a shade of regret dimmed the brightness of his eyes.

Den did not care for anything or anybody, very much, Sally told herself. His pleasure in the prospect before him was all he was thinking of: his passion for horses what was taking him to Warrinup. He would put up with cows and milking machines if only he had a few horses to handle and could drive young stock to the sale yards. She had told Fanny that, and was sure Fanny would humour Den about being her new stockman.

Dinny had given Den a five-pound note to spend in Perth, and Den felt a millionaire with all that money in his pocket. But he had no idea of the wrench his going would be to Dinny, until Dinny hobbled off, blinking as if he had got a speck of coal dust in his eyes.

'Strike, mum,' Den exclaimed, sprawling back, in the train, when it was moving at last, 'Dinny seemed quite upset about me going away.'

'He was so proud and pleased when we called you after him,' Sally said. 'Feels you belong to him, in a way. I do think Dinny loves you more than anything in the world, Den.'

'Gosh!' Den stared at her. 'I never thought of that.'

His brow wrinkled.

'But it's on your account,' he added shrewdly. 'Dinny thinks you're the goat's tail, mum.'

'Den!'

Den's face crinkled to an urchinish grin.

'Doesn't sound too complimentary! But you know what I mean.'

They slept that night, leaning back on the hard seats of their second-class compartment in the train, and were in Perth next morning. Sally had taken rooms at a boarding-house kept by Vicky Molloy's husband's sister, on Adelaide Terrace. Theresa was staying with Mel who had married and got a butcher's shop in one of the suburbs.

Den's eager curiosity and enjoyment kept Sally in good spirits next day. The city had grown and changed a good deal since she had last seen it. She was amazed at the new buildings and big shops which had sprung up, though the streets looked very narrow and cramped after Kalgoorlie's wide thoroughfares.

Old houses, with beautiful gardens, still stood along the Terrace, and the oleanders round the medieval looking castle which was Government House were covered with rosy bloom, throwing a fragrance of almonds into the street. But the river was what Den gazed and gasped at, most of all. The river lying blue as the sky at the end of the streets, and stretching across to the misty shores of South Perth. He would have spent all day exploring its winding course and making little trips on the ferry boats: envied the half-naked youngsters playing about on the jetty and swimming off the beaches at Como and Applecross. They were living an enchanted life to a lad brought up on the goldfields.

Den had learnt to swim. Lal had taught him in the pool Kalgoorlie boasted of since coming of the water, though the water was often filthy and stinking: stiff with men and boys on the hot summer days. Never before had Den seen so much water. He bought himself trunks, determined to go for a dip next morning before breakfast. It would have to be from the bathing enclosure, Sally insisted. There were sharks in the river. Children only splashed about in the shallows. Perhaps after the parade, Lal could take them to one of the sea beaches.

The sea! Den had never seen the sea.

There had been free excursions to the sea for goldfields children, but Sally could never swallow her pride sufficiently to let her children take advantage of charity, always promising herself that some day she would take the boys for a summer holiday herself.

'Gee, mum,' Den queried, 'why in the name of blazes have we lived all those years on the fields, when there was a place like this to come to?'

He was amazed by the trim, quiet city, the beauty of its tree-lined streets and shining waterway, with red-roofed suburbs stretching away to the dim blue wall of the ranges.

'Dad always hoped to strike it rich on the goldfields,' Sally told him. 'Some day, we thought we might be able to live here.'

They had watched the march that day. Sally could never forget it: standing in the street for hours under a hot sun, jammed with Theresa and Den in a crowd of excited men, women and children, patriotic fervour at boiling point. The men were mostly old, or middle-aged, and full of bombast: what they would do to Kaiser

Bill and Little Billy. Win the war? Of course we would! Wait till our boys got there!

The women were more subdued. Mothers and wives looked stunned and uncertain as to how they should take this going to war of their sons and husbands. Whether with pride in the spirit of their men: or without any attempt to disguise the sadness and fear consuming them. There was no hiding the sorrowful eyes, and the heaviness of many a woman's heart, though faces smiled, and lips held firmly, repressed a persistent sobbing going on behind quiet appearances.

But the crowd was good-humoured and ready to be amused by any incident which would relieve the tedium of waiting for the troops to pass.

A red-faced, elderly man in a white helmet and tussore suit, being addressed as Colonel by a woman with a long scraggy neck and beflowered hat—which was all you could see of her—talked in a loud voice about India, China and the Boers, as if he wanted everybody to know he had been on service in several wars.

People shifted and shoved this way and that to see the speaker.

'I've got two sons going,' a woman near her said to Sally. 'It's all I can do to crack hardy.'

'We've got to keep bright and cheerful. Not let the boys know how we're feeling,' another woman exclaimed.

'That's the worst of it,' Theresa chipped in. 'I feel more like howling, meself.'

'It's unpatriotic to start snivelling. You ought to be ashamed of yourself!' The hat piled with faded flowers turned on Theresa. Sharp eyes squinted from a withered face. 'If I had ten sons I'd give every one of them to fight for his King and Country.'

'How many sons have you got?' Theresa asked.

'That has nothing to do with it.' The flowered hat tossed back and turned away, completely blocking Theresa's view.

The crowd laughed, and somebody remarked: 'And old maid, I'll bet!'

'I've got four sons, and they're all in the army,' a shabby, little woman with a patient, pleasant expression and bare, workworn hands said. 'I can't say I gave them to the army. They wanted to join up, and I'm glad they did, if they thought it was their duty. But it's hard to put up with all the same.'

'That's right!' one woman after another cried. 'That's the way we all feel.'

'Is it their duty?' a young woman with a baby in her arms asked. 'We're sending the pick of our men overseas, and what's going to happen here?'

A heated argument arose. The young woman with the baby defended herself, angrily, one or two men supporting her.

There were cries of:

'Shut up!'

'Get your bumps read!'

'She's mad!'

The old Colonel barked:

'Outrageous! What? A red-ragger! Damned dangerous letting foreign agitators undermine the war effort. Ought to be shut up—or shot!'

The crowd surged forward anticipating a brawl. But a few well-timed guffaws, and shouts of:

'Stand back!'

'Keep your hair on!'

'Take it easy!'

restored good humour. Over-wrought patience and expectancy found an outlet in chiacking the Colonel as well as the young mother and her supporters.

Then children along the edge of the pavement squealed: 'They're coming! They're coming!' And the blare of a military band could be heard with the cheering of crowds along the route of the march. Outbursts of cheering soared and swelled, droning away with a moan in their fall, as if people were not so sure, after all, that to see these columns of marching men and their war equipment was a matter for cheering.

Those splendid lads on their solid, well-groomed horses, with feathers flying in their cocked hats; of course, everybody was proud of them; exulted in their physical fitness! What perfect specimens they were of young manhood, sun-tanned, tough and stalwart! But cheers were choked in many a throat. How could their kith and kin cheer these lads to their death?

The men themselves were riding as military discipline required, rigid as wooden gods, undisturbed by the clamour in the streets. Eyes right, they swung along in their youth and valour, demonstrating to fellow-citizens that they had become well-trained soldiers, though now and then, a grin and a gesture indicated that a trooper had recognised a familiar face in the crowd.

It was anguish to think what they were going to face, these lads from the back blocks, from cattle stations and farms, from the wheatlands and country towns, Sally realised. They were the fathers, brothers and sons of women like herself.

As they passed through the beflagged streets, the cheering crowds: as the rows and rows of men and horses paced smartly to the hilarious music of the bands, through all the honour and glory flung about them by national sentiment, she wondered how many of them would return to their homes after the war had ended. How many of them would hear the crazy, tumultuous cheering of crowds in the streets for victory and peace?

Only the children, girls and a few old men, could let themselves be carried away by the delirium of war fever. For the children the parade was a spectacle. They liked to wave their little flags and see the horses and guns: hail a father, brother or someone they knew among the soldiers.

Girls in their white and brightly coloured summer frocks clustered in groups, throwing kisses and flowers, calling gaily to the marching men, all of them so virile and handsome, almost any one would do for the sweetheart or lover of her dreams.

Who could blame the girls if they were throwing themselves into a reckless pursuit of men in uniform, as people said they were doing? War stirred the sex instinct. And men going to wrestle with death, naturally became greedy of every joy life could give. Both men and girls were responding to a fundamental urge, Sally thought, as they sought to defy the threat of extinction forced upon them.

'Lal!' It was Den's eager cry drew Sally's eyes from scrutiny of the close-packed ranks. So many men and horses, looking very much alike, how was it possible to distinguish one's own lad from the others? She could not be as sure as Den of recognising Moppingara. There were hundreds of dark bays with a white blazed nose like Moppin among the horses. And every man in his khaki uniform, polished belt and leggings, rifle slung over his shoulder, cocked hat with the tuft of emu feathers, looked as brown and well set up as Lal. It was almost as if they were all her sons: every mother's son had lost his identity in this muster of Australian men and boys. Sally thought of them all as Lal.

But following the jerk of Den's head and the restive plunging of a horse, by standing on tiptoe, stretching and craning her neck, she caught a glimpse of a sun-burned face turned towards Den in a three-quarter glance: laughing eyes flashing beneath a felt hat brim. Then there were only Lal's broad shoulders and the back of his head to gaze at.

'Did you see, mum?' Den yelled. 'Mop knew my voice and Lal had a job to hold him.'

Sally nodded. Everything blurred before her: the blare of the band broke in shattered fragments. For a moment she felt numb and in darkness. But the crowd jostled and surged round her and presently she was part of its tumultuous emotion again, knowing Lal had come and gone: passed with those hundreds of other khaki-clad men, sitting stiff and square shouldered on their well-trained horses.

'Perthy! Perthy!' Theresa screamed.

Sally could see him quite clearly, the lean, sharp-featured warrigal of the Molloy tribe who had become a light horseman, as solid and well set up as the rest.

'As magnificent a body of men as ever I saw,' boomed the old Colonel. 'The sort of men we ought to breed from.'

'How many of them will come back to breed?' Sally asked bitterly.

'We pay a great price for our Empire, ma'am.'

'We pay?' Sally flared. 'Who pays? Nothing anybody pays is comparable to what those boys are going to pay. An empire isn't worth it.'

'Eh, what! But, damme, ma'am. . . .'

Sally was carried along by the crowd surging after the troops. The Colonel's outraged spluttering followed her.

'These red-raggers—damned dangerous! What? Ought to be shot!'

CHAPTER XXVI

LAL dashed out to see them after the march, making quite a stir in the boarding-house. With laughing exuberance he strode through the house, swinging his shoulders, spurs jingling on the polished leather boots which reached nearly to his knees. He knocked over a pot plant on the hallstand, as he passed; and was hugging his mother, and apologising that he hadn't seen the blasted thing as he came in from the sunlight, all at once. Then it was Den's turn to be grabbed and shaken, while Lal demanded what the devil he meant by making Mop play up and disgrace the regiment.

'Gee, Lal, where is he? When can I see him?'

Den wanted to go off there and then, find Moppin in the horse lines and see how he was being treated by the army. But Lal had other plans.

'We're going down to Cottesloe,' he explained gaily. 'Dick and Amy are staying at the pub, and there's a good surf at the North Beach. I'm meeting a girl on the third breaker at five o'clock.'

Lal insisted on taking a taxi, and within an hour they were on the beach. Dick and Amy were there in bathers, sprawled on the sand, waiting for them.

Lal and Den lost no time getting into their bathing togs, and

Sally sat watching as they splashed into the sea and swam out to the breakers which rose from the blue sea and hurled themselves along the beaches, bearing a swarm of boys and girls, shouting gleefully. Dick and Amy stayed talking to Sally for a while, then they too ran off, swallow-diving from the beach, with the easy grace of young people familiar with the sea.

Amy had spent many summer holidays here, at Cottesloe, Sally remembered, and Dick had learnt all the tricks of surfing on the Sydney beaches.

It was a glorious afternoon, hot, with scarcely a breath of wind to ruffle the crest of the surf, breaking in three lines of green rollers towards the shore.

Sally wished that she had a bathing suit, and could join the boys in the breakers. It didn't seem so long ago that she was Den's age, and had run as eagerly into the sea with her sisters. The family used always to drive or ride from Warrinup to camp at the coast for two or three weeks during the summer months. The year Morris had gone with them, mama made new bathing costumes for all her girls: queer shapeless garments of blue spotted print, or red turky twill, with long pantaloons and skirts to hide their figures. Mama, herself, had taken a dip wearing a big straw hat and an old dressing-gown. Sally could see her again, bobbing up and down in shallow water and thoroughly enjoying herself.

Of course, Morris was not expected to see the Misses Ward in their bathing costumes. But one never knew what accidents might happen at the seaside! Cecily, or Grace, might get out of their depths and a rescue have to be effected. Sally smiled, knowing how romantically her mother's mind would work over the possibilities of such a situation.

Papa took Morris and Bob to swim in a deeper pool beyond the headland. They could dive in there without bathers. Sally always objected to splashing about in the shallows of what was regarded as the women's part of the wide, sheltered bay, under her mother's eye. She and Fan had learnt to swim when they were children, and sometimes when papa took Morris and Bob for a day's fishing at Cape Naturaliste, she and Fanny would go for a walk to that deep pool, where the men bathed, peel off and practise diving in their skins.

Could this middle-aged woman sitting here on the beach, with a weathered face and silver threads in her hair, be the same girl who used to dive naked from a rock on the south coast? Sally could see as in a dream the dark forest behind her, and the shining water stretching away into the distance. How surprised her sons would be if they heard about such goings-on! And how shocked mama would be to see boys and girls, disporting themselves in the sea together, as they did nowadays, in brief, close-fitting garments which revealed every line and curve of their beautiful young bodies.

Yes, those were her sons, frolicking out in the sea, Sally mused. She had come a long way since the days on the south coast with mama and the girls. It was a long time since she had experienced the thrill of playing about in the sea, being rushed along and tumbled about in the surf like this.

The sparkle of the sea water tempted her to rush off, undress and plunge into it. To-day the sea was the blue of water hyacinths, under a heat haze, lying along the horizon. The haze lifted now and then to a light breeze which just feathered the long lines of green rollers lolling in towards the shore. But she had no bathers. Could she afford to buy a smart black woollen bathing suit, like the one Amy was wearing, Sally asked herself. No, she thought not. It would be foolish to spend so much money, when she might only be able to use the suit for a few days. Perhaps she could hire one from the dressing shed, further along the beach, to-morrow? But was there going to be a to-morrow? How many to-morrows would there be before Lal sailed? He did not know.

Dick had said those long grey shapes lying out in the roads were warships, and that big ships alongside the wharf at Fremantle might be transports.

Here on the beach, it was difficult to believe there was 'a war on', as people kept reminding each other. Here on the beach, in the hot sunshine, everything seemed so peaceful. Men and girls were romping about in the sea with shouts of laughter and careless gaiety: Lal, and other soldiers, who had come down from the parade for a cool off, among them. Just two or three hours ago they had been riding, rigid and grim, equipped for the fighting front, and in a few days would be on board the transports, steaming across the blue water, passing the outlines of Rottnest Island— going beyond the horizon. Where? Nobody knew exactly, except that it was being whispered Egypt, not France, might be the destination of these Australian forces. All the horror and bloodshed of war lay beyond the pale blue fall of the sky and the misty horizon from which those men and boys in the troopships would be vanishing.

She must not think of it, or of Morris and Tom, Sally told herself. Her eyes had strayed to the wharves and white-roofed buildings of Fremantle under haze, in the distance. Memory of the grey-stone prison there made her heart ache. How incredible it was that Morris and Tom should be couped up in that place, instead of being here on the beach with the rest of the family.

Lal and Dick had both been to see them, and Lal had told her, coming down in the taxi, that he was worried about his father's appearance.

'Tom's all right,' Lal said. 'Good old Tom! He'd stand up to anything. But dad's whipping the cat. Thinks he's brought disgrace on us all. Wish we could get him out, mum.'

'I've done all I could,' Sally said.

But here she was enjoying herself, sitting on the beach, gazing at the sea and dreaming, as if Morris and Tom did not exist, and there was no war to carry Lal off into all that madness of death and destruction. It was because of Lal she was here, she consoled herself: because Lal might have so few days in which to make the most of the sun and the sea.

The sea breeze was freshening and whipped loose wisps of hair from the braid round her head. Her face was strained and sad when Dick threw himself down beside her. Amy had stopped to talk to some friends, nearby.

'What's up, Sal-o-my?' he asked tenderly.

Sally smiled to reassure him. 'I was feeling a bit mopy,' she said. 'How are you, darling?'

'Good!' Dick's glance gave her inside information about himself. He looked rested and more mature for these days of honeymooning by the sea. 'But Amy and I must go home, to-morrow. Wish we could stay to see Lal off: but a man mustn't risk losing his job now.'

'Of course not!' Sally smiled at his half-laughing, half-serious air.

Den came running up the beach then, dripping sea-water and grinning delightedly.

'Gee, it's great, mum,' he cried. 'You can get a big wave out there where they're breaking on the sandbank, and shoot right in on it.'

Lal was standing with a group of girls on the water's edge. Such a splendid figure of a man in his short trunks, bare brown limbs gleaming, throwing back his head to laugh with lusty abandon!

'Lance-Corporal Gough's very popular with the ladies,' Dick commented.

'Strike!' Den quizzed, when Lal came loping alongside. 'How many girls have you got on the string, Lal?'

'None of your cheek, young feller!'

Lal rolled Den over, and they started scuffling, trying wrestling holds, and tumbling over each other like a pair of puppies. But Lal was in good training and too powerful for Den. Presently Den cried for mercy and Lal sat back, laughing and slinging off at the cocky young brother of whom he was so fond.

Amy dropped into the sand beside Dick. 'We'd better make a

move, darling,' she said. 'It's the Red Cross concert and dance to-night, don't forget.'

'Wouldn't you like to have a dip before we go up, mum?' Dick asked.

'I'd love to,' Sally replied. 'But I haven't got any bathers.'

'You could have mine,' Amy said dubiously, 'if they would fit.'

'Go on, mum!' Lal urged.

'I'll race you to the sandbank,' Den cried.

So Sally went up to the dressing shed and changed into Amy's bathers. They were wet and cold, a little tight on her bosom and thighs; but she was still slim enough to wear Amy's suit comfortably. She scolded herself for feeling self-conscious, when it came to running back over the beach, half-naked, with Amy's red cap tied over her hair. But the boys laughed and cheered as she waded out and dived under a breaker.

It was ecstasy to be wrapped in the sea again, to feel the rough caress of the blue salt water, wrestle with the breakers and lose all sense of the cares of existence.

Breathless, with eyes and nose streaming after being buffeted about by the waves, she ran up the beach and dropped down on the sand beside Amy and Dick, grabbing one of their towels.

'I'd no idea you had such a good figure, Sal-o-my!' Dick exclaimed teasingly.

'Don't be absurd,' Sally gasped. 'I don't run to fat, that's all.'

It was then Colonel de Morfé strolled along, and hailed the group, hilariously.

'Well, I'm blest, a real goldfields party!'

Dick swore beneath his breath, and presently he and Amy found that they had to speak to some friends further along the beach.

Frisco sprawled on the sand beside Sally.

'As a matter of fact, my dear, I wondered who Lal's new charmer might be,' he explained mockingly. 'God, Sally, you strip well.'

Sally's eyes sparkled with anger.

'Why do you talk like that?'

Frisco enjoyed her discomfiture. 'The only way of getting behind your defences, I suppose, Mrs. Gough.'

'Well, you don't,' Sally declared. But his lean brown figure stretched on the sand beside her, Frisco's eyes with their demand and derision, stirred the deep current which had always run between them.

'Shut up,' Frisco growled. 'Let it be— just you and me, and the sea—like eternity before us—for once. Give me these few moments, Sally!'

Dazed by the sun and the sea and the agitation which Frisco's appeal had aroused, Sally sat clasping her knees and sea-gazing. He lay beside her, as if asleep, tensely quiet, and lost to the gay moving crowd about them. Other couples along the beach were spread about in the same attitudes of repose and abandonment. But were they held in the same intimate communion, which had come to her and Frisco, Sally wondered.

She and Frisco had been absorbed into each other, caught in an emotion that was like the sea, wrapping them in its warm, irresistible flow, rushing them along with rough, inexorable breakers. Sally was tossed about by them: lost herself in a drowning swirl. Trembling and with startled eyes, she withdrew from the spell Frisco had put over her.

'I must go,' she said breathlessly.

Frisco's eyes opened to gaze at her with a sun-dazed brilliance.

'You can't get away from me, now—or ever, Sally,' he said.

Sally ran across the beach to the dressing shed. The boys were waiting for her when she came out, 'clothed, and in her right mind', she told herself. Lal said they were going to have dinner at the hotel with Dick and Amy. It was his shout. Then they would go afterwards to a concert and dance in the beflagged little restaurant at the end of the jetty.

CHAPTER XXVII

AFTER all Lal did not sail that week, or for over a month after the parade. There were other wonderful days of sun-baking and surfing at Cottesloe: swimming and picnicking at Rockingham where the 10th Light Horse went into camp.

Sally and Den took the small steamer which at the week-end chugged down the river and along the coast between the islands and the mainland, to the collection of scattered shacks, shops and bungalows which was a popular resort for summer holidays. Den had the time of his life with the horses and men looking after them. He rode and groomed Moppin, took him splashing into the sea, went to dances and vaudeville shows with Lal.

But at the end of a fortnight, when Lal said it looked as if the regiment was to do at least a month of intensive training, Den said suddenly:

'I reckon, if Aunt Fan really needs me, it's up to me to go, now, mum.'

Sally could only agree. So Den left for Warrinup by an early morning train, two days later. Sally went to see him off. Lal and Den had said good-bye the night before in their own jaunty and joking fashion, though there was a thickness in their voices, a choking understanding of what this parting might mean, as they broke away from each other.

Lal had said: 'I'm proud of the kid, making up his mind to go to the aunts, when he wants so much to knock round with me.'

'So am I,' Sally told him.

She wished Den could have had these last days with Lal; but Fanny had written to say that her old man had left to take charge of his son's shop in the town, and she was just about desperate for some help with the cows and all the work that there was to do on the place.

So young and coltish Den looked when he stood on the platform just before the train pulled out. His underlip quivered and it was hard for him not to blubber as he used to as a kid, when he had got a crack that could not be taken with manly fortitude.

'Lal will be all right, mum,' he said, 'won't he? Nothing could happen to Lal: it just couldn't!'

'Lal's always been lucky,' Sally said to cheer him. 'We must back his luck now.'

'That's right!' Den's grin rewarded her. 'I told him to keep his fingers crossed, like Dinny says.'

Den had hugged and kissed her and jumped on the train as it was moving.

'I'll be down to see you, soon,' Sally called after him. 'Give a hand with the next muster.'

'Gee, mum, that'll be great!'

Den's face lighted and his eager yell flew back to her, as the carriages rattled past.

Then he was gone, and Sally felt lonely and depressed as she returned to the boarding-house where she was staying. So many separations she had had to face lately: seeing Morris and Tom taken away to prison, then Dick going off on his honeymoon, and there was still her farewell to Lal which must be gone through with. That would be the worst of all. She must not grieve about Den's going to Warrinup, she told herself. She had wanted him to go: wanted to get him away from the infection of war fever, although if only Den could have waited until Lal sailed, it would have been so much easier for both of them.

Still the boys were right, she decided. Lal said Den's job on Warrinup would be a bit of active service and part of the struggle to win the war. He had to hop in and get on with it, as Lal himself would have to obey marching orders.

Every day there were fresh rumours as to when the troops would be embarking. A raider had been sunk in the Indian Ocean, and Lal thought departure of the troops would not long be delayed now. Sally was determined to stay and see Lal off, even if it meant remaining much longer in Perth than she had intended.

She had gone each week-end to the camp at Rockingham and spent long afternoons on the beach with Lal. Several times Colonel de Morfé had joined them. Once or twice his wife had been with him, and his manner had been aloof and reserved.

But it was he who told Sally the date had been fixed for embarkation, and his strapping figure was the last Sally could distinguish on the crowded deck of the troopship when it steamed out of Fremantle harbour.

She had stood for hours, in the blazing sunshine, with the crowd waiting to be allowed on to the wharf. When men and horses were on board, and the troopship swung out from her moorings, the crowd stampeded through the barriers, and Sally was carried along with it. In that dense throng of friends and relations, struggling madly for a position from which they could see their men, she despaired of even catching a glimpse of Lal.

The khaki-clad figures were swarming everywhere on the deck of the transport. They hung over the bulwarks and clung to the rigging, dwarfed by the height and distance of the ship from the wharf, until they looked no more than dun-coloured larvae of the gum moth, writhing together, inextricably bound by some mysterious purpose and sense of direction. Sally could not distinguish one man from another, and her cry: 'Lal! Lal! Where are you, Lal?' was drowned by the shouting of thousands of soldiers, their mothers, wives and sisters, fathers and brothers, calling last messages.

Then she heard the whistling call her boys used between each other, and at last discovered Lal, on the shoulders of another man. The crowd had made way for her to struggle to the edge of the wharf. She could not hear what he yelled in the chorus of good-byes and good-lucks being shouted out all round her, and feared Lal would not have heard her last shrill, foolish words:

'Take care of yourself, darling! Take great care of yourself!'

But another gay, reckless voice bawled over the water: 'Don't worry, Sally! He'll be all right!'

She had seen Frisco shouldering through the press of men near a shrouded gun, and pain gripped her heart, as she realised that he, too, was going out of her life for ever, perhaps. Tears streamed down her face as she fluttered the rose-coloured scarf she had promised Lal to wave to him; but she did not see him again, although the whistle of the Gough boys drifted back to her, as the troopship steered for the open sea.

The crowd shed its noisy, cheerful clamour as figures on the troopship became blurred. Many men and women ran after it along the wharf. Others stood watching until the grey hull of the steamer, moving slowly and heavily, passed out of sight beyond the mole. Women were sobbing now, fathers and friends trying to comfort them.

'You've got to be brave,' they were saying.

'It's no use worrying!'

'The boys'll be back within a year!'

'They'll give the Kaiser hell: clean up the bloody mess in no time!'

Most people were sad-eyed and heavy-hearted as they walked away from the wharf. Everybody knew that some of those lads on the troopship would never return. Fathers and mothers were fighting down gloomy presentiments; but there was still a lot of sturdy bluff and bravado. Australia had to show the stuff she was made of. If there was a scrap on, the boys wanted to be in it! You couldn't stop them! 'Rule Britannia, Britannia rules the waves.' That was all right. But she couldn't do it without the help of the Australian expeditionary forces. Men went off to reinforce their patriotism in the pubs. Women, like Sally, could only curse the war and long for it to end.

Next day, she went to the prison to see Morris and Tom. They were only permitted one visitor a month, and Sally was glad now she had let Lal visit them last month.

The grim, fortress-like building on the hill above Fremantle appalled her when she had seen it several times lately. It was infuriating to think of Morris being treated like a criminal behind those high walls, surmounted by cut-glass bottles and barbed wire.

As she walked up the hill, she could not help thinking of the day she and Morris had been married in Fremantle. Such a romantic affair it was, running away from home, catching the coastal boat from Bunbury, and being married by special licence in the old church, near where the railway station stood now. Her handsome and debonair young husband, who could ever have thought he would be a prisoner in that hateful jail?

How happy they had been: what a gay, irresponsible life they had led in Perth and Fremantle: going to dinners and parties at Government House, and being made a fuss of by everybody. Then Morris had bought Booingarra Station.

If only that had not been such a disastrous failure! If only he had not lost so much money, and put what was left into the mines at Southern Cross! His family had broken with him then: refused to help him any more. From the 'Cross, Morris had tramped beside the first team on the track to Coolgardie. He had learnt what hard work and hardships meant, prospecting on the early goldfields. He had forgotten he was ever an English gentleman. But what did that matter? He was a better man for all those gruelling experiences.

Sally was proud of the way Morris had been able to work with all sorts of men on Coolgardie and Hannans. It was something for him to have won their respect and confidence. Poor Morris, he hadn't had much luck prospecting. Now and then, perhaps, he had done fairly well, and put everything 'back into the ground', hoping it would be a good investment.

He had never got over the rush to Black Range. His health was never the same, and he had lost hope of ever striking it rich. He had worked underground, and it had nearly been the end of him. But nothing he had ever done was harder for him, and showed more grit, than taking on an undertaker's business.

If ever a man had redeemed the follies of his youth, Morris had! That young husband of hers was a criminal perhaps, spending money lavishly, foolishly: not caring where it came from, or how he got it. He had never thought of money as something which should be earned or that he should do any manual or menial work! He had taken it for granted some men and women were born to wait on him, minister to his comfort. But now, when he understood it was absurd and infamous to live like that, he was put in jail!

Sally would not admit that Morris had been guilty of any crime in what he had done. He had been foolish: he had taken a risk which hundreds of other men took on the fields: that it was the custom for a man to take to help another in a tight corner. He had been 'framed'. That was what everybody knew in Kalgoorlie, and yet Morris had been sentenced to six months' hard labour—and Tom with him.

If Tom had not been involved, Sally thought, Morris could have taken his conviction with the easy philosophy of a man who accepted the goldfields' code. But, from what Lal said, Morris was allowing a sense of defeat and disgrace to overwhelm him.

Sally hoped she could make him realise that he must not let this happen: she hoped she could arouse him from his despondency. If he did not let this experience hurt him, it would not, she must assure him.

She felt a little sick and nervous, as she lifted the heavy knocker on the guard house and a constable spoke to her through a small barred window.

The guard house was small and stuffy, every window closed. Oh, that was the prison smell she had heard of, Sally thought, as the musty odour of the place struck her.

It was a surprise to be addressed rather curtly. She explained that she had come to visit her husband and son. There was some discussion between the two policemen as to whether the prisoners had received the visitor they were entitled to for this month. But Lal's visit they decided came within the period of the previous month.

Heavy keys clanked, and a thick iron-studded door was rolled back, giving on the interior of the prison yard with its cobbled roadway, strip of green lawn, administration quarters and stacked rows of barracks. There was a sentry in a wooden box on the high wall, and an old convict in dirty, yellowish prison clothes branded with black arrows, pottering about digging weeds from the lawn.

Surely Morris and Tom would wear their own clothes to receive visitors! It was a shock when a warder showed her into a narrow compartment with drab yellow walls. There was no chair. Only at one end, a row of iron bars with a narrow passage and what looked like a cage with more iron bars before it, on the other side of the passage. It was into this passage Morris shambled. Sally did not recognise him until another warder called his number, and a bowed and trembling figure in the same clothes as the old convict she had seen on the lawn, stood in the cage before her.

'Morris!' she cried, feeling as if her heart would break, at the sight of his sunken eyes, ghastly face, and the grey scrub on his jaws.

Morris gave no sign of being pleased to see her.

'You shouldn't have come,' he said irritably. 'I told you not to.'

'My dear,' Sally cried, clinging to the bars for support, 'as if this makes any difference! You know I've wanted to come, all the time, but Dick's wedding and Lal's going away—I had to wait.'

She chattered on brightly then, trying to control her agitation, and give Morris some courage to overcome his humiliation.

It was terrible to have to talk to him through two rows of iron bars, and to know that the warder at the end of the passage could hear every word she said. He was a decent sort, though: had turned away once or twice. Sally wished she could have kissed Morris; but those two rows of iron bars, and the passage between, separated her from him.

The few minutes she was permitted to talk to Morris dragged, as a matter of fact. They were the longest minutes she had ever known, and misery for him, she felt. She told him all the news about

Dick and Lal, and about Den going down to help his aunts on Warrinup. There seemed nothing left to say then.

'Don't be discouraged, Morris,' she begged. 'You'll be home soon. And this doesn't mean anything. Lal's depending on you to give him the football and boxing news. "Tell dad," he said just the night before he sailed, "he's the only one I can trust to tell me how the old team's carrying on." '

'Did he say that? Did Lal say that, Sally?' Morris queried.

'He did,' Sally lied glibly. 'And Lal will be looking forward to his letters from home, Morris. Oh, you know how he'll need them !'

'Yes,' Morris said dully. 'He'll need them.'

'Time !' The warder's voice broke harshly on that moment when thought of Lal had re-established their mutual bond.

The warder unlocked his cage and Morris shambled away, escorted by another warder. Sally had to suppress an hysterical inclination to cry out and weep furiously because Tom was coming.

She was trembling and struggling to control her distress when he appeared, dressed as Morris had been. He, too, was unshaven, his hair rough and on end. Sally had never seen her men so unkempt. The prison had made them look like criminals, she told herself. Tom seemed well, though, harder and stronger than she had ever seen him. Prison had not broken him. His spirit shone in his eyes, proud and defiant, immune to any indignities harsh regulations could put upon him.

'Hullo, mum,' he greeted her as he strode behind the warder into his cage. 'Don't let this place get you down. We'll soon be out of it, and dad's better than he was. Lal's coming to see us bucked him up. Tell me about the old chap. The transports've sailed now, I know. We get all the news here, though we're not supposed to.'

Sally pulled herself together to talk to Tom as cheerily as she had to Morris. It was not so difficult to chatter and gossip about the things that would interest him, though Tom saw through her spurious brightness and said, gently :

'Take it easy, mum. You don't have to play up to me.'

He wanted to know what was happening on the fields : how people were taking the war. His questions were guarded though, and she understood from his glance at the warder, that she must be careful not to say anything which might make trouble for Charley O'Reilly or any of his friends in the I.W.W.

'How's Mrs. Owen ?' Tom asked anxiously.

Sally told him about Nadya's visit, and that she had gone to the sanatorium. Sally, herself, was minding some of her books. Eily had brought them over because she said Nadya wanted Tom to have them. Eily had promised to read some of them to Sally when she went home.

'She's a great kid, Eily,' Tom smiled. 'Give her all of the best from me, and Charley and the boys.'

'They're planning a great reception for you,' Sally said.

'Knock that on the head, mum.' Tom's voice was very firm. 'I don't want any fuss.'

'The hug and kiss I'd like to give you now, will be waiting, son,' Sally promised.

'That'll do me.' Tom's eyes had their grave smile. 'It's the only sort of reception I want. And a good meal! Grilled steak with a poached egg on top and apple pie. Bet dad feels that way too.'

'You'll get them,' Sally promised. How reliable and reassuring he was, her dear Tom! It was like him to say something to buck her up: make her feel that there were practical and commonsense things she could do to help Morris and himself.

As she crossed the prison yard, escorted by a warder, another visitor was leaving also. An old man, screwed up with rheumatism, but walking briskly.

'Holy smoke,' he exclaimed, 'if it isn't Mrs. Gough!'

In the guard room, as the visitors were being checked off, he explained to the stiff, solid figures buttoned up in their blue uniforms: 'Ye've had a distinguished visitor in the prison to-day. One of the pioneer women of the goldfields.'

The policemen were not interested or impressed. They might never have heard of the goldfields, or understood what it meant for a woman to battle along there, in the early days.

As she walked away from those grim stone walls, Sally was overcome by an enervating nausea. The sunshine dazzled her: her legs felt weak and as if they would not carry her. Was she going to faint, she wondered.

'It was such a pleasure to see you, missus,' a sharp voice broke in on her ebbing consciousness. 'For the life of me, I couldn't help singin' out. You don't remember me? But I remember you from the days you was campin' on Hannans with Morrey. Bert Screech is the name. Did fairly well at Kanowna and pulled out.'

Sally could not speak.

'Feelin' crook?' the kindly voice went on. 'There's a seat handy. We can sit down for a bit. Cripes, I know how it feels visitin' here for the first time.'

He steered Sally to an open shed facing the prison, and sitting there, she recovered from that bewildering weakness.

'Thank you, Mr. Screech!' she said, after a little while. 'I feel better now.'

'What's wrong?' the old man asked. 'Morrey hasn't struck trouble, has he?'

Sally told him what had happened.

'Don't you worry, missus,' Mr. Screech said cheerily. 'Morrey'll be all right, and your boy. Folks on the fields know when a man's been framed like that—though they don't hold it against a workin' miner if he does get away with a bit of stuff. I come along to see an old mate in the can, now and then; and know how to work a few points with the warders. Got a son-in-law who's a jockey,' he whispered slyly, 'and can give 'em a good tip for the races, sometimes. They don't forget it. I'll see Morrey gets a few extras in the way of tucker and tobacco while he's here.'

'That would be good of you.'

Mr. Screech simmered to Sally's smile.

'It'd be funny if I couldn't do a little thing like that for an old mate,' he chortled. 'Why, Morrey and me, we tramped with the first team along the track to Coolgardie!'

Those words were like the refrain of a familiar song, and Sally found her spirits rising to it.

She had a cup of tea with Mr. Screech in a shop in Fremantle, while he made eager inquiries about the old mates, gossiping all the time of mining camps and rushes he had been on in 'the roaring 'nineties'.

Sally took a train back to Perth. There was nothing to keep her in the city now, so she packed quickly and caught the express for Kalgoorlie.

As the train rushed through the night, she sat up in the corner of a shabby, hard-seated compartment, too tired to sleep. The train rocked and swayed like a dilapidated buggy on a rough road; but she was indifferent to its jolting, the noisy chatter of wheels on the rails, the spasmodic conversation, drowsy grunts and snoring of other passengers. Empty and bereft of any emotion, she could think of Lal—and Frisco—somewhere on the high seas: of Morris and Tom shut in the airless cells of that prison on the hill at Fremantle. The train seemed to be running through the starry night, carrying her away from the harrowing experiences of the last few days.

The first hot breath of the dry, inland plains was balm to her weary senses: the smoke of burning-off fires like incense. Embers near isolated camps glowed as if they were jewels in the darkness, and surely, that was a fragrance of paper daisies on the air! Sally remembered how the paper daisies spread white as snow over miles and miles of country when she and Laura had gone up on the coach with Alf Brierly to Coolgardie.

In the first light of dawn the names of sidings made a singing in her brain. Koorarawalyee, Warri, Boorabbin, Woolgangie!

When the sun rose, it showed red earth, and the sea of scrub, spindly snap and rattle, pale blue cotton bush and saltbush, the darker mallee and mulga, spreading away and away into the distance. Goldfields country lay before her, as it had done for the first time, so long ago. How could she love a country that had been so indifferent to her joys and sorrow, Sally asked herself? Yet she did love it. That was something that soothed and rested her in the very sight of its infinite distances, its ineffable blue skies.

She understood now what Morris had meant when he said: 'This country will get you.' It had got her, Sally realised. She felt that she belonged to it. Her roots were embedded in its soil, as much as roots of the silvery grey mulga, which had weathered so many droughts, and could still cover itself with golden bloom.

She was glad to be home again, Sally told herself. She was glad to have work to do which would enable her to weather the war, and a guilty awareness that her love for Frisco was not as dead as she had hoped it might be.

CHAPTER XXVIII

DEN's letters were the bright spot of these days after Sally returned to Kalgoorlie.

Gough's boarding-house on the Boulder Road had never looked such a ramshackle, elongated old humpy, so shabby and weather-beaten, with the white paint peeling off its corrugated iron roof, and the creeper over the front verandah sagging untidily. And it was so empty!

Despite the four boarders who slept in the bunk-house across the yard, and came into the dining-room for their meals, and Chris and Dinny who still occupied rooms on the back verandah, Sally was oppressed by a feeling of emptiness in the place.

It was the boys she missed, of course. Life was very dull and flat without them. For so long the house had reverberated to the racket of their voices: their comings and goings, laughter, quarrelling and joking with each other. She had gone about her housework in a whirl of happy activity. Now, there was very little to do: flies sang in the silent rooms and they were too tidy. Linoleum on the floors shone and she dusted the furniture. But what satisfaction was there in keeping a house like a new pin for nobody's benefit?

209

To be sure Dick and Amy dropped in to see her one evening, and Eily had run along to hear the news of Tom. Marie came almost every day for a few minutes. But still, Sally confessed, she felt like a hen whose chickens have all turned out to be ducklings and taken to the water. She scolded herself for moping, went to Red Cross and Comforts' Fund meetings, read some of Tom's books, and argued with Chris and Dinny about the war. No news had come from Lal yet; but Den's letters were something to look forward to, so fresh and breezy: full of his new importance and the fun he got out of his experiences on Warrinup.

Sally read Den's letters to Chris and Dinny, and again to Marie and Dick, until she knew them almost by heart.

During his first week, he had gone out into the back hills to round up clean-skins with Charlie and an aboriginal stockman, who had come back to Warrinup when old Martin left. It was very wise of Fanny to have arranged that excursion, Sally explained laughingly. She must have guessed that nothing could please Den more. And the Charlie Aunt Fan had talked of as being such a good neighbour, and giving her a hand before Den arrived, was a girl, it seemed. 'You could have knocked me over with a feather, mum,' Den wrote in his first excited schoolboyish scrawl 'when I found out Charlie wasn't a he, but a she, and has been helping her father on their place since her brothers went to the war.'

He was amazed by the organisation of all the work on Warrinup, the number of cows milked, the way the milking machines were driven by an engine that pumped water from the river too, turned the separator, and flushed out the bails and pig pens, each night and morning. 'The floors of the bails and pig pens are as clean as a china plate,' Den declared rapturously, 'and everything is so up to date, it's no wonder Charlie says Miss Ward has made Warrinup a model dairy-farm.'

Den was astounded that two old maids could have done such a thing, and carry on the work of the place. 'Though it's getting too much for them, now,' he observed complacently, 'and I can take over all the outside jobs. Aunt Fan says she'll look after the milk and cream, but I'm to be responsible for bringing in the horses, yarding the cows, taking cream in to the siding and rounding up cows and calves in the bush.'

'That'll suit Den,' Dick laughed.

'Suit him down to the ground,' Dinny chuckled.

'We've been losing a lot of calves lately,' Sally went on reading Den's letter, 'the dingoes are bad, and when a cow drops a calf in the bush it's an easy meal for a dingo. But Aunt Fan thinks there's been some two-legged dingoes about, too, and they've been selling any clean-skin they can pick up to the butcher at the siding. I'm going to keep a look-out for those swine and give them something to go on with, if I catch them at it.'

Everybody had to laugh at the bluster of the young cattleman.

'Gee, mum, Den exclaimed, it was great the other day, when Aunt Fan was introducing me to one of the neighbours, she said: "This is Sally's boy, Denis Gough—the new manager of Warrinup." Wish she meant it! But I reckon if I can show the aunts I *would* be a good manager when I learn all about cows and butter fat, Aunt Fan won't be slinging off when she says that.'

'You bet she won't!' Dinny beamed, backing Den to get his own way in whatever he was after.

'Aunt Phyll's a funny old duck,' Sally went on reading, 'very fussy and deaf. She's always saying: "The boy looks very thin, Fanny. We must feed him up." Or "Give the boy a quiet horse, Fanny. We'd never forgive ourselves if anything happened to him here." And gosh, mum, you should have heard Aunt Fan telling her I can ride. "He's as good a horseman as his mother was, Phyll," Aunt Fanny bawls. "Oh, yes," Aunt Phyll says, "he's very like dear papa, I know—and fond of horses. But don't let him ride Dartigan yet. And don't shout, Fanny! I'm not deaf."

'Dartigan is the best horse on the place, mum, and you bet I'm breaking my neck to ride him. He's a big bay gelding, the dead spit of Moppin; and it gives me a pain in my gizzard to see Jigger on him. Jigger's the abo stockman, who used to work here years ago and only came back from a walk-about up north, lately. He's a blinkin' marvel with horses, and breaking Dart into stock work. Aunt Fan says some day I can ride him if I stay here long enough. Golly, mum, can you see me budging till I get that nag?'

Sally was pleased to say she could not see Den leaving Warrinup while the bay gelding was there.

'But they're bonzer old girls, the aunts, Den wound up, and I reckon we'll get on all right, if only Aunt Phyll doesn't butt in too much. She likes to think Fan can't manage without her, and Fan humours her all the time, though she does all the bossing of the show, and Phyll just potters round the house. It's funny to hear them fussing about each other.

' "Now, Fanny dear, do have a little rest."

' "Phylly, dear, did you take your medicine?"

' "Yes, my sweet."

' "No, dearest!"

'You'd think they were a pair of love-birds the way they go on to each other, mum. And they don't know quite what to make of me. Phyll thinks I'm a kid: and Fanny tells her that I've left school—am almost a man, now.

'But I think they like me, mum, and are quite pleased about having me here. "It's just like when Morris came," Aunt Phyll said when I arrived. "If only poor papa and mamma could have seen Sally's boy." And then they both cried a bit and kissed each other and gave me a hug, and we went into the sitting-room and had tea. And they wanted to know all about you and dad and the boys. I didn't say anything about the dirty trick Paddy Cavan played us, though, mum. Thought they mightn't understand, and by and by I can explain to them properly.

'That's all for the present, and tell Dinny I'll write to him soon. Your loving son, Dennis M. Gough.

'P.S. Don't forget about coming down soon. I like it here, but gee, I miss you and Lal, mum.'

'Bless him,' Sally sighed, and smiled at the thought of Fanny and Phyll with Den like a hobbledehoy cuckoo thrust into their quiet nest. How strange it was to realise they were old women! They had always been as attached to each other as if they were twins, although Fanny was a year younger than Phyll. What a mercy that Den was trying to accommodate himself to living with them, and that the girls did like him.

There was a letter from Fanny, which said Den was 'a dear boy', and already being a great help to her. She was sure she and Phyll were going to be very fond of him. They only hoped Den would settle down and be happy with them on Warrinup.

Sally hoped so too, and Dick said emphatically:

'Best thing that could have happened to the kid, sending him to the south-west, Sal-o-my!'

Dick called in on his way home from work sometimes, but never had more than a few minutes to spare. Amy was taking her domestic duties very seriously, Dick said, and didn't like him to be late when she had cooked a dinner.

'You mustn't keep her waiting, dear,' Sally agreed, and Dick would fly off on his bicycle, so that Amy should not be ruffled or disappointed, if he were later than usual coming home.

Sally had gone to have tea with them one Sunday. Amy called the meal supper; and served it a little later than usual, which was just as well, because it gave her time to feed her boarders first.

It was a great comfort to see Dick and Amy in their own home. They seemed very happy, even if it was rather like a new toy. Everything was so fresh and pretty, and Sally thought Amy and Dick had all a young couple could desire to start housekeeping with in Kalgoorlie: wire-netted doors and windows, cool safes, and a beautiful bathroom, besides their new furniture, chintz curtains and covers. Already Dick had made a garden, and planted a lawn on which a sprinkler was flashing the evening Sally visited them. And in the spare bedroom Amy showed her the basinet she had just bought, all decked out with white net and blue ribbon.

CHAPTER XXIX

PADDY CAVAN was back in Kalgoorlie. Amy had run into him at the 'Western Star' when she went to see Tim McSweeney. Tim was a sick man and going into St. John of God's hospital for an operation.

Tim pooh-poohed the idea that anything much was wrong with him. He had never been ill in his life, he said, and didn't want the quacks cutting him open and making a mess of his inside. But Laura was worried. The doctors suspected an internal growth, she told Amy. They had put Tim on a strict diet; but still he could not eat without suffering acute pain.

You would never know Paddy, Amy declared. He had spruced up extraordinarily, and was strutting about as if he owned the place. His trip abroad had certainly made a great difference to him. It was cut short by the war; but Paddy had spent a few months in London, staying at the Hotel Cecil, and meeting important men in the mining world. He was going to Melbourne to interview Federal ministers and put through a big financial deal, he had told Amy.

Tim said Paddy was blowing his bags about all the money he had subscribed to the war loans. He talked loudly and proudly about a man's duty to the Motherland; subscribed liberally to Red Cross funds.

When Mr. Cavan spoke at a public meeting about 'the need for every man to do his bit supporting the war effort', he referred to 'the grand fight our boys are puttin' up on Gallipoli'.

Somebody in the audience yelled:

'Why aren't you there, y'rself, Paddy?'

Paddy replied sturdily:

'By God, there's nothing I would like better, than to be with the boys dealing out hell to the boches, and thim-there haythen Turks. But the British Government's got a job for me; and I'm goin' to do it to the best of my ability.'

'One of the "Would-to-Goders," ' somebody shouted derisively.

'I'm a bigger man than ye've any idea of, me dear,' Paddy said confidentially, when he drove Amy home from the hospital in his car, one afternoon. 'This war's made me: don't mind how long it lasts. There's fortunes bein' turned over in contracts and munitions, and war loan's a good investment.'

'You ought to be ashamed of yourself to say so!' Amy cried indignantly.

Paddy laughed.

'Ashamed? What would I be ashamed of? They want money to carry on the war, don't they? And I've got it to lend at a fair rate of interest.'

'Men fighting don't get any interest on their lives,' Amy said. She had heard Tom say that.

'More fools they,' Paddy growled. 'I'm fighting in me own way, and I don't intend to let the military big wigs and political shysters squander my money to suit themselves. When the war's over, it's the men who've kept their heads—not let themselves be carried away by a lot of highfaluting talk—will rule the roost. Oh, I'm a good patriot, me dear! Patriotism pays when y' know how to handle it.'

'You're a scoundrel,' Amy said.

'Surre, I'm a scoundrel,' Paddy agreed, all good-humoured amusement at her indignation. 'On the top of the world where I've been, they're all scoundrels, would cut your throat for two bob. But if there's any throat cuttin' to be done, I'm doin' it—not them, see.'

Amy said she was sorry she had allowed Paddy to drive her home; but she was very tired when he picked her up at the hospital, and he had taken her unawares.

Laura and Amy visited Tim every day. But the operation was not a success: he died a few days afterwards.

'Poor Tim,' Laura said when Sally went to see her. 'You couldn't help becoming fond of anyone who was so kind and generous.'

Amy wept passionately. 'I loved Timmy! I loved him more than you did, mother. No one's ever been so good to me. I'll never forget what it was like when I was little and came home from school. Tim was so glad to see me. I could cuddle up to him and feel quite happy.'

Everybody was surprised when it was known that Tim McSweeney had left most of his money to Catholic organisations in the town. There was an annuity and a bungalow for Laura. The bungalow was next to the one he had given Amy as a wedding present and was to be hers at Laura's death. But otherwise Amy was not mentioned in the will.

Laura could not believe it. Tim had always told her he loved Amy as if she were his own child and would leave her 'well-provided for', she said. But, apparently, during his illness he had made another will, realising his duty as a true son of the faith, which neither Laura nor Amy would accept. There was nothing to be done about it. Laura had not a word of reproach for Tim.

'He suffered so much,' she said. 'If it gave Tim any comfort at the end, to make his peace with the Church, it was better that way. Amy and I wouldn't like to have been a burden on his conscience.'

When he was dying, though, Tim had whispered: 'It's too bad about Amy—but I couldn't help it, Laurie.'

'I didn't know what he meant at the time,' Laura explained. 'I just kissed him and said: "We both love you, Tim." '

'He looked so pleased, Sally. I feel he did know we'd understand, and was happy, at the end. It was the least I could do for him.'

The hotel was to be sold, and Laura went to live with Amy until she could move into her own house.

Nadya's death in the sanatorium at Wooroloo occurred the same week. Eily came to tell Sally about it, her eyes red and swollen with crying.

'Oh, Mrs. Gough,' she said, 'it'll be awful for Tom! Why did Nadya have to die? Why did she have that cruel, beastly consumption of the throat? Why couldn't they have done something for her at the San? It's terrible to think of a wonderful person like Nadya having to stop living. We needed her. Everybody needed her so much.'

'What will happen to her children?' Sally asked.

'Mum has been minding them while Nadya was away,' Eily said. 'But it's too much for her, really, with all her own kids to look after. Claude says he'll try to get a housekeeper.'

For days, Sally found herself thinking of Nadya and her children: wishing she had known Nadya better and wondering how her death would affect Tom. She had caught a glimpse of the fire and purity of the woman's character, her intellectual brilliance and infinite sympathy. It was not surprising, she thought, that Nadya had made such an impression on Tom. She was a rare bird to have drifted on to the goldfields, and Tom had been hungry for the sort of companionship and stimulus she could give him. Sally hoped that Tom's feeling for her would not have gone too deep, and that Nadya's death would not destroy his capacity for loving Eily, or another girl, some day.

'She was a remarkable woman, Mrs. Owen,' Dinny said. 'Everybody who came in contact with her felt that. You'd be surprised if you heard how the men are talking about her in the pubs and on the mines, ma'am. They know she was fighting for them—even when they didn't agree with her. I feel, meself, as if the workers've lost one of the best friends they've ever had in Boulder.'

It was a great thing for a woman to have won such a tribute, Sally thought. A woman who had come among people of the goldfields, ill and a stranger, and yet stirred them to more vigorous thought and struggle in the trade unions and political organisations of the labour movement. Her name might be forgotten, the very fact that she had ever existed, be submerged by the debris of time; but her influence on Tom, and other men with whom she had been associated, would remain, Sally was sure.

She was thinking about Nadya the afternoon Violet O'Brien called.

Violet had put on weight; was handsome and statuesque these days. From time to time, Sally had heard all sorts of tales about her lovers and love-affairs, and brushed them aside as the usual gossip about a good-looking woman. Violet, she knew, owned the pub where she served drinks, herself, with other barmaids. Her whole family lived on the premises. She sang in the bar and at charity concerts in the town, her voice as beautiful as ever, full and clear, with melody in every note. But Violet herself no longer attached any importance to it. She had given up all idea of becoming a professional singer. It was too late for that, she said, so she had become hard and practical. It was necessary in the hotel business, and she was determined to make money and enjoy life, to compensate for having to throw her dream of becoming a prima donna on the mullock heap.

'Oh, well,' she said lightly, that day, 'I'm going to be married at last, Missus Sally. Not as young as I was, you know, and not wanting to be left on the shelf.'

'My dear,' Sally exclaimed, 'who is he, and when?'

'Mr. Isaac Potter,' Violet replied as if she got a sardonic amusement out of the idea. 'I'm doing very well for myself, don't you think? He's a bit older than I am, of course; but well in. Oh, money-lending and land mostly. I'll be able to sit back and play the lady. Won't it be marvellous? I'm so tired of wrestling with things: singing to drunks and making money. I've been doing it all my life, Mrs. Gough, and now, I'm going to give up. Feels rather like throwing in my hand: but Ike is really a good sort: wants to take care of me. And, God, I want somebody to take care of me, now.'

There was a desperate note in Violet's voice: some repressed emotion surged behind the mask of her face. It had an unhealthy pallor. Her features had thickened, Sally observed. She did not know what to say, and Violet continued:

'Don't talk to me about love. I'm sick to death of men making love to me. "Expense of spirit in a waste of anguish," as Bill Shakespeare says, is all that's ever meant to me. It's much better to marry a decent old bloke like Ike, and be a good wife to him.'

'If that's the way you feel about it . . .' Sally agreed.

'I do,' Violet assured her. 'I'm going to have a nice, comfortable home, with a music room, and sing and play to myself for hours. Never see the inside of a pub or bar again. And, really, the best part of it all, is that Ike does know something about music. We'll have that in common at least—and kids, I hope.'

'Well, good luck!' Sally replied, feeling that optimism was all Violet required of her.

'Never expect the moon, and you can put up with a carbide lamp —that's my motto,' Violet told her. 'Come and see me when I'm Mrs. Ike Potter, won't you, Missus Sally.'

CHAPTER XXX

Tom and Morris came home a few days sooner than Sally expected. When they walked round the corner of the house in the blinding light of the midday sunshine, she was dazed for a moment, thinking that she had visualised what would soon happen. But the figures stood firm and solid before her: did not fade, waver and vanish. She ran out to catch hold of them, put her arms round them, kiss them and exclaim: 'Oh, darlings! My darlings!'

Those shabby figures kissed and spoke to her. They felt like self-contained parcels of Morris and Tom, carefully packed to cover their emotion. Sally brought them into the kitchen. They sat down while she made tea, got a meal ready for them, exclaiming and chattering crazily in her joy and excitement.

So quiet and strange, Tom and Morris were at first. They seemed unable to shake off a weight the prison had put on their spirits, or to get rid of the depression and apathy which had come over them in jail. But soon Tom was getting up and striding about, throwing back his shoulders and stretching his legs. He started to say something, over and over again, and broke off with a grin to exclaim:

'Cripes, it's good to be home, mum!'

But Morris sat slumped in his chair, dumb and inert. He had no energy or interest for anything: looked an old man, ill and broken. His clothes hung on him. A paunch and smooth, round cheeks had given him the air of being a prosperous business man before the trial; but they were gone now. The neat, hooked nose which had maintained a fastidious aloofness through all the vicissitudes of his life on the fields, jutted from the slack, sallow skin of his face in a bony crag. His eyes were dull behind their smudgy glasses.

'Oh dear,' Sally sighed, 'it's dreadful to see your father like that, Tom.'

'Give him time,' Tom said. 'His heart's been playing up a good deal. The doctor down there said he'd have to take things easy when he came home.'

Morris exerted himself, more than he had yet done when old mates and neighbours came round to welcome him and Tom. He talked to them and took their cheery greetings and good wishes in the casual, sporting way he knew they expected.

'It's knocked Morrey a bit, this business, missus,' Dinny said. 'But don't worry, he'll get over it.'

During the next few months, however, Morris could rarely be roused to take much interest in anything. When old cronies, like Sam Mullet, Eli Nancarrow, and Tassy Regan came along for a yarn or a game of cards, Morris sat listening to them, dull-eyed and silent. He went to sleep over the cards. Lal's letters were the only things which stirred the dreary lethargy overwhelming him. He would sit up and listen eagerly while Sally read Lal's letters aloud: study a map of Gallipoli, and discuss problems of military strategy with Tom and Dinny in the evening.

Lal's first letters, describing life on the troopship and the first days of the regiment in Egypt had been light-hearted and amusing.

But very soon came news of the landing at Gallipoli, and of heavy casualties among the Australian and New Zealand forces. It was Sally's birthday, April 25th, the day on which Australian troops received what was described in the newspapers as their 'baptism of fire'. But it was a baptism which brought death to so many, that never again did the day dawn without mourning and sadness for her, and for hundreds of mothers throughout Australia.

Lal cabled almost immediately that he had not been in the landing, so for a few days Sally breathed more freely. His next letter explained that the Light Horse had been dismounted, and was going into action in support of the infantry.

Friends and neighbours were eager to hear Lal's letters, as well as Tom and Morris, Dinny and Dick.

Sally read the one describing the landing on Gallipoli over and over again.

'The 11th Infantry Battalion and the first crowd from the West in the landing party, mum,' Lal wrote, 'got a particularly hot time. Seventeen of their thirty officers were killed or wounded. I've had yarns with some of the wounded, and our officers—Capt. Peck in particular—say it was a marvellous performance. We started to land at half past four on Sunday morning and as the boats neared the shore, machine guns and artillery and rifle fire simply poured into them from all directions. From three boats that started early in the piece not a man landed. But the other chaps simply went mad. They were ordered not to fire a shot and as each party landed, they simply extended and charged with the bayonet. Everyone says the language was something frightful. They roared and yelled and cooeed and frightened hell's bells out of the Turks. Then the NZees came on and joined in with their Maori war cries.

'The Turk sharp-shooters did good work, but on the whole their rifle fire was bad, or it is believed our poor chaps would have been wiped clean out. The buggers wouldn't face the steel at any price, and as our chaps got anywhere near them they ran for their lives and they were better sprinters than our fellows in most cases. At any rate none of them were "running off weights". I've heard several chaps say they had seen our men drive bayonet and rifle clean through a Turk when they did get a go at him.

'One little chap, over here in hospital, was shot through the groin and dropped in the open. Couldn't budge an inch and a cow of a Turk within a hundred yards started sniping at him. He had eleven pots and couldn't get closer than putting one through his cap. Then a couple of Australians came along and the Turk ran, but our lads had too much foot for him.

'There seems to have been a tremendous amount of this individual fighting, little bunches of twenty and thirty or a hundred men getting together, very often without an officer and simply bogging in. At any rate they were expected, and given, till six in the evening to land and take up their positions. But by ten in the morning the jobs were finished.'

Several scrappy letters had come from the trenches on Gallipoli when Lal was in the thick of the fighting there. Letters on paper torn from an army notebook, and in faded lead-pencil. Then the long letter arrived which made Sally's heart ache and rage in anguish for her boy. Lal had been wounded and wrote from hospital in Heliopolis:

'You will gather from my last letter, mum darling, that we were expecting a big attack from the Turks, towards the latter end of July. The "big bird" used to sail over us and over to the Turks daily, and reports were that over 50,000 of them were reinforcing their already mighty strong troops opposing us. Night after night we expected them and those of us not in the outpost (we shifted later on) would be "called to arms" from 8 to 9, 10 or 11 sometimes, and then again just before daybreak. We got a shift right up to the main firing line on Saturday, July 31st. This was to be for a fortnight when we were supposed to get a spell. It was very solid going, as we were pretty stale and sleep was a hard thing to get. Perthy Molloy blew along, I think on the Wednesday or Thursday. It was good to see him, but we only had a short yarn.

'Then on the Thursday we knew we were going to strike before the Turks had a go at us. Thousands of troops, English and Gurkhas, principally, landed on Thursday night from Lemnos Island. Of course, the Turks knew as much as we did. Their dicky birds got very cheeky and used to fly over us, dropping a few eggs. Usually aimed at our supply and ammunition stores, but never did any harm.

'On Friday we packed all our spare gear in our packs and left them with the Quartermaster, keeping out our overcoats and oil sheets (although these too were supposed to be handed over), two tins of dog, water bottles filled, tea, sugar and biscuits. As many as we could carry were served out. Strips of white calico to each man too. Piece round each sleeve and on back: our tunics were to be left with the Q.M. or packed in our little haversack—which meant that we were to fight in our old flannels. All our war paint of course was aboard us—each man carrying 200 rounds. Orders stated "no cartridges to be in the magazine". This meant that we were to charge with bayonets and no one would be able to stop and fire. Orders like these may be all right for some troops, but our chaps to a man intended having ten of the best in the magazine and one in the barrel for luck. And I expect it was realised. At any rate I believe the order *was* altered at the death knock, allowing us to load.

'On Friday afternoon, at 5.30, the right flank made a start. Some of our chaps saw it from a high spot. It was an awe-inspiring sight from all accounts, to see our chaps hop out like one man right along the flank and charge. I was just on my way to have a look when we got the order to "stand to arms," and so missed it. The battleships, of course, were dealing it out to the Turks, covering the advance. The idea was to make this advance on the flank, and naturally the Turks would reinforce from the centre and other flank. When they did, our other flank was to have a fly. Well, I won't write about what I heard, I'll stick to what I know.

'We, in the centre on Walker's Ridge, were supposed to have a pie job. Our gunboats were to have bombarded the artillery and machine guns opposing us, and our job was to go for their trenches with the bayonet, and we would only be opposed by rifle fire. That's all we knew of our little affair. We were the 8th and 10th Light Horse. The 9th, our other regiment of the 3rd brigade, reported "unfit for duty" during the week. Why I don't know, as we had all landed the same time, and we reckoned the 10th did more graft by a long way than both the others, but that's by the way. There were two lines of the 8th to go out before us, we making the third line to go out from the centre. Our go was to take place about 3 a.m. That night after "stand to arms" when we were allotted our positions for the morning, I dug out some goldfields blokes and we had a good wongie, also a drink for luck.

'Rum, of course, is served out each morning in the trenches and it's wonderful how the thimbleful bucks the chaps up. I tried it several times but couldn't come at it, so Harry Mullet and Ross Lee used to come in for mine as a rule. That was one of my many little jobs, whacking out the rum to the chaps in our troop. Harry was made acting sergeant the day before, and had to go to another troop, much to his chagrin (if old Harry has such a classy commodity). Still it was bad luck to get parted from us all at the very rise of the barrier.

'I remember asking Harry whether the guard would wake us on the a.m., but he said: "You chaps won't get any sleep with all this firing going on."

'He, I might say, had only been with us a week or ten days and had not become accustomed to the noise. Anyway sleep we did, and were all sound when he came himself and said we were running late. Well, we filed in behind the 8th. Their first line went out, and then we moved up a piece, and watched the second line go over the parapet and took their places.

'We knew something had gone wrong, long before this, because the Turks were enfilading ("end on" firing) our trench besides hopping shrapnel and the 75 shells right on us. These were supposed to have been blown out by the gunboats. Chaps were dropping back in on top of us, and we could hear the bullets pinging into the sandbags just above us, so we had a faint idea we were in for a rough time.

'I'm getting ahead of myself a bit. Should have said that our 4th line was to comprise part of the 10th, with sandbags, picks and shovels. Each man of us took two sandbags with us. The first line of the 8th were to take the first trench, their second line go right over them and take the second trench, while we were to go further on still and take the third. So that, when we knew the first and second lines of the 8th were only about ten yards out, instead of a hundred or so, we guessed things weren't too good.

'As a matter of fact, we should never have been ordered to go: the small number of us left. I'll have something more to say about this on the verandah at home, tell Dinny.

'Well, anyhow, we got the order to hop out, and over we went. I was one end, and the other sergeant the far end of the thirty of us.

'The leader of "A" troop went into a dead faint twice while we were waiting to charge—just excitement I expect. I went along and spoke to him; but he said he couldn't understand it. Poor beggar's dead now.

'Speaking for myself, mum, and the chaps nearest me, we never felt the least bit excited or nervous: Perth Molloy was next to me and he's a splendid chap.

'There was a slight delay in giving the order to "go"; but when it came, we got off the mark well, so far as I could see of the chaps near me. We had been told there might be a bit of barbed wire entanglement near the first two trenches. They were quite close, and not the ones we were aiming at, as they were unoccupied.

'I remember wondering as I got fairly close to them, whether I'd be able to clear the barbed wire without coming a cropper, when I ran against "one", ten to fifteen yards out. Haven't the faintest recollection of actually falling, but remember it felt more like a punch on the chest. Anyhow I hit the ground good and hard, found plenty of pals round me, knocked over too.

'I was down for some time before I tumbled just exactly what had happened. Things began to choke up inside and I found I was coughing up the real thing. One chap about ten yards from me, sang out: "Where did you cop it, pal?" and I pointed to my chest. "Fair on the ninder, me,' he said. He was lying on his back and was half propped up. A few minutes later a shell burst just behind me—and rolled him over.

'We seemed to be out about an hour, but it really wasn't more than ten minutes, I suppose. The bullets were simply hailing round us and shells bursting everywhere. It seemed suicidal to shift as there was a slight rise to our left. Perthy with a bad wound in his leg got back O.K., and then I had a try.

'I started to back with my belt on, left my rifle. But couldn't manage it. So after a good deal of trouble I unbuckled my belt with my left hand. The right wasn't in too good working order, through the bullet going through my chest muscles, and then I rolled over and over until I got pretty close to the trench when a chap threw out a puttee with a stone on the end. I promise you I didn't miss it. After that I was good-oh!

'Harry Mullet blew in about the same time, and we battled along through communication trenches to our Red Cross chaps. They tied us up temporarily, and then we walked down to the Red Cross tent where scores and scores of our fellows were. Of course, those who were very badly wounded were carried down on stretchers, and those who'd got their legs knocked about, but a great number of us just padded along. The chaps thought I was going to the clouds as I bled pretty freely and kept spitting up blood, but really I didn't feel too bad.

'Well, we were fixed up by the doctors in the Red Cross hut and then put in different shelters until the time came for us to go to the beach. They have a system of tags for the wounded, giving name, number, reg., etc., and then details of wounds, so that when you get to the hospital they can draft the patients easily without worrying questions. Many chaps were beyond talking. A white label simply means 'wounded' or ill, white with red border 'serious', and all red dangerous. I got one with a pretty red border and intended sending it along to you as a "small token", mum, but these blanky orderlies grabbed it.

'I'd been in the dressing station some time when they brought round a jug of good hot tea and some biscuits. I thought it was midday but found it was only 9 o'clock.

'The sailors in a steam pinnace towed in three or four big barge affairs to a temporary landing stage, and after a bit of trouble we got towed out to the hospital ship *Delta*. We were shelled a few times before we got well out, but they were aiming for a couple of our 6-inch guns which were just near the beach—and we couldn't blame the Turk.

'We were drafted to different wards on the ship and you have no idea the glorious feeling of relief it was, to be able to lie down on a comfortable bed, get your wound dressed, and not have to worry about anything at all, bar the fact that some of our boys were still amongst 'em. But I knew our crowd couldn't charge again. I quite expect to hear of the 10th being back here to spell any day. At the same time I have a slight idea of what you and dad must be feeling, mum—all the time.

'More than half "A" Squadron were killed or wounded. I lost some of my best pals.

'Tell you another time about Lemnos Island and all the scores of battleships, transports, destroyers there. We landed at Alex., then were put on the Red Cross train bound for Cairo.

'A couple of days afterwards, I began to get a bit bad, and hit the bubble up to a shade under 104°—which they reckon is pretty good for a mug. Anyhow doctors had a screw, and I was on the operating table inside half an hour. A bad abcess had formed on the chest. This was over a week ago, and I'm pretty right again—expect I'll be back in the line before long.

'Don't worry, mum, and tell Den one of the boys who came in from the horse camp told me the other day Mop's in the pink.

Your friend Colonel de Morfé's in hospital here, too: got a lump of shrapnel in his eye, watching the show on Walker's Ridge. He tried to stop it, he says, and finally Major Todd did get down to Brigade Headquarters, seeing red about the order to attack coming up, again and again, when the regiment was being smashed to blazes, and nothing gained by it. Frisco reckons the British troops at Suvla Bay were expected to cut off the Turk's reinforcements, but it didn't happen. We got it in the neck because "Somebody" had bungled the operation. Three-quarters of our squadron was wiped out. It's worse than being wounded to know the whole thing was a wash-out, and so many of a man's best mates dead. Those of us who went over the top and got back don't blame Johnny Turk so much as some of our dug-out colonels. We reckon we could settle Johnny Turk if we got a fair go, and will, when we can tackle him in the open.'

'Oh Lal! Lal!' Sally cried, appalled by what had happened to her boy.

She hoped his wound would keep him out of action for a long time, and wondered how on earth she was going to endure the torment of knowing he was in the fighting again.

CHAPTER XXXI

Tom got back his job on the mine.

Mine owners contended that gold production was part of the war effort. Australia and the Empire needed gold in order to secure dollar credits in America. Many miners had gone into the army; but experienced men were regarded as being engaged on essential war work. Managements were cutting down clerical and technical staffs, however, in an effort to speed up recruiting.

Sally shivered as she thought of it, and of Dick. Posters and songs were urging young men to join the forces. And the Government had issued cards, asking every man of military age whether he intended to enlist, and when. If not, why not?

Tom was safe enough, it seemed, unless he caught the war fever, and felt impelled to volunteer. He also had received an anonymous letter containing a white feather. Tom wore the feather in his hat until his mother begged him not to. A man working underground, and risking his life every day of the week, could afford to laugh at that white feather, she said. Already the controversy about conscription for overseas service was raging. The only choice before a young man, apparently, was going to be whether he would join the forces as a volunteer or a conscript. Sally fretted and fumed over the consequences to her sons whenever this question of conscription arose.

Did Morris realise what those consequences might be, she wondered. He was all for conscription: talked like any jingo about shirkers and slackers being made to fight—as if every man who was not in uniform should be regarded as a shirker or slacker. Sally suspected the tradition in his blood. Morris had fostered Lal's hankering for a military career. But she could not believe Morris wanted Dick, and Tom, and Den to be drawn into this disastrous war.

Tom was so pleased to get back to work: to regain his status of a working man, earning fairly good wages, that for a time nothing else mattered. Those months at Fremantle made no difference to his work mates, and he could find his way through dark tunnels of the mine as if he had never left them.

Even shrilling of the mine whistles in the morning did not diminish a sense of freedom he was enjoying. He jumped out of bed, showered and dressed, whistling in scrappy, joyous little outbursts. Getting into the rough and tumble of men in the change room, hearing the curt instructions of the shift boss, and swinging a shovel for Ted Lee again, was a real thrill, he told Sally. He was surprised and amused at being like a duck going back to water.

It was a sense of freedom he was revelling in, Tom said. Freedom from that musty cell which shut him off from the work-a-day life of his fellow men: freedom from the harsh, deadly discipline and mechanical drudgery of prison labour. There was a sweet taste to toil a man was doing with his mates, sweating, cursing and chiacking with them. He was free to tell the underground foreman what to do with his job, if he wanted to. He could have himself hauled to the surface and walk off the blasted lease, if he felt so inclined.

Free he was not, Tom knew, in the sense that he, or any other working miner, could afford to ignore the need to work for wages. But that was part of a system they recognised as inevitable. For the time being at any rate. There was no such thing as absolute freedom, Nadya used to say. It was romantic nonsense to talk of a freedom without obligations, or social duties, as the anarchists did. The only sort of freedom a man or a people should expect, was the freedom to ensure community well-being, the freedom for every man, woman and child to grow in physical and mental vigour, towards perfection of the human race.

He could think of Nadya now, without the black desolation which had gripped him when he knew she was dead. It was as if the light of her life had left a glow in his heart which would burn steadily through the years.

But Tom had been disturbed by Lal's letters. He wanted to rush off and stand by his young brother. He wanted to buck into that rotten job on Gallipoli: do something to help Lal and the hundreds of Australian lads who were fighting against terrific odds among those barren, foreign hills.

Recruits were being called for. Tom wished that he could throw up everything he had ever stood for and volunteer. He could not bear to think of Lal wounded, and talking of going back again to the trenches. It was damnable to realise what Lal had gone through under that shattering enemy fire, crawling back to shelter, with the dead and dying all round him. The horror and misery which had torn Lal, clawed at Tom as he thought of so much valour and so many lives thrown away because 'someone had blundered': failed to check up on the strength of the enemy position, and persisted in an adherence to the plan of attack until three-quarters of the men taking part in it were wiped out.

But war was all waste, and a colossal blunder, Tom was convinced. Or worse: part of a criminal intrigue between the Great Powers for markets, raw materials and spheres of influence. Behind that intrigue he saw a system of economics which forced governments to fight for supremacy and national privilege to plunder the world. A system which bred war: made war between rival states inevitable. That was why behind the barrage of talk about the rights of smaller nations, German bluff of defending the dignity of her Austrian ally, declarations of Tsarist concern for the woes of religious brethren in Serbia, the war had developed into a bid for prestige and power between the most powerful states. A trade war, as Charley O'Reilly was saying.

Tom had heard Charley addressing a crowd in the street one night soon after his return.

Standing on a box, a gaunt, impassioned figure with the grey hair ruffled back from his bare head, Charley shouted:

'War has slashed a highway of ruin through the ages, a highway strewn with wreckage, reddened with fire, lined with crosses, prisons, corpses, skulls and graves.'

He was quoting from a pamphlet just issued, Tom knew. Overcoming the hostility and muttered resentment of the crowd, which threatened to get out of hand if he made any reference to the war in which so many of their sons and brothers were fighting, Charley went on:

'War mistakes brutality for bravery, madness for manliness and homicide for patriotism. War has damned the world with hate.

War has stained the earth with blood and tears, broken the health, and shattered the limbs of millions of the world's strong men, and filled the highways with hobbling cripples. War has crowded the world with widows and orphans, with broken hearts, broken homes and broken hopes. War places the conqueror above the educator and the assassin above the artist. War, as organised force and cruelty, spits on religion, adopts the ethics of the tiger and the shark.'

Tom agreed with most of what Charley said, but there were some differences of opinion he wanted to thrash out with him. Dinny and Eily, Charley and he, had sat by the roadside after the meeting, and Tom told them that he wanted to enlist.

'What does it matter to the workers,' Charley asked, 'which capitalist state, or group of capitalist states, bosses the show? The workers get the same raw deal under the capitalist system anywhere. It's against the system you've got to fight, Tom: not against fellow workers in other countries. Let the capitalists fight their own wars if they want them. Working men are fools to spend their blood and guts to bolster up the capitalist system no matter whether it's British or German.'

'But,' Tom objected, 'you've got to look facts in the face, Charley. The workers under capitalism in British countries have got democratic rights they haven't yet won in Germany. Here in Australia we've got a stronger trade union movement, a stronger labour party, chances for organisation, that the German workers haven't got. With a conscript army the German ruling class can put the boots into the workers, any time they like—and keep on making them wage-slaves, and slaves to their military machine. We don't want a German victory because, with a powerful conscript army Germany could dominate Europe, and worsen conditions for the workers everywhere. She could plunge the world into future wars, like she's done now. That's what's worrying me. I reckon all we've got is a choice of two evils. We're better off under British capitalism than we would be under German, and we can't afford to let the war be a walkover for Germany.'

'What about Karl Liebknecht? Charley snorted. 'A socialist deputy in the Reichstag who spoke against the war, and refused to vote the war credits? The German workers've got leaders who are organising against the war, don't forget.'

'In prison?' Dinny quizzed. 'That's where most of them are. And you can still spout from a soap box in the street, Charley. And so can socialists in London. Though there's a lot of conscientious objectors being jailed there—and it looks to me as if we'll be havin' that sort of thing here if they bring in conscription, like Billy Hughes reckons on doing.'

'And you talk of fighting conscription in Germany, Tom, when it's on your own door mat,' Charley scoffed. 'Christ, I never thought you were such a bone-head! You'll see what happens to democratic rights if they bring in conscription here. Conscription's the big stick the bosses want to break the trade union movement in this country.'

'We'll have to organise against conscription, Tom,' Eily said, as if she were appealing to him, but unflinching in her own conviction.

'That's right!' Dinny said. 'I've got a pretty good idea how y're feeling, lad. But, after all, there's thousands of young men will fight for the victory of British capitalism, and mighty few who'll fight for the interests of the working class in this war. I reckon your fight is with the workers against capitalism and against war. If you and the chaps like you drop everything now, well, the labour movement's going to suffer, and we'll get conscription, sure enough.'

Tom brooded a moment.

'I guess you're right, Dinny,' he said. 'I'm on guard for the workers—whichever way the war goes.'

Eily squeezed his hand.

'Oh, Tom,' she said, 'I knew you would be.'

'You've chosen the hard way, son,' Dinny said when they were walking home together. 'But, I reckon, it's the only way for you.'

Dick had almost hugged Tom when he saw him that first night Tom and his father got back from Fremantle.

'God, lad, it's good to see you,' he cried.

Tom thought Dick looked as if he had been doing a term of hard labour, rather than himself. Dick was lean and nervy, pretending to be happy and carefree; but Tom did not like a line of worry on his forehead, and the strained weariness of his eyes.

'What's up, old man?' Tom asked bluntly, when they got a chance for a word together.

'Nothing. At least nothing much,' Dick replied; but the habit of talking things over with Tom was stronger than the resolution to wrestle with his own difficulties as he thought was incumbent on him.

'It's a bit heavy going, being a married man, at first. That's all. No joke trying to make your screw spin out to cover exes. And Amy's going into hospital any day, now. Poor kid, she's had a bad time: been very sick. Sally says she'll be all right when the baby comes; but a man feels rotten, having let a girl in for all that. And the worst of it is . . .'

Dick paused, the attempt to make light of his worries falling away from him.

'The worst of it is,' he went on, 'the company is bringing a good deal of pressure to bear on eligible men to join up. I've had the tip my services could be dispensed with. If a man joins up his job will be waiting for him when he gets back. If he doesn't join up, well, it's the sack, anyhow.'

'Cripes,' Tom exclaimed, 'they can't do that!'

'Can't they?' There was a cynical twist to Dick's query. 'They're doing it, Tommy. I had to have a word with the manager about my position—and came to some sort of understanding with him that I could hang on until the baby's born.'

'That doesn't mean you've got to go into the army,' Tom objected.

The mine owners are all weeding out non-essential men on the surface staffs,' Dick said. 'It's a patriotic gesture. But get me straight, Tommy, if it weren't for Amy and the kid I'd feel I ought to do my bit. Things look bad, and we've got to win this war.'

Tom put his point of view, and tried to dissuade Dick from volunteering for active service abroad. Dick agreed that Tom's arguments were sound for him. Somebody had to safeguard the home front and all Tom stood for; but Dick said he still felt he had to fight with the men who were going overseas.

'Mind you, Tommy,' he said, with his wry smile, 'Amy won't object to being a soldier's wife. She'll rather enjoy being in the fashion, as a matter of fact—though she'll expect me to be an officer —not just a foot-slogger in the ranks. It's Sally who'll cut up rusty. My God, you'll have to help me break the news to her, when I've got to.'

CHAPTER XXXII

AMY's baby was born the following week. Dick dashed into the kitchen one morning as Sally was lighting the fire. He grabbed and kissed her, crying: "I've got a son! A son, Sal-o-my!' It seemed the most gloriously exciting and amazing thing that had ever happened to him. Sally was thrilled, too, by his news: that her first grandchild was blinking and yawning in the bright morning air.

He wasn't much to look at, yet, this son of his, Dick admitted. More like a grub just out of its chrysalis, than anything, all red and puckered up; but the doctor and nurses said he was all right, weighed seven and a half pounds, and Amy was fine: sitting up in bed and having a cup of tea when Dick saw her. She was going to call the baby Wilbur—and Alfred—to please her mother. So long as he got Bill for short, Dick didn't care. Dick was more like Den in his overflowing exuberance. Den and Lal must be sent telegrams to let them know of their new dignity as uncles, he remembered.

Tom's hand had locked with Dick's as they stood side by side, as if renewing some secret compact over the birth of this baby. Morris threw off his apathy to beam at Dick and say: 'It's a great day for the family, my boy!' And Dinny chuckled and gurgled, calling Morris grandpa, and Sally gran.

Sally and Morris were very pleased with their grandson when they called at the hospital to see Amy. He was a fine, sturdy youngster, they assured her; and she looked as pretty as a picture, with a dainty bed jacket over her shoulders and a lace cap on her head.

When Amy went home Laura took charge of her and the baby, and for several weeks you would have thought that Dick's little home was the happiest on the goldfields. Dick seemed to have thrown off his financial anxieties. He walked over to see Sally pushing the baby's pram, with Amy trotting along side. She said Dick was wonderful in the house, did all the sweeping and polishing, washed the dishes at night, and got up ever so early to take young Bill for a walk, so that she could sleep in a little longer.

Then the blow fell. Dick lost his job on the Boulder Reef. What was he to do? He knew what was expected of him, and talked the matter over with Amy. She wept a little, but soon was reconciled to the idea of Dick going into the army. After all, it did mean that Dick would be earning something, and she couldn't expect to be better off than so many of her friends whose husbands were in the forces.

Sally was distracted. She could not believe that there was nothing else for Dick to do.

'You ought to think of your wife and child,' she said.

'I'm thinking of them, darl,' Dick said. 'Amy will get my pay, and a pension for life if anything happens to me. I can't be sure of being able to provide for them any other way just now.'

'Oh Dick,' Sally wailed, 'we could manage. We could all manage together.'

'We couldn't,' Dick said firmly. 'This has got to be faced, Sal-o-my, and the less said the better.'

For a week or two Amy looked woebegone and pathetic: she went about saying that she was 'a soldier's wife now, and must be brave'.

Sally thought Amy took Dick's enlistment far too easily. She seemed to be actually enjoying all the sympathy she got, and the sensation of being noble and patriotic. Had Amy any idea of how utterly against the grain military service was going to be for Dick, Sally asked Tom. Had she realised the terrible danger Dick was going into?

'She must know, mum,' Tom said.

When Dick went into camp Amy decided to shut up the house, and go down to the coast. She had taken a cottage at Cottesloe, she said. It would be better for the baby during the summer, and she would see more of Dick when he was on leave.

Dick came home to see his mother twice before he sailed, several months later. Once, just after she received the news of Lal's death. She did not even know that Lal had rejoined the regiment in Palestine, the morning she went to meet the post boy. When last they had heard from Lal he was attending an officers' school, and expected to get his commission. That meant a great deal to Morris. It was nearly a year since Lal had been wounded.

Sally herself had taken the telegram from the boy who came on his bicycle from the post office. Just an ordinary, skinny, sun-scalded goldfields lad, he was, with a red band on his shirt sleeve. She had torn open the envelope, little thinking that youngster could be the bearer of such bad news.

As the words on the telegraph form struck her, her brain reeled. Then they sprang before her, as if a branding iron had seared them on the flimsy paper: 'We regret to inform you that Lieutenant Laurence Fitz-Morris Gough was killed in action on April nineteenth.'

Sally's cry, her one broken cry, brought Morris shambling towards her. There was no need to tell him what had happened. So many people in the town had received those heart-breaking telegrams. All the time Lal was in action Sally had dreaded to open a telegram. But with Lal in hospital, still alive and recovering from his wound, she had lost that dread.

Oh Lal! My darling Lal!' she cried and stumbled into Morris's arms. They clung together, she and Morris, in the first onslaught of their grief.

When they went back to the house Morris took the telegram and read it himself. He had dropped into a chair near the table, and slumped over it, racked by a heavy, uncontrollable sobbing.

There was nothing to say which would comfort him, or herself, Sally knew. She felt as if Morris were suffering more than she. He had been so proud of Lal, loved him in a way he had not loved his other sons. Even as a little chap, Morris seemed to have made up his mind that Lal was going to be 'his boy'. It had always been Lal and dad who were doing things together. The sort of understanding and tenderness had grown up between them, that Sally herself had for Dick more than for Tom or Den, though she reproached herself for it.

It was Lal who most often had gone off with his father to see a fight or a football match. Lal he had trained to be a good boxer and footballer. And Lal who had gone into the carpenter's shop to give his father a hand. She had thought Lal was just lazy and good-natured about that, satisfied to have a chance to earn easy wages, and boast of the good thing he was going to make of the undertaking business, some day. But she knew now that Lal had hated the dullness and dreariness of it. His military training had been a way of escape.

Dear laughing, happy-go-lucky Lal—he had enjoyed his brief hour of military glory; strutting about in his smart uniform with spurs jingling, the emu feathers in his hat flying! But it had all ended now. How? How had it ended? That was the thought which tortured her. In pain and despair? Did Lal know when his life was being blotted out? What was he thinking? Was his heart sick with longing for a word from one of his family? Did he struggle against death? Had he wanted, desperately, at the last, to live and enjoy his man's life to the full? Did he think it had been worth while to fight and die as he had done?

Sally cursed as she thought of her boy being pot-shotted at and killed; or blown to pieces by a bursting shell. She could see Lal lying on a stretch of shell-blasted ground, or in a casualty station. Dying, and dead, she could see his stiff white face and maimed body: her mind whirled crazily in her rage and grief.

How did women come to tolerate this insane business of war? How was it possible to let young men be taken in their strength and beauty, and smashed to bloody pulp? Friend and foe alike. Why do women bear sons if this is to be the end of them? Why do they make their sons fine, fit men—to be slaughtered? Why are there wars? What's the cause of them? Through her sorrow and passionate resentment of Lal's death, Sally remembered Dinny's and Tom's talk about the causes of war. She remembered what Nadya had said.

Morris and she were alone in the house when that youngster brought the telegram. He had gone off on his bicycle, whistling, as Lal himself might have done not so long ago.

It was early in the afternoon. Tom came in at about five o'clock.

'We've got to take this like Lal would want us to, dad,' he said. 'We've got to stand up to it.'

'If only we knew what happened,' Morris muttered. 'How it was . . .'

'We'll get word soon,' Tom assured him.

Each of them knew that nothing could mitigate the fact that Lal was dead, and yet they had to try to comfort and sustain each other. Tom went out to send a wire to Dick.

When Dick came home at the week-end he hugged his mother with brimming eyes.

'I can't believe it,' he said. 'He was so full of life, Lal. I thought nothing could happen to him.'

'That's how we all felt,' Sally said.

Although Tom and Dick were concerned for their father and her, Sally knew nothing had ever hit them so hard as Lal's death. It was the first break in the family circle, and in something the brothers had shared from which even she and Morris were excluded.

Dick asked: 'Has anyone told Den?'

'I'll write to him to-night,' Sally said. Dick promised to do it for her.

Seeing Dick in khaki added to her sadness. He looked well, brown and strong, as a result of his training and living in the open air. But the rough, sloppy uniform he was wearing made her feel that Dick's life would be treated as of even less value than 'Lal's had been in this brutal business of war.

She decided not to go down to Fremantle to see Dick off. It was more than she could bear, she thought, to see the troopship pull out, and realise that Dick had become just one of those swarming, khaki-clad figures, so much alike, so much just figures stuffed into drab, evil-smelling clothes for the killing and being killed. With Lal it had been different. She had never doubted that Lal would return. But Dick, how could she hope that she would ever seen him again?

CHAPTER XXXIII

In the months that followed Sally was grieving not only for Lal, but for the thousands of Australian men and boys who had died on Gallipoli, or in the blue waters of the Aegean Sea along its coasts.

People were stunned by news of the withdrawal from Gallipoli. Official explanation that an important delaying action had been fought on the Peninsula, and tributes to the incomparable valour with which Australian and New Zealand troops stormed the beaches and held their positions, could not dispel the impression that many lives had been sacrificed. The Gallipoli campaign was referred to as a colossal blunder.

Sally swore to herself that she would never forgive that blunder. But she felt helpless in the war madness swirling about her. Australian troops were fighting now in Palestine and in France. Dick had sailed and expected to be sent to France. Every day screaming shells and shattering bombardments would be breaking over him. He would be marching across a devastated country-side, crouching like a rat in some muddy trench or dugout, and taking part in those desperate charges with fixed bayonet, under a hail of enemy fire, which Lal had described.

Sometimes, Sally felt she would become insane with realisation of the fiendish cruelty of war. She could not throw off the horror and misery of knowing what Dick was going through: of what thousands of mothers like herself were suffering. But it was no earthly use to curse and wail: she must be calm, she told herself. She must think about this scourge which afflicted humanity: find out whether there was anything in what Charley O'Reilly, Dinny and Tom were saying—that this war could be stopped, and the outbreak of future wars prevented.

After moments of such intense consciousness, she found it difficult to go to her Red Cross meetings: sit quietly knitting or sewing, and listening to arguments about the need for conscription.

So many people had become accustomed to the war that they read the newspapers quite casually. They read of battles in which thousands of men were killed and wounded, almost unmoved. They read of ships blown up, and towns in ruins as if no new horror could make any impression on their minds. Such people seemed to develop a callous tissue, some sort of indiarubber covering for their minds, from which unpleasant truths bounced off, leaving no mark, Sally thought.

She was amazed at the way men and women went about the affairs of their households and businesses, almost unaffected by the war, complaining of small hardships and deprivations; but enjoying their pleasures, shopping sprees and social junketings, just the same. The shopkeepers boasted that 'business as usual' was their motto; and crowds flocked to the annual race meeting as they had always done.

There were returned soldiers now in the streets: men without an arm or leg. The hospitals were full of more serious cases. Returned soldiers had been appearing in the courts on charges of being drunk and disorderly, obtaining money on false pretences, or creating a disturbance. Some of them who had been discharged from the army, were already looking for work. Socialists and members of the I.W.W. had been imprisoned for making speeches against the war and against conscription.

The strike of engineers on the Clyde in Scotland created a stir on the goldfields, indicating as it did dissatisfaction in the Old Country with profits which were being made out of the war.

A statement of the case in the *Miner* rallied support for the engineers among workers on the goldfields.

'Not a single man of all those refusing to work who would not willingly sacrifice time and labour for the good of his country and in order to defend the lives of his fellow countrymen at home and abroad,' it said. 'But they refuse absolutely to allow themselves to be made the tools whereby large profits may be piled up. Their unanimous demand is for the government to take over these armament and ship-building yards and control them in the interests of the nation.'

Nationalisation! Socialism! That was what lay behind the demand of the Clyde engineers, the daily press all over Australia declared. Mining magnates, politicians and military leaders were loud in their abuse of the treachery of the Scottish workers.

Mr. Patrick Cavan, interviewed by an Eastern States newspaper on his experiences abroad, expressed the opinion that German spies and their agents were stirring up trouble on the Clyde. The same influences, he stated, were at work in the anti-conscription movement. He considered that the government must take strong measures against foreign agitators, disruptors and strikers, whose sole object was to sabotage the war effort.

'Can you beat it?' Dinny snorted. 'Paddy Cavan talkin' as if he and his sort, exploitin' the war and the nation, aren't sabotaging the war effort more than anything else.'

'They make and break wars to suit themselves,' Tom said bitterly.

Mr. Cavan had been a good deal in the news, recently. His marriage to the widow of a Melbourne brewer aroused no end of curiosity and was treated rather as the latest joke in Kalgoorlie and Boulder. Gossips soon fossicked out the details. Paddy had married money, they said. Her first husband had left Mrs. Mary Ann Gaggin a fortune and two daughters; but she was no oil-painting, and according to all accounts a quiet, stay-at-home little body, who disliked publicity and the whirl of fashionable society. When Paddy came west on a business visit, during the summer, Mrs. Cavan did not accompany him.

Dinny and Tom scoffed at the idea that foreign agitators had anything to do with working-class resentment of profiteering, or with the anti-conscription movement. When it was a question of using foreign workers on the mines to lower conditions and weaken the union, Mr. Cavan was all for the foreigners and keeping up the profits on gold production, Tom said. Tom was concerned about a serious situation which was developing on the mines.

Foreign workers were being employed to replace miners who had enlisted. The foreigners were using palm grease pretty freely to get jobs. Australian workers had always been opposed to greasing the palm of underground bosses and foremen to ensure that a man would be picked for a good job. But foreign workers had brought the custom with them from other countries, and regarded it as necessary to secure work.

There were shift bosses making handsome additions to their wages every week, as a result of sling-backs from the Dings. The shift bosses favoured the employment of foreign workers in the mines for this reason, although they protested that the foreigners were better workers, more easily handled. As a result of language difficulties, Tom pointed out, the foreigners, frequently, did not know when they were being used to work under bad conditions and ignore the regulations.

Workers flocked to Kalgoorlie and the Boulder from other States where the closing down of industries had created serious unemployment problems. In the west, too, unemployment was growing. The pearling industry had been brought to a standstill, luggers were laid up on the beach at Broome, and workers swarmed to the goldfields from all over the State, in the hope of finding work on the mines, or the trans-continental railway.

Kalgoorlie was to be western head of the new railway which was being built across three thousand five hundred miles of arid country from the South Australian border. The project had been launched for strategic reasons; but was absorbing hundreds of the unemployed who, camped out there on the wide grey Nullarbor Plains, were laying the shining rails which, it was boasted, would form the longest straight stretch of railway in the world.

Thought of that railway fired the imagination of goldfields folk. It was going to link them with the other great cities of Australia and guarantee the future of Kalgoorlie: that it would never fall into dust or become merely a collection of ramshackle, deserted huts about a solitary pub, which had been the fate of so many goldfields towns.

During the war, construction of the railway brought hordes of the unemployed to Kalgoorlie. Many tramped a hundred miles out into the desert country, hoping to find work on the railway. Many were forced to tramp all the way back again, and hung about the town, derelict and destitute. They resented the fact that foreign workers could find jobs on the mines, while they were unemployed and starving.

Why didn't they enlist? Why didn't they go into the army? Most able-bodied men did; but there were scores physically unfit for military services: the weedy, undersized larrikins of city slums, battered, middle-aged toilers with defective eyesight and rotten kidneys: some conscientious objectors, also normally healthy; and lads of the I.W.W., determined not to fight in this war.

Charley O'Reilly and Claude Owen made an attempt to organise the unemployed. They 'couldn't organise a dog fight', the unemployed men said. But the fact of the matter was Charley and Claude would not attack the employment of foreign workers on the mines. They said any man had a right to work, though not to grease the palms of the bosses for a job, or to let himself be used against the interests of fellow workers, by undermining union organisation and conditions the union had fought to improve on the mines. Union representatives made that clear to the foreign workers, and many of them had joined the union. But the point of view was not popular with workless men drifting about the town: neither were Charley and Claude. They became pitiful figures, waving their arms wildly and shouting themselves hoarse, in order to make workers and workless understand the causes of war, and the need for international solidarity of the working class to end war. It was all regarded as disloyal and unpatriotic propaganda.

Both Charley and Claude had been set on and beaten up by groups of drunken larrikins. Charley was run out of the town by an angry mob after a patriotic meeting, and Claude Owen had been arrested and imprisoned for speaking against the war.

'You can't help admiring them for what they're trying to do,' Sally ventured.

'Men's lives are at stake,' Morris said harshly. 'Fools can't be tolerated when there's a war on.'

'Who are the fools?' Tom wanted to know.

'You got to admit it, Morrey,' Dinny said. 'One of the English generals has been talking about trade unionism as the "rot of the national soul". "One remedy, one alone, can eradicate this state of rot," he says. "Martial law will cure it." Conscription will put the workers under martial law. It has in France. Huge profits are bein' made out of the war, and the workers are gettin' it in the neck. If conscription's necessary to win the war, let the rich men put in what they've got. Not force a poor man to put in his all, while they go on making more money out of his sacrifices. Why, accordin' to Billy Hughes they've even been selling zinc and other war materials through neutral countries to the enemy since the war began.'

'That's got nothing to do with the issue,' Morris contended. 'I've got no time for the profiteers—and I'm not boosting the system. But while men are under fire on the battlefields, all I say is, they've got to have reinforcements. I don't care how they get them so long as they get them.'

'Conscription isn't the way in Australia,' Tom contended. 'And it's depriving men on active service of the very things they're fighting for. There's not a daily newspaper in Australia will print a line about the reasons for the opposition to conscription for overseas service. They try to make out it's only spielers and crooks, racing touts and pacifists, socialists and wobblies who are opposed to conscription; but as a matter of fact, many people are just using their common sense and saying: "We don't see the necessity!" Conscription will give a reactionary government too much power: be a sell-out of democratic rights the Australian people have won through years of struggle. And besides, there's the national aspect. Isn't Australia to be defended? Isn't this country to have any means of self-defence? You know—everybody knows—when the Defence Act was introduced to provide a citizen army, we were told the Japs were only waiting for a chance to swoop down on Australia. Japan was the enemy we had to fear. We had to be ready to defend ourselves.

'In the event of war, the British navy was supposed to be equal to dealing with defence of our shores. Australian taxpayers subscribed to navy estimates on that understanding, and then started to build an Australian squadron to make sure that if Britain had her hands full in the North Sea, we'd have some battleships handy in the Pacific. But what's the position? British financiers have been subscribing to the Japanese Loan, helping the Japs to build an army and navy; become a power in the Pacific.

'What happened when the first Australian contingents left for service overseas? We know now. There were Jap warships in the convoy escorting our troopships. They even cleared out one night, a returned man was telling me the other day, sort of indicating that the Australian troops were at their mercy! It was hard for the boys to swallow—being handed over to the Japs—after all the talk there's been for years of the menace of Japan and the need for compulsory military training, a citizen army and navy to defend Australia from the Japs.

'And you bet the Japs weren't convoying our troops for fun! They were getting their pound of flesh, and we've got a pretty good idea what it was, with Japanese goods being dumped here, and Jap agents swarming everywhere. They've grabbed what they wanted in China, and although the Japanese threat to Australia was never greater than it is now, not a word critical of British policy towards Japan; or of the attitude of the Australian government towards these evasions of tariff and immigration regulations, can be uttered. The censor puts red ink through any reference to them in a newspaper article or speech. Men and women have gone to jail for defying the censorship and trying to let the people of Australia know what is the actual state of affairs.'

'They've got a right to know,' Dinny muttered. 'But Billy Hughes is scared stiff the Japs will take advantage of havin' warships in our ports to start something.'

'They've been some nasty incidents in the north—in Brisbane and Cairns,' Tom went on. 'Jap sailors are swaggering round, and boasting openly that some day they'll be ruling the roost there. The wharfies and returned soldiers have been warned against giving them any excuse for a brawl. There were Jap warships in Brisbane waters, quite recently, and the Jap commander threatened to open fire on the town if any unfriendly incident to a Jap sailor occurred.

'It's a very difficult situation that's been created: a situation in which the government has to spar for wind. But one also in which the Australian people are entitled to know the facts and be prepared to defend their own interests. Our job is to put up a fight for the right of the Australian people to develop as a nation, prepared to defend their own country, capable of defending it. It's not good enough for us to be just a pawn in the game of British financiers. Conscription for overseas service will make us that. Voting "NO" on this issue will defend Australia and the democratic rights of the Australian people.

'You've got the gift of the gab—even if you haven't got the guts to fight,' Morris said angrily.

'Morris!' Sally cried, appalled that he could say such a thing to Tom.

'I'm sorry. I'm sorry, lad,' Morris added hastily. 'I didn't mean that. I know you've got guts for anything. That's why I hate to see you barking up the wrong tree about the need for conscription.'

CHAPTER XXXIV

WITH Dick in the trenches in France, Sally could think of conscription only as a means to get reinforcements to him. If there was the shadow of a doubt about reinforcements being available, she

239

agreed with Morris, the government must take action. Dick wrote about 'the mud and bloody muck' of Flanders: a charge at dawn in drizzling rain, wiping out of his platoon under heavy fire: crawling back to a dug-out that was demolished by shell-fire a few hours later. He had missed that shell by a fluke but it got most of his cobbers. Dick said only the men's loyalty to each other kept them fighting and set on victory.

The controversy over conscription for service overseas increased in bitterness and intensity as time for taking of the referendum approached. It created the atmosphere of a civil war, splitting the community into hostile factions, tearing placid family relationships to pieces, obscuring even the war news in importance for the time being, although no one forgot that it was against the background of war decisions had to be made.

Sally thought the referendum could have only one result. War fever was still at its height, and patriotic frenzy excluded the anti-conscription point of view from the daily press. Many publications were made illegal. Public halls could not be obtained for anti-conscription meetings, and even those held in the street were broken up by rowdy patriots and soldiers.

That Tom was opposing conscription was a tragedy to his mother. It was all very well for him to argue conscription would be used against the working class and against the trade unions: but that was of less importance to her than sending relief to the men under fire, men living day and night on the battlefields in Flanders. She was frantic when she thought of it; felt as if she were fighting for Dick's life and the life of thousands of other Australian boys.

'Surely, Tom,' she pleaded, 'you don't want to refuse to send reinforcements to the men fighting. It's like saying Dick and those boys in France can die of exhaustion, but you won't make some of these loafers and I.W.W. windbags give them a helping hand.'

'Don't talk like that, mum,' Tom said, his face drawn with pain. 'You're taking the thing personally. It hurts like hell to think of Dick out there. And Lal—but I've got to do what I believe to be right, not only for Dick, but for Australia—and all our men on active service.'

'Who are you to judge, my son?'

'A working man,' Tom said. 'And I'm not making a fortune out of the war, or backing those who think that the life and rights of Australian workers are of less value than profits.'

'Well, you've got to give Hughes credit for showing up the base metal industry in this country,' Morris said angrily. 'He pointed out it was still under German domination a year after war was declared. He said the Australian Metal Company was linked up with the Metal Gesellschaft with headquarters in Frankfurt, and that the company which "determined how much zinc Australia should produce, its price and destination, and also copper, was of German construction". Lead was in the bag too.'

'That only proves what I've been saying,' Tom replied. 'Billy Hughes says too, that someone in this country sold coal to the *Emden, Gneisnau* and *Scharnhorst*. The cruisers were supplied with Australian coal, and British sailors murdered when their ships went down by the men who sold it to the Germans. And yet he wants to put the labour movement in pawn to the mob that does that sort of thing!'

'He wants to win the war,' Morris shouted.

'Conscription isn't necessary to do it,' Tom shouted back at him. 'The voluntary system hasn't failed. Catts, head of voluntary recruiting in New South Wales, says recruiting was held up in some districts this year, because the military authorities couldn't cope with the number of recruits. Over fifteen thousand men had to be kept waiting over three months.'

So it went on. In a world riven by war, the chaos and misery brought by it, the disorderly brawling of political factions, it was necessary, Sally thought, to have peace in the home and keep family affections unimpaired. But the war had invaded her home. Morris and Tom were always at loggerheads over the conscription issue.

Morris could not refrain from abusing anti-conscriptionists, and goading Tom into an angry defence of them. Never before had an atmosphere of such antagonism been generated in the house. Tom and Morris when they were arguing seemed to forget that they were father and son. They shouted and snarled at each other as if they were bitter enemies. Sally's head ached with the clangour of their voices and the tension their conflict created. She was terrified where it would end: that Tom would leave home. She only saw him for a hurried meal in the morning and evening. Every night he was out until all hours: got very little sleep before it was time to be up and going off to work again.

'Don't argue with your father, Tom,' she begged. 'He's an old man and can't get rid of some of his fixed ideas.'

'I don't want to argue with him, mum,' Tom protested. 'But I've got to stand up for the things I believe in.'

Tom had been working on an anti-conscription committee in the town. He was addressing street meetings: spending every afternoon and evening canvassing, arguing and urging people to vote 'No'. Morris distributed leaflets and handbills in favour of conscription.

Tom and Morris ignored each other's activities as much as possible; and Sally endeavoured to prevent clashes between them. Tom came and went like a stranger in the house.

It was from Eily that Sally learned what Tom was doing. She, of course, was working with Tom on the anti-conscription committee: typed letters, helped to organise meetings and distribute illegal documents. But she, too, was troubled about the way Tom was driving himself, night and day, with very little rest, and a desperate, indefatigable energy. He had quarrelled with her father, also, Eily said, because Tom did not see eye to eye with him about the war.

'But Tom's right,' Eily said, fiercely loyal. 'I know he's right. Dad says Tom's no revolutionary, but Tom says the defeat of German militarism is as much our job as the defeat of conscription in Australia. What's the use of beating the conscriptionists here, if the most powerful conscriptionist power in the world is victorious in this war, and can dictate terms which will keep the workers in chains everywhere. Tom says we've got to fight on two fronts: at home and abroad. It's illogical to think a scrap in your own back-yard's of more importance than the big fight going on to decide whether you're going to have any back-yard.'

'Oh dear,' Sally sighed, 'I wish I was as sure Tom's right as you are, Eily.'

Eily's eyes held a naïve pity.

'It's not only because I love Tom,' she said. 'I really believe he's right.'

'Tom's very lucky to have you believing in him and helping him,' Sally said.

'Oh, that!' Eily's smile fluttered. 'I'm happy just to be with him, and do anything I can to help. Some of the committee don't understand. They think Tom and I—well, that we're too friendly: ought to be engaged, or something. Miss Barbury—she's a pacifist and very prim and proper, you know—but a sweet old thing, said to me the other day: "My dear, I don't like to mention it. You won't mind, will you? But, do you think you ought to go about quite so much with Mr. Gough? I know you're heart and soul in your work for the cause—but people are talking, and a young girl has to be so careful of her good name." "Don't worry about that, Miss Barbury," I told her. "Tom and I have been comrades for years." I could see from the shocked look on her face that she thought I meant we'd been living together. "But we're not even sweethearts," I said to reassure her.'

'Aren't you?'

'No.' Eily met Sally's glance with clear, smiling eyes. 'Though I wish we were. A long time ago Tom used to kiss me when he took me home after a dance. But that was before he met Nadya. Sometimes I think he cared so much for her he won't ever feel fond of anybody in that way again. I don't blame him, of course, for loving Nadya. She . . . she was so wonderful. And I know she loved Tom, though she never said so. Mum gets a bit annoyed with me sometimes for "running after" Tom, as she says: being always at his beck and call. But she's fond of Tom, too. Since Claude Owen's been in jail, and she's been looking after his children, Tom's been sending her money every week to help with their keep — and it's not easy for him, mum knows, with all the expenses he's got now, paying for printing and sending speakers to out-back camps when there's not enough money in the committee's fund.'

'I didn't know Tom was doing that,' Sally said, realising that was why Tom no longer asked her to bank a portion of his pay, although he still handed her half of all he earned.

'Oh, yes,' Eily went on. 'And he won't spend a penny on himself if he can help it. Even on Saturday or Sunday when we've been out canvassing all day, he never thinks of stopping for a meal. I have to say: "I'll simply drop, Tom, if we don't have a bite to eat, or get a cool drink somewhere." Sometimes if I can get him to rest for a few minutes at midday he falls asleep, and is so cross with me for letting him lose an hour or two! But it's worth it, knowing he's not so terribly tired when we go on.'

'I'm glad Tom's got you, Eily,' Sally said impatiently, glimpsing the fine ideas driving these young people, but unable to approve of such reckless expenditure of youth and energy. 'Some day, I feel sure, Tom will discover how much you mean to him. I'll be very happy, anyhow, when I hear you *are* sweethearts.'

'Oh, Mrs. Gough!' A lovely light welled behind Eily's blue eyes. 'Will you, really? If it could be like that, some day!'

CHAPTER XXXV

LAURA went down to Cottesloe to join Amy after Dick left. Amy had let her house at Mullingar, and would remain at the seaside until Dick returned, she said. She was doing all sorts of war work, it appeared, and wrote asking her mother to come and help her with the house and the child.

Sally heard nothing of them for months, although occasionally she saw Amy's name mentioned in the social column of weekly papers. Mrs. Dick Gough was a member of The Golden Butterflies concert party, which was giving performances to entertain soldiers in camp and raise money for Red Cross and comforts funds, she read. Mrs. Dick Gough had worn smart green linen suit at the races, and flame-coloured georgette at the Red Cross ball in the Town Hall. 'Among devotees of the surf and sun at North Beach, Mrs. Dick Gough could always be numbered, with an escort of naval and military men.'

When Laura returned to the fields at the end of the summer she brought Billy with her. He was toddling now, a sturdy, obstreperous youngster with a shock of dark hair, and 'the wicked look in his eye of a regular young warrigul', Dinny said.

'I don't know what's come over Amy,' Laura wailed to Sally. 'Of course, she's raised a lot of money for patriotic funds. But there's too much flying about with colonel this and major that, for my liking. And, above all, with Paddy Cavan! Amy says she has to keep sweet with him because he contributes generously to patriotic funds. Paddy's staying at the Ocean Beach Hotel and making a great splash with his money to impress the crowd Amy gets round with. She sings that "Honeysuckle" thing at the concerts, you know: "I am the honeysuckle, you are the bee", and it would make you sick to see Paddy sitting looking at Amy, all goofy, and as if she meant it for him.

'A whole crowd of young people will come in from a dance in the early hours of the morning, and start frying bacon, or fish: wake the child and me, and Amy's a nervous wreck next day. She won't listen to a word I say about it's not being fair to Dick. Just bursts into tears and says I don't understand. She's got to try to forget Dick's in France, and this is the only way she can do it. But it's very bad for Bill, and I just couldn't stand it any longer. Amy promised if I brought him home with me, she'd drop everything and come back to the fields for the winter.'

Sally was concerned on Dick's account. She had just heard that Dick had been wounded and was in hospital in England. He was making good progress, and there was nothing to worry about, he said. It was some relief to know he was temporarily out of the trenches; but she hoped that news of Amy's gallivantings would not reach him.

Their grandson was a new bond between Sally and Laura. A little jealous and apprehensive of each other's overtures to win the little chap's affections they might be; but very pleased with him as the seal of their friendship. Sally was quite reconciled to the idea that Laura should have first claim on Bill: that he should turn to her as if she were his mother and natural protector, though Sally was afraid Laura was giving in to him too much and making him a terribly spoilt, little brat. Still she saw to it that Billy learnt to like his visit to Grandma Sally: the gay, easy way she had with him, and the strange, exciting toys she produced for him to play with, letting him wander about the house and do as he pleased.

Amy ran up to see Billy during the winter months, but she did not stay long. She was restless and irritated by the quiet life of Kalgoorlie after the hectic whirl of the summer in Perth, and the pressing demands of her war work.

Soon after she returned Paddy Cavan, too, paid Kalgoorlie a visit. He put up at the Palace Hotel, and astounded everybody by playing the mining magnate in great style, giving dinner parties, and shouting with unusual generosity in the bars. Paddy had presented an aeroplane to the Royal Air Force it was rumoured, and put half a million into war loans. He had made so much money out of various deals in the Eastern States that he was reputed to be one of the wealthiest men in the Commonwealth.

Sally found it difficult to forgive Amy for going to Paddy's dinner parties in Kalgoorlie; and for driving about with him in his big black car. Laura told her she had remonstrated with Amy.

'It used to be horses, now it's a Rolls Royce, Paddy's courting you with,' Laura had said.

'What nonsense!' Amy tossed off the insinuation. 'Paddy's a married man, with a wife and two children, now. Surely, I don't have to cut him dead because he made love to me once.'

'Don't try to throw dust in my eyes, Amy,' her mother replied. 'Paddy's as much in love with you now as he ever was.'

Amy's laughter rippled.

'Well, I'm no more in love with him than I ever was. But I can't just sit at home and mope until Dick comes home, can I?'

'You could show a little more consideration for Dick's family,' Laura suggested. 'And a little more personal dignity, than to allow Paddy Cavan to take you about so much. People are beginning to talk.'

'Let them talk,' Amy exclaimed lightly. 'I'm going down to Cottesloe again for the summer, and taking Billy with me.'

She went off singing that little song Laura so much disliked and which she was always singing or whistling, these days:

> *You are my honey-honeysuckle,*
> *I am the bee;*
> *I'd like to steal the honey sweet*
> *From those red lips you see,*
> *I love you, dearly, dearly . . .*
> *And I want you to love me. . . .*

CHAPTER XXXVI

AFTER the first referendum Sally hoped that Morris and Tom would forget their differences and settle down to a normal tolerant attitude towards each other. She hated to hear them bickering, and to see the antagonism that flared so easily when this subject was mentioned. Home had become merely a place in which they flung the most vicious hostilities of the campaign at each other.

Morris still could not forgive Tom for the part he had taken in defeating the referendum—though he thanked God, the West had voted solidly for conscription.

The Prime Minister said he would accept the verdict of the people, but Tom was sure the last had not been heard of the matter. Already voices were raised declaring that the referendum had been a mistake. A bill should have been introduced to enforce military service for overseas, or regulations promulgated under the War Precautions Act which would have had the same effect.

It was generally admitted that Mr. Hughes might have tried either measure, had he been able to muster a majority of Labour members in support of such proposals. But this he could not do and was loath to precipitate an election. His expulsion from the Labour Party for persisting in a policy to which a majority of the members was opposed, created a situation that split the party and before long made an election inevitable.

The election campaign took a more or less normal course, with a few stormy meetings: but little doubt—in the minds of most people, that the elections would reflect decisions of the referendum. When it did not many Labour members lost their seats, and the Opposition 'swept the polls'. Even Morris was disturbed, although conscriptionists everywhere whooped jubilantly. The elections were regarded as a personal triumph for Hughes and the 'win-the-war' policy. Had the people regretted their verdict on conscription? Or was the election merely proof that the people of Australia would go any lengths to win the war, short of conscription. It was obvious after Hughes' policy speech that another referendum was on the cards.

The first referendum had stirred a lot of muddy water. Facts in relation to it were well known before the second referendum was taken.

On the goldfields, revelations in connection with the Maltese affair were a decisive factor in making many people vote against conscription. Everybody knew that before the first referendum there were hundreds of unemployed tramping the country in search of work. Mr. Hughes was accused of bringing a shipload of Maltese to work on the transcontinental railway. He denied that he was doing so. But after the referendum the facts leaked out. The French steamer *Gangé* was approaching the West Australian coast with two hundred and forty Maltese on board, when the French consul in Sydney was authorised to instruct the captain of the ship not to touch any West Australian port. He was directed to coal at Adelaide, and put the ship in quarantine: give out he was bound for Noumea and reduce speed so as not to reach Melbourne until two days after the poll. Tom had copies of the telegrams which were sent.

In relation to the soldiers' vote, there had been suppression of the results for a long time, and then a widespread impression gained ground that they had been 'doctored' to give a 'yes' majority.

All the prosecution, censorships and vilification levelled against men and women opposed to conscription, were continued with renewed violence during the months before the second referendum.

Most people smiled, but did not attach any importance to a poster which read:

'To arms, capitalists, parsons, politicians, newspaper editors, and other stay-at-home patriots! Your Country needs you in the trenches! Workers, follow your masters!'

It was hard to believe that the man responsible for that poster had been arrested and sentenced to fifteen months' imprisonment.

Soon afterwards twelve men of the I.W.W. were arrested in Sydney and sentenced to ten and fifteen years' imprisonment and the I.W.W. was declared an illegal organisation. Then nine men in the West were charged that, together with these members of the I.W.W., they had conspired 'to raise discontent and dissatisfaction amongst the subjects of our lord, the King'.

Among the accused men were Monty Miller and Mick Sawtell. Sally knew them both. Monty was eighty-four: a white-haired champion of the rights of working men, as courtly and dignified in his manner as a foreign aristocrat. Dinny and he were old mates. Monty had often sat on the verandah, expounding his views on socialism and industrial unionism, or reciting in a powerful, sonorous voice whole essays from Emerson, and speeches from the plays of Shakespeare. As a lad of eighteen he had fought in the Eureka stockade, and Sally had often heard him reminiscing about the historic struggle of the miners at Ballarat. Mick was a few years older than Tom, but they were good friends. A red-headed young man, full of fiery ideals and pacifist zeal for 'the emancipation of the working class', Mick was a bit confused in his ideas about practical organisation, Tom said. But Sally liked to listen when Mick talked to Tom about the books he had been reading. He was fond of poetry, and had given Tom a poem in a plain folder by Furnley Maurice, a young Australian writer. 'To God from the Weary Nations' it was called. Sally could remember Mick's voice, intoning passionately in the dark:

> *The dreamers wait. What can the spirit urge*
> *Against the madness of this sorry day?*
> *How can the timid form of Peace emerge*
> *Unless the marshals let the dreamers say?*
> *And they are few and most forsaken, Lord,*
> *Who slaved and suffered for their human hope,*
> *Though Thou shalt give the martyrs to the sword,*
> *Preserve the future from the hangman's rope.*

Sally had learnt the verses. They haunted her, their lines recurring and running through her head as she went about her work, worried about Dick, the war and the referendum.

The trial of Monty and Mick on that seditious conspiracy charge disturbed her a good deal, although it gave Tom and Dinny a lot of ironic amusement.

Monty had defended himself and cross-examined Mick in order to make their point of view clear to the court.

Monty asked Mick whether he agreed with Emerson: 'That every government was one of force. A government of love had never been known, but if one ever was it would bring to their knees in contrition and tears those members of the community, previously looked upon as useless and criminals.'

Mick quoted Emerson back at him, to the effect that a government was a conservative force. If there was no one to come forward and risk jail, or at least prosecution, the world would never progress.

'Do you consider that Socrates was a good citizen?' asked Monty.

'Yes, and he died because of his good citizenship,' said Mick.

Between them, Monty and Mick traced the history of the struggle for progress from the time of Plato to the present prosecution, quoting from memory Shelley, Godwin, Tolstoy, Kropotkin and Marx: outlining revolutions in architecture, music and aesthetics, and defending 'the sacred right of members of the I.W.W. to work in the interests of the working class to make the world a better place to live in'.

Even the daily press referred to 'the dramatic force and flow of language with which the two accused had held the attention of those in court'. Mr. Justice Burnside, sentencing the men, said they had been found guilty, and he had to accept the verdict as being correct.

But he was entitled to form his own opinions as to the circumstances in which these men had found themselves. 'Against not one of them had he heard anything stated to show that they were other than men of good character . . . The gravamen of the charge was the distribution of literature for which he did not think they were really responsible, and which he thought, in their calmer moments, they would themselves strongly denounce.'

There was a good deal of truth in this, Dinny admitted. The accused were released on a bond to be of good behaviour, keep the peace and to obey the laws of the land.

Before the second referendum was taken, Sally was satisfied that Tom and Dinny were right. Their reasons for opposing conscription had been justified by the course of events.

She had read a book, exposing manipulation of the war loans in the interests of financial combines, the *Nation*, and other illegal publications which Eily and Tom were distributing. Why were those papers and books illegal, Sally asked. She resented being told she must not read something of vital interest to her. If information was false and unreliable, it could be disproved: if not, people were entitled to it. Women like herself felt the lives of their sons and husbands were at stake: the future of their children. It was outrageous that any government should tell grown men and women they must not read criticism of the way the war was being conducted, or hear what anybody had to say about the causes of war.

Sally felt as if she had been buffeted about in the suffocating heat of a goldfields dust storm. First of all, prepared to accept all the Prime Minister said as gospel, and agreeing with Morris that reinforcements for the men on active service must be kept up at all costs. Then wearing herself out in endless arguments with Tom and Dinny: shattered by the conflict between Morris and Tom. But now she had seen how the rights of the people were ignored by censorship and prosecutions: how unnecessary violence had been used against anti-conscriptionists, and that there had been a cynical abuse of law to incriminate them for putting the facts of their case before the people.

Dick had been wounded and was in hospital: she could think more clearly. He wrote that he had voted against conscription, and that most of the men in his platoon, in France, had done likewise. None of the boys were so favourably impressed with life in the army that they believed every single man in Australia ought to be run in to it.

'Happiest day of our lives,' Dick had written, 'will be coming home, and getting out of the army. We've had a bellyful of it, Sal-o-my! All very well for Billy Hughes to say "Allied generals have learnt much" since the Somme offensive and Pozières (20,000 casualties a month!). But most of us reckon we'd have to have a lot more confidence in army methods before we'd give the military a free hand with our young brothers. It sticks in the men's gizzards that in England it's against regulations for a common soldier to eat or drink in a pub frequented by officers. You wouldn't believe what a big effect this, and the everlasting saluting, has had on the attitude of Australian troops towards the military having any more rights over them. Tell dad I'll put on the gloves and give him a go round the yard if he votes for conscription.'

Morris was shaken by Dick's letter, but said Dick was influenced chiefly by concern for Tom and Den. Both of them were in reserved occupations, and Morris asserted conscription would not affect them. But in any case the wider issues had to be considered. There was a falling-off in recruiting, and the war had to be won.

He took it for granted Sally would help him to hand out leaflets advocating a 'yes' vote, as she had done before.

'No, Morris,' she said firmly. 'I don't any longer believe conscription is in the best interests of the Australian people. Reinforcements have been kept up, and I wouldn't trust this government any further than I can see it.'

CHAPTER XXXVII

TOM had come home one evening looking dirty and dishevelled. There was a nasty cut on his forehead and his face was bruised and bleeding. Eily was with him, not in much better shape.

'Had a bit of a dust-up with a couple of drunken soldiers,' he explained casually to his mother and went off to wash.

Eily was trembling and on the verge of tears.

'They got Tom down and kicked him, Mrs. Gough,' she cried. 'I don't know what would have happened if I hadn't yelled. Barney Riordan, Peter Lalich and two or three miners came along and got Tom away. He'd been speaking in Hannan Street, and all night these men had been trying to break up the meeting, but there was a good crowd round us. Somebody sang out: "Heigh, boys, Tom Gough's a mate of ours, and we want to hear what he's got to say. If you don't—clear out." Then the soldiers rushed the platform and there was an all-in fight for a few minutes. The chairman closed the meeting and Tom and I got away. But three men followed us, and I was scared something was going to happen. Tom walked on, and told me to keep out of the way if they tried any funny business. But how could I?'

'She just hung on to them and yelled until Barney, Ted Lee and some of our chaps arrived,' Tom said, coming back into the room. 'And those toughs handled her pretty roughly while she was about it.'

'Are you all right, Eily?' Sally asked anxiously. 'And you, son?' She went to get a basin of water to bathe Tom's head.

'Just a bit groggy, mum,' Tom said, trying to hold himself together. 'Don't worry. A kick in the groin was the worst part of it. Fair doubled me up.'

Sally was shocked and alarmed. It was proof to her of what Tom said, that there was a war within a war. Because Tom was opposing conscription in the interests of the working class, he was being treated like an enemy of the people and of his country. She wanted to send for the doctor, but Tom would not hear of it.

'I'll be all right after a night's sleep,' he said.

Going up to bed he looked back at Eily with a shy smile.

'Thanks, comrade,' he said gently. 'She's a great little girl, isn't she, mum? Keep her here to-night, won't you?'

Eily broke down when Tom had gone.

'Oh, Mrs. Gough,' she sobbed, 'it was awful—I thought Tom would be killed. Those men weren't soldiers: they were just toughs in uniform. They don't belong to the fields. They've came up with a recruiting sergeant, and are trying to make brawls and get our men arrested.'

'I'd rather Tom were in jail if this is what is going to happen,' Sally said grimly.

Next morning Tom could not move without pain and was passing blood. Sally sent for the doctor. There was some internal injury, he said. A few days' rest might give it a chance to mend. If necessary he would arrange for an X-ray and admission to the hospital.

Tom fretted and fumed through those days in bed, but the haemorrhage ceased, and at the end of the week he was declaring himself as fit as a fiddle, and insisting on going back to work.

He was not well, Sally knew, not well enough to work underground. The injury to his back and kidneys was still giving him a good deal of pain. But Tom insisted on starting work again. Not only in the mine, but with the anti-conscriptionist committee.

'I'm a soldier on active service too, mum,' he said. 'On active service for the people, and I can't afford to loaf on the job.'

Eily had continued with her work, delivering leaflets and even

251

speaking at street meetings instead of Tom, while he was on the flat of his back.

The fighting spirit of the girl amazed Sally.

'Oh, my dear,' she said, 'how can a little girl like you influence people to think and act differently?'

'I don't know,' Eily replied simply. 'But I've got to try. If there's nobody else to tell them the things they ought to know I've go to try. If there's nobody else—I've got to do my best.'

It was all against the tide, unpopular and thankless work she was doing. There were no bouquets or pretty speeches for a girl who, after working in a restaurant all day, sat up half the night typing reports of speeches made in the Eastern States, roneoing them for distribution, then walked round throwing them and illegal leaflets over garden fences in the small hours of the morning. Eily's strenuous, self-imposed tasks were very different from what Amy called her war work, Sally realised. Amy boasted of the good time she was having, dancing and surfing, being escorted hither and thither by officers of the army or navy. She was complimented and cheered: had made quite a name for herself as an organiser of patriotic concerts.

Of course, Tom and Eily were fanatics, Sally told herself. Yet she could not help admiring their fanaticism. They were prepared to sacrifice everything, including their love for each other, to their crazy notion of serving the working class.

Sally had no doubt that Tom did love Eily. Since that night when he had been beaten up by drunken hooligans, his eyes had sought Eily's with a new, appreciative tenderness. Eily was walking on air.

'Every night, now, Tom kisses me good-night,' she told Sally. 'And sometimes he just holds me in his arms and says: "My love, my dear little love." '

'I'm glad, Eily,' Sally told her. 'I do hope you'll be married soon, and have some happiness together.'

'We haven't talked about that yet,' Eily said hurriedly. 'I don't think Tom wants to, until after the war. He said once: "We've got no right to think of ourselves until all this is over, Eily." '

"What nonsense!' Sally exclaimed.

'I don't think so,' Eily said, stubbornly. 'You see, I feel the same way as Tom does about it. There's so much to do—and so few of us to stand by the workers in this struggle against conscription, injustice and oppression. I love Tom, and it's heavenly to know he loves me. But we can't desert our comrades in jail and fighting at the front, just to be happy together.'

'I'm not a public meeting,' Sally told her crossly.

'Oh, dear,' Eily laughed, 'I'm getting quite a stump orator, aren't I?'

She was so unaffected and sweet-natured, Sally could not help loving her; but she wished that Eily and Tom would be a little more like ordinary people in their ways and ideas. They seemed to be wrapped up in their enthusiasms, and strenuous activities in connection with various committees: would rather attend a stuffy meeting or study economics and industrial history together than do anything else, Sally complained.

At least they had the satisfaction of knowing that the energy they put into the campaign against conscription was not wasted. After defeat of the second referendum, even people who had voted for compulsory overseas service began to say: 'You've got to take off your hats to the anti-conscriptionists. After all, in circumstances of extraordinary difficulty, they saved Australia from drastic legislation which wasn't necessary!' As it was, the war effort was no worse off, and recruiting continued at a rate to justify reliance on the voluntary system.

Oh yes, Sally assured herself, there were compensations for young people like Tom and Eily who hitched their waggon to a star. They could go on star-gazing no matter what harassed them. Rotten eggs, abuse, being kicked and knocked about did not affect them. They would work themselves to frazzles for the things they believed in, and be quite content if some almost mythical people they called 'the workers', or 'the workers of the world', benefited by their labours. Of course, Tom and Eily had been through a tough time during the conscription campaigns. But, after all, they could have the satisfaction of knowing they had backed a winner. And now the revolution in Russia was a feather in their cap. Tom went about as if he were personally responsible for it. Sally had not seen him so lit-up and lively for some time, as he was that night when he and Eily came to tell her the news.

Tom heard it when he came off shift: the pubs were full of it: men shouting each other hilariously, and singing 'The Red Flag' and 'Solidarity for Ever'. There was a general feeling that this was a victory the workers should celebrate, and that although the war might drag on for a while the end was in sight.

At the newspaper office Tom had seen the cables; but no more information about them was available. He went off to find Eily. It was the busy time for her: the 'Home from Home' restaurant, where she worked, full of men waiting for their dinner. But Eily had heard the news and flew about among them, taking their orders, as if she were dancing. She carried her heavily loaded tray as if it were a featherweight, beaming at everybody and exclaiming: 'Isn't

253

it wonderful? Isn't it marvellous?' When she saw Tom she could only grab him for a moment, and say the same thing over and over again.

Tom sat down and had dinner at one of her tables, so that as soon as she finished work they could walk home together.

A gash of gold, from the setting sun, thrust aside dark clouds over the sky as they walked along the dusty road. They knew a thunder-storm might be brewing: but their whole world was steeped in glowing light.

'If only Nadya could know,' Eily whispered.

'I was thinking that,' Tom said.

It seemed as if some unbelievably miraculous thing had happened: something they had dreamed of, yet scarcely believed could be anything more than a dream. But it had happened! This was the reality for which Nadya had struggled in that far country of which she had talked so much. In their rejoicing, it was enough that Tsarism had been overthrown. They were confident the first step had been taken towards fulfilment of her faith: that the workers of Russia would evolve a new social system after they were released from the old oppression.

Morris refused to be impressed. All he could see was the effect on the Western Front, and a weakening of the Allied offensive in Flanders.

Den's letters were like a refreshing breeze through the turbid atmosphere of those months when Morris and Tom were snarling at each other over conscription, the war and the revolution in Russia. Den gave Sally a breath of the green and quiet southern countryside, as he wrote proudly of the number of cows he was milking: what percentage of butter fat they gave: how his steers had brought top prices in the sale yards. She could feel that somewhere it was still possible for people to live sane and useful lives. And Den's accounts of talks with Charlie, jobs he had done for Charlie, visits to Three Creeks, gave her an inkling of what Fanny wrote later.

Fanny said Charlotte McLean was the daughter of their nearest neighbour. Her two brothers had gone off to the war and she was practically running Three Creeks. Her father had thought he could carry on with a half-caste stockman when the boys left home. But he was almost crippled with rheumatism, and Charlotte took charge as a matter of course.

'The young people have a good deal in common,' Fanny wrote, 'and get on very well together. Although, usually, they seem to be quarrelling, and "slinging off at each other", as they say. Charlotte was rather scornful of Den at first and treated him as if he were a greenhorn. But often now Denis gives her a hand with stock, and odd jobs, so do not be surprised, my dear, if there is a romance in that quarter.

'Indeed, Phyll and I don't know how any girl could help falling in love with Denis. He's such a dear boy, so full of life and good spirits, always whistling and yodelling about the place. I don't know what we'd do without him. He really has taken over management of everything now, and although at first we were a little afraid to give him a free rein, we have let him buy pedigreed stock at an enormous figure, and we're quite satisfied with the results. Only too thankful not to have to slop about out of doors in all weathers.'

From his letters Sally gathered that during the conscription campaign, Den had been a little unsettled: thought he ought to volunteer. 'I've been trying to think things out, mum,' he wrote. 'Remember what Lal said? "Food supplies have got to be kept up. You'll be doing as good a job on Warrinup, lad, as you would in the army." Aunt Fanny and Phyll couldn't manage without me, now, Charl says, and she couldn't either—helping her to muster and brand, and taking her cream cans along with ours to the factory. "You're doing the work of two or three men on Warrinup, Den," Charl said. "You can't just drop it to go into camp."

'I don't see how I can, either,' Den concluded. 'Though sometimes, it doesn't seem fair for me to be stowed away down here, when I think what Lal and Dick have been up against—and Tom.'

'You can't blame me for wanting to keep Den out of the army,' Sally exclaimed defensively, after reading this letter to Morris and Dinny.

'I'm thanking God, myself, for Charlie and Warrinup,' Morris admitted.

CHAPTER XXXVIII

A ROCKET soaring into the night sky told people of the back-country the good news. Peace, it said, and a shooting star fell into the darkness again.

Sally saw it that evening when rumours of an armistice being signed had been circulating for hours. The end of the war was like the breaking of a long, dry summer to her. An infinite relief, unutterable weariness after the tension of nervous anxieties, left her little energy for rejoicing. She could feel the silence of the guns which had thundered over distant battlefields. The earth seemed becalmed after the fury of the storm which had swept it.

That Dick would be coming home was almost too good to be true. His wound had healed, and he had expected to leave for France within a few weeks, when last he wrote. But now, there would be no more fighting for him! Sally's heart swelled to the bliss of that thought. She knew how so many women were feeling whose sons, brothers, lovers and husbands were coming home. She knew, too, how those were feeling who would never see their men again. Her grief for Lal resurged.

Next morning the mine whistles were all shrilling madly. The men had tied them down when they stopped work and went off to join in the celebrations. Soon the streets were filled with racketing crowds of men, women, boys and girls, surging along, singing and dancing. Strangers stopped to hug and kiss and frolicked on.

Never had there been such a riot of rejoicing. Flags flew from every building. In the pubs beer was flowing like water and the uproar was terrific. It went on all day and night, until people dropped with exhaustion. What did it mean, Sally wondered. Was some primitive instinct of the life force expressing itself? An instinct as irrational as that which had expressed itself in hysteria at the beginning of the war? Did this jubilation mean that people had learnt the value of peace, and would do something to preserve it? Or did it mean that the celebrations were just an excuse to forget the holocaust of the war, and to enjoy the excitement and licence of an unbridled holiday?

Morris would take no part in the celebrations. He was satisfied that the armistice had been signed and Allied victory was assured; but he could not rejoice, because Lal was dead. That, he felt, was the price he personally had paid for victory and peace. Her own gratitude for them was too deep and awed, Sally found, to join the orgy in the streets. Friends and neighbours came in to tell her about it and laugh over absurd incidents. Marie and Dinny, Tom and Eily, brought their accounts of the gay furore. It had been a great day for Kalgoorlie and Boulder.

A few weeks later, when Sally saw a stalwart figure in the uniform of the 10th Light Horse push back the garden gate and walk along the path towards her, a spasm of joy almost blinded her.

In the dusk, for a moment, she thought it was Lal, and clung to a verandah post, trembling. But the broad-shouldered, solid figure approaching her lacked Lal's jaunty swing and stride! When the soldier had come quite close, and she could look into the lean, hard face, burnt bronze, she saw the kind, brown eyes, so like his mother's. Sally recognised Perth Molloy. Sergeant Molloy he was now, she knew, and had been decorated for valour. The narrow magenta ribbon on his shabby tunic recorded that. But Perth was thinking only of why he had come to see her, as he met Sally's eyes. He was thinking of Lal, she realised, as he gripped her hand.

'I was with Lal, Mrs. Gough,' he said. 'Thought you might like to know what happened.'

Morris shambled along the verandah and they sat down there, in the cool of the evening, with blossom on the potato creeper shedding its warm, musky fragrance round them, to hear what Perth had to say.

'Lal and me were together on Gallipoli, until we both copped it at Walker's Ridge,' he said. 'Lal got his commission as soon as he left hospital and was breaking his neck to get back to the regiment, when we went into camp for reorganisation and training. I got my stripes, after a bit—and reckon I owed them to the good word Lal put in for me. And, gosh, it was great to know I'd be serving under him—we could stick around together.

'The boys were in good heart getting back to their horses and out into the open—though it was tough going what with the sand and the heat. There was good country in Palestine all the same: you'd see an old Arab pushin' a wooden plough, and fields of barley and olive groves, pass a Bedouin village now and then, or cross a wadi —like a dry creek bed.

'We reckoned we were evening up the score for Gallipoli in the fighting round Bir Hamisah, El Arish and Rafa—but Gaza was a tougher proposition. It was an old town with a big hill sticking up behind. Ali Muntar, they called it, and it was covered with cactus hedges and trenches, and fortified like Gibraltar, our spies said.

'I had a good yarn with Lal the night before we rode out of Jemmie, before the second battle of Gaza. Artillery was to bombard the Ali Muntar and Gaza defences for an hour at dawn, and East Force, 52nd, 53rd and 54th infantry divisions, attack and capture the positions. The Imperial Mounted Division, 3rd Light Horse Brigade and our regiment, as part of it, got the job of assaulting the redoubts to the south and holding on to prevent reinforcements reaching the Turks.

'We struck along a wadi and dismounted: left our horses in the wadi and crawled into a crop of barley to wait for the dawn. The barley wasn't a foot high, so it wasn't much cover: and the Turks started sniping. Then the roar of guns on the other side of Gaza began, and that was the longest hour ever I put in, Mrs. Gough. We got a fair shower of machine-gun fire and had to lie still till the word came to go forward. God, how the boys hopped into it when we got the signal! We took the first outpost in broad daylight, and pushed on: captured a ridge, and by that time the Turks were giving us all they'd got, artillery fire, shrapnel and high explosives. I saw Lal in the thick of it and men falling all round him.

'We'd routed the Turks out of some shallow trenches and rifle pits, and were about one thousand two hundred yards from the position we were supposed to capture. There was an open stretch between the ridge and the Turkish stronghold, with a wadi running through it. They'd got the range and reckoned on wiping us out here. We fell into the trap: you could hear the roar of artillery round Ali Muntar and we hung on all the afternoon. If some of our guns were brought up we reckoned we could finish the job. But our Hotchkiss and machine gunners weren't in the race at that distance. Then the Turks got a big batch of reinforcements and the order came for us to retire round about sundown.

'I looked round for Lal. We'd got separated during the fighting. Somebody told me he was dead, lying out there in the front line below the ridge. I had to be sure, and crawled out when it was dark. Lal was just about all in when I found him; but he knew me. "Good old Perthy," he said, "go it Tigers!" The old football team'd like to know that. I yelled for stretcher bearers. The Turks'd been pretty decent not firing on our stretcher bearers. I did what I could for Lal . . . but it was no use.'

'Thank you, Perthy,' Sally said.

'Was that all he said?' Morris asked.

'His last words,' Perth said carefully, 'were: "Give my love to mum—and dad, and the boys." '

Sally knew he was lying: that Lal had not been able to think of anything but that this lad from the fields was with him. It was hard for Perth Molloy to express his feeling for Lal, she knew. What he had done, told more about it than anything he could say.

'Something went wrong with the second battle of Gaza,' Sergeant Molloy went on. 'It was like Walker's Ridge. The worst bloody mess of the whole campaign. I was talking to Colonel de Morfé, the other day, and he says the plan was cock-eyed. The Turks had a better intelligence service than we had. It cost us fifteen thousand casualties. But there were changes in the High Command afterwards. When Allenby took charge everything was different. You could feel better organisation in every move that was made. We smashed the Turks at Beersheba, swung back at Heira and Tel-es-Sheria and pounded hell out of 'em at Gaza. Oh, well, you know all the rest, Jerusalem, Galilee, the Jordan Valley and Damascus. I got laid out with malaria in the Jordan Valley, missed the last stunt of the regiment at Damascus. The boys reckon I've got ten lives to've pulled through so far. I'd give most of 'em, Mrs. Gough, if Lal could've been in at the finish!

'Christ,' he added, brokenly, 'we'd been through so much together. There was nobody like Lal! The men would've done anything for him. He'd put heart into them, take a shovel and do a bit of digging, start joking and chiacking when things were toughest. I lost the best mate I ever had when Lal went out to it at Gaza. . . .'

Tom and Eily celebrated peace in their own way. They were married quietly at the registrar's office, with Dinny and Sally as witnesses. Sally had made a cake for them, and Eily's father and mother, Marie, Dick and Amy, and a few of Tom's friends, Barney Riordan, Toni Mattina and Peter Lalich, came along for afternoon tea. Danitzça, Old Peter's daughter, was Eily's best friend. They had played together as children at Kurrawang and were working in the same restaurant. Toni was Danitzça's young man. So it was quite a nice little wedding party, after all, Sally said.

Morris and Tom had forgotten their differences over conscription; but after Sergeant Molloy's visit Morris relapsed into the lethargy in which he had sunk when he returned from prison. He had roused himself to fight stubbornly through the conscription campaigns; but Lal's death and the end of the war seemed to deprive him of any interest in life. He dragged himself from day to day, as if the effort to speak or move were too much.

The doctor said his heart was in a bad way, and that he must not be allowed to exert himself. Morris had been subject to attacks of pain and sudden weakness ever since work underground strained his heart. The shocks of recent years, his arrest and imprisonment, the war and Lal's death, had put a burden on it, greater than it could bear, Sally realised. She was very gentle and tender with him during those days when he sat dumb and half-dead, already, in his chair on the verandah. Often he fell asleep there, and it was scarcely a surprise to find one afternoon that he would not waken.

For weeks Dinny had been helping to dress and move Morris. He ran out to the verandah when he heard Sally's cry of distress. But Morris was dead. There was nothing they could do for him, Dinny said. Sally knelt beside Morris's heavy quiet figure, weeping not only for him, but that so much disappointment and sorrow had shadowed their life together.

CHAPTER XXXIX

RETURNED soldiers were fêted and welcomed home with socials and dances, shouted in the pubs, promised land and homes and jobs by the politicians, fleeced by specious rogues with attractive propositions for earning a living, and reinstated by employers prepared to honour their pre-war pledges. But soon the 'Would-to-Goders' were talking of the change over of industry from war-time production to the production of less profitable commodities: the need to reduce expenses: the unsuitability of soldiers for the steady, exacting routine of business offices. 'Many of the returned men were nervous wrecks,' these patriots protested. 'They can't do a decent day's work, and think they've got to have all sorts of concessions. Will sling up a job and walk off at a moment's notice.'

The first enthusiasm for returned soldiers had worn off when Dick came home.

Sally scarcely knew him. He looked so much older: his face was thin and lined, his dark eyes held a pain and horror he tried to hide from her anxious gaze with a smile of his old loving raillery.

Nothing was left of the good looks and insouciance of the Dick Gough who had married Amy Brierly. Dick walked, dragging his feet in their heavy army boots. He was stooping as if his shoulders had become set to crawling through dug-outs and carrying his soldier's pack. His voice sounded harsh and brittle.

'Well, I got through after all, Sal-o-my!' he said, jauntily.

'Darling!' Sally's joy enveloped him. 'Nothing else matters.'

'Not sure Amy thinks so.' Dick's voice was jerked out of him. He seemed not to know what to say, or how to say it. 'It was a bit of a shock to her, seeing me look the worse for wear—and expecting "a wounded hero".'

'It will be difficult for you both at first, I suppose,' Sally replied briskly. 'Settling down and getting used to a humdrum life again.'

'You wouldn't believe,' Dick said wearily, 'how I've dreamed of doing just that. And never thought it could happen. It didn't seem possible with bombs bursting all round you, and your mates being blown to blazes every day. I still can't believe I'm here— and it's over. Heaven won't seem half as good as my own little shack with Amy and the kid.'

Dick had spent a few days with Amy at Cottesloe before going up to see his mother. Amy wanted him to return to the coast for a while. But Dick was anxious to see about his job, and be ready to start work as soon as he was discharged.

'I can't suffer the crowd Amy's getting round with,' he told Sally, with a twist to his lips that was meant for a smile. 'They seem to be sorry the war's over. Can't talk about anything but the good times they've had.'

His son was a surprise and delight to Dick. He had brought Billy with him and they stayed with Sally until Amy could arrange for somebody to take over the seaside cottage.

'Cripes, he's a great little chap, isn't he?' Dick exclaimed to his mother. 'I'd forgotten kids grow so quickly. Bill cottoned on to me at once. I'd no idea it would be such a thrill to hear him say daddy.'

Amy expected to be up by the week-end, so Dick went over to Mullingar and opened up the bungalow. He had aired and cleaned out the whole place for her when she arrived.

There was some delay about his being taken on at the Boulder Reef. Two younger men had been doing his work, and the management made rather a favour of finding a place for Dick. All Dick cared about was getting back to a normal way of life; and already returned soldiers were finding it difficult to pick up the threads of existence where they had left them. Business firms were making retrenchments. Hundreds of soldiers found employers had forgotten their pledges to recruits, and repatriation schemes were failing to keep up with the need to find work for men discharged from the army.

Dick thought he was lucky to get his job back, and went off every morning, wearing one of the cheap, ill-made suits being turned out for returned soldiers. He looked as eager as he had done the first day he went to work on the mine.

But it was not easy for him to adapt himself, Sally thought, not only to some slights which had been put on him in connection with his work in the smelting room; but to the demands of domesticity and the social life which Amy liked. Dick could not reconcile himself to the fact that people at home had been living during those war years much as they had always done.

The shops were full of fruit and vegetables, meat and groceries, and women's clothing made the usual gay display. Crowds swarmed through the streets, laughing and chattering. They filled the pubs and restaurants, picture theatres, trains and trams, as if every day were a gala day, and there were no aftermath of war to be reckoned with: no unemployment problem: no hospitals where pain-racked, shattered bodies, and where the blind and the maimed, the insane and diseased wreckage of war, clung to the threads of existence.

The war had made no difference to the ordinary life of the average citizen, Dick said. And he was right, Sally believed. The 'business as usual' slogan of the business men, 'the good times' girls and young married women like Amy boasted of having had during the war, were an indication of that. There were people who admitted they were sorry the war was over, as well as stock brokers and profiteers who had made fortunes out of war loan and government contracts for food, clothing, building materials, munitions and other equipment for the military forces.

The east-west railway was finished, and hundreds of men drifted to the goldfields when they were paid off. They hung about looking for work, tried their luck prospecting, soon found themselves without money or any means of escaping from the goldfields towns. Returned soldiers resented the swarms of foreigners and outsiders who had taken their jobs during the war years.

Out of uniform returned soldiers swelled the ranks of the unemployed. Disillusioned and desperate, they sought some solution of their grievances. The only one they could see was preference to returned soldiers on the mines, and for any work offering. That meant the displacement of foreign workers. Tom said the Miners' Union would not support discrimination against a man on racial grounds, or any move likely to weaken union organisation. Preference to trade unionists was the union's reply to the contention that foreign workers were taking an unfair advantage of wages and conditions won by Australian workers in the mining industry.

Dick had a lot of sympathy with the returned soldiers; but he saw Tom's point of view: that the only protection soldiers would have in any industry was the union behind them; and that soldiers and unionists should pull together in the crisis that was looming.

He had an uneasy feeling that his reinstatement was a concession to popular sentiment, and that his services would be dispensed with on some pretext before long. A month later a slip in his pay envelope informed Dick that owing to a falling off in production it was necessary to cut down expenses. A reduction of staff had been decided upon. The company regretted to inform Mr. Gough that it would be forced to dispense with his services from the beginning of the New Year.

Dick lost no time applying for a position on another mine. But it was the same story everywhere: mine managers on the Golden Mile had no vacancies for innumerable returned soldiers who applied for jobs as metallurgists, clerks, mechanics and process workers.

A strike on the woodline interrupted a regular flow of firewood from the out-back country to the mines, and the mines closed down. Thousands of men were out of work and a serious situation developed between unionists, foreign workers and returned soldiers.

During those months Dick was one of the unemployed he looked ill and worried. Amy wanted him to go away and try to find work somewhere else. She had been restless and dissatisfied ever since the end of the war. Hated Kalgoorlie, she said: the dullness and dreariness of life on the fields. And Dick was changed too.

She had never imagined Dick could change so much, she told Sally. He used to be good-natured and charming with everybody. Now he was nervy and irritable. had been positively rude to some of her friends; and wouldn't let her ask them to the house, or take her to dances.

'Dick's just worried about being out of work, and having to economise,' Sally said.

'Even if he is,' Amy said fretfully, 'that's no reason for him to go round looking like a scarecrow and being so moody. He used not to be like that.'

'Not before the war,' Sally said, the bitterness of knowing what the war had done to Dick in her voice. 'How can you expect him to be as light-hearted and easy-going as he used to be?'

'Other men haven't changed so much.' Amy clung to her grievance, her fair, pretty face hard and peevish. 'I met Colonel de Morfé at the Palace the other night. He's lost an eye, but hasn't let the war get him down like Dick.'

After a moment she went on quickly: 'Dick was furious with me for having dinner there with Paddy Cavan on Saturday night. Paddy asked us both, of course: but Dick wouldn't go. And I couldn't turn Paddy down, after having dined with him so often before, just because Dick was home. Besides, I wanted to ask him to do something about getting a job for Dick.'

'Amy!' Sally gasped.

'Well, why not?' Amy asked defiantly. 'He said he would do what he could.'

Sally felt sick and angry. 'How can you be so silly?' she exclaimed. 'Hasn't it occurred to you that Paddy Cavan's about the last person who would do anything to help Dick? Do you think he's forgiven you for marrying Dick?'

Amy's face puckered to her irritation.

'I'm sick and tired of hearing that,' she cried. 'Mother's always harping on it. But Paddy never makes love to me. He just wants us to be friends.'

'Does he?'

Amy flinched to the inflexion of Sally's voice.

'Paddy swears,' she continued heatedly, 'he had nothing to do with Mr. Gough and Tom having got arrested in that gold-stealing case—though you'll never believe it, he says.'

'Paddy's always most dangerous when he's lying,' Sally said quietly.

She was glad to hear that Paddy had gone off to the Eastern States soon after this talk. He intended to live in Melbourne most of the time now: had a splendid home at Toorak, and another at Macedon, Frisco had told Marie. His wife was a quiet, rather plain little woman, religiously inclined and a good deal older than Paddy. Paddy had married her to get possession of big interests she held in a brewery combine. She had twin daughters, and she and Paddy got on quite well together, although Paddy was disappointed that Mrs. Cavan had failed to do her duty by him and produce a son.

Frisco said that Paddy had made a lot of money during the war: invested half a million in war loan, presented a battle plane to the Royal Air Force, and contributed thousands to patriotic funds. The government was indebted to him for some valuable advice with regard to reorganisation of the metal industry which had been dominated by German interests at the outbreak of the war. What was Paddy going to get out of it? Paddy had not been spending money and throwing his weight about for nothing, Colonel de Morfé declared.

He came to see Dinny when the New Year Honours list was published.

'Sir Patrick Cavan!' he roared, and his laughter was as boisterous as in the old days. 'I guessed Paddy had something up his sleeve. That's what you get for being an ardent patriot and a philanthropist, Dinny!'

Frisco himself was in financial difficulties. His business interests had suffered during the war, and Paddy had manœuvred him out of his share of a big deal in which they were partners, he told Dinny. Litigation was pending, and he hoped to take the wind out of Sir Patrick Cavan's sails when the facts of the case were known.

'Paddy hasn't got a leg to stand on,' Frisco crowed. 'Will have to unload to the tune of a few thousands.'

'Paddy's got more legs than a centipede when it's a question of wriggling out of anything,' Dinny warned him.

'I know all about that.' Assured and confident Frisco smiled at Sally. 'But I've got him just where I want him.'

It was the first time she had seen Frisco with that black shade over his eye, Sally's heart quailed as she looked at him. He was still in uniform and carrying himself with the swagger and devil-me-care grace she knew so well, though he was older and tougher. His face had an expression that the fighting on Gallipoli and in Palestine had put there, she thought. Deep lines grooved the dark skin from his nose to his mouth. His lower lip was thrust against the upper, forcing it to a grim firmness beneath his scrubby moustache.

Sally knew Frisco had come to see her rather than Dinny, though being down on his luck had always brought him along for a yarn with Dinny and Morris, as though old mates could be depended on for some warmth and friendliness, when other associates cold-shouldered him. His wife had left him, and he had divorced her a few months ago.

'Don't be sorry for me, Sally,' he said roughly, with a flash of his old derisive gaiety, as Sally walked with him to the gate. 'The war may have broken me—because I forgot everything else when I was out there with the boys. But it's made me more the sort of man you wanted me to be—if it's any good to you to know that.'

CHAPTER XL

'WHEN Noah Hedges, Chairman of the firewood company, addressed a deputation from the timber cutters,' Dinny said, 'he congratulated them on "the glorious record" employees of the company had put up as soldiers during the war. They'd earned honours rangin' from the Military Medal to the Victoria Cross. "This record would compare favourably with that of any industry in the State." But he "and his colleagues could give no increase in wages, nor grant any improvement in existing conditions".'

'The men wanted to discuss clauses of the new contract separately,' Tom reminded him. 'But any consideration of their claims was just brushed aside. They refused to sign the new agreement.'

'You can't blame them,' Eily declared heatedly. 'Dad's been working on the Kurrawang woodline and he says the workers had a three and a half years' contract with the firewood company. There's been a big increase in the cost of tools and stores the firewood company sells to workers on the far-out timber-cutting camps. Nobody denies the cost of living had risen enormously during the war, and that the firewood companies, running the only stores on the timber camps, have had the workers at their mercy. But when they asked for an increase in wages to meet the increased cost of living, before signing the new agreement, it was a case of nothing doing.'

'It's not a strike, but a termination of agreement,' Tom said.

'What's the difference?' Sally exclaimed, impatiently. 'Thousands of men are out of work, and storekeepers say they can't feed the unemployed in Boulder and Kal any longer. Returned soldiers are blaming the foreign workers for stirring up trouble, and unionists for supporting them.'

'We're organising the unemployed,' Tom said. 'We've got government relief for families in distress, but the rations are being whittled down. When we held a meeting outside the Workers' Hall to protest about it, returned soldiers tried to break it up.'

'That was because you sang the "Red Flag" and uttered "revolutionary sentiments",' Sally retorted.

'There's a crime, now!' Dinny chuckled. 'Don't forget there were returned soldiers singing and uttering them too. It's only this bunch in the Kalgoorlie Returned Soldiers' Association is making trouble. Mind, missus, I can see the point of view of returned men who say "they were promised everything and've got nothing". But the workers are not to blame for that. Soldiers are being blinded to their own interests when they can't see any fight for better wages and conditions is their fight. It's the high cost of living and the scare about there not bein' jobs for all, that's at the bottom of this business.'

'I know,' Sally replied. 'But things have never been worse on the fields, Dinny! There's never been so much bad feeling among the workers themselves, Kalgoorlie and Boulder men, unionists and non-unionists, foreigners and ourselves.'

'As Edmund Burke said,' Chris muttered in the background, ' "I like a clamour when there is an abuse. The firebell at midnight disturbs your sleep, but it keeps you from being burned in your bed." '

Everybody laughed, and the talk drifted to a rush on the Hampton Plains which had been causing a good deal of excitement during the firewood dispute. It was not often now that sensational finds took a stream of prospectors out into the bush.

Tom and Eily were living with Sally until they could furnish a home of their own. Tom was reluctant to leave her after his father died, and Eily quite happy to help Sally in the house, though most of her time was given to work on the committee which had been set up to assist the unemployed. Tom, himself, was out of work as a result of the strike, which continued to be called a strike whatever its actual character.

The committee sometimes met at her house, and Sally learnt to know all the ins and outs of the struggle between the foreign workers and returned soldiers: the indignation about an anonymous letter which the secretary of the Kalgoorlie Returned Soldiers' Association had taken seriously, and the brawls which were occurring between disgruntled soldiers and hot-tempered foreigners.

Many workers on the timber camps were Italians, but they did all the heavy work, the firewood companies claimed. Australians and Britishers got the lighter jobs. Returned soldiers, however,

266

were not rushing poorly paid labour on the timber camps, or hankering after being dumped hundreds of miles out in the bush without social amenities of any sort. They were quite prepared for the foreign workers to supply firewood for the mines; but not for them to hang on to more highly paid jobs on the mines.

The dispute dragged on for months, with anger and resentment growing between the firewood workers, foreigners, the unionists who supported them and Kalgoorlie returned soldiers. Boulder soldiers were with the union, Tom said, because most of them were working miners: the Kalgoorlie Returned Soldiers' Association was being run by conservatives, non-unionists and men who had been recruited from business offices, although there were some miners among them.

The atmosphere became more sultry and ominous, as it was when a thunder-storm was brewing. The government had been urged to do something to prevent the soldiers' threat about running foreigners off the fields from being translated into actual violence. The most insignificant incident might incite soldiers to take the law into their own hands everybody felt. Only a spark was needed to set ablaze their accumulated grievances about unemployment and foreigners earning good wages.

'Returned soldiers are being blinded to their own interests, and induced to play the bosses' game,' Tom said. 'They've been sidetracked from the real issue, which is unemployment, to attack the Italians and Slavs. Who brought Maltese to work on the railway? The government and the employing class behind it: and why? To break the power of the unions to bargain about decent conditions of work and pay. Wasn't one of the employers saying in parliament, the other day, he was "sure that in nearly every case the aliens, or Italians, will give better work for the money than Britishers". Look at kaffirs on the Rand. He believed if we had the same cheap labour which is obtainable in South Africa, more white men could be employed here as bosses.'

'All men are equal in the sight of God,' Chris muttered.

'Good Christians say they believe that,' Dinny said. 'Well, what's wrong with a government supposed to uphold Christian principles recognisin' if the working man has equal rights with his boss in the eyes of God he should have 'em from a government, and individuals who reckon they exercise authority by the will of God?'

'That's the gist of the matter,' Tom agreed.

Charley O'Reilly and Claude Owen had dropped in to discuss the situation with him that evening.

'Me, I was brought up a catholic,' Charley said with his rollicking, gusty good humour, 'and I know what the Church said about it. "It's easier for a camel to go through the eye of a needle than for a rich man to enter into the kingdom of God." That's why the Church has got all its time cut out scrapin' the rich men into heaven. But a poor man can go straight to glory. If you take his poverty away from him you take his chances of glory.'

'I went to jail because I was a pacifist during the war,' Claude remarked, in that mild, unctuous voice of his. 'The parsons say that the ten commandments are the basis of morality. Christians must obey the law: "Thou shalt not kill." But there are special circumstances in which Christians need not obey the commandments. Who is to decide what are those special circumstances? Either the law is valid, or it is not!'

'Capitalist economics decide the special circumstances,' Tom said.

' "The ruling ideas of each age," ' Chris muttered, ' "have ever been the ideas of its ruling class." '

'And I fell out with some of my theosophist friends,' Claude went on placidly, 'because they argued the Germans were "young souls". Death to them was a chance to reincarnate in other lives, progressing to realisation that only by doing good to their fellow men could their souls achieve happiness.'

'That's a good argument for bumping off the capitalists,' Charley roared. 'We should regard them as "young souls", and ourselves as benefactors for bumping them off—giving them a chance to get on their way to a happy ever after.'

'It wouldn't help us to organise the workers,' Tom pointed out in his sober, matter-of-fact fashion. 'That's the job we're up against at the moment. If you could knock some common sense into returned soldiers who are threatening to run foreign workers off the fields: make them see that, as unionists, the foreigners can't do us any damage, and, as unionists, the returned men themselves would be in a stronger position to force the government to deal with unemployment, we'd be getting somewhere. The foreigners won't take rough-handling easily, and things are going to boil over pretty soon unless we can stop it.'

Mothers and wives like Sally, who knew something of the dangers lurking in a situation where men were exasperated and desperate, heaved a sigh of relief when the strike was settled. A new forest area was made available near Widgiemooltha, four hundred miles from Kalgoorlie, and the government offered the firewood companies a reduced rate of freight to the Golden Gate siding. On the basis of the old agreement as to rates and conditions; but on condition that the firewood companies would supply stores and tools at the prices then obtaining, the wood cutters were going back to work.

Miners had hustled the wood cutters into patching up their

differences with the firewood companies, Tom said, because mine managers were saying that if the water rose any higher in some of the mines it would be questionable whether work could be started again. Firewood must be made available to the gold mining industry soon, or it would cease to exist on this field.

The shadow of another slump was darkening the horizon, and miners and mine workers were alarmed at the prospect of giving the proprietary companies any additional pretext for closing down of the mines.

Earlier in the year mine managers had said that the gold-mining industry of the West was in a parlous and dangerous condition. The output of gold had dwindled to an alarming extent during the war years, due to the enlistment of miners, the cost of materials and retrogressive legislation in the form of a war-time profits tax. From sixteen thousand men employed in the industry the number had been reduced to round about nine thousand. A demand was being made for removal of the embargo on the export of gold and that the Federal Government pay a subsidy on gold production: subsidise the employment of returned soldiers on the treatment of low-grade and otherwise unpayable ores, and subsidise prospecting parties.

Cost of the war to the Commonwealth had reached a staggering figure when it was considered how small a population had to meet this liability. It could only be liquidated by increased production. The mine owners maintained that they had to have assistance before production on the mines could be increased.

'The Mining Act has been used by all sorts of adventurers to hamstring gold production in this country,' Dinny said, yarning with some of his old cronies. 'Take the miles of gold-bearin' ground locked up by the Hampton Plain's company, and at Wiluna. The southward trend of the Golden Mile is practically untapped. Why shouldn't the big dividend payin' companies've been made to set aside a portion of their profits for prospectin' outside their workin' leases. They could put profits earned on this field into gold mines in Ashanti, Nicaragua and Mexico.'

'The Great Boulder Proprietary was workin' a mine in Alaska,' Speck Jones butted in.

'The Minister for Mines said the other day twenty-five millions sterling in dividends have been paid out by the mines of the West, and practically the whole of it's gone out of the country,' Dinny went on. 'But now the mining companies want the government to give 'em a leg up so as they can go on ridin' on the backs of the workers, and make more money to send overseas.'

269

'Makes y'r heart bleed to hear some of the big boys beggin' for a gold bonus,' Sam Mullet murmured, gazing off into space.

'It's the experienced prospectors can do most to open up new fields,' Tassy Regan ruminated behind the blue smoke from his black, stuffy pipe. 'Wasn't it the old prospectors put them on to all the gold ever mined in this country? "The man who," as Mart Walsh used to say, "wint out into the wilderness with his pick in wan hand, his water bag in the other, and his life in the other." And didn't he go, begorra, "where the hand of man niver set foot, and the only signs of life were the bones of the dead men who wint before him"?.'

'Y're right there, Tassy,' Eli Nancarrow's voice cracked as he spoke, though he was still as spunky and alert as he had been twenty years ago. 'Old prospectors like you and me, and Dinny and Sam and Speck, we'd find gold where these new chooms'd walk over it!'

Tom had been sitting on the verandah step listening to the old men.

'We reckon,' he said, 'It's not only prospecting that's needed. The government could establish plants for the manufacture and supply of mining chemicals and explosives on the fields. The cost of mining supplies would be reduced, and prove more effective than either a gold bonus, or the higher price for gold, to improve living conditions in Kal and Boulder. Work would be provided for the unemployed, mining costs be reduced and production increased. The government showed what could be done when it took over production for war. We say it's up to it to apply the same principle to meet the needs of the people now.'

'When we got State batteries that was a move in the right direction,' Sam pointed out. 'The State batteries gave prospectors a chance to run their own show, increased production and kept money in the goldfields towns.'

'That's right, Sam,' Tom went on. 'We're organising the unemployed to make demands not only for immediate relief, but to subsidise prospecting parties, build roads, make dams and bores to improve water supply in the back country, and start State enterprises which will give more men a chance of earning a living in Kal and Boulder.'

'There's one thing some of the mine managers are beginning to realise 't any rate,' Dinny could not resist giving his old mates something to smile at. 'That unionists are good fighters. Did y'r see what old Ham-and-Eggs said at a welcome home to some of the boys the other night in Boulder? Tryin' to keep sweet with men on the mine, I suppose. But he said: "an overwhelming majority of the men who went to the front were unionists", and says Ham:

"Unionists stormed the heights of Gallipoli. They taught the Germans their lesson in Germany and Mesopotamia." '

'Be the Great Livin' Tinker,' Tassy chortled, 'he must've been lit up. But he's not a bad sort, old Ham!'

CHAPTER XLI

IT was cold and frosty the night Dick came in after midnight and went up to Tom and Eily's room.

Sally heard them talking.

'What's the matter, Dick?' Eily asked.

'There's been a dust-up between returned soldiers and a bunch of Italians,' Dick said.

Tom muttered sleepily.

'Sorry, old man, but something's got to be done about it.' Dick's voice was urgent.

'What's that?' Tom was awake now and concerned.

Sally could hear Dick saying:

'I had to go to the football smoke social, and coming home passed the Majestic café. There was a crowd on the footpath. A fight on inside somebody said. Then a Dago ran out with a knife in his hand and half a dozen returned men after him. More Dagoes after them. And the crowd followed. You never saw such a free-for-all: the Dagoes were outnumbered, bashed, kicked, knocked down with two or three men on top of them.

'Then another lot of Dagoes came along from Outridge Terrace, started a barrage of bricks and stones and the crowd scattered. But the brawl broke out again opposite the brewery, and I heard somebody yelling that a soldier had been knifed. It was Tom Northwood, the butcher's son, and he was bleeding pretty badly when they carried him away. Another chap was stabbed too. Then the police arrived and everybody did a bunk, the Dagoes running towards the Terrace and the soldiers who'd been in the thick of the shindy back to town.'

Tom was beginning to dress.

'I'll go along and see the Union secretary,' he said. 'Some of the foreigners are good unionists, and we'll have to protect our members.'

'You don't have to tell me that,' Dick said. 'I came along so as you'd get busy.'

'Some of us've got a pretty shrewd idea there's a move on to use returned men against the union,' Tom said. 'That showed up in the lumpers' strike, didn't it? A colonel moved the resolution in support of the government's action on the wharves to protect scabs. But the soldiers shouted it down. They stood by the lumpers.'

'The position's a bit different here, Tommy,' Dick argued. 'I know as well as you, and a lot of returned men do too, that the newspapers and political stooges have been trying to create bad blood between the workers and returned soldiers. But I can see the Kal men's point of view. A man can't help feeling mad if he's put in the last two or three years in the bloody trenches in France, and comes home to find himself out of a job and hard up.

'The Italians have been flourishing while he was away: hundreds of them in the mines now. They own wine shops, pubs, fruit shops and restaurants. You've only got to see them in town on a Saturday night, all dressed up and carting girls around. Down-and-out soldiers aren't in it with the girls, or the restaurant-keepers: get the glassy eye. Our men get back on them by slinging off, calling the Dagoes stinkers and dingoes, and treating them rough whenever there's a chance: jostling them off the footpath and pushing them out of the way in a pub. Dingoes and Dagoes mean about the same thing these days. In this shindy to-night the Dagoes' blood was up and they fought back. If Tom Northwood dies . . .'

'Let's hope he doesn't,' Tom said.

They had gone off together then. Tom did not return until the early hours of the morning: had time only to snatch a couple of hours' sleep before he went to work. One of the neighbours called over the back fence to ask Sally whether she knew that Tom Northwood had died. Eily hurried off to the Workers' Hall. Dinny went out to hear what was happening in the town; but news of the riots had spread like wildfire before he returned.

'Gosh, missus, you wouldn't believe what's goin' on in Kal to-day if you hadn't seen it,' he gasped, looking dishevelled and exhausted.

'For goodness' sake tell me,' Sally exclaimed irritably. 'I hope Dick wasn't in it. I've heard nothing but the wildest yarns about soldiers wrecking shops and pubs run by Italians, and chasing them out of town.'

'That's what they've been doin',' Dinny said. 'And a mob of loafers and larrikins trailing round with them. I saw Dick for a few minutes, but he was goin' round with a couple of soldiers tryin' to stop the rampage.'

He paused for breath.

'It started, Dick says, after the R.S.A. meeting in Kal this morning. A bunch of soldiers marched off to the Glen Devon hotel where several of the Dagoes who'd been mixed up in the fightin'

272

last night were living. The police were on guard at the front entrance, so the mob swung round and broke open the back door. The Italians had got away, but the mob smashed windows and doors, looted the liquor and ran amuck through the whole place, helpin' themselves. There were cockatoos and parrots let out of their cages flyin' all round, and horses turned out of the stables gallopin' down the street.

'A resolution urging the Federal and State Governments to deport Italians from the fields had been passed before the attack on the Glen Devon hotel,' Dinny explained. 'It demanded that Italians be given until Saturday to clear out, the State Government bein' asked to provide special trains to take them to Fremantle. There was a lot of talk about the soldiers "maintaining law and order", Dick said. But everybody knew what was going to happen.'

'The baker told me a young chap named Gotti says he stabbed Tom Northwood and has given himself up to the police,' Sally interrupted. 'Gotti thought it would stop his countrymen being blamed and further damage done.'

'That's right,' Dinny went on. 'But the mob was mad with booze by that time, rushin' from one Dago pub to another, smashing doors and windows, grabbin' every bottle in sight and cartin' off barrels of wine. At the "All Nations" Orsatti and his wife were scared out of their wits. The crowd was three or four thousand strong by then, and Orsatti tried to make a speech from the balcony. He was dragged back and nearly choked before a cop rescued him.

'Dick says Colonel de Morfé and one or two of the R.S.A. officers arrived, and got a couple of hundred soldiers to march off to a paddock behind the "Shamrock" hotel. Frisco and the others pitched into the soldiers: tried to make them listen to reason. But all the afternoon the raids've been goin' on, and Italians are bein' hunted out of their homes, men, women and children, scuttlin' off into the bush in fear of their lives.'

'It's a shame and a disgrace,' Sally exclaimed. 'How could such things happen here, Dinny?'

'The R.S.A. is blamin' larrikins and hooligans in the mob that followed the soldiers for doin' all the damage, of course.' Dinny mopped his face with a dirty handkerchief. 'But there's no doubt it was the soldiers set the ball rolling.'

Tom had come in from work then and Dick soon afterwards. Tom said the Miners' Union and the Boulder R.S.A. were going to oppose the Kalgoorlie resolutions aimed at driving Italians off the fields. Dick told him that he had been doing his utmost all day to knock some sense into ringleaders of the disturbances; but they were full of bluster and cock-a-hoop about the way Italians were clearing out already. There was to be a raid on Boulder that night. The hotels were closing at half-past seven by proclamation; but the lust for destructive violence was still running hot and strong in a majority of the men who had been wrecking and looting Italian pubs that afternoon. Tom would not wait for his dinner. He went back immediately to Boulder to try to organise some protection for the foreign workers.

When he returned towards midnight there were three terrified women with him, one with a baby in her arms.

'These are friends of mine, mum,' he said. 'Can you put them up for the night? They've been turned out of their homes. Scores of women and children are sleeping out in the bush and hiding among the dumps.'

'Of course, son,' Sally said, a little flustered but anxious to be cordial. 'Come in, please!' She turned to the women: 'I'm so glad to be able to do something for you.'

She recognised only Danitzça, who had come to see Eily sometimes. Tom had often spoken of her father, Peter Lalich, who lived at the Kurrawang. Both Danitzça and her father had been at Tom's and Eily's wedding, Sally remembered. Danitzça was a lovely girl with blazing dark eyes and firm high breasts; but her face was pale and angry that night, her black hair hanging in loose strands, her dress torn and dirty.

'This is my sister, Marietta, Mrs. Gough,' she said. 'She is married to Adamo Fiaschi who has a wine shop near the "Golden Horseshoe". And this is Toni Mattina's grandmother. Toni and I are going to be married soon. We're grateful to you for taking us in. Many people in Boulder to-night are afraid to shelter Dagoes.'

'It's been a rotten stunt, mum,' Tom explained while Sally and Eily bustled about making tea and toast.

Marietta sobbed quietly, suckling her baby, and old Mrs. Mattina muttered and rocked herself, wailing: 'Toni! Toni!'

Nobody understood what she said except Danitzça and she was trying to comfort the old woman.

'Several hotels were broken into,' Tom said. 'There were flying stones and smashed glass everywhere; but the "Horseshoe Inn" and the "Golden Horseshoe" got the worst of it. They were looted and wrecked in a few minutes. The mob was like a pack of lunatics when it got to the drink, shouting and yelling, and threatening to beat up any Dago in sight. The men cleared out when they saw what was coming. Women and children ran off to hide behind the dumps and in the bush, frightened out of their wits.

'I found Danitzça and Marietta and Mrs. Mattina in a pothole near Fiaschi's wine shop. Somebody had gone round "warning" the Italians in Boulder the soldiers would kill any of the men found in town to-night. Toni was working alongside of me till the mines closed down. He's a decent chap, born and bred on the fields and a good unionist. But he's young and single: one of the men the Kalgoorlie mob want to get rid of.'

Eily tried to reassure Marietta and Danitzça as she poured out tea and passed round thick slabs of hot buttered toast.

'You'll feel better after a cup of tea,' she said cheerily. 'Nothing like a cuppa when things go wrong. Don't cry, Marietta! It's bad for the baby. Tom will look for Toni, Danitzça. Everything will be all right.'

Sally was glad she had spare rooms in the bunk-house. Danitzça helped Eily to make up the beds, and presently the unexpected guests were all comfortably stowed away for the night.

Danitzça wanted to take her sister and Toni's grandmother to the Kurrawang next morning but Tom advised her not to.

'You'd better stay with mother until things settle down,' he said. And Sally added: 'You're very welcome, my dear.'

She was pleased to help Tom and Eily, she told Dinny; and to show how she felt about the way foreigners were being treated, although it was rather a trial to have three strange women and a baby on her hands for the next three days. Toni's grandmother sat on a sofa muttering and moaning all the time: tears coursed down her brown, wrinkled cheeks.

'Mrs. Mattina says it was a pogrom,' Danitzça explained. 'Just like what used to happen in Russia when she was a girl, and a crazy mob attacked the Jews.'

Toni's grandmother was a Russian Jewess who had been a ballet dancer in her youth. She had married Luigi Mattina, a successful prospector, when he had sold a gold mine and was spending a holiday abroad. Extravagant living and speculation ruined him before he returned to the fields. He had gone out prospecting again, taking his young wife with him. But no more luck had come his way. He died soon after his only son was killed by a fall of earth on the Golden Horseshoe. Toni's mother had re-married and left Toni with his grandmother. Her whole life was wrapped up in Toni and he was devoted to her.

'That's it,' Dinny said, elated to have found a reason why so many working men had turned against the foreigners and taken part with soldiers in the riots. 'It was a pogrom. When the Tsar's government wanted a scapegoat, it would turn the people's discontent against the Jews. And here the returned soldiers and unemployed've been stirred up to turn on the foreign workers, instead of looking for the real cause of their troubles.'

'You're right there, Dinny,' Tom said. 'But it's not only foreign workers they've been stirred up against, but unionists, and anybody making a stand in the interests of the workers. Wobblies and socialists are being warned they'll be run out of town if they go on uttering "Bolshevik sentiments".'

'Jay Gould, the American millionaire, said: "I can always hire one-half of the workers to kill the other half",' Dinny reminded him. 'And don't forget, soldiers've got out of the way of thinkin' for themselves in the army.'

'But this mob in Kal haven't got things all their own way,' Tom said. 'The statement of the Boulder R.S.A., which is just out, condemns "the lawlessness and looting" which took place yesterday. There was a unanimous decision to disassociate itself with the whole business.'

'That's the stuff, Tommy!' Dinny said, his spirits rising.

'The union statement has cleared the air, too,' Tom continued. 'It protests at the failure of the government to protect Italian citizens, demands the immediate withdrawal of instructions given for them to leave the district, and pledges the union to protect fellow unionists and our members.'

'I haven't been able to look a foreigner in the face these last few days,' Sally confessed. 'It's good to think there's something to show a few bullies can't run amuck and expect decent men and women to support them in this town.'

'That's what a lot of people are saying, mum,' Tom said.

There was no doubt that most people were shocked by the riots, particularly the old timers. Her neighbours told Sally about a sick girl who had to be carried into the bush because nobody in the street where she lived would shelter a Dago. When the drunken mob was rampaging nearby, an Italian woman with seven children had given birth to another, in the open, on that bitterly cold night.

In response to this feeling the Kalgoorlie Returned Soldiers' Association changed its tune. In an interview with Orsatti and several other Italians, regret was expressed that the wives and children of some Italians had been so frightened by reports of what the soldiers would do to their homes that they had taken shelter in alluvial holes or slept in the bush. Married Italians, especially those who had married Australian women, would be allowed to remain, so long as they behaved themselves 'decently and orderly', it was announced; but single Italians of eligible age must leave the district.

Many Italians with their wives and children had already left for the coast. But numbers of single men who had taken refuge in the scrub had no money or means of getting away. When a director of one of the firewood companies promised them credit for a tent, tools and stores to go wood-cutting on the Kurrawang line, which stretched far out into the bush, they accepted this offer.

'Suits him all right,' Dinny commented. 'Gets labour for his job and the foreigners under his thumb.'

In his evidence at the coroner's inquiry into the death of Tom Northwood Jim Gotti said:

'I took the knife from the fish shop. Had to take it for my protection . . . rushed out into the street. Saw the crowd in Parker Street and Madalina on the ground: said "Leave him alone, he's had enough." Someone say: "Here's another Dago!" Hit me in the mouth and knocked me down. I got up. "Leave me alone," I say, "I got nothing to do with you people." They knock me down. "Leave me alone!" I say, "or I give you this in the guts." I pulled knife and got away. Crowd followed me. Heard my mate Zapelli calling. He was down on the footpath with four or five men on top of him. I thought they would kill him: caught Zapelli by the legs and tried to pull him away. A big man caught me by the neck and pulled me down on the knees. The crowd was on top of me. I pulled knife and stabbed the man who had hold of me. He let go. I got away and went back to Glen Devon Hotel.'

Gotti was charged with wilful murder, but a jury in Perth returned a verdict of manslaughter with a strong recommendation to mercy.

After hearing an appeal regarding the law of self-defence the Full Court squashed the conviction. A section of the criminal code protects a man acting under 'reasonable apprehension of death or bodily danger'; and it was held the jury's recommendation to mercy was made on the grounds that Gotti 'honestly believed that he was in danger when he used the knife'.

CHAPTER XLII

'LORDY, isn't it lovely?' Eily exclaimed happily when she knew she was pregnant. 'Though I feel I really shouldn't be having a baby when there's so much to do just now.'

The ferment over the riots had subsided; but Eily went on working on the unemployed committee and organising a waitresses' union.

Such a slight, scraggy little thing she was: had worn herself to frazzles earning her living as a waitress and throwing her energy into various committees. But Sally put her foot down now. Eily had been very sick for weeks and must rest, Sally told Tom. She was going to see that Eily took things easily and got some flesh on her bones. Sally herself had become very attached to Tom's wife, and was delighted when Eily began to bloom as a result of her care.

Eily's happiness filled the house. A heavy quietness had hung about it since Morris's death. The enlarged photograph of Lal which hung in the sitting-room now, reminded Sally, too, of the sadness which would never quite leave her. Dinny might yarn and chuckle with old mates on the verandah, Marie and Theresa Molloy come along in the afternoon to gossip and joke over a cup of afternoon tea; but it was not until Eily and Tom were living with her that Sally could smile and laugh easily again.

It was heart-warming to see Tom's and Eily's love and happiness. They were like two people who had found refuge in a storm: so surprised and delighted that they could enjoy the simple satisfaction of being together; and that it had given them this joy of the baby which would be theirs. Sally thought she had never known two young people so united mentally and spiritually as well as by their love. From their own resources of serenity Eily and Tom could dispense some, and give everybody about them a sense of well-being.

Tom went off to work as usual, sometimes in the early morning, sometimes on night shift. But when Ted Lee took him on as mate he had risen to the dignity of a machine miner. He was making good wages and planning to build a house.

For the first time in her life Eily said she was having a holiday. It was marvellous not to be rushing round a restaurant and run off her legs all day. She sang all manner of revolutionary songs as she went about helping Sally with the housework: dusting and sweeping as if she were really enjoying herself. She was very proud of, and amused by, her bulky appearance and making baby clothes which Marie had cut out for her. When she sat on the verandah to sew she loved to talk about Tom, and listen to Sally's stories about her babies and the boys' pranks when they were growing up. Sally liked to read Den's letters to Eily, and Dinny was always sure of an audience for his yarns when she was about.

Eily refused to drop all her usual interests, however. She went to meetings with Tom on Sunday, and every night read from some heavy book and made notes industriously.

Nothing pleased her more than when Dick said: 'Well, how's my little sister?'

Amy and Eily did not get on so well. They looked at each other with their fur rising, Sally said, which was to be expected since their ways and ideas were so different. But they were very polite to each other: smiled and spoke sweetly, when probably they would have preferred not to do anything of the sort. If they had let fly some of their reasons for disliking each other, it might have done some good and created a better understanding between them, Sally thought. She still loved Amy, and despite her affection for Eily was prepared to defend and excuse Amy's rudeness and slightly patronising attitude towards Tom's wife.

Sally explained to Eily that Amy was a little jealous, perhaps, because for so long, even before she married Dick, she had been almost one of the family, and did not like to see another girl take her place. And Amy was in a curious frame of mind just then, missing the excitement and social whirl in which she had been caught up during the war: frightened, too, by Dick's lack of money and work.

Poor Amy, she was a bird caught in the rain, Sally said. You must make allowances for her. If she was behaving like a spoilt child it was understandable. She could not get used to living on short commons, being frugal and having no fun. And Dick, being nervy and irritable, made everything more difficult for her.

Sally did not want to lose her confidence in Amy, nor Amy's in her. She promised herself to have a word with Dick about being considerate, and not forgetting little lover-like attentions which would make up for some of the pleasures of which Amy was being deprived. It was so easy for young people to drift apart when they were fretting about financial difficulties, although it was incredible, Sally assured herself, that any serious trouble could crop up between Dick and Amy.

She was horrified when Dick said:

'Oh, the gilt's off the gingerbread, I'm afraid, mother. Amy's never been the same to me since I came home. She says I've changed, and am not in love with her any more. I think she means she's not in love with me now. But, maybe, it's just war nerves and being hard-up that's got us down.'

Dick paused, trying to drag his troubled thought to expression.

'All I can think of is providing for her and the kid. It's a new sort of love I've got, deeper and better.'

'Don't let anything come between you,' Sally begged. 'Amy's a dear girl—but it wasn't easy for her to keep her head all the time you were away, and so many people flattering and making a fuss of her. You've just got to be patient, and try to help her to get through this slump between you—as well as on the mines.'

'I know,' Dick's smile flickered. 'But I'm not sure that Amy wants to be helped.'

It was a great shock to everybody when Laura was knocked down by a motor car in the main street of Kalgoorlie a few weeks later. She died on her way to hospital. Sally remembered the beautiful girl she had known when they first came to the goldfields together; and the unhappy woman Laura had become trying to adjust herself to living without Alf. Alf's wife, the 'Lady Laura', the mine he had called after her, memories of them flitted through Sally's mind as she talked to Amy, who wept inconsolably after her mother's death. It was easier to think of them than of Mrs. McSweeney with her fair, flabby face, complaining voice and breath smelling of brandy.

Brandy had something to do with the accident, Dinny said. The driver of the car protested that the lady was 'under the influence': stopped, swayed unsteadily, then ran forward when he tried to pass her. Amy could not understand or forgive Laura these lapses from proper behaviour for a mother, which had made her so absurd and pitiful.

'But after all, she was my mother, and I did love her,' Amy wailed. 'It was a terrible thing to have happened to the poor darling. I'm all alone, now.'

'You've got Dick and Billy,' Sally reminded her.

'Oh yes,' Amy admitted grudgingly. 'But they're not the same as one's mother. Even if we didn't always get on well, at least I could depend on mother to stand by me—no matter what happened.'

'I'd like you to feel that about me,' Sally said gently.

'You expect me to be different than I am—and I can't,' Amy sobbed. 'Mother knew that.'

She looked very pathetic and woebegone, with tears washing her face and her perky little nose red and swollen: but before the funeral she was wearing deep mourning, and had used a little eye shadow to accentuate her sorrow. Her tears could be controlled to a dabbing of her eyes with a lace handkerchief and a discreet sniffing.

Dick was all tenderness and concern for Amy. She was deeply affected by her mother's death, he believed, despite that almost unconscious posing for effect which had surprised Sally. It surprised him that Amy should be pleased to see all the flowers on her mother's grave, and to receive so many letters of sympathy. No one had realised, Laura least of all, that she would be remembered with such goodwill and kindness. An obituary paragraph in the *Miner* was something Amy could be proud of. It had been copied by Eastern States newspapers because her mother had belonged to a well-known Melbourne family. Reference was made to 'the gracious presence which had adorned the early goldfields', and to the 'musical talents with which the deceased had delighted many audiences'. The tragic manner of her passing, it was stated, would be mourned by all who had known Mrs. Tim McSweeney.

Dick and Amy seemed to be drawn closer together after Laura's death. Laura had done her best to prevent friction between them: Dick's ally in all that might interfere with the security of their marriage, and yet a soft bolster for Amy to lean on when she chose. Amy was turning more to Dick now for something stable and all-loving in her life, Sally thought. And Dick was more anxious than ever to get a job, so that he and Amy could regain some of their first happiness in each other.

CHAPTER XLIII

Tom hired a buggy and pair of horses to drive across to the Kurrawang for Toni's and Danitzça's wedding. Eily sat beside him, very large and careful of herself, but as delighted as a child to be having this outing. Dinny and Sally bumped up and down on the back seat.

The wedding party was held at Peter Lalich's house. And what a gay, friendly gathering it had been! You would scarcely believe, Sally said, that so many people could have squeezed into one room —though they overflowed on to the verandah, and into the back-yard where a kid and a sucking pig were roasting, slung over smouldering fires. They wafted a rich savoury odour over everything. And the noise! A joyous clatter of laughter and exclamations in half a dozen languages resounded, with outbursts of singing nearly drowning the shrill, merry blither of the tamburiças several men were playing. This Slav instrument was like a guitar in different sizes, and Peter was very proud of the orchestra he had organised among his countrymen to play on festive occasions.

Radiant with happiness, Danitzça sat beside Toni for the wedding feast. She was wearing the gala dress of a Jugoslav peasant girl: a full white skirt flowered with red roses, and bordered with red and green, and a gaily embroidered blouse. A wreath of coloured flowers and wheatears, shaped like a diadem, stood up from her vivid face and was tied with coloured ribbons falling in long streamers behind. The dress had been her mother's before she came to Australia, and Marietta, also, had worn it for her wedding.

Old feuds and religious differences sometimes had caused ill-will between Italians and Slavs on the goldfields. But nobody remembered them that night. Perhaps because Peter's and Toni's friends did not attach any importance to these differences of thought and custom among work mates. Then, too, the riots had brought them together as foreigners; and everybody was rejoicing at the mating of such a handsome young couple as Toni and Danitzça. To a certain extent it symbolised a new unity between the Italian and Slav peoples.

The riots had not been forgotten, and fear still lurked in the minds of some men and women about dangerous undercurrents in the life of this country, to which many of them had come as a place of refuge from persecution and hard living in the old world. Tom and Eily, Sally and Dinny, were the only guests not of their own races. They had been invited, Tom said, because Peter and he were old friends, and because Danitzça was grateful to Sally for sheltering her, Marietta and Toni's grandmother, 'on that terrible night of the pogrom'. As well as Peter, Danitzça and Toni wanted everybody to believe that they had good Australian friends who were not to blame for what had happened. There was no shadow of a grievance against them in the genial and friendly greetings which hailed Tom Gough and his family.

The wedding feast was sumptuous and uproarious, with piles of pickled cucumber, beetroot, onions and olives, to whet the appetite, and a whole chicken for every guest, as well as cuts from the roast kid and sucking pig. The noise and heat were too much for Eily. She went out on to the verandah, where some of the younger women with babies were waiting until the first sitting had finished, to have their meal. Sally went on eating until she could not stow away another crumb in case her host might imagine she was not enjoying his wonderful meal. She marvelled at the quantities of food people were consuming. Spaghetti and ravioli, as well as jellies, preserved fruits, iced and spiced cakes, all washed down with tumblers of red wine from three wicker-clad demijohns standing against the wall. These had been sent to Peter for the wedding by countrymen who had vineyards along the Swan River and down near the coast. There were toasts and a merry shouting of congratulations to the bride and bridegroom.

After the meal the table was carried out and a space cleared for Danitzça to do a folk dance, while friends and relations sat round, singing and beating out the rhythm with their feet.

It was the custom in the village her father and mother had come from, for the bride to have her last fling of youthful freedom like this, and for the bridegroom to rush in, join her in the dance, capture and carry her off. Danitzça's family knew, of course, that Peter had been teaching Toni the steps of this dance for days past. There was a gale of laughter and delighted applause when he bounced after Danitzça, following her graceful, whirling figure with every step and turn of a young man of her own people, claiming his bride.

On the narrow verandah, when the guests had drifted out for a breath of fresh air, Sally talked to Marietta and her husband.

Marietta's husband was still sore about the losses he had suffered during the riots. His business had been ruined, he explained to Mrs. Gough. He had been robbed of his stock and driven out of his wine shop. The government's decision not to renew the licences of aliens remained in force, and he, Adamo Fiaschi, was now working on the woodline with Toni.

'Very good for him,' Peter declared. He was better pleased to have a son-in-law who was a working man than proprietor of a wine shop.

Toni's grandmother complained bitterly that she had had to leave her home in Boulder when Toni could no longer work on the mines. She had been living with the Lalichs until Toni and Danitzça were married.

'Never mind, gran,' Danitzça said. 'We'll soon have a nice home in Kurrawang, with a garden and goats, and a vine growing over the trellis at the back.'

She was going out to the timber camp with Toni and would be living in a tent for a while. Mrs. Mattina was to stay on and look after Peter until Toni could build a house of his own.

The old woman shook her head, exclaiming lugubriously and setting the big, gold ear-rings jiggling beside her withered face.

'She says Toni has deserted her,' Danitzça laughed. 'She has nowhere to go: nowhere to rest her old bones. But don't you believe it, Mrs. Gough. Gran had quite a lot of money hidden in a box, and all her jewellery, when the house was raided, so she's quite well off: has nothing to growl about, really !'

Other women were better dressed at Danitzça's wedding than Mrs. Mattina. Their striped silks and flowered prints made a bright setting for the slight figure of the old woman in her old-fashioned dress of black sateen with a high collar, tight bodice and full skirt. But Mrs. Mattina was decked out like a gipsy. Necklaces and bracelets adorned her bosom and arms. Her boney brown fingers glittered with rings.

She sat near the door talking to herself until Toni bounded over to her.

'Come on, gran, show a leg,' he cried gaily.

Mrs. Mattina protested querulously as Toni bent over her, love and laughter in his eyes.

'But you promised to dance at my wedding,' he said: picked her up and dumped her in the middle of the floor.

The tamburiças struck up a lively air, and the tiny black figure began to move, stiffly, like a marionette. Gaining confidence, Mrs. Mattina held up her skirt and stepped out briskly. Forgetting time and place, as the rhythm of the music drove her, she danced with gestures of incomparable grace and a joyous abandon.

Sally knew, of course, that Toni's grandmother had been a ballet dancer in her youth; but she had never imagined anything like the magic that slight, insignificant looking little woman in an old black dress, threw into her dancing. It transformed her and transported the crowd of excitable foreigners watching her to a passion of admiration and applause. How they cheered and clapped, stamping their feet and shouting, while Toni's grandmother bowed and blew them professional kisses! Then Toni picked her up, kissed her and carried her to her chair near the door.

There was more singing and dancing; but Eily looked fagged and Tom thought it was time to be going home.

'I haven't enjoyed myself so much for a long time,' Sally exclaimed, when they were driving along the wide, dusty road by the light of a waning moon.

'It's good to think we can still be friends with the foreign workers,' Dinny said. 'And that they don't bear us any malice for the recent troubles.'

'Peter Lalich and Toni don't because they understand the cause,' Tom replied. 'But there's a good many numskulls among them as well as among us.'

'One thing foreigners can show us,' Dinny chuckled. 'How to enjoy life. I don't think we ever get as much fun out of things as they do. Really let ourselves go, bein' jolly and free and easy like they did to-night.'

'I wish we could feel as happy,' Sally sighed.

'Don't we?' Tom queried.

'I do,' Eily said softly.

'We don't show it,' Sally protested. 'We sat round to-night with tight little smiles on our faces trying to be sociable; but all the time tied up somehow, and not being naturally as lively as the others. I'd have liked to drink a lot, kiss somebody and dance like Mrs. Mattina.'

'Oh, mum, why didn't you?' Tom laughed.

'I don't know. Because I was afraid of looking foolish I suppose,' Sally admitted.

'Isn't that just what I was sayin',' Dinny crowed. 'I'd give a lot meself to do what I feel like doin' and think about it afterwards.'

'Spontaneity's all very well,' Eily said, as if this were too serious a matter to joke about. 'But it can do a lot of harm. I'd rather think first and act afterwards.'

Then there were the lights of Kalgoorlie and Boulder spread out before them! Tom and Eily exclaimed, almost in the same breath with Dinny and Sally, at the beauty and wonder of that swarm of golden stars twinkling and glittering far out over the plain, the misty grey scrub of the still untamed wilderness stretching beyond for hundreds of miles.

CHAPTER XLIV

HERE in these out-back towns of the Western goldfields the welter of world affairs had its repercussions. Every worker read his daily newspaper, the *Kalgoorlie Miner*. Although conscious of his isolation from the storm centres of international politics, a miner felt that he held one end of a golden thread inextricably tangled in the intrigues for economic supremacy going on overseas. No more than a toiler producing the gold which weighed so heavily in deciding the fate of nations he might be; but that knowledge drove him to watch more closely what was happening in other countries and to discuss its bearing on his own life.

Men like Tom Gough, Ted Lee and Barney Riordan were deeply concerned about every shift and change of the international barometer, as it indicated fair or foul weather for the working people of the world. They took care to introduce topics into the yarning at crib times on the mines, in the pubs and at the street corners, in order to show the significance of the daily news and its bearing on local affairs.

The talk would swing from Japanese demands on China, and the menace to Australia of islands Japan had seized in the Pacific, to the setting up of a republic in Germany: the wrangling of victorious powers at the Peace Conference: the farce of a League of Nations which would exclude the United States of America and the Russian Union of Socialist Soviet Republics. Strikes and race riots in America, the suppression of a general strike in England and strikes occurring all over Australia, were the subject of heated discussions.

Everybody knew it was not only on the Golden Mile that unemployment and the high cost of living were causing problems with which working men had to wrestle.

A gloomy background for creation of the new order of society based on just and humanitarian principles which the Allied nations had promised their peoples—after the war! Not many business men, or trade union leaders, believed anything would be done to give effect to those promises.

'Only a few optimists like Missus Sally thought something might come of them,' Dinny said. 'And she's always quoting an English member of parliament who said "the war will abolish class distinctions and inaugurate a new era in Great Britain".'

'He said,' Sally defended herself, 'that: "the sense of brotherhood in the services was affronted by what the civilisation of 1914 offered to the average citizen, and it may be that the Utopias, conceived in many a muddy trench, or under the burning sun of the Orient, will be put to practical test in order that Great Britain and her dominions, to-morrow, will be a vastly happier place within which to dwell."'

'Looks like it, doesn't it?' Dinny's quizzical grin faded. 'With unemployment and starvation facing the workers everywhere, and Lloyd George talkin' about the fortunes of "astronomical dimensions" munition manufacturers made in the first years of the war?'

In Kalgoorlie and Boulder the future of gold was a burning question. On the production of gold these out-back towns, so remote from the thaumaturgy of international diplomacies, depended. Kalgoorlie and Boulder were a source of supply which used to be considered vital to the stability of an economic system that had dominated existence for centuries. But the value of gold had depreciated with the creation of paper currencies during the war. Economists were saying that the value of money now was only two-thirds of what it had been ten years ago. Material prosperity must be gauged not on the number of pieces of paper printed, or the totals of banking figures, but on goods produced. A prime requisite of the gold-mining industry was the revival of production in other industries, and the return to a currency on a par with gold. But could a senile financial system effect this acrobatic feat?

The Western mines had produced a great deal of the gold shipped to the United States to pay Great Britain's war debt. A number of miners and prospectors could tell you, that according to Winston Churchill, four hundred million pounds' worth of bullion had been shipped to the States, and a thousand million of other securities. Immense hoards of gold were stored in the vaults of the Yankee banking houses and United States Treasury; but the war debt was far from liquidation. And still the United States had not got enough gold. A commission had been appointed to inquire into the question of paying a higher price for gold production within its own boundaries.

The stock exchanges of the world were disturbed by the forecast of a period of lower gold production, which, it was asserted, would cramp credit and trade expansion, lower wages and result in increased unemployment.

An article in the *South African Mining Journal,* quoted in the *Kalgoorlie Miner,* was widely discussed on the mines and throughout mining towns of the West.

It said: 'A falling gold output will jeopardise industrial peace.' And the *Miner* went on to comment: 'The journal urges that all gold-mining combines should contribute towards State subsidies to low-grade mines to prevent the loss of twenty per cent. in output. The withdrawal of notes needs both caution and time. The present extravagant demands of labour destroy confidence, prevent enterprise, cause unemployment and threaten revolution. The whole question of the standard value of gold should still receive expert inquiry in order to stabilise prices, protect high-class labour against that of inferior races, and to guard against depreciated currencies.

'Looks like as if this bloke was sayin' stabilise the gold producin' industry and you stave off revolution,' Dinny remarked.

'And that the value of gold is a problem only socialism can solve,' Tom said quietly. 'For us that means strengthening the organisation of the workers: the trade unions and the political representation of the working class. We're going to have a tussle here presently.'

'It was a great fight the lumpers put up against a scab union on the wharves,' Dinny reminded him.

'You've said it, Dinny,' Tom agreed, his face grave and set to thought of the struggle for union principles which was brewing on the fields. 'The disruptors didn't get away with anything on the wharves and we reckon they won't on the mines.'

When Sam Mullet, Eli Nancarrow and Tassy Ryan came along at the week-end to yarn with Dinny, Sally would hear them turning over the news of the world with the same, casual familiarity as the news of the fields. They talked of Lloyd George and Wilson, Lenin and Clemenceau, as if these men were old acquaintances like Paddy Hannan, and Mullocky O'Dwyer, Fardown Mick, or Florrie Driscoll. From shrewd comments on the peace treaty the conversation would drift to reports of the collapse of the Soviets in Russia, the latest gossip about the Hampton Plains rush, or the row brewing between the Miners' Union and returned soldiers in Kalgoorlie.

And in the background Chris would be making his muttered

comments. Sally remembered the last night he had sat there with Dinny and his cronies.

Chris was chanting to himself a long poem she had often heard him murmuring before. The poem was by Lucretius, a Latin poet who had lived in the first century before Christ, Chris told her. That night he had raised his voice a little to say:

> *And all the pageant goes, whilst I with awe,*
> *See in its place the things my Master saw;*
> *See in its place the Three Eternal Things—*
> *The only three—Atoms and Space and Law.*

> *Hearken, oh Earth; hearken, oh Heaven bereft*
> *Of your old gods. These ageless fates are left,*
> *Who are at once the makers and the made*
> *Who are at once the weavers and the weft.*

Three days later Dinny came in from Bulong to tell Sally that Chris was dead.

'His heart must've konked out on him, missus,' Dinny said sadly. 'We was sittin' by the camp fire, same as we always did of an evening, and Chris'd been talking about some of his old cobbers. I got up to turn in. Chris started to follow me and sat down again in his bag chair.

' "Come on, Chris, time to get a bit of shut-eye," I ses. But he didn't answer. I knew something was wrong and went over to him. He was jest layin' back there with his mouth open.'

Dinny brought in some books for Tom and Eily, and one for Sally in which she found that poem underlined. Chris had written in the book: 'For Mrs. Gough from Christopher Montgomery.' That his name had not been the one he used was all they ever knew of Chris.

Dinny missed his old mate so much that he sold the show they had been working on and came to live at the Goughs.

The riots and withdrawal of single Italians from Kalgoorlie and Boulder had not made much difference to the employment of returned soldiers. Some of them got jobs on the mines; but many were still at a loose end. A floating population of workers from the great east-west railway also continued to scrounge about, picking up a few days' work, now and then. Living in shacks of bagging and rusty kerosene tins on Misery Flat, or in the open cut of the old Maritana mine, they hung on, hoping that when the mining industry got into full swing again there would be work and wages for all.

288

Dick was desperate. He had been playing two-up, Dinny discovered, trying to make a little money, gambling with other workless men who collected around the big ring among the sandhills near the 'Sun Inn'. Dick would have taken any job on the surface, or underground, but no jobs were available. Dinny lent him money to keep away from 'the sway', and wanted to take him out prospecting.

'It would be a good thing if Dick could get out of town for a while, don't you think, dear,' Sally said to Amy.

'I don't care what he does,' Amy cried defiantly. 'I'm just about fed up with things as they are.'

'Amy!' Sally could not hide her surprise at a settled grouch and ill humour in Amy's voice.

'It's not only being hard up,' Amy explained shamefacedly. 'But Dick and I just can't get on together. It's no use trying.'

CHAPTER XLV

DICK had been out of work for six months when he was offered a job at Wiluna. A rich field, near Lake Way, three hundred and sixty odd miles from Kalgoorlie, it had been opened up in '96 but struck difficulties in the treatment of low-grade ore. Several companies, experimenting with new processes, lost heavily and closed down. The field had a bad reputation not only among miners because of the arsenical content of the rock carrying gold, but also among investors and mining magnates.

In rough, inaccessible country, it was out of the question for Dick to take Amy and Bill with him to Wiluna.

Dinny tried to dissuade him from accepting the post of assistant metallurgist which a newly formed company, proposing to take over an old plant and experiment with Wiluna ore, had offered him.

'Crikey, I'm not turning it down, Dinny.' Dick said. 'Not on your life.'

'Wiluna's the worst bloody show in the country, Dick,' Dinny said. 'I remember when George Woodley and his mates went out with camels from Cue, and started prospectin' round about Lake Violet. It was a good season, and the lake a sheet of fresh water, covered with wild duck, curlews and ibis: even a few seagulls was knockin' around, I've heard George say. Lennan picked up the first gold on an outcrop half a mile east of where the main camp was set up later. He pegged and called his mine "The Black Swan". The party picked up four hundred ounces of alluvial and located gold-bearin' reefs. They pegged the Monarch lease and George Woodley got the Reward claim. There was a rush and capitalists on the tail of it.

' "Wee-loon-ah" they started to call the camp, and some of the boys thought it was the abo word for "windy place". But it was the cry of the curlews named it an old abo told me. "Wee-loon-ah! Wee-loon-ah" that's the way the curlews cry, and they were cryin' over the place night and day.

'Jack Kimber started a one stamp crusher on the Essex, used to work it by hand from a windlass. And when Percy Martin yanked out a lump of quartz weighin' six hundred ounces—four hundred of 'em pure gold—we thought Wiluna was goin' to play merry blazes with the prospects of Kal and Boulder. Machinery was carted out from Cue by camel team. A small syndicate set up the first treatment plant.

'Simmy Darling—Mr. Darlington Simpson—who'd taken over "The Black Swan", entertained the Governor, Sir Gerald Smith once, and apologised for not havin' his dinner service of beaten gold handy. It's a fact the boys say, a blacksmith on one of his mines at Peak Hill had made Simmy a dinner service of beaten gold. But before long, gold in the oxidized zone began peterin' out, and the companies on Wiluna struck trouble.'

'I know,' Dick said impatiently. 'It's not only sulphide ore they've had to contend with up there. Attempts to treat Wiluna ore by roasting failed. Ben Howe claims to have perfected a process for volatisation, but couldn't make a payable proposition of precipitating the gold. Cost £ 30,000 to recover three ounces. Operations ceased and the mines were abandoned. But the crowd I'm going up for have got some new ideas and a lot of money behind them. Even if the job does peter out I'll get a chance to do some interesting experimental work.'

'That's all very well,' Dinny grumbled. 'But if y'd seen the men I have, sufferin' from arsenic poisoning, y' wouldn't be rushin' it, Dick.'

'I've seen plenty,' Dick said. Hearing Sally's gasp of consternation, he added quickly: 'I know how to look after myself. Used to mucking about with cyanide, don't forget.'

Dinny plunged into his reminiscences again in order to side-track Sally's anxiety.

'Remember the floods on Wiluna, missus?' he queried. 'They haven't stopped talking' about 'em up there yet! In 1900, it was, the lakes brimmed over and spread over the plains for miles. Y'd think they were pullin' y'r leg when y' see the dead, dry country all round to-day. But it's a fact they had boats on the lake and started a sailing club, held a regatta there that year. Could sail for a hundred and fifty miles. Got dinghies and yachts the six hundred miles up from the coast by train to Cue and camel packed 'em the rest of the way.

'But that was after the water subsided a bit. At first work stopped on the mines and the camp was cut off. The mail coach couldn't get through. The last driver who tried had to unharness his horses and leave the coach stuck up in the middle of Lake Way, with the mail bags and a thousand ounces of gold on!

'Stores were runnin' low, and things lookin' pretty serious, when Tom Tweedie steered the warden through with a buggy load of flour, sugar and tea.

'For two or three years y' never saw anything like the seasons they had round about. There was herbage and game everywhere and the abos were fightin' fit. They had a great scrap, two tribes of 'em, near Lake Violet. The stench from dead bodies got so bad the warden hired Charley de Goose, who'd come over from Cue, to bring 'em in and bury 'em at thirteen bob a head. Charley was makin' quite a good thing out of diggin' up the corpses again as soon as he'd planted 'em—until the warden took a tumble to what he was up to.'

'Some people don't have any luck,' Dick grinned.

'Charley de Goose and Micky, the Priest, had plenty runnin' gamblin' joints at Cue in the roarin' 'nineties,' Dinny mused. 'But talkin' of luck—Jack Carlson struck tough luck on Wiluna. He was prospectin' about fifty miles east and came on the remains of Bob McKenzie and his mate who'd done a perish out there. Jack decided to bring Bob's body in, and was packing it on a camel with the rest of his gear when the dead man's gun went off and shot him through the leg. Jacky had the hell of a time pullin' through himself. But he stuck to Bob and saw his mates gave him a slap-up funeral.

'The quartz reefs were peterin' out and there wasn't much doin' when I was on Wiluna soon afterwards. Herbert Hoover came along that summer. He and John Agnew reckoned Wiluna had seen its best days. I reckon it had too.'

'Don't go, dearie,' Sally pleaded. 'There's always been a hoodoo on the place.'

'The blacks wouldn't camp there in the early days,' Dinny said. 'And they were a fierce, wild lot: came down to the lake like ants now and then. Canning struck trouble with one of the tribes further north when he was puttin' through the stock route from Hall's Creek. That was a great job, Dick, chartin' a track eight hundred miles long through what was supposed to be desert country. But

Canning located water all the way and some pretty good stretches of feed for his horses and camels. Was out eighteen months, and only lost one of his men, Mick Tobin. He was speared by blacks.'

'I remember,' Sally butted in. 'Big Bill Matheson was with him, wasn't he?'

'You bet he was,' Dinny's little laugh gurgled. 'Bill never let you forget it. He swore by Canning, reckoned he was the best all-round bushman he ever struck. But the first stockmen bringin' cattle over the track had a crook spin. They was two blokes by the name of Thompson and Shoesmith, with a couple of Kimberley natives and a mob of two hundred cattle and twenty horses. Shoesmith was jest about blind with the sandy blight when the mob stampeded, and Thompson ran a mulga stake through his arm gettin' after 'em. Y'r know the hell of a time a mulga scratch can give a man, festerin' and poisonin!' Well, Thompson and his mate were in a bad way, and the blacks knew that when they attacked. Both of 'em were speared near the same well where they got Mick Tobin. The whole outfit was lost, cattle and men and horses. A year later, another stockman comin' through picked up Thompson's diary; but he had a stronger party and was well armed. All the same, stockmen and drovers'll tell you they've got to keep their eyes skinned, and sleep away from the camp fire on the Canning Stock route.'

'Well, thank goodness, Den's safe in the south-west, and not droving for northern cattle stations like he wanted to,' Sally exclaimed.

But her anxiety about Dick going to Wiluna was uppermost in her mind. She knew well enough what arsenic poisoning meant. Had seen men with the cartilege eaten out of their noses, and been told how it destroyed their virility. Dick would be working on a new process, not only to reduce costs in the treatment of Wiluna ore, but to make the arsenic content a profitable commodity.

'I can't bear to think of you taking the risk, Dick,' Sally said. Dick's smile sent a pain to her heart.

'Risk?' he queried. 'I'd take any risk to get out of the dead end I've been in lately. The trenches in France weren't so bad, Sal-o-my, as breaking my neck to get a job and seeing Amy and the kid go short of things they ought to have, these last few months.'

Sally could have wept at the bitterness in his voice.

'Don't worry, mother,' Dick said gently. 'I'll be all right: know how to take care of myself. It's a great chance, really! Why I might discover the process that'll make Wiluna ore a payable proposition.'

'The Great Fingal at Daydawn paid all right,' Dinny said.

'They got a million and a half out of it, but the miners died like flies—even the women and children livin' round about got the white dust that was always in the air when the mine was working. Though that was quartz dust, not arsenic. Now the big dump's standing like a mountain with the snow on it, and they say the sands'd go four 'weights. But the town's deserted, a couple of eagles'd built their nest on the old poppet head of the main shaft last time I saw it.'

'It'll be a long time before the eagles build on Wiluna if I have any luck,' Dick declared gaily.

'Y'd much better come out prospectin' with me,' Dinny grumbled.

But Dick's mind was set on going to the Wiluna field now. He went off before the end of the week: was travelling by car for a day, then when the tracks got too heavy would pick up a camel team taking stores through the last stretches of dense scrub to the mine workings and miners' shacks scattered over rising ground near Lake Violet. There were still a few parties working small shows and crushing at the State Battery, although most of the mines had been deserted for years.

'Afraid I've given Amy and the kid a crook spin lately, darl,' he said to Sally. 'But they're going down to the coast right away. Amy'll like to be there for the summer.'

CHAPTER XLVI

EILY's daughter was born in August.

Such an old sobersides Tom had always been, and now he was full of joy about the child and Eily's motherhood.

'Eily had a bad time, they say at the hospital, mum, but is all right now,' he told Sally, looking fagged after being up all night, although the brightness of the early morning was on his face. 'And the baby's the dead spit of you! She's got fairish hair though, and the prettiest little hands.'

'Well, she's not to be called Sarah,' Sally cried, hugging and kissing Tom, more excited and delighted about this baby than she had been even when Billy was born. 'You know, I've never forgiven my parents for naming me after an estimable great-aunt. I'd have liked to be called Daphne.'

'Daphne, she'll be,' Tom grinned. 'Eily'll love that.'

The public hospital was still a big rambling building of corrugated iron, but there were trained nurses and capable doctors in attendance. Eily was in a ward with several other mothers when Dinny and Sally went to see her. She looked 'a sight for sore eyes', Dinny said, sitting up in bed with a pink woollen jacket over her shoulders and her baby in her arms, a smile ,of infinite tenderness and wonderment on her face. No one on the goldfields was a happier girl than Eily Gough, Sally knew.

'Tom and I both hoped we'd have a daughter,' she told Sally. 'We're going to call her Daphne.'

When she left the hospital Eily and the baby came back to live with Sally. There were more empty houses about, owing to the slump. Many of them were being sent by rail to the coast, and Tom had his eye on one he intended to buy when Eily was strong enough to arrange about furnishing a home of her own.

Dinny was in luck again. He and Tassy Regan had gone out prospecting together soon after Dick left for Wiluna. They pottered about on a spot which Dinny had fancied for some time, always intending to give it a trial. When they picked up a couple of floaters they thought they were on to something: loamed in every direction until a small leader was located. Following this down, at a depth of fifteen feet it had gradually widened to two feet. Eight tons from this leader yielded thirty-five 'weights to the ton over the plates. The sands gave good assay value, and formations alongside the leader a dish value of twelve 'weights.

There was nothing sensational about the show; but in these days when the exploitation of low-grade ores was becoming more profitable, and the possibility of a gold bonus was 'in the air', any new find aroused excitement and expectation. So Dinny and Tassy soon had a rush round them and sold their lease at a satisfactory figure.

'The ground's pegged a mile and half south of the Breakaway,' Dinny reported gleefully. 'And for nearly a mile to the north. Takes the old timers to locate her! I wish to God Dick'd come out with me, missus, like I wanted him to, instead of chasin' that wild cat at Wiluna.'

Dick wrote that he was pleased with his job, however. He had been doing interesting experimental work—though operations might have to be suspended until more money and gear were available. He hoped this would not happen for a few months, and that Amy and young Bill could stay on 'at the coast until the end of the summer.

Then Den's letter came announcing that he was going to be married in a few weeks!

He and Charl had decided it was no use trying to cope with the milking on two places any longer. When they were married Den proposed that they should install extra milking machines, and do the milking for both farms on Warrinup. The aunts were willing: thought it was a grand idea. Sally must come down for the wedding. Den felt she had to be there to complete his happiness, and the aunts were dying to see her. If Dinny could come too Den would throw up his hat and turn hand springs. 'Gosh, I'd give anything to see the old snoozer, and show him Dartigan,' he wrote. 'Tell him, his godfather ought to stand by a bloke at his wedding, and he can be my best man if he'll come.'

Dinny was more rattled than tempted by the idea of being best man at a wedding. But he asked eagerly:

'D'y' think we could go, missus? D'y' think maybe we could? Strike, I'd like to see the lad again.'

'It's out of the question, my going,' Sally said weakly. 'But you go, Dinny. I don't see why you shouldn't.'

'Not without you,' Dinny said.

'Cripes, mum, why don't you go?' Tom wanted to know. 'You ought to. Think how Den'll feel if you don't, and we owe it to the aunts. Eily and I'll look after things here, if that's what you're thinking of.'

'Of course we will,' Eily said. 'Go on, mum, let's send a wire and say you and Dinny'll be there.'

'Oh dear,' Sally faltered, 'I'd love to go, but . . .'

'No buts,' Tom decided. 'You're packing!'

The next week passed in a whirl. Dinny bought a complete outfit: a new suit, shirts, socks, shoes, pyjamas, half a dozen ties and a felt hat. He was so fussy and excited, Eily and Tom got a lot of fun out of teasing him about his preparations.

Dinny had been to see Marie and asked her to buy the few clothes Sally would need for a visit like this.

'Time was I'd've spent all me money on booze,' he explained apologetically. 'If I'm not doing that now, Missus Sally's to blame —and'll have to put up with the consequences.'

Tom wanted to pay for his mother's railway ticket, but Dinny was aggrieved at the idea.

'Y' wouldn't deprive me of the pleasure, Tommy, would y'?' he said. 'We're goin' to do things in style, travel first class, have a motor car to the station, and whenever we want one. It's going to be the holiday your mother's dreamt of for years, goin' back to see her own folks. She's earned it. And well, I never reckoned I'd have the luck to be goin' with her—and to see Den runnin' a place like that.' So they had gone off looking like a honeymoon couple themselves, with Tom and Eily on the station to say good-bye and trying to make the baby wave a little fat hand.

'We had a slap-up time,' Dinny said when they got back a fort-night later. 'Best time I've ever had in all me born days.'

He could talk of nothing for days but Den's wedding, Miss Fan and Miss Phyllis and Charlie: the horses and dairy herds Den was handling. Sally, too, went over and over everything that had happened during that brief visit to her old home.

After leaving Kalgoorlie in the late afternoon they had arrived in Perth next morning: taken an early train for the south-west, next day, and towards evening reached Warrinup where Den was waiting for them with a buggy and pair of lively young horses. Just to show how well he could manage them, Sally was sure.

'And there was y'r mother sniffin' the air like a dog on the trail,' Dinny burbled.

'Oh, it was good to smell the damp undergrowth, that smell of ferns and wild thyme in the southern bush, Tom,' Sally said. 'Every turn of the road brought back memories. And to see the river flowing away into the distance, and the old house huddled against the timbered hills, a feather of smoke drifting up from the chimneys, just as it was when I last saw it! I could scarcely believe so little had changed, although of course there were new roads and bridges, and ever so many more homesteads scattered about.'

'It's a grand place they've got down there, and no mistake,' Dinny declared.

'Den looked so well, ruddy and brown,' Sally rattled on, 'and about twice the size he used to be. But he's just the same, really! Our dear, bumptious laddie, full of tricks to get his own way, and getting it mostly. Fan and Phyll think he's marvellous. He does what he likes with them. Charlie won't let him boss her too much, though. And Den knows it. She's a nice girl, rather plain and matter of fact, really, though she looked quite pretty in her wedding dress. She and Den talk mostly about cows and the price of butter-fat. How they ever found time to fall in love I don't know. But they did, and there you are!'

'Den's found runnin' a dairy-farm's no picnic,' Dinny carried on. 'And you've got to hand it to him for the way he's doin' it. He's forgotten about the work on a big cattle station he was always hankerin' after. Does a bit of musterin', brandin' and breakin' on Warrinup, but it's cows keep him busy most of the time. And he works hard! Gawd, he works hard, Tom! And Charlie, too. But they like it. So that's all to the good.'

'It was an old-fashioned wedding in the little church at War-rinup,' Sally continued blithely. 'Charlie wore a white silk dress and a veil and orange blossoms, and there were two bridesmaids, and Dinny didn't forget the ring, and escorted the bridesmaid down the aisle as if he were used to doing that sort of thing every day in the week.'

'Don't you believe it, Tom,' Dinny protested. 'Me legs were shakin' under me. It was all I could do to get to the church door, with so many strangers lookin' on and wonderin' who was the funny old sod Den Gough had got to be best man at his wedding.'

'Then there was the wedding breakfast at Three Creeks, and a dance afterwards when they'd cleared away the tables and chairs,' Sally broke in. 'A real country wedding, Eily, with Phyll playing polkas and barn dances, like when we were girls, and men and women I'd known then coming round and saying: "Is it really you, Sally?" I'd never've known them either. Most of them'd got so fat and old. I never realised I'd got old until I saw them. Oh dear, it was funny and sad, too! But Fanny and Phyll were very sweet and loving. It was wonderful to hear them say: "Welcome home, dear Sally!" and to see all the tables and chairs in the old home, just as they used to be.

'Fan and Phyll took a great fancy to Dinny. They'd heard of him so much from Den they felt they'd known him for a long time, they said. They want you and Eily, Tom, and Dick and Amy, to go down and spend a holiday with them. Dinny's to go whenever he wants to, and I've promised some day to pay them another visit.'

Dinny beamed as Sally talked. He had been thrilled to be received as a friend of the family, and to hear Den introducing him at the wedding as: 'My godfather, Mr. Denis Quin, an old mate of my father's and a pioneer prospector of the Coolgardie goldfields.'

Life at Warrinup was a new experience to Dinny. The greenness of the cleared paddocks, abundance of water everywhere, and the busy, hard life of the farmers and orchardists awed and surprised him, though he felt cramped and closed in by the forests and hills: was quite ready 'to make tracks' when Sally began to get restless.

A letter from Eily had mentioned casually that Dick was back from Wiluna. The company he had been working for was closing down. 'But don't worry, mum,' Eily wound up cheerfully. 'Dick's got the chance of another job on the Boulder.'

But Sally was worried, and she still felt rather a black sheep with her sisters. Their ways and ideas were so different to her own now. From the daily newspaper she had seen there was likely to be a strike on the mines. And she knew what that meant. No work or wages for hundreds of men. Her boarders would not be able to pay her, and Tom would be short of money. She felt she must go home to look after things. Besides, after she had discussed the family news with Fanny and Phyll: heard all about Cecily's and Grace's children, and the details of births, deaths and marriages in the district, there was nothing else to talk about, except Den and the wedding, of course, and Warrinup.

The evening before she left, Phyll said: 'We think it's only fair to tell you, Sally, that Den has taken a load of anxiety off our minds. We were afraid we might lose Warrinup a few years ago. You know we had to raise a mortgage on the property in order to install milking machines. And it was very difficult to keep up the interest on that borrowed money when I got ill. Fanny couldn't've carried on much longer. But now, with Den helping us, we're meeting our payments quite easily. How pleased dear papa would be to know a grandson of his is looking after the place.'

'Phyll's trying to say,' Fanny added, 'that Warrinup will be Den's when we are dead. But we do want to spend the rest of our days here.'

'We offered to go away and let Den have the house when we knew he was going to be married,' Phyll explained apologetically. 'But Den wouldn't hear of it. The dear boy! Of course, we won't interfere with the young people in any way. And Charlie says she'll be quite happy living with us.'

'If only you knew what it means to me,' Sally told them, 'to see Den settled down here.'

They were such simple, unworldly old dears, Den said. How on earth they had ever managed to run Warrinup for nearly twenty years he could not imagine. But they were both better pleased to potter about the house and garden; or to make jam and jellies than to be out in all weathers rounding up cows and taking cream into the butter factory.

It had been a grand holiday and Dinny enjoyed every minute of it: but he was glad to get back to the goldfields.

'A man can't hear himself think down there,' he said. 'The trees are always crowdin' in on you, and nobody talks about anything but cows. Up here y'r eye gets used to distances and big ideas.'

Sally, too, felt like that. She had lived so long in that ramshackle house on the Boulder road that she could not rest or sleep anywhere else, she confessed. And besides she had been anxious about the strike: how it would affect Tom and Dick.

During their one day in Perth on the return journey, Dinny hired a taxi and they went to see Amy in her cottage near the sea at Cottesloe. But Amy was not there. A woman leaning over the garden gate of the house next door, told them that Mrs. Gough had 'gone out with the fat gentleman in his big black car'.

'Did she take the little boy?' Sally asked.

'Oh, no, she never takes him,' the neighbour replied, an edge to her voice. 'She leaves him at the grocer's shop round the corner.'

Sally went to the grocer's shop: explained that she was Billy Gough's grandmother, and asked to see Billy. She found him playing in the back-yard with two other small boys, very grubby but well and happy.

'Mrs. Gough leaves Billy with me quite a lot,' the grocer's wife said. 'I don't mind. Got three kids of me own, so one extra doesn't matter—and she pays me to look after him.'

Sally felt inclined to kidnap Bill and bring him back to Kalgoorlie; but contented herself with buying apples and sweets for him.

As soon as he had said: 'Hullo, gran!' and let Sally kiss his dirty little face, Billy wanted to return to his game, and ran off shouting gleefully.

'Oh dear, what has come over Amy?' Sally exclaimed when she and Dinny were on their way back to Perth to catch their train.

'Y' don't want to worry about what that neighbour woman said,' Dinny tried to reassure her. 'A born scandal-mongerer if ever there was one.'

They both guessed who the fat gentleman in the big black car might be and were concerned about Amy's friendliness with Paddy Cavan.

CHAPTER XLVII

DICK was working underground on the Boulder Reef, Sally discovered. Not only that, but he was spalding on the ore bin.

She hated him to be doing this, merely laborious work. But Dick took it rather as a joke, or pretended to take it that way.

'It's only a temporary job, Sal-o-my,' he said lightly. 'Good to get my muscle up. The Wiluna crowd are chasing more cash. They're keen to have me with them when they start operations again.'

But Dick, too, was going to be out of work as a result of the strike.

'It's the same old struggle,' Dinny said. 'You might say the first round on this field was over alluvial rights, and this looks like bein' the second.'

'It's a vital principle of unionism that's at stake,' Tom said. 'Dragging in the old Coolgardie Union is just a stunt to cloud the issue.'

'That's right,' Dinny agreed.

'What's happened?' Sally asked anxiously. 'Since we've been away, I mean.'

'The most important thing,' Tom said, 'is the ballot. By an overwhelming majority miners on the Golden Mile have voted against working with non-unionists. They are members of the Miners' Branch of the Australian Workers Union, of course, and say the Coolgardie Union has been resurrected and is being boosted, at the moment, to defeat the miners' move to strengthen their organisation. The Coolgardie Union carried a resolution condemning the ballot as "a piece of trickery, framed for the purposes of intimidation and carried out by a lot of Bolsheviks". It says it's going to stick to its guns and fight if necessary to defend the miner and his country from these foreign agitators.'

'Easy seen where that sort of talk comes from.'

'That's what we say, mum,' Tom said. 'We reckon no miner who's got any nouse would be taken in by it; or let himself be used to weaken trade union principles. There's a few old boys who've been kidded into thinking they're patriots because they voted for conscription, and wouldn't pay levies to help fellow workers in the lumpers' strike. But the fact remains they're playing the bosses' game to break the unity of the miners and force us to work with scabs.'

'The snag is the C.U. was registered in the State Court, but not the Federal Arbitration Court, it seems, Tommy,' Dick said.

'But it's got no funds or membership to fight for an award, and we're out for a hearing in the Arbitration Court,' Tom pointed out. 'We'll do all the fighting and bear the costs.'

'There's some blokes mean as they make 'em,' Dinny interrupted. 'They'd let others do their fightin' and shellin' out—and pick up the plums jest the same.'

'Rat-bags!' Eily said fiercely. 'No decent miner'd be seen dead in the same street with them.'

'Early this year,' Tom went on, 'all branches of the Federated Miners in the West decided to join the A.W.U., become a branch of that union. All except the Coolgardie branch. It's been practically dead for years: didn't have sufficient membership to vote itself out of existence even, when other branches joined the A.W.U. An attempt was made to organise a General Workers' Union to counteract miners' amalgamation with the A.W.U. The A.W.U. opposed registration of the new union in the Federal Arbitration Court, on the ground that the A.W.U. covered workers on the goldfields. The Coolgardie union was dragged out, and a branch set up in Boulder to become the mouthpiece of anti-working-class interests on the field.'

'How about the returned soldiers?' Sally asked. 'What are they doing?'

'The Boulder men are with us,' Tom said, 'but you know what to expect from the Kalgoorlie bunch.'

'Can't see beyond the nose on their faces,' Dinny grumbled. ' "Preference to returned soldiers" is all they can think of—not realisin', as workers, the only hope they've got of makin' a decent living is a strong union.'

'We applied for cancellation of the Boulder branch of the Coolgardie Union.' Tom's logical mind returned to his statement of the miners' case. 'Because it was not observing the rules of a miners' union. Shopkeepers, publicans, all sorts of men not associated with the industry are being admitted. A list of members and officials has not been sent to the registrar, annual returns have not been submitted, or accounts audited. And because there was already an industrial union in Boulder when this bogus branch of the C.U. was dumped there.'

'Oh dear,' Sally sighed, 'I suppose you're right, Tom. There had to be a show-down. But I wish the returned soldiers could have been kept out of it.'

'So do we,' Tom said. 'We reckon it's an industrial dispute and returned soldiers shouldn't butt in.'

Sally dreaded the deprivations and harrowing anxieties a strike imposed on the miners, their wives and families. To her a strike was a tragic drama in which the chief actors were always abused and vilified by those who had no understanding of the real causes, or the courage and fortitude which underlay industrial struggles. She knew the miners on this field well enough to realise that they were not easily moved to down tools, lose wages and see their wives and families go short of food. The conditions in which miners habitually worked were so bad, the foul air and sweltering darkness, with accidents occurring every day because of defective machinery, dangerous ground and the pressure a man put on himself, even when he was 'dusted', to earn a decent pay, that it seemed as if only some extraordinary crisis stirred them to desperation and rebellious action.

'Grime kissed and death kissed,' as Jabez Edward Dodd, a poet among them, had written, 'they work below ground'. Every miner who had sweated for several years in those foetid caverns of the Golden Mile knew he was doomed. So many men were dying of tuberculosis that a commission had been inquiring into ways and means of arresting spread of the disease.

Dr. Cumpston's report cleared up a lot of misunderstanding about miners' phthisis, or miners' disease as it was called. Most miners understood now that there was a difference between tuberculosis and fibrosis, or silicosis, although it was a shock to learn that within two years, or even sooner, the lungs of a miner working in dust and fumes usually became affected with fibrosis. Tuberculosis spread in the dank underground atmosphere as the result of a germ infection: but fibrosis, or silicosis, was due to the breathing of dust and fine particles of silica which lodged in the lungs predisposing them to all sorts of weaknesses, including tuberculosis.

Sally was panic-stricken when she remembered how long Tom had been working underground. She begged him to try to find some other way of earning a living; and she was terrified for Dick, who was as thin as a rake, and had looked ill ever since he returned from the war.

But how much worse off most of the men working in the mines were! The majority of them, according to recently published figures, suffered from some stage of silicosis or tuberculosis, men with wives and children to provide for. The death rate from tuberculosis had increased alarmingly; but many men were afraid to give up a job they were accustomed to, on the off chance of finding other work. There was talk of pensioning them off, but so far nothing had been done about it. And the miners were so loyal to a sick mate that they would do half his work for him and disregard the danger of infection to themselves, rather than see him paid off and reduced to the last stages of despair.

Everybody knew that although some of the recommendations of a commission on the ventilation and sanitation of mines had been embodied in the regulations the most important had been either amended or left out.

With a powerful union behind them the miners were sure they could enforce inclusion in the regulations of more adequate measures to safeguard health, and bring pressure to bear on the mine owners for the improvement of their living and working conditions. That was why they were striking now.

'Never known the men so solid and determined,' Tom said. No wonder, Sally told herself. It was their lives they were fighting for, and an organisation which would enable them to bargain more effectively for recognition of their value to the mining industry.

When Tom came home at noon next day the strike had begun.

'Before the day shift started work,' he said, 'our stewards went round asking for a show of union tickets. Members of the C.U. were not regarded as unionists. Then our officials approached the mine managers and told them that unless every mine worker took out an A.W.U. ticket, not a man would start work. The managers

302

said they would not discriminate between unions, unionists, or non-unionists. So we walked out and the mines are at a standstill.'

Next day was Labour Day, a workers' holiday. The procession swung through the town in hot sunshine, with banners flying and a brass band making a merry din. At the sports, on the recreation ground, the miners' leaders were hailed with enthusiasm. They spoke about the struggle which had begun: warned the miners and their wives that it might be a long and bitter one; but that what they were fighting for was a fundamental principle of unionism. They pointed out what most working men and women knew, that only organisation gave them any power to improve wages and conditions of work. And it was a fair thing to demand that those who benefited by the victories and awards won by the Miners' Branch of the A.W.U. should share the hardships and costs. A scab was the meanest thing on God's earth, because he not only took all he could get from the trade union movement, but did nothing in return except indulge in strike-breaking tactics aimed at defeating their fellow workers.

The great majority of men and women who had lived and worked all their lives on the goldfields understood that; and that any opposition to union policy was being engineered by the mine owners, because it threatened their grip on the mining industry which, like a giant octopus, had drawn colossal profits from the very life-blood of the workers, and these inland towns, for many years.

A thunderstorm in the late afternoon overcast the holiday mood of the great crowd, and sent hundreds of men, women and children scurrying for home in torrential rain. It was like an omen of the stormy and depressing weeks which lay before them.

The Kalgoorlie Returned Soldiers' Association, which had joined forces with The Imperialist League, and changed its name to the Returned Soldiers' League, came out with a resolution which showed how deep the cleavage between this group and the working-class community had become.

This resolution declared bluntly that all returned men must stick together and put the R.S.L. first in all matters. 'That this branch of the R.S.L. is in favour of all returned men belonging to a union, but refuses to have anything to do with the A.W.U. unless it recognises preference to returned soldiers.'

'Law and order must be upheld,' one speaker said. 'The Kalgoorlie R.S.L. is united against the forces of Bolshevism and other influences, which tended to corrupt Australian life and institutions.'

'Why drag in Bolshevism?' the miners asked. 'What we're defending is union organisation.'

Their laughter was harsh and bitter. Why did men who should

be fighting with the miners in their own interests voice the opinions of mining magnates and their political rouseabouts? Surprise, anger and disgust shook the workers of Boulder when the Kalgoorlie R.S.L. offered its services to the police and two hundred of its members signed on as special constables.

Somebody went round with a bell, and Kalgoorlie returned soldiers held a meeting in Hannan Street to put their views to citizens. 'The soldiers must defeat the A.W.U., otherwise Australia will be akin to Russia,' one speaker said. 'Bolshevism must be stamped out.' Cheers from their supporters and howls of derision resounded.

'Seeds of discord have been sown on the goldfields by emissaries from foreign places,' another speaker declared. The booing of the crowd drowned the 'Hear, Hears!' of his friends.

But when Harry Axford announced that 'returned soldiers must not fail now. They were fighting for all loyal citizens and for the maintenance of the purity of their mothers, wives and sisters', the rage of listening miners boiled over. The insinuation that the men on strike would be a menace to females, if their union became more powerful, outraged a tradition of chivalry towards women which miners and prospectors had prided themselves on since the earliest days of the fields. Miners surged towards the platform in a rush which would have cost Axford his life had not the police contrived to get him away. The meeting was closed and the crowd dispersed, seething with indignation.

The Miners' Union denied responsibility for the action of its members on this occasion and on the first day of the strike when some of them were accused of rough-handling scabs. The union announced that it would not countenance acts of individual violence. It urged the miners to maintain a calm and disciplined attitude, and not to fall for any provocation.

'These wild speeches and the enrolling of special constables are intended to enrage you,' Tom Bradley, secretary of the Miners' Union told the miners. 'You know Bolshevism and foreign agitators have got nothing to do with the strike. You know what we're fighting for—a hundred per cent. unionism—and the Chamber of Mines, and the returned soldiers know it, as well as we do. They're trying to stir up hostility to the miners and create disturbances. I'm not here to tell you what to do. You know what to do. But don't fall into the trap and give them an excuse for arrests and prosecutions which will divert attention from the strike and the policy of the union.'

At the same time the union protested at the arming of citizens, and stressed the dangerous effect which this putting of weapons into the hands of one section of the community, to use against another, could have on the morale of the miners. Because there were unruly spirits on both sides, ready for a brawl, the miners' leaders approached the Kalgoorlie R.S.L. not to organise processions or demonstrations likely to cause a riot; and the Miners' Union agreed to refrain from organising similar processions and demonstrations. But the enrolment of special constables continued.

'The resident magistrate, who's supposed to be impartial, is up at the Soldiers' Institute swearing men in as specials,' Tom told Dinny. 'George Callanan says they're enrolling lads of seventeen and eighteen, and one old man of seventy's a special now. Some of the worst crocks and spielers in the town are swaggering round armed with rifles and revolvers.'

'They didn't dare come at that in the alluvial troubles,' Dinny exclaimed.

'Only armed the police and talked of bringing up the York militia,' Sally reminded him.

Two thousand miners assembled at Fimiston, near the Block below the mines, at seven o'clock on the morning after the holiday. Union men on three shifts turned out to ensure no scabs worked that day. In a few hours the wildest rumours were flying through the town about how unionists had stormed the mines, flung scabs down shafts, or beaten them up, and the mines had closed to prevent further disturbances.

Eily was in a fever of impatience for Tom to come home, and Sally anxious about Dick. He was more likely than Tom to have got mixed up in a fight, she thought. That was what the war had done to him: made him reckless and uncompromising in whatever he did. She was glad to see Tom and Dick coming up the garden path together.

They laughed at the idea that union activity had been as violent as the rumours implied. There had been a scrimmage here and there; but on the whole they were satisfied with the result.

'As a matter of fact,' Tom said, 'our plan worked out fairly well. The meeting on the Block was quick and lively. Pickets went off to each mine and took up their position. For the most part they advised men to join the union: argued with them about going to work when we were on strike. And a good number joined up, or just walked off.

'Things got out of hand here and there. The boys were mad when they saw one man carrying on as usual. They told him to knock off. He's been talking big ever since the riots against foreigners, and blowing his bags about what he'd do if anybody told him to stop work. Well, he started a fight and was getting the worst of it,

305

when somebody hopped in flourishing a revolver. But it was grabbed off of him before he did any damage.'

'A scab tried the same game on the Percy,' Dick went on. 'He's the bird who's been threatening returned soldiers would go along and smash up a store because a while ago the bloke who runs it painted his shop red. Didn't like the idea when we told him there was nothing doing on the mine: he'd better go home. Was laying about him, kicking and punching, till he got pushed up against the embankment and toppled over.'

'Serve him right,' Dinny chuckled.

'The worst incident happened on the Boulder,' Tom added. 'Tom Bradley caught some crazy galoots holding a scab over a winze and threatening to drop him down. Bradley straightened them up and told the bloke to scram. But the news got round and scared other scabs. On the Boulder five men had been advised to clear out, but were hanging round, waiting to go below. They changed their minds and walked off.'

'There's always a few hot-heads liable to do their block,' Dinny commented.

'I know.' Tom's face was grave and hard. 'But that sort of thing reacts against us.'

When a deputation from the miners went to interview representatives of the Chamber of Mines, they agreed to advise non-unionists to join the A.W.U. But this concession was wrung from them at the pistol point, they told delegates from the Kalgoorlie R.S.L. later, and withdrew their promise. Angry crowds surrounded the building, and a stone was thrown through a window, the miners' leaders said. This was the pistol shot which alarmed the mine owners. The crowd burst open the back and front doors and surged into the Chamber. A spokesman for the Chamber of Mines announced that the promise had been given to induce an angry mob to leave the premises.

'Looks as if they want to make the miners so mad they won't know what they're doing,' Eily exclaimed.

'That's what we think,' Tom said. 'The men have been warned. If a fight starts, there's no knowing where it will end. We're unarmed, and standing on our rights as trade unionists. Say the government's asking for trouble to arm "specials" against us.'

During the next few days the tension increased. Hotels were closed by proclamation. 'Kalgoorlie was preparing for war,' people said. The Soldiers Institute was referred to as 'the war office.' Marches of 'specials' with fixed bayonets horrified men and women in the streets. Their sympathy turned more and more towards the miners. The Chamber of Mines refused to negotiate any further with the Miners' Union. It agreed to pay two-thirds of expenses incurred by the force of special constables. At the Perseverance Mine the police were entrenched, armed with rifles and bayonets. A big fitting shop was converted into a dressing station. At a mass meeting of over two thousand miners the decision not to work with non-unionists was re-affirmed by men, resolute and incensed by the attempts made to intimidate them and defeat their purpose. A defence committee had been set up, and a fund opened to provide food for the families of miners out of work through closing of the mines, and money was coming from working-class organisations all over Australia. Members of local unions and branches of the Miners' Union on the northern goldfields levied themselves to support the struggle of the Boulder miners.

But what reinforced their courage and determination more than anything were the resolutions passed by the Boulder returned soldiers.

Tom's face beamed as he read them to his mother and Eily:

' "That this meeting condemns the action of the Kalgoorlie R.S.L. executive, as in our opinion they are fighting the battle of the Chamber of Mines and acting in a manner detrimental to the best interests of ourselves as workers, and we form ourselves into a vigilance committee to protect and fight for our workers. That this largest meeting of returned soldiers ever held on the Eastern Gold-fields, advise all our returned soldier working mates to link up with A.W.U. That we have every sympathy for the A.W.U. and pledge our solid support for the union. That this meeting censures the Kalgoorlie executive of the R.S.L. for interfering in industrial matters." '

'That's something like!' Dinny declared gleefully.

'It's put the boys in great heart,' Tom said. 'Nobody can say, now, that bunch in the Kalgoorlie speaks for returned soldiers on the goldfields, and that the Union isn't justified in the stand it has taken.'

The days dragged on, torpid, nerve-wracking days in which the exasperation of the miners was at breaking point and tempers smouldered dangerously: clashes seemed inevitable. It was rumoured the miners had caches of arms which would be used if there was any shooting or injury to their mates. Still no scabs were working on the mines, and it was well known that the miners would not tolerate any attempt to work them under the protection of armed guards.

The miners sought a conference with the Kalgoorlie R.S.L. in order to find some common basis from which their differences could be overcome. But the miners' leaders maintained that their further action must be decided by a ballot of the membership, and the R.S.L. maintained that it would not differentiate between unionists and non-unionists, so nothing was gained.

Tom came home one afternoon sweating with fury.

'It's almost more than the men can stand, the way the specials are carrying on,' he said. 'They take their revolvers from their pockets and start polishing them up before us. Swagger round, sniggering and jeering, until all you can think of is bashing that look off their faces.'

'Don't let 'em do that to you, Tommy,' Dinny warned.

Tom threw himself into a chair. Sally had never seen this steady, even-tempered son of hers so shaken and over-wrought.

'I know: keep calm: stick to the union plan. Don't let the swine pull your punches. That's what I say to the boys. We'll fight if we've got to—but in an organised way. Solidarity for ever. But, cripes, it's hard, Dinny!'

"Course it's hard, son,' Dinny agreed. 'But public opinion's swung our way. Everybody can see what's happening. People are sayin' it's a miracle the miners've managed to control themselves. If the union hadn't've had good leaders, the fat would've been in the fire before this.'

'That's a fact,' Tom conceded. 'But there's a move to open the mines on Monday. Steam will be up and everything ready for a start, the managers say. If they try working with scabs . . .'

'Christ a'mighty,' Dinny gasped. 'There'll be a flare up and no mistake.'

'You've said it,' Tom agreed wearily.

CHAPTER XLVIII

SALLY awakened to hear the tramp of heavy feet on the road. She looked out of her window, and in the wan moonlight of the small hours before dawn, saw rows of men with rifles and fixed bayonets marching in military formation towards the Boulder.

Tom and Dick had seen them too. She heard them moving about quickly as they dressed.

'What does it mean?' she asked anxiously when Tom stood beside her.

'It means there'll be bloodshed on the mines to-day, if we can't put a stop to this blasted provocation,' he said. 'The men are swearing they won't go unarmed if arms are used against them.'

The next minute Dick and he were gone, without a cup of tea or a bite to eat, Sally remembered, reproaching herself.

Dinny went out to scout for news a few hours later. He came back, limping quickly along the road, his eyes bright with anger.

'They've arrested eleven of the union leaders,' he exclaimed. 'Went to their homes, and caught them off their guard.'

'Tom?' Eily queried breathlessly.

'They haven't got him, the boys tell me,' Dinny said. 'He's been up at the Block tryin' to steady things down.'

'What about Dick?' Sally asked.

'He showed up at the Boulder Reef ready to start work if there were no scabs on the mines, and walked off with the men when they found there was a surface worker not in the union.'

'Was there any fighting?'

'No. Everything went off as if it was a Sunday School picnic, like it was planned, to let the armed forces see they were makin' fools of themselves.'

When Tom came home at midday he verified what Dinny had told them. On every mine, except the Australia, he said there were two, sometimes three non-unionists. On the Ivanhoe and the Horseshoe the managers advised the men to join the union. In every case, after the miners' representatives had informed the manager that the men would not work with scabs, the men walked off the lease. Only the Australia, which was a hundred per cent. unionist, was manned and started work.

'Surely they'll see we can't be beaten now,' Eily exclaimed.

'The men have been committed for trial in Perth,' Tom said. 'Bail's been refused, and they're being shanghaied on to the train this afternoon.'

He was indignant and depressed about the arrest of so many active members of the union, and the short shrift they had got from the magistrate.

'They're being charged under a section of the Criminal Code,' Tom said, 'in connection with what happened the other morning when our chaps hustled two or three scabs off the mines. Accused that they "then and there, tumultuously disturbed the peace".'

Sally minded the baby so that Eily could go with Dinny and Tom to see the arrested men off at the railway station.

'It was like it was in the alluvial struggle,' Dinny said. 'Y' never saw such a crowd, missus! And the boys jest about ropable, and bustin' to have a crack at them damned specials, standin' in a row to guard the prisoners.'

Amy came home that week, because Dick had written to tell her that he could not afford to keep on the cottage at the coast during the strike. Dick was delighted to see her and Billy. He had opened up the bungalow at Mullingar and was looking forward to turning over a new leaf with Amy. He wanted to make amends to her for the bad time he had given her while he was unemployed, he told Sally. Of course, it was tough luck that Amy should have to come back in the midst of the strike; but he had a few pounds in the bank to draw on now, so they wouldn't have to depend on relief or strike funds.

Although he had been working underground for the last month or so Dick was in good heart. He had heard that the Wiluna Company expected to start operations again soon, and would send for him. Meanwhile, to be in this fight with Tom and the miners had bucked him up extraordinarily. The spirit of the men, their grit and loyalty, the sense of something heroic in this struggle, which aroused them to face a period of workless and wageless anxiety, even hunger for themselves and their families, in order to defend what they regarded as a 'fundamental principle of union-ism', made him forget his grouch about being reduced to the ranks of the unskilled workers. Dick said he got a real kick out of being accepted as a mate by the miners. He was full of enthusiasm for their guts and hardihood. He would stick to them, through thick and thin, for the rest of his life, he told Tom, no matter what sort of a job he might get later on.

But Amy was not pleased to know Dick was on strike: not just stood down because the mines were idle, and the miners playing up about something or other.

She had been surprised to discover Dick was working as a 'common miner', and that he was actually taking part in the strike. It was mortifying and most inconsiderate of him, she said. What would her friends say?

Dick thought by explaining the reasons and causes for the strike he might win her sympathy. Amy shrugged her shoulders. She was not interested.

She continued to be on friendly terms with mine managers and their wives who were doing everything in their power to defeat the miners. Dick pointed out that it put him in an awkward position.

'You've put yourself in it,' Amy said wrathfully.

She was incensed to discover she was not so popular among these old friends as the wife of a miner on strike. This meant that she had to stay at home a good deal, moping and miserable.

'Poor Amy,' Dick exclaimed ruefully. 'She's very sorry for herself and thoroughly ashamed of me.'

He did his best to reconcile Amy to her hard lot: courted and cajoled her more assiduously than he had ever done: helped her with the housework, and minded Bill when she wanted to go to a party or dance. Sally marvelled at Dick's patience and good-humour. His son seemed to compensate him for Amy's discontent and peevishness. Dick looked quite happy playing with the young-ster: often brought Bill, sitting in front of his bicycle, when he came to see Sally in the evening.

Amy never came with them, so Sally went to see her, determined that there should be no estrangement between them. But Amy was as cool and off-hand with her as if she were a casual acquaintance.

'You would have thought I was to blame for Dick working under-ground,' Sally told Marie indignantly.

' "What on earth's the matter with you, Amy?" I said, riled at the way she was behaving. "I suppose you're worried and upset about the strike." '

'She was smoking and giving herself no end of airs and graces, Marie,' Sally went on, after a moment's hesitation. ' "Don't talk to me about the strike," Amy said, "I'm sick to death of it. If Dick wants to get mixed up with that sort of thing, he can't expect me to drag along with him all my days. He'll never get a decent job now. My friends think he's just crazy." '

'Mon Dieu,' Marie cried. 'What did she mean?'

'That's what I'd like to know,' Sally said, out of a troubled thoughtfulness. 'But Dick came in then and I couldn't ask.'

CHAPTER XLIX

DURING the first week of the strike, when she went out in the early morning to pick up some kindling for her fire, Sally found Kal-goorla crouched by the wood heap.

Kalgoorla looked just a bundle of dirty rags, squatting there on the ground. She rose stiffly, the dilapidated man's hat shadowing her face. But her eyes sought Sally's, a brighter gleam in the dark-ness behind their matted eyelashes.

'Bin find'm that feller, Fred Cairns,' she muttered.

Sally's mind moved slowly from her worries over the strike and the turmoil of the last few days, to recollection of that name and what it had to do with Kalgoorla. She remembered Maritana's death, Kalgoorla's anguish, the disappearance of Fred Cairns, the packing off of Maritana's children to State institutions, Kalgoorla's finding of Maritana's body in the disused shaft. Now, evidently, she had tracked Fred Cairns and was ready to settle their score.

'Where is he?' Sally asked, wondering what she should do.

Kalgoorla might have her own ideas about summary justice, she realised: think a man of her tribe could dispose of Fred Cairns with a well-flung spear. Sally knew only too well that the aborigines would suffer for it. Kalgoorla and her kinsman have to pay the penalty for killing of a white man.

'Bin come along old camp,' Kalgoorla told her. 'Kick'm up shindy. Two feller work there. Tell Fred get the hell—not give'm money. Fred tell'm "inform the pol-eece". They feller tell'm: "Go ahead, you lose neck." '

'Is he there still?' Sally asked.

'Wiah.' Kalgoorla's face relapsed into its sullen gloom. 'Track'm, sun jump up, sun lie down, sun jump up, sun lie down. Bin find'm show longa Pingin.'

Sally sent her off to wash while she rooted out an old dress. When Dinny and Tom came along the verandah for breakfast Kalgoorla was already there, her hair still wet, and her face shining, a blue print dress of Sally's flapping about the thin sticks of her legs.

Their greeting, jolly and joking, banished her sombre brooding for a moment. It pleased her to be treated like an old friend. Dinny had just the right way with her, and Tom's affection, carried over from his childhood, Kalgoorla sensed surely enough.

'Bin find'm Fred Cairns,' she told Dinny and Tom; and went on with her story as if she could think of nothing else.

Over breakfast Dinny and Tom agreed that the police should be put on the track of Fred Cairns. But Kalgoorla, as Sally feared, had her own ideas about that.

'Tell'm pol-eece nothing,' she said, looking sullen. 'Pol-eece not find'm Meerie. Pol-eece not find'm Fred Cairns.'

'But they wanted to,' Dinny pointed out. 'If they catch Fred Cairns now, they tell'm you kill Maritana, maybe. But if one of you feller black feller, spear'm Fred Cairns, they kill'm black feller.'

Kalgoorla's eyes shifted from his face. She knew that what Dinny said was true; but suspicious and resentful of the way the police had treated her before, she could not believe that Fred Cairns would get his deserts at their hands. She had more confidence in tribal justice. After all, it was only an aboriginal woman who had been killed, and other native women had died without white men being made to suffer any penalty. Kalgoorla remembered the massacre at Menankilly, and she had a suspicion of powerful interests concerned to protect Fred Cairns.

' "If I'm nabbed make it hot for some people",' she muttered, as if dragging from her memory words carefully stored there.

'Did he say that? Did Fred say that?' Dinny asked.

'Eh-erm. Tell'm Big Jo in old camp.'

'Looks as if he might squeal,' Tom said. 'Better let the police handle this, Kalgoorla,' he added gently. 'It's too big for you.'

Kalgoorla's bleary eyes turned to him. It was hard to relinquish her vengeance. But her eyes held a trust and devotion as she looked at Tom that Sally had never seen her show anyone.

'You tell'm, tell pol-eece,' Tommy,' she said quietly, 'me tell'm.'

Dinny had gone with her to the police station and helped her through the ordeal of making her statement.

For days Sally and he expected news of Fred Cairns's arrest: Tom was too pre-occupied with the strike to give more than a passing thought to wondering whether Fred Cairns had been warned and escaped. Kalgoorla knew first what had happened. She had gone bush after her visit to the police station, and trailed into the yard a week later, slumping wearily down by the wood heap; but there was sullen fury in her eyes. She had walked all the way to Pingin and back again.

'Pol-eece, nothing!' she spat contemptuously. 'Him bin get away.'

The strike had dragged on for nearly two months. It was the chief topic of conversation in Kalgoorlie and Boulder. Everybody was affected by it. The business life of the two cities had been brought to a standstill. Neighbours and strangers talked to each other about it. In the shops and streets, in the trams and in he pubs, there seemed nothing to discuss but the strike and the trial of the arrested miners which was pending.

The whole community had been drawn into this struggle of the miners; but while a campaign against it was still being waged by the Chamber of Mines, the sympathy of ordinary citizens swung to the miners and their wives, who tight-lipped and gloomy-eyed, maintained a dogged resistance to any suggestion of a settlement which would defeat their purpose.

Relief funds and capable organisation were providing food, so that men no longer collapsed from hunger and exhaustion as they did in the first weeks of the strike. Miners' wives might grumble among themselves about the deprivations the strike had imposed on them and their children; but they defended it, and their men, with fierce loyalty.

CHAPTER L

'SEE Sir Patrick Cavan's payin' a brief visit to the goldfields,' Dinny remarked, looking up over his spectacles, as he read the morning's *Miner*.

'The briefer the better,' Sally snapped.

' "Sir Patrick is disturbed about the situation on the mines," ' Dinny glanced back at his newspaper. 'Thinks, "as a result of his long experience in the mining industry, he may have some useful suggestions to make for settlement of the dispute".'

'He'll settle it all right, if he gets a chance.' The dishes clattered as Sally washed up. Dinny usually read the morning news to her, sitting in the kitchen, like this, as she cleared away after breakfast.

The strike had dragged on for nine weeks, with conferences and mass meetings, at which the miners maintained a resolute defence for the principles for which they had ceased work. Failure of their application to have the Coolgardie Union deregistered in the State Arbitration Court, however, struck a blow at their hopes of putting it out of action.

No doubt they were defeated on that score. It was a bitter pill to swallow, although the Miners' Branch of the A.W.U. still refused to recognise the Coolgardie Union as a bona-fide miners' union. But with an undertaking of no victimisation from the Chamber of Mines, the men who had been on strike were in good spirits when the mines re-opened early in the new year.

'You don't want to get down-hearted, Tom,' Dinny said. 'This strike's been the longest and toughest ever put up on the fields. But if y've come out of it with a stronger union, a bigger membership, and a better organisation to fight with later on—well, y' haven't done too bad.'

'That's what we reckon,' Tom said, with his slow smile. 'Mines in the back country from Westonia to Wiluna are working on our ticket, and on the Golden Mile only twenty boneheads still refuse to join up.'[1]

After remands, protest meetings and a delay of over three months, the men who had been arrested were brought for trial before the Criminal Court. Every day, as they drove through the streets of Perth from the lock-up to the court in the prison van, these scapegoats for the working miners sang lustily. Crowds cheered them as they passed; and when the Black Maria broke down one day, and

---

[1] The Coolgardie Union was deregistered in 1947.

they were marched back to their prison cells, a crowd of men and women followed, shouting goodwill and sympathy.

But it was the defending lawyer who created a sensation by his address to the jury. Never had the case for the miners been more forcibly put than Dickie Haynes put it on that occasion. He flayed the magistrate who had sent the case, "with a cloud of witnesses", out of the district for trial.

It was the first case of riot that had ever been tried in Western Australia, Mr. Haynes pointed out. Hitherto, cases of assault had been disposed of in the police courts with fines of thirty or forty shillings. On this occasion fisticuffs had been magnified into a riot. The reason why the prosecution had been made was clear. Members of the Chamber of Mines were not mine owners. They were the servants of foreign companies. They had no interest in the country at all. Their interest was to screw as much out of the mines for their bosses as possible. The Chamber of Mines was a dignified name, but let us tear off the mask.

The unfortunate miners had been out of employment before this strike, for seven weeks or more, as a consequence of trouble on the woodline. They had to deplete their resources to live. If the Chamber of Mines could postpone from week to week the miners' approach to the Arbitration Court to obtain betterment of their conditions, it could hope to defeat them, and hence it was that it had set about weakening them, and fostering that 'mongrel union' the Coolgardie Union.

How could there be industrial peace with these two unions in the field, the one fostered and pampered by the Chamber of Mines and the other liable to be 'stouched' at any moment? The best way to deal with a snake was to scotch it straight off, and when the miners saw this bogus union entering their life they decided to bring things to a crisis. They tried to get the erring one into the fold.

The Chamber of Mines was the only society Mr. Haynes had ever known, or read of, which contributed to the payment of officers of justice, and granted them douceurs—backsheesh—at the end of the year. It was a reversal of the first principle of the Constitution. It was striking at the very foundation of justice. Would these detectives bring to justice a Chamber of Mines offender? No. They would not get their bonus at Christmas if they did so. It was a most blackguardly thing to allow anybody to have a thumb on an officer of justice. This Chamber dominated the whole of Kalgoorlie. No business man there dared to offend it. He might as well pack up and leave the town if he did.

'Remember the accused are your brother men,' Mr. Haynes

appealed to the jury. 'What happened to them may happen to you in the near future unless you check it. The accused men compare more than favourably with members of the Chamber of Mines.'

Bringing in two or three foreigners was intended to create an impression that the dispute had been incited by them, Mr. Haynes continued. The Crown had filed an information without the least hope of getting a conviction, for the purpose of subjecting the accused to the ordeal of a trial. It was crucifying them. It was a conspiracy to build up a case of riot.

The judge summed up in favour of the Crown, but the jury disagreed and had to be discharged. The accused miners were remanded to the next sitting of the Court. But the Crown advised that a *nolle prosequi* would be entered, so that when the men appeared in court again they were all discharged.

There was great rejoicing the night the news reached the goldfields. It was the first time for years that Dinny had got drunk. He and Dally came home together, embracing each other and stopping every now and then to sing 'Solidarity for Ever' in their cracked old voices. From every pub on the Golden Mile the chorus arose and rang along the dusty streets. There were cheers for Dickie Haynes who had so completely vindicated the miners' case and for the men, who for over three months had been enduring the cat and mouse game the law was playing with them.

Not since release of the fighters for alluvial rights in the 'nineties had there been such a triumphant celebration. This 1919 strike would be remembered as the great fight for unionism in the West, Tom said. It would have a significant place in industrial history.

Sally suspected that even he and Dick had been 'bending the elbow' more than usual, when they came in laughing and joking together as lightheartedly as when they were schoolboys. It was a long time since she had seen them so jolly and carefree; and Eily was as lively as a cricket, bouncing all over the place, exclaiming, and asking questions.

But when Dick called in on his way to work next morning Bill was with him. Dick was carrying a small suit case: his face drawn with pain and anger.

'Will you look after the kid for a while, darl?' he said to Sally. 'Amy has cleared out with Paddy Cavan.'

'Dick!' Sally could imagine that Amy had been willing to flirt with Paddy; but that she would leave Dick for him was unbelievable.

'Knocks the stuffing out of you, doesn't it?' Dick queried, wincing. 'I'm getting used to the idea. But at first I thought it was a joke. When I got home last night I found a note on the dressing-table in our bedroom—like the husband does at the pictures. "Dick, darling, I'm going abroad with Paddy. Can't stand things here any longer. It's no use trying to stop me. Look after Bill, Love, Amy." '

'But she can't do it,' Sally cried. 'For her own sake, as much as yours. I'll go to Perth and try to find her.'

'No, mother,' Dick said. He had come to a decision Sally perceived and did not wish to argue about it. 'If this is what Amy wants, we'll leave it at that.'

CHAPTER LI

The months slipped away quietly after reverberations of the strike had died down and the arrested men returned to their homes. Only scabs on the mines were finding 'the game wasn't worth the candle', as Dinny said. No decent unionist would drink or have anything to do with them: they were slung off at and ostracised wherever they went. Their clothes and boots and cribs were tampered with in the change room, and all sorts of accidents happened to them underground. Before long most of them were 'snatching their time' and leaving the fields.

Tom and Eily found an empty house in a long street of small, weatherboard miners' dwellings and went to live there. Dick and Billy remained with Sally. Dick, she thought, was getting over the hurt of his broken marriage, taking his work underground as a matter of course, finding interest and pleasure in watching his son grow from a noisy, obstreperous urchin into a sturdy, self-reliant, little lad.

Bill was going to school now and plaguing everybody with questions. He swung on the gate, watching for Dick to come home: loved the romp and games he could expect for an hour or so when Dick came in from work. Dick bathed the child every evening, and read to him before putting him to bed. They were great mates. But Dick made no attempt to get another job.

'What does it matter how I work as long as I can earn a crust?' he asked.

'It doesn't, of course,' Sally said, 'if you're not interested in using your brains.'

'But nobody wants my brains, Sal-o-my,' Dick replied lightly, bitterly.

'That's when you use your brains to make them wanted,' Sally said. 'Things don't just fall into your lap, son. You have to battle for everything worth while in this life.'

Dick made inquiries about the job at Wiluna soon afterwards. He had been keenly interested in those experiments with arsenical ore. Sally had to stifle her fear of them, and her reluctance for Dick to go back to Wiluna, if this work would enable him to regain his standing in the industry and overcome the hurt and humiliation of Amy's desertion. She promised to look after Bill, though Eily, too, had offered to take charge of him if Dick went to Wiluna.

For the benefit of the neighbours and a few busybodies, Sally talked vaguely about the small legacy Mrs. Richard Gough had received from her mother's relations. She had gone to England to fix up legal matters in connection with the legacy, Sally said. She hoped that if Amy returned some day, this little fiction would make it easier to account for her absence, although Dick refused to be a party to it. At first there seemed to be no scandal-mongering. But before long it was 'all over the town', Dinny said, 'that Mrs. Dick had done a bunk with Paddy Cavan'.

Dinny denied there was anything in the gossip.

He could not admit to himself that there was. He was terribly upset by it.

'I've always been real fond of Amy,' he told Sally, sweating profusely and mopping his face. 'She might've been a bit of a flibbertigibbet, but I never thought she could do a thing like that. You'd never've believed it of Alf's daughter, would you, missus?'

'If she'd been very much in love with Paddy, I could understand it,' Sally said, stirred by a vagrant memory. 'But she couldn't've been. It's only his money, and having a good time, Amy cares about.'

When Violet came to see her, during the week, Sally understood how it was that everybody was talking about Amy and Paddy Cavan.

Violet was portly and prosperous looking. Mrs. Isaac Potter now, and the mother of two children; but there was something about her which had not changed. A certain strength and independence of character. Placid and self-contained, she might appear; but Sally sensed in the full-blown Violet the essential quality of the girl she had known.

'Of course, you know why all Kalgoorlie's talking about Amy and Paddy Cavan,' Violet said. 'Mrs. Archie Malleson and Mrs. Bob Dowsett were staying at the same hotel in Perth. They say Amy and Sir Patrick left by the *Orion* for London.'

'Why couldn't they hold their tongues?' Sally wailed.

'Amy's a bitch,' Violet declared flatly. 'Everybody knows she's been playing up with that old swine for some time. I hope Dick will divorce her and be done with it.'

318

'I don't think he will,' Sally said. 'Dick's extraordinarily faithful to the thing's he's loved, and Amy's the only girl he has ever cared for really. I think he feels Amy may need him some day, and for the child's sake . . .'

'You're all like that!' Violet said impatiently. 'Got some queer idealistic streak! I shed all my highfaluting ideas long ago . . . No, I haven't . . .' The husk of a superficial complacency fell from her. 'I've tried to, but some of them still cling. I can't forget I wanted to be a prima donna, and what destroyed my chances. But I don't mind much now. I'm very fond of Ike and the children—and I can still sing for people here, like I used to. I might've sung at Covent Garden and the Grand Opera House in Paris, but would I have got out of it what I get here? You know, it makes up for a lot when I see a crowd of miners before me: all those tough, worn faces looking rapt and lit up when I sing to them.'

'The men think the world of you,' Sally told her. 'You're still little Vi'let O'Brien to them.'

'At that concert for strike funds I thought they'd raise the roof.' Violet smiled to a recollection which pleased and flattered her. 'You never heard such a bawling and stamping, cheers and encores.'

'I was there,' Sally laughed, 'bawling and stamping too. You never sang better, Violet.'

'Ike and I had a great row about it,' Violet said blandly. 'But I just said to him: "I've always sung for miners, and I always will. I know too much about mining not to believe a working miner's entitled to all he can get. So when there's a strike on, I'm with the miners. If you don't like it, you must just lump it, old dear." '

'Did he lump it?' Sally asked.

'He did.' Violet smiled. 'He's very good to me, Ike. And I've reached the stage of being satisfied to let him be; but that doesn't mean I haven't got a mind of my own, and won't use it when I feel inclined. Living like I've done, on the goldfields all these years, Mrs. Gough—well, you just can't help standing by the miners when they're up against it.'

'That's how I feel,' Sally said. 'More than ever now, with two sons working underground. My heart's in my mouth every time I hear the siren of the ambulance. But, thank goodness, Dick's hoping to get back to metallurgy when the Wiluna Company starts again.'

'I'll have a word with Ike,' Violet promised. 'He's backing that show to make a lot of money presently.'

CHAPTER LII

ON that black morning when she heard the siren of the mines' ambulance shrilling in the distance, Sally dropped what she was doing and ran to the gate.

Tom met her on the garden path. There was no need to tell her that the ambulance siren was shrilling for Dick. Tom's face, his eyes, communicated what he could not say.

'Is he dead?' Sally asked, hearing her voice as if it were a long way off. She was conscious of the hot sunshine beating down on her, and of the new white ambulance which had passed the house.

'Yes,' Tom said.

Everything went dark. Recovering consciousness in her own room, Sally became aware that Tom and Marie were with her. The brandy they had given her was burning her lips, driving away a stupifying darkness. She could hear Tom and Marie talking in an undertone. Dinny's query reached her: 'Is she coming round? Will I go for the doctor?'

'No,' Sally forced herself to say, 'don't go for the doctor.'

She sat up, looking at Tom with dazed eyes.

'Tell me,' she said, 'what happened.'

Tom sat on a chair beside the bed, holding her hand, trembling himself, and trying to speak steadily.

'I don't know exactly,' he said. 'We went down in the cage together and started work. I didn't see Dick again until they sent for me. Seems there was a heavy run of ore, he got thrown off his balance and fell. . . .'

'Oh God,' Sally moaned, 'it's too much. I can't bear it, Tom.'

'I feel like that too, mum,' Tom said.

'Why did it happen?' Sally moaned. 'Why did it have to happen just when Dick seemed to be so much better, and it looked as if he would get that job at Wiluna?'

Tom hoped that she would not want to see Dick's body. He had seen many mutilated and smashed by accidents on the mines; but seeing Dick's head crushed and bleeding, his arms broken, his legs limp and dangling in his blue working clothes, had shaken him beyond self-control. He staggered drunkenly from the sight unable to arrest the sobbing breath that racked him.

'Somebody's got to tell y'r mother, Tom,' Barney Riordan had said.

That pulled Tom round.

'I'll tell her,' he said, and had been able to reach Sally before the ambulance passed.

Sally insisted on going to the hospital. Before entering into the room in which Dick's body was lying Tom had begged her not to raise the sheet covering it.

'I must say good-bye to him,' Sally said.

She had raised the sheet and gazed at the bloody mess of that beloved face, with only the strand of dark glossy hair above it by which she could recognise Dick.

'My precious! My precious!' she whispered, dry eyed.

She sat there beside the sheet-covered body, her hands locked in the unutterable agony of knowing that her first-born, her beloved son, Dick, lay there: dead and remote from all the joy and suffering they had shared for so long. Tom remained with her, suffering for her as well as Dick, Sally knew, although she could feel nothing but that Dick was dead.

'Come, mother, we must go now,' Tom said at last.

Sally had walked out of the hospital with him, indifferent to anything that could happen to her any more.

Early next morning an eerie wailing came from the back-yard. Sally knew what it was. Kalgoorla had come to lament with her, and was sitting by the wood heap. Tom got up to go out and ask her to be quiet. It was too harrowing, he thought, that shrill keening and moaning. But Sally called to him:

'Leave her alone, Tom. It's the way I feel.'

She could not arouse herself for the funeral which left the house that afternoon. Eily took charge of everything that had to be done. Violet had come and taken Billy away to stay with her and her children for a few days. Sally would not go to the cemetery or look at the procession of miners which followed Dick along the Boulder road. Hundreds of men tramped behind the old hearse which Morris had driven so often. They were burying Dick with all the honours they could give a mate and a good unionist who had been killed on the mines.

'What does it matter?' Sally said wearily. 'What does anything matter? Dick's dead. That's all that matters.'

She had asked for Dick's clothes to be brought to her: the clothes he had worn to the mine that day before he changed into his working flannels and dungarees to go underground.

Marie was with her when she went through the pockets of the navy blue suit, took out Dick's small belongings: a clean handker-chief, a pocket book, cigarette holder, stub of pencil and a few letters.

There was a letter which had been opened recently, and crushed, before being thrust back into his pocket. Sally opened that out and read it.

Marie saw swift anger and an expression of horror cross her face. 'What is it?' she asked.

'A letter from Amy,' Sally said. 'Dick got it the day before. I knew he was troubled about something, but I can't believe . . .'

'Did she want to come back to him?'

'No.' Sally glanced down at the letter. 'Lady Cavan died recently, she says, and Paddy wants to marry her. Amy asks Dick to divorce her.'

Marie was aware instantly what Sally was thinking. She knew as well as his mother how Dick would hate to take divorce proceedings which would expose Amy's association with Paddy Cavan. She could not know, as Sally did, that Dick had cherished a lingering hope Amy would realise she had made a mistake and want to return to him.

'Don't believe for a minute it wasn't an accident, darling,' Marie cried. 'Dick wouldn't've done a thing like that. He wouldn't willingly have hurt you so much.'

'I can't believe it,' Sally said passionately. 'I just can't! But I knew he was troubled. He looked . . . like he did the day he brought Billy to me—dazed and stricken.'

When Tom came to see her later she asked how Dick had been that morning when they yarned for a few minutes before going underground.

'He was a bit quiet,' Tom said. 'I asked him what was the matter. "Nothing," Dick said. "At least not much. Tell you about it by and by."'

'Did he say that, Tom? Did he really say that?'

'Yes,' Tom told her. 'He looked worried and the truckers say Dick was sort of absent-minded: didn't seem to hear when they yelled to him. He stepped back, lost his balance somehow, and fell. . . .'

Sally gave Amy's letter to Tom.

'This came the day before,' she said.

Tom swore angrily as he read the letter.

'Tom . . .' Sally faltered, 'was it an accident?'

'Of course it was an accident,' Tom said. 'You don't think Dick would throw his life away for Amy, do you? I'm sure he wouldn't. I reckon this letter was on his mind though: made him careless, perhaps. That's how it was, mum. I see the whole thing now. He wouldn't've said he'd tell me "by and by", what was wrong, if he had thought there wasn't going to be any by and by.'

'No,' Sally agreed. 'Only . . . it makes things so much easier for Amy, this way.'

'Forget it, mother!' Tom tore the letter across. 'I don't believe we meant so little to Dick, you and I, and young Bill—particularly Bill—that he'd do this to oblige Amy. But if ever I see her again I'll let her know what I think of her—and Paddy Cavan, the old sewer. God, what I'd give to get my hands on to him!'

CHAPTER LIII

'TIME, only time, will soften the blow of Dick's death on your mother, Tom,' Dinny said.

And time moved slowly for Sally. From the dry, incandescent days of summer it passed to a winter of torrential rains and wild, icy winds. Sally did not care whether the earth blazed a fiery red under the summer sun, or the men stamped mud on her floors after the rain. She was eating, working, sleeping mechanically, because Dick was nowhere in the world. Never again would his mere presence fill her with inexplicable joy: their eyes meet and laugh together in mutual understanding: his voice sound like a song in her ears with its gay, tender greeting:

'Well, Sal-o-my, how's things?'

For a while she had been ill. It was as if Dick's coldness and stillness, that last time she saw him, had swept her. Her faculties were numb: her mind a blank. She lay in her room making no attempt to overcome her desolation. Then Marie's eyes penetrated her clouded consciousness: Marie's dark eyes sharing her anguish and pleading with her. The realisation that Marie, worn out with work and worry, was watching over her drove Sally to exert herself and struggle against her sorrow.

Tom and Eily had taken Billy to live with them. Dinny and Marie between them were cooking for the boarders and doing the housework. But Marie had her old father-in-law to look after as well. When she began to take up her daily work again, Sally reproached herself for having given Marie so much fatigue and anxiety.

Marie exclaimed: 'Oh, darling, for me it is good to be with you and see you well again.'

She flitted in and out of the house every day for months, eager to divert Sally's mind from its sadness by talk of Tom and Den: their need of and concern for her. But Tom and Den did not need her as Dick had done, Sally said. And somehow she had failed him: failed to realise how deeply he loved Amy, and how her desertion had affected him.

For a long time Sally's face looked hard and stiff: she could not smile. When Dally and Dinny were talking she did not hear what they said. Their voices made a meaningless clatter in her brain. Usually she was thinking about Dick: wondering why a woman should have borne a son, reared and cherished him, striven to fit him for the struggle of existence, ensure for him a measure of security and happiness, and have had to see him deprived of all that made life worth living.

Dick had met with more disappointment and disaster than his brothers. Lal, after all, achieved some sort of fulfilment. He had wanted to be a soldier, enjoyed the honour and glory of his brief military career. Sally still rebelled at the cutting short of his young life and grieved for Lal. But Lal had died fighting, and that for him would have been a logical conclusion to the way he had chosen, she believed. If Lal had not gleaned the satisfactions of mature manhood, at least he had been spared its agonising disillusionments. The pain of Dick's death was greater than any she had felt when he was born.

Perhaps, if Amy had been different, all the rest wouldn't have mattered, Sally argued with herself. Then, too, if Dick had been different, less sensitive and vulnerable, he would not have been so hurt by the defeats he had suffered in his work and marriage. Had she made Dick too finely tempered steel to fight effectively in 'the brawl for the stomach's crust'? Sally asked herself. Lazy, careless and a little selfish he might have been in his youth, she thought. But not since the war! Not since he had been aroused by the horror and suffering created by war and its causes. Not since he had known what it meant to have a child of his own. A son for whom he was responsible: must provide some opportunities of health and happiness. Oh, young Bill was something Dick had got out of life that was a joy to him! His love for Amy and the first years of their marriage, too, had brought him a radiant happiness.

But there was small comfort remembering these things when Dick was dead. It was so dull to live without looking forward to seeing him: enjoying the intimate, flippant familiarity of their relationship, not only as mother and son, but as prospectors seeking some mysterious treasure they could share.

Sally had been wrapped for several months in her mourning for Dick when Dinny said:

'They say Frisco's in a bad way—got the black 'flu, and livin' in a shack on Misery Flat.'

324

'What? What did you say?' Sally asked, as if she had only half heard what Dinny was saying.

Dinny repeated his remark.

'What is he doing out there?' Sally queried.

'He's broke, from all accounts,' Dinny replied. 'Lost his case against Paddy Cavan—and is down and out, Tassy was tellin' me. Says he's gone back to camp life because he can't get round like he used to now he's blind.'

'Blind?'

'It's been comin' on him ever since he lost his right eye in the war,' Dinny said. 'Last time I saw him he was jokin' about havin' to get a dog to lead him around. Thought I'd go over and see if there's anything I can do for him.'

Dinny spoke as if he had been trying to make up his mind on the subject. He could not forgive Frisco for the part he had played in the alluvial struggle, in the riots and in the big strike, siding always with the mine owners to defeat the working miners, although some of the unemployed camped on Misery Flat had told him Frisco was as sore as most of them about the rotten system which starved and flung a man on the scrap heap when it had no further use for him. Dinny could not credit that; but it was some sort of an excuse to make if Tom and Charley O'Reilly accused him of being a silly old galoot to be acting soft about Frisco.

After all, Tom and Charley had not come foot-slogging along the track to Coolgardie in the early days, and Dinny was bound by his code of an old prospector to succour a mate in distress. Even if Frisco had not been a mate of his, in the fullest sense of the word, Dinny felt that he would have to do something for Frisco. You couldn't let a man die like a dog when fate had dealt so hardly with him.

Blind, ill and broke to the wide the boys said Frisco was, lying out there in a shack made of rusty kerosene tins flattened out, with the rain pouring through. It would be inhuman not to go out and see whether Frisco would go into hospital, if Dinny could arrange to have him taken there. After all, Frisco had had his good points. When he had plenty of cash he had stood by many an old timer. If he, himself, were in similar straits, Dinny knew Frisco would have rushed along and done everything possible for him. He was always generous and ready to help an old mate down on his luck, you had to say that for Frisco.

Dinny had broached his intention of going to see Frisco with some perturbation, remembering Sally's resentment of Colonel de Morfé's attitude when Morris and Tom were charged with gold stealing, and her disgust at his business connections with Paddy

325

Cavan. He did not expect to arouse her from her indifference to what was happening about her by what he had said: was astounded when Sally exclaimed:

'I'll go with you.'

'No need to do that,' Dinny said, alarmed at the prospect of Missus Sally going into one of those filthy, dilapidated shacks on the flat and of taking her into contact with the black 'flu. An epidemic was raging, the hospital crowded and several deaths had been reported.

'Y're not well enough y'rself, ma'am, to go traipsing over there,' he protested. 'I can do all that's necessary.'

'You can't,' Sally said obstinately. 'Have you forgotten what Frisco did for me when the natives carried me in from the Darlot track? We'll go at once, Dinny. Just wait till I get my coat and put a few things in a basket.'

Dinny was vexed with himself for having mentioned Frisco and his plight: but it was no use arguing with Missus Sally when she spoke like that.

As they walked along towards the Boulder, and then took a side street towards a fringe of scrub at the back of the racecourse, Dinny was surprised to find Sally stepping out briskly, and talking with more animation than she had shown for many a day.

She wanted to know how long Frisco had been blind and living with the unemployed and dead-beats on the flat. Why no one had told her that he had lost his lawsuit against Paddy Cavan, and was in such financial difficulties? How many unemployed were there? And what was being done for them?

'Maybe we talked about such things; but you haven't been able to interest y'rself much in the news of the town lately, ma'am,' Dinny said.

'I've been living in a bad dream, Dinny,' Sally told him. 'To-day I seem awake for the first time since—since Dick's death.'

Her voice stumbled at those words and a shadow fell over her face.

'But now y're y'self again,' Dinny agreed hurriedly, anxious to chase away that shadow. 'And ready to help others, like y've always done.'

'That's how it is, Dinny,' Sally said.

Dinny was horrified at the muck and disorder around those scattered shacks in the shelter of a few spindling trees. Rickety, patched-up boxes of bagging and rusty kerosene tins flattened out, they stood on the wet earth: some more like native wurlies, so low that a man could scarcely stand up in them, with a hole on one side to crawl through, and a fireplace outside. Here and there an old timer and good bushman had made an attempt to brush and clear up the rubbish about his own ramshackle dwelling: but refuse had collected round most of the huts. The stench of decay and mouldering filth overhung the place.

A white cur, gnawing a bone, barked frantically at the sight of strangers, and the head and shoulders of an old man appeared over the half-door of one of the shacks.

'Wait here till I find out where Frisco is,' Dinny said.

He went to have a word with the old man, whose skull, covered with close-cropped white hair, rose from behind his barricade. Sally stared about her, aghast that humans were living in such hovels. They were worse than fowl houses or goat pens. Never on the old rushes had she seen men living like this. On Ding Bat Flat, it was true, scores of foreign workers had run up shacks made of rusty tin, pieces of bagging and corrugated iron, but these places had the semblance of houses: here there were the sort of crude mounds animals might throw up to protect themselves from the weather.

When Dinny turned away from the old man and dived into a mound of bag and rusty tin, a few yards from her, Sally walked along to the entrance and stood there, looking into a cave-like darkness.

She could just see the stretcher on which Frisco was lying, covered by a dirty blanket: a tousled head and face overgrown by a ragged beard. She heard a hoarse, fluttering voice raving and moaning, begging for water, cursing feebly.

'It's all right, Frisco,' Dinny said, dipping a jam tin into the bigger tin of water beside the stretcher. 'Take it easy now.'

Frisco dragged himself up to drink. He fell back with a gasping rattle that might have been laughter.

'For Chris'-sakes, Dinny! . . . Who'd've thought it?'

'Shut up!' Dinny growled. 'I'm goin' to get you out of this dump, Frisco, and see y're looked after.'

Sally dived into the hut and stood beside him, saying urgently: 'Go for a car, Dinny. I'll wait till you get back.'

'Sally!' Frisco flung an arm over his face. 'God damn and blast you, Dinny!' he shouted. 'Take her away! Clear out, both of you. I'm done for. What's the game, anyhow? What the hell's the game? Come to gloat over a man when he's down, eh? Or am I magnoon—seeing things? Get out! Get out!'

Frisco's raving broke on a filthy oath. He fell back exhausted, sobbing and distraught, as Dinny dragged Sally out into the bleak sunshine.

'We'll take him home, Dinny,' she said.

'You can't do that,' Dinny protested. 'I'll see if I can't get him in at the hospital.'

'The hospital's full,' Sally said. 'They're calling for volunteers to help with the nursing. Get a car, Dinny—or must I go myself?'

'But ma'am . . .' Dinny demurred.

Sally went back into the shack, and Dinny tramped off along the track to the township. At the first pub he rang up for a car, and returned to the flat.

When he peered into the darkness of the shack in which Frisco was lying Sally was sitting on a box beside him. She had spread a wet handkerchief on his head, and Frisco was sleeping. Sally motioned Dinny to stay outside and came to him.

'I've given Frisco a couple of aspirins,' she said. 'When the car comes you can wrap the blanket round him, and you and the driver can help him into the back seat. We can give him a wash and clean clothes when we get him home.'

'Lord,' Dinny groaned within himself, 'what have I done?'

There was no denying Sally was a new woman, with a glow and wilful energy about her he had not seen for many a long day. Dinny had heard the old rumour of a love affair between Frisco and Missus Sally, but had never given it any credence. Whatever truth there might have been in the gossip had died out long ago, he was sure. Yet how could Missus Sally look at that pitiful wreck of a man with such concern, and be so determined to nurse him herself if there were not something between them?

Dinny fretted and fumed in the throes of his uneasiness and consternation, feeling responsible for having drawn Sally into this business of salvaging Frisco, and yet helpless to interfere with what she was determined to do. What would Tom say? He would not like his mother to be looking after Colonel de Morfé, Dinny knew. But what could Tom, or anybody else do, if Sally had made up her mind about it?

Frisco had been installed in Tom's bedroom, and Sally nursed and tended him assiduously until he was well enough to be stalking about again.

Barbered and wearing the clean shirts and pressed suits Sally laid out for him, Frisco regained some of his gay and jaunty manner, though he had to move carefully, feeling his way about, guided by Sally's voice or her hand in his. The shade over his eyes was a reminder that Colonel de Morfé could never again be the good-looking rake he had once been; but there was still sufficient virile devilry in the man to make him dangerous where a woman was concerned, Dinny feared.

Sally could laugh at Frisco's blandishments: make no bones about ridiculing his pretensions to a change of heart about the interests of a mining community, and the need for a clean up of the industry which would give miners and small investors a fairer deal. But that black shade over his eyes, and his helplessness, Dinny thought, were winning Missus Sally to a devotion for Frisco which was disturbing.

It was almost more than Dinny could endure to see the way she waited on Frisco, anticipated his slightest wish, bustled about looking delighted to be doing anything for him. Dinny, himself, had been willing enough to perform any service for Frisco while he was still weak after his illness. He helped Frisco to shower and dress, shaved and led him about. But Frisco had quickly learnt to do most things for himself: could find his way in the house, when he was familiar with it, almost as if he could see. That was the worst of it.

Now that he was well, Frisco showed no sign of moving on: had settled in at Mrs. Gough's as if he were the star boarder. And Dinny resented it. He was jealous of all the attention Missus Sally lavished on Frisco: grumpy and miserable, because Frisco seemed to have taken his place in the house.

CHAPTER LIV

THERE was a good deal of gossip when it was known that Colonel de Morfé was living at Mrs. Gough's. Old timers, particularly, remembered the whispers there had been, years ago, about Frisco's designs on Morrey Gough's good-looking young wife.

Of course, Frisco was an elderly man now: bankrupt and blind, though he contrived to carry himself with his usual swagger. A lean rakish figure, he could be seen walking beside Mrs. Gough, laughing and talking to her with his old reckless gaiety, as she steered him along the road or as they sat in the small park, which was an oasis in the city now. As oblivious of people about them, as if they were young lovers, they went about together.

It was all very well, people were saying, for Mrs. Gough to play the good Samaritan when Colonel de Morfé was ill and destitute. Old timers stuck to each other when they were in trouble. Even Dinny had been willing to forget the record of Frisco's palmy days. But Mrs. Gough could not expect respectable people to approve of the way she was 'carrying on' with Colonel de Morfé at present. She did not, Sally admitted, when Dinny screwed up his courage to tell her 'people were talking'.

Dinny was hurt and offended by her laughter and indifference to his concern.

'Maybe I'd better clear out, if that's the way you feel,' he said.

'Don't be silly, Dinny,' Sally said impatiently. 'This place has always been your home, and always will be, I hope. But it's my home, too; and I'll do as I please in it.'

It was the nearest they had ever come to quarrelling, and Dinny shied from the idea that he could have a serious difference with Missus Sally. The indefinable affection there had been between them for so long forbade that.

'I'm not presumin' to say you shouldn't, ma'am,' he said, ill at ease and unhappy. 'But Frisco and me, we never did get on well together, and livin' under the same roof's not goin' to be easy.'

'But he's different now—you know he is,' Sally pleaded.

'He's learnt his lesson a bit late in the day,' Dinny growled. 'And I reckon it's only skin deep. If Frisco got a bit of luck he'd be barking with the top dogs again.'

'Maybe you're right,' Sally admitted. 'But it means a great deal to me to have Frisco here. I'm happier than I've been for years. I can say this to you, Dinny, because we're old friends. How on earth could I have managed without you, many times? And I couldn't bear you to go away: feel you weren't at home in this house, just because . . .'

'If you want me to stay—well and good,' Dinny said. 'You don't have to worry about me, ma'am. I'll always be standin' by if you need me.'

Sally explained all this to Frisco. He laughed and said he was not jealous of Dinny. He had no desire to usurp Dinny's position in the household: was quite prepared to placate Dinny, show him they could be good friends, so long as Dinny understood that he, Frisco, and Sally were lovers. The only right Frisco aspired to, he said, was the right to take her in his arms. He was in no position to make terms. If Dinny was not in love with her, and could put up with Mrs. Gough having a lover on the premises, well, Frisco would only thank his stars and render unto Dinny the things that were Dinny's: his privileges as Sally's guide, philosopher and right-hand man in domestic emergencies.

Having settled this matter of how Frisco and Dinny and she were going to live peaceably in the same house to her own satisfaction, Sally found herself as happy and light-hearted as a girl. She bloomed extraordinarily in this belated summer of her love affair with Frisco: took more interest in her appearance: was careful

330

to dress up and put a little colour on her lips when she went out with him. She looked years younger and very handsome, with her grey hair, finely etched brows and wide brown eyes, alight and smiling.

Dinny and Frisco got along quite well, on the whole. Dinny by ignoring what did not please him at Mrs. Gough's these days; and Frisco by taking care to keep on good terms with Dinny. He was very considerate and good-natured, Sally thought, humouring Dinny, yarning with him about old times and deferring to him continually. Dinny was more fidgety and irritable than Sally had ever known him. She got impatient with him sometimes, but Frisco could often laugh off his quirks and cantankerousness. There was nothing flagrant in Sally's and Frisco's love-making. They had decided 'to observe the decencies', as Sally said: not obtrude the fact that they were lovers on anyone's notice.

Of course, Dinny understood the situation between them and was resigned to it. He spent quite a lot of time with Eily and Tom and went to bed early. So long as he could close his eyes to what was going on under his nose he did not seem to mind. But occasionally Frisco let fall a 'sweetheart', or Sally a 'darling', and these endearments riled Dinny more than anything else.

Things did not always run as smoothly between Frisco and Dinny as Sally could have wished. Dinny was furious if Frisco took his chair on the verandah, or Frisco's temper flashed because Dinny had moved his pipe and tobacco pouch. Then, too, Frisco would be aggrieved if Sally left him to work in the garden with Dinny, and Dinny become grumpy if she went out two nights running with Frisco.

'The silly old men,' Sally exclaimed to Marie. 'What am I going to do with them?'

'It is not every woman of your age has two men crazy about her,' Marie commented gaily. 'You must marry the one and give the other his *congé*, I suppose.'

'I don't want to marry either of them,' Sally declared.

'Oh, la-la! And so you will be a scandale, chèrie!'

'A joke, you mean.' Sally smiled. 'You should see the winks and grins go round when Frisco and I walk along the street or into a pub. Surely, now we're grey-headed, we ought to be able to live together without people making a fuss about it? Dinny's been part of the family so long nobody notices him.'

Tom's disapproval concerned her most. He could not overcome his distrust and dislike of Frisco: hated to see Frisco lounging in the sitting-room at home, and to hear Frisco addressing his mother with easy familiarity.

'How on earth you can suffer that man, I don't know,' he said irritably.

'I don't suffer him,' Sally spoke firmly. 'I like him to be with me. It's not easy to explain, son. I told you enough once before. I've done what I ought to for a long time. Now I'm going to do things because I want to do them.'

'All right, mum, have it your own way,' Tom said.

'I intend to,' Sally told him.

But Tom did not come to see her so often. Eily and the children usually spent an hour or two with her every week. Tom and Eily had three children, a girl and two boys. And Billy often ran in after school, shouting: 'Hullo, gran!' He was a wiry, keen-witted, irrepressible youngster, always hungry and ready for the rock buns, or an apple, Sally had stowed away for him.

It was a comfort to hear from Eily that Tom was talking of giving up work underground. He had not been looking well for some time; and Sally was distressed to know that Tom had got his 'dirty ticket' at the first medical examinations held in the new Commonwealh Health Laboratory. It had been opened recently in Kalgoorlie in order to arrest the ravages of disease in the mining industry.

Since 1905 four royal commissions had been appointed to inquire into conditions in the mines and their effect on the health of miners. Evidence and reports revealed an appalling waste of life caused by dynamite fumes, dust, lack of sanitation and bad ventilation, apart from deaths by fatal accidents, which on the register of the Miners' Union were noted as due to 'natural causes'.

Sally remembered the chairman of one of the commissions had said:

'We are not considering the diseases of the men and the interests of the mine owners, but the value of the men to the State. Every working adult lost to the State means a loss to capital.'

Dinny snorted over that. 'Miners are dying like flies,' he said. 'But all some people can think of is profits on their labour.'

Sally had learnt a great deal from the facts and figures the commissions brought to light. How fatal his job was for every working miner, for one thing, even though he did not meet with a disastrous accident. She had always been aware of tragedy overhanging work in the mines: been terrified for Tom, and begged him to give up work underground long ago.

Almost every woman who was the wife or mother of a miner knew the gist of those reports. She knew that: 'A man taking up underground employment in the average minefield where siliceous rock exists, at the age of twenty, will be probably incapacitated before the age of fifty, and possibly much sooner if he continues in that occupation. In other words, at least a third and possibly more than one-half of his normal industrial life has been forfeited.'

The doctors agreed that almost every person working in the dust of a mine developed some fibrosis. 'Once fibrosis, always fibrosis,' Dr. Mitchell had said. Although in the early stages fibrosis did not prevent a man from working underground, or apparently impair his normal health, continued work in the dust and fumes surely and steadily killed him.

'The average miner is a man who works till he drops. He is suffering not from T.B.: he is suffering from silicosis,' one medical witness had said. And there had been terrible instances on some of the mines like the Great Fingal at Day Dawn, where nearly fifty per cent. of a batch of young Italians died within five years. One miner on oath stated that nearly all the men he knew working on the Great Fingal, ten years ago, were dead, especially the Italians who had been working in rises. The silicotic dust on the great dump there affected the wives and children of the miners, too. And the same was true of Bonnie Vale, where white quartz broken under the stampers was still blowing about the miners' homes and cutting into the lungs of men, women and children.

The rock of the Boulder areas was supposed to be of less damaging a quality; but all the same, dumps piled in grey and yellow hummocks and jagged peaks beside the mines were the curse of the town. Every breeze stirred their loose sands, pouring them down on the houses of Boulder and people in the streets. The Kalgurli and Lake View and Star were running their dumps out in long barricades now, rather than piling them up; but still women blamed the Golden Horseshoe dump, towering like a mountain over the town, when their floors and kitchens were covered with grit. It was a ceaseless and hopeless task to keep them clean.

No wonder a health inspector reported that the homes of the workers were ill ventilated and windows rarely opened. Women fought the dust as best they could, trying to prevent the germs in dust blowing over open sanitary pans and the expectorations of hundreds of tubercular miners in the street, from reaching their food safes and living-rooms. On the leases over four thousand foreign workers, with their wives and families, were living in shacks of scrap iron and bagging. It was said they earned good wages and could build better homes; but costs of building material were high, and there was always an uncertainty about how long a man's health would last to earn any wages at all.

Most of the foreigners wanted to save money and leave the goldfields: return to their own countries, or set themselves up in business at the coast. When they did build, their houses were the sort of places they dreamed about, gay, fantastic, little villas that stood out from the drab monotony of most miners' dwellings, streets and streets of them all alike, weathered wooden and corrugated iron boxes, whitewashed and dust-raddled.

Although there had been an improvement in conditions on the mines since the first commission made its report, the miners were not satisfied that recommendations of the commission were being carried out. Some of them were embodied in new regulations, but many important recommendations had been either amended or ignored. Arrangements for underground closets and crib places were better, change rooms provided better washing facilities, ventilation had received some attention, but still not enough. The men complained that the size of shafts was still the same. The main shaft down which the cage passed, in some mines, was the only opening to ventilate a dozen levels and the stopes above, equal to another dozen levels. They could name levels where there was no ventilation: where they were working three hundred feet from an air current, and there was neither winze nor rise to take off fumes and dust. The smoke from an explosion got away the same way as it went in. They could smell it on their breath when they went off shift.

Mines of the Golden Mile had a bad reputation these days. When they were smaller and worked by hand labour they were not such death-traps, old miners said. The working pace was harder now, and mining at depth, the increased use of compressed air drills and explosives had brought about a worsening of the health of miners and a heavier death roll. Men knocked up working in deep levels for long periods as they did not in shallow levels. And 'the more dynamite the more dust', the miners said. They grumbled a good deal about winzes and passes being mullocked up: disused winzes being used as mullock passes instead of being kept open as air passes.

Shrinkage stoping, it was contended, increased dust. The ore in the ore channel was broken down and passed to the mill in a heavy fog of dust. Rill stoping, many believed, caused less dust, was safer and healthier for the men and cheaper for the companies; but if the back was bad, rill stoping meant greater danger of accidents. On the Great Boulder for that reason the rill method could not be used.

In the Fingal and other mines men had worked in rises which went up a hundred or two hundred feet. That meant they were working in falling dust all the time, and sometimes the dead ends were seven or eight hundred feet from an air course. Rising, Tom said, was a man-killer, and should be abolished except where absolutely necessary. The Holman hoist had practically done away with the need for rising higher than twelve feet. But a great deal of rising went on, and it was admitted that men, hungry for money, worked above the regulation height of a rise.

Tom blamed the contract system for a lot of the risks the men took. Most machine men worked by contract: truckers and shovellers were on wages. Contract men had to quote against each other to get good positions. If they got a bad place they had to work for all they were worth to make a living wage. Sometimes they made more, often less. That was why they were 'measurement hungry', rushed back into rises and dead ends where the smoke and dust were so bad you could scarcely see a lighted candle at arm's length.

Men suffering from T.B. had worked underground for years: spitting and coughing in the heavy humid atmosphere which bred germs. There was a regulation forbidding men with the disease to work in a mine: but it had only recently been enforced.

Miners knowing a mate had no other means of earning a living would not give him away, or agree to enforcement of the regulation unless he and his family were guaranteed compensation or a suitable job.

Every pay the miners were subscribing to support a mate who had broken down, and every day helping some sick and desperate toiler through with his plod. The situation had become so serious that at last the Miners' Phthisis Act was passed, providing for the medical examination of all miners, and compensation or suitable work for tubercular men found to be unfit for work underground.

The new Commonwealth Health Laboratory which had just been opened was a beacon of hope, Sally thought. Most men who had been working underground for long went for their first examination with fear in their hearts. The young and vigorous who received normal certificates flourished them proudly: others were dumb-founded when their X-ray plates showed the first signs of fibrosis. The older men groused gloomily at having their worst fears confirmed. But at least something was being done to arrest the spread of T.B. and to give men suffering from silicosis a chance of living longer.

Tom was one of those who had received a verdict of silicosis, and Eily was very upset, Sally utterly miserable. Tom laughed at them both.

'I'm damned lucky it's not worse,' he said. 'I've been working underground for twelve years, and a machine man for more than half that time. Of course, I've been careful; but it might've been T.B., and then I'd've been on the scrap heap. As it is, I can work out my contract, and start right away looking for a surface job.'

Sally and Eily both knew that the damage done by those fine particles of sharp dust to his lung tissue could not be repaired. Yet if he avoided increasing the damage by not working in dust there might still be many years of life ahead of him.

Tom was wise: he had pulled out of the mine as soon as possible. But it was not easy to get a job on the surface. So many men were in the same plight as himself. On the crackers there were still clouds of deadly dust, and on the ball mill: the roasters, cyanide vats and filter presses were not likely to improve an already weakened constitution. Finally Tom had taken a job on the brace, pushing full trucks to the bins and tipping them. But all the winter he had been coughing, catching one cold after another, looking so weary and washed out that Sally's heart ached as she thought of him.

What could be done to minimise the risks of a short, hard life for the average miner?

Tom and his mates demanded that silicosis should be regarded as an industrial disease, and the burden of providing for disabled miners be borne by the industry. So far, only miners suffering from tuberculosis were being removed from the industry, and obtaining compensation from the government. An incapacitated miner on relief, from the Mine Workers' Relief Fund, rarely lived more than twenty months. But a scheme was being mooted to settle tubercular miners on the land: men who had been excluded from the industry but were not yet suffering from an advanced form of the disease.

The union urged that the system of working three shifts should be abolished, and that work in stopes, firing out in dead ends or rises, should be done in two shifts with four hours between, so that going back to work the men would not be breathing so much dust and smoke. Also that a workers' inspector should be appointed to check the carrying out of regulations.

The mine owners objected that they could not maintain an output large enough to pay interest on two shifts.

'Output is not so important as the health of the miners,' a miner had replied to one of the commissioners.

CHAPTER LV

WHEN Dinny bought a broken-down motor car from an old mate down on his luck, he thought he might as well learn to drive it.

But the car had held him up with punctures and a leaky radiator several times, skidded over a culvert and tipped him out on to the

336

roadside. The crank handle had nearly broken his shoulder. After a week or so Dinny swore he'd sell the damned thing for scrap, or give it away, rather than make a fool of himself trying to master such an infernal contraption.

'I'll drive it,' Sally said. 'I used to be quite good with horses, and I've always wanted a car, Dinny.'

'You're not driving her till she's in good working order, sweetheart.' Frisco liked to air that lovely authority Dinny found so irksome. 'Tell you what, Dinny. I know a chap who's a wizard fixing up old buses. We'll get him to overhaul her, and maybe, if she's all right, Sally could try her hand driving.'

The 'wizard' had given Dinny's motor car a new lease of life and taught Sally to drive. Dinny almost wished he had not. He had been nervous of driving himself; but his heart was in his mouth all the time, sitting in the back seat, while Sally was at the wheel. She dashed along the road recklessly, cutting corners and taking any side of a track that suited her. Dinny heaved a sigh of relief when she brought the car to a standstill with a triumphant jarring of brakes.

Frisco, of course, could not see what was happening, although he joked and uttered a word of warning when the car rocked and swayed like a ship on a stormy sea, or Sally threw him and Dinny out of their seats with a bump over a rut in the road. Before long, goldfields folk learned to know when Mrs. Gough was coming and keep out of her way. That was the only reason she had escaped a serious accident, Dinny was convinced.

Sally confessed that she liked the road to herself when she was driving. It was just as well for other cars to give her a wide berth until she got more used to humouring Jiggledy Jane. They had decided to call the car after a well-known character of the early days. If it was a bucking colt she had to deal with she would have known what to do, Sally said, but the mechanics of locomotion by any other than horse sense were beyond her. In a resurge of her youthful, adventurous spirit, however, she enjoyed learning to use them; and was delighted with Frisco's suggestion that they should make a tour of the outlying goldfields when the weather settled and the tracks were in fairly good order.

'How about it, Dinny?' Sally asked.

Dinny was dubious about going anywhere far from a garage, or without a motor mechanic.

'With you to show us the tracks, old man, and give a hand in case of breakdowns, we'll be all right,' Frisco declared.

After a lot of inquiries and arguments about tracks, a route was decided on which would take them to Leonora and Laverton, where they hoped to strike a track to Wiluna, and return by Day Dawn and Cue to Sandstone, Payne's Find, Golden Valley, Southern Cross and Coolgardie. Stores and camping equipment were collected in case Jane played up and stranded her passengers in the bush for a few days. Sally expected to be away for a fortnight or three weeks, and Eily had agreed to come over and look after her boarders.

Dinny could not resist the temptation to throw some prospecting gear into the back of the car, and Frisco was looking forward to getting inside information about the Sunset mine at Lawlers in which he had acquired a few shares. He stowed his guitar with Dinny's prospecting dishes for the sake of old times.

It was a bright sunny morning when they rattled out of Kalgoorlie, turning north, and Sally felt gay and excited to be going off on this grand tour of the old rushes. She had heard their names so often; but they were almost as remote and romantic places to her as Paris, New York or London.

Dinny and Frisco were in high spirits, too, looking forward to revisiting the sites of rich finds on which they had pegged, and put in many a day's back-breaking toil without much to show for it; dashing over the tracks along which they had tramped, or goaded their camels and horses, short of food and water, and haunted by the prospect of doing a perish out there in the grey scrub of mulga and salt-bush, running into stretches of spinifex and thorn. They were full of yarns about those days, recalling rows with 'ghans found polluting the water at the rock-holes near Broad Arrow; encounters with natives round about Bardoc, where a hostile tribe used to let fly spears on unwary prospectors. Dinny chuckled and exclaimed, jubilantly, at the speed with which the car was eating up distances it had taken him weeks to cover.

'My God, if we could've got about like this in the early days, Frisco, we wouldn't've had to worry about tucker and water!' he shouted above the clatter and gusty wheeze Jane made, bumping over the rough tracks.

'We'd've whizzed over many a good bit of ground, more than likely,' Frisco yelled.

Snap and rattle was bright green round the whitewashed mine buildings at Comet Vale. Leaves on the saplings flashed like glass in the sunshine and the tall sticks of their trunks were pink and bronze. The blue-grey of cotton-bush and salt-bush grew beneath them on the red earth, with here and there false sandal-wood in a rounded bouquet of yellow-green, then the mulga, sage-green and silvery spread away to where the humped backs of blue hills struck paler blue of the sky.

338

'Why do we talk of this as a grey country?' Sally exclaimed eagerly. 'See all the colour in it!'

A few miles further on she stopped to give a lift to a man tramping along towards Yunndaga, with his swag on his back.

He was a miner, he said, when he settled down in the back seat: had been working on the Comet for the last couple of years.

'It's one of the worst mines in the country, I reckon,' he told Dinny. 'I'm all over sores and boils, and most of the men get that way from the water pourin' out of the walls. And the water pourin' out like that makes 'em dangerous. There's been too many falls of rocks and accidents lately for my likin'. When my mate copped it, I ses to meself: "Bob," I ses, "y'd better snatch y'r time." So here I am. Pity, too, when y'r come to think of it. I was workin' on a rich patch from stone piled up on the floor of the stope; but had a quarter of a mile to crawl to the place where I was workin'. Got a feelin' I wouldn't be workin' there long, though, if I didn't pull out.'

Sally thought it was her lucky day when several miles out of Menzies she got her first puncture, and the miner was there to give Dinny a hand, jacking the wheel, patching up the tyre and replacing it.

'Done a good bit of this sort of thing,' he said cheerfully. 'The mate had one of these here boneshakers, and we'd wind her up and make for the nearest pub of a week-end. Often as not didn' get there: would spend the whole bally time, tinkerin' with her by the roadside. He was a great bloke, Bert Parker. . . .'

Bob liked to talk as he worked. He was talking most of the time, in the back seat of the car, when Sally drove on again.

'We started truckin' in the Horseshoe,' she heard him saying, 'Jeeze, did that mine stink! And the walls were crawlin' with cockroaches. They'd eat a man's crib, and y' couldn't get the musty, fusty smell off of y'. Even after y'd had a wash and been up a while y'd smell like a rat. Bert couldn't stand it, so we pulled out and came up here.'

He didn't say what had happened to Bert; but Sally guessed that Bert was probably the mate who had 'copped it', and Bob was still too raw about his death to be able to talk about it.

They chuntered into Menzies in good style, and Bob left them at the pub, after shouting drinks, and taking a couple with Dinny and Frisco.

Menzies sat on a tableland: the flat top of a low ridge. Its bare red earth, dumps and poppet legs, were clear against china-blue of the sky. Dumps beside the mines, ochre, greeny-grey, burnt sienna, and creamy-white, stood in high banks, wedges and huge pyramids: miners' shacks scattered beyond them, rusty with age, or whitewashed, cut out of the glare, with not a blade of grass or herbage anywhere. Men walking in the main street made black silhouettes against the sky, and crows flung themselves across it in black heiroglyphics, uttering their harsh ka-kaing like a warning.

Frisco could remember the time when Menzies was competing with Kalgoorlie to be the centre of the goldfields. He said there was a lot of German money in the place; but Florrie O'Driscoll had pegged a big acreage. Dinny himself had seen lumps of solid gold that came out of the Queenslander and other mines; and a splendid spring of drinking water at eighty feet on the Picton leases.

With two pubs, a row of shops, a town hall of red brick, the township still had an air of smug prosperity.

'Wish I had the wad of shares I dropped on the Lady Shenton,' Frisco mourned. 'She was badly opened up, and a lot of rich stone wasted on the plates, either overloaded with mercury or smothered in dirt and sand. But with a new manager, she came good: is the hope of the town, now, they tell me.'

They stayed the night at the red-brick pub. There was no need to bustle. Dinny and Frisco wanted to prowl round the mines and Sally was looking forward to a good night's rest.

Early next morning they were off again, making for Leonora: passed through Niagara, where heaps of rubble and broken beer bottles marked the site of a once flourishing township. Here and there a wall of mud bricks still stood, and a row of pepper trees thrust bunches of bright green along what was once a street. Thousands of miners used to swarm round shops and pubs, there, in the evenings. Now, only big white dumps, like snow-covered hills beside the deserted sky-shafts of old mines, bore witness to the busy past of the town.

Kookynie was in no better shape, with the same heaps of rubble and glass, the same walls of mud bricks crumbling back into the red earth. The dumps round abandoned shafts were sulphur-yellow, mauve and terra-cotta, as well as white, and in a tumbled down humpy Dinny found an old fossicker, who said he still got a few 'weights on the dumps. He and his goats and dog were the only live things in sight.

Jane trundled along obligingly all that day, and swung round the dark bluff which was Mount Leonora, just as the men were coming off shift on the Sons of Gwalia, the big mine on the far side of the ridge. Miners trooping up from below were soaking wet and filthy, their figures black against the sunlight: faces yellow and ghastly. Some of them slumped down on the ground near the shaft, too exhausted to move: others streaked way to the change room, and their homes—white huts standing in rows along the road below the ridge. Trim and foreign-looking the small houses were, with coloured doors and green trellises: a vine or bougainvillaea flaring, and white goats coming in for the milking.

'Little Italy, they call it, round here,' Dinny said. 'Most of the miners on the Gwalia are I-talians or Sicilians.'

Surface workings of the big mine were stacked high up on the side of the hill: whitewashed, weatherworn sheds and offices, treatment plants, ore bins, foundry, gigantic wood heap and dump of grey slimes looking out over a dry salt lake, which glittered in the late afternoon sunshine as if it were filled with clear water.

The rough red-brown back of the ridge, rearing itself from black ironstone mail of the plain, stretched for nearly two miles into Leonora. A shabby little township with several shops, two or three pubs, a church, school, hospital, picture show and a merry-go-round in the street, Leonora was doing its best to be an outpost of civilisation for miners working on the Gwalia, and prospectors coming in from shows scattered through the hundreds of miles of mulga scrub and bare flat plains to the east.

Frisco remembered Leonora when it had been a roistering camp, and there was good cattle country round about. The lake used to be a mile wide after heavy rain, and the plains carpeted with herbage and wild flowers. Some enterprising pastoralists had started cattle stations: a few of them still held hundreds of acres running about a sheep to thirty acres. After a long drought they were lucky to feed any stock.

In the old days drovers would bring cattle into Leonora from over the Queensland border, Frisco said. It was a trek of over two thousand miles through the Northern Territory; and nowadays, with the country as dry as the hobs of hell, you wondered how they did it. Couldn't've been done except in a good season. And ten years of drought had just about left a desert behind with sand dunes piling over the stock routes and filling the wells.

'There was a drover used to rule the roost when he hit Leonora,' Frisco chortled. 'A wild, powerful blackguard, everybody was scared of him, drunk or sober. He went around flourishing a revolver and would shoot at anything for a bit of practice. I've seen him potting at a jam tin on an abo's head, and he'd blaze away at a blowfly if it annoyed him.

'Those first squatters up Leonora way reckoned somebody was getting away with their cattle and there wasn't much doubt as to who it was. The Hawk, as he was called—Jack Hawke was his name—would come in with a mob, sell most of 'em in the yards, all but a few good beasts, and go back along the track, pick up some clean skins on the way, brand 'em and turn up, in a few months, with another mob. Everybody knew what was going on, but nobody dared to tackle him. The policeman would drink with him in the pub. The Hawk would be singing and playing merry blazes, shouting all comers, and disappear suddenly. He was a likeable chap: had a way with him, and old Dooley wasn't risking his skin to please the squatters. It went on for years.'

The road to Laverton was a dusty swale of wheel tracks, twisting and turning over red earth under black ironstone pebbles, or through endless miles of dying mulga, red with dust by the roadside and brushing the sky with brown and yellow brooms at a little distance.

The scrub had been cut for sheep in some places, and once Dinny saw two sheep nosing over the stony ground for seeds and scraps of dry herbage. How they managed to survive was a mystery. Men in Leonora, who had known the country since it was first prospected, told him they had never seen it in such a bad way. Dinny groaned over the drought-stricken prospect lying before them.

Jane did not like it either. She began to splutter and protest. Dinny got out and inspected the radiator, found it was leaking, and thanked his stars he had put a small tank of water in the back of the car. A little further on a tyre blew out with the crack of a pistol. Dinny and Sally set to work cheerfully to repair the damage. They found a spike of mulga, as sharp as a steel blade, embedded in the tyre. Frisco laughed uproariously when a second and third puncture had to be dealt with. Sally and Dinny, dusty and sweating though they were with lifting the wheel, patching and swinging it into place again, kept up their spirits by slinging off at him and chiacking each other.

They hoped they might find a handy man in Malcolm who could repair the radiator. But that was just another deserted mining township in ruins: the walls of the big red-brick hotel standing without a roof, the name of a bank blazoned over a heap of rubble, abandoned shafts and broken bottles everywhere.

Murrin was no better, and Jane running like a lame duck when they came to Morgans after innumerable stoppages to let her cool down while Dinny tinkered with the radiator. Morgans, too, had become a derelict, although one mine on the ridge above appeared to be working. Nothing was left of the town's former prosperity except mounds of rubble and glass and the walls of a roofless, gutted pub, still showing faded wallpaper in the sections where bedrooms had been. A pink house with empty blue eyes stared out on the desolation.

Dinny and Frisco climbed up to the mine and found an old miner who said nothing much was doing underground. His job was to keep goats from falling into the cyanide vats. The flocks of goats, left behind when the mines closed down and men and their families left the township, were a regular pest. He was pessimistic about anybody being able to repair the radiator, except a lad who ran a truck for the mine and he was away in Leonora.

There was nothing for it but to push on, after filling the water tank, and try to reach Laverton that night.

Over the stony ridges they went, and through the miles and miles of mulga which could be seen from rising ground, grey as a vast inland sea. But on the horizon a line of hills stood up, faintly blue, changing to cobalt and indigo as Jane trundled nearer and nearer. Tired and exasperated though she was, Sally found the sight of those blue hills exhilarating. She was determined to get to the top of them. It was there the township of Laverton dozed on a tableland.

Thunder rumbled in the later afternoon and suddenly Dinny got fidgety. He was sure they were off the main track. Then Jane bucked and came to a standstill. What on earth was the matter? Dinny investigated and could find nothing wrong. Frisco made suggestions. Dinny and Sally both crawled under the car and lay on their backs examining the dusty, complicated mechanism of her interior. But it was nearly dark and they were disgusted with Jane's tantrums.

'We'll have to camp for the night and see what we can do in the morning,' Dinny said gloomily.

Sally thought that was a good idea. When they had lighted a fire, boiled a billy of water for tea and made a meal of tinned dog and damper, it was like old times. She was quite happy to stretch on a rug and gaze into the blue dark of the night sky with its diamond dust of stars. Dinny plucked 'mulga feathers' for her to lie on when they wanted to sleep. Trust an old prospector to know how to make you comfortable, Frisco said. He asked Sally to bring him his guitar. When he started to strum and sing Sally was satisfied that this was the best part of the trip.

'After all,' she said lazily, 'I don't mind if Jane keeps us here for a day or two.'

Frisco sang: *She was a good girl, a decent girl, and her hair hung down in ringlets,* mixed up with:

> *My pretty Jane, my dearest Jane,*
> *Ah, never look so shy,*
> *But meet me, meet me in the even-ing.*
> *When the bloom is on the rye.*

'That's all very well,' Dinny grumbled, 'but I'd rather have a string of camels in this country while the drooth's on.'

343

He pottered about the car all next morning, cleaned and oiled her. Sally helped him, testing every adjustment which might induce Jane to move. She humoured and coaxed her. Dinny kicked and cursed. But not a budge could be got out of 'the contrairey female', Dinny reported to Frisco.

'No need to get windy,' Frisco said easily. 'Somebody'll come along and give us a hand or a lift into Laverton.'

'Might be a week on this track and nobody go by,' Dinny growled.

'If it's water you're worrying about . . .'

'Shut up,' Dinny muttered. 'Missus Sally'll hear you.'

They were still there next day and no car or truck had passed. In the afternoon there was a thunder-storm and a few drops of rain fell. All day, through the blazing heat, Dinny sat scanning the track and Sally began to suspect what was on his mind. Again towards evening thunder rumbled and lightning threw jagged spears over the hills. Dinny squatted silent and moody in the darkness, near embers of the camp fire, after the thunder-storm died away; but Frisco still strummed and sang, flirting with Sally and making jokes about their grand tour.

The situation looked serious on the fourth day: there was very little water in the tank, and only enough flour in the tucker bags for a small damper. But that evening the thunder cracked and crashed in terrific explosions, lightning tore the sky with its dazzling live wires. Then the rain began, pouring down in sheets which lashed the dry earth and obliterated everything a few yards away.

Dinny had the tanks out in an instant, as well as every billy and dish he could lay his hands on. He was soaked to the skin when he joined Sally and Frisco in the car. Jane was a poor thing to depend on even for shelter. The rain swept into her and dripped through her shabby hood. All night it poured down but Dinny grinned and applauded.

'Send her down, Hughie!' he cried, as the diggers used to on Coolgardie and Hannans.

Wet and cold, Frisco and Sally sat huddled together on the front seat until early morning, Sally trying to get a little sleep by resting her head on Frisco's shoulder, while Dinny snored peacefully as he lay on top of the dunnage piled across the back seat.

He had lit a fire, and Sally and Frisco were standing beside it to dry their wet clothes, when a truck pulled up and a cheery voice called:

'All right?'

'Cripes, no!' Dinny yelled and rushed over to interview the driver.

That young man cast an experienced eye over Jane, crawled under her and reappeared covered with red mud.

'Looks like she's broke her universal,' he said. 'I'll try and fix her so as we can tow her into Laverton.'

That's what he did. And it was a nerve-wracking experience for Sally, watching the truck ahead and trying to keep Jane to the erratic pace of their good-natured saviour.

She was more than pleased to dump Jane at the blacksmith's and arrange with his striker, who was supposed to be 'a bit of a motor mechanic' as well, to put her in working order.

The joys of camping by the track had faded. Even Frisco and Dinny were glad of a bath and comfortable bed at the hotel in Laverton. It was several days before Jane was considered ready for the road again; but Sally enjoyed walking over the great table-land which dominated hundreds of miles of outspread plains, and their curled scrub, the colour of water hyacinths, under rising mists, after the rain. The huge blue bluff which had been her objective driving along the track was beneath her feet now. The Lancefield mine had burrowed into it. Rows of miners' huts spread in a scattered settlement at the back of the mine.

Frisco and Dinny spent most of their time visiting shows round about. They yarned with old prospectors. Sally heard them talking about Skull Creek, so called because there were so many aboriginal skulls washed down in it. Natives had speared prospectors' horses in the early days and prospectors had taken savage vengeance.

Somebody remembered Stone Soak Jimmy, an aboriginal, who was being taken down to Leonora soon after the railway was built. Handcuffed and in chains, he had dived through the train window and got away: made back to the wild and still unexplored ranges to the north. The natives round about Laverton were always fierce and treacherous, Frisco said.

It was out of the question now to go on to Wiluna. Rain had made the tracks boggy, and more than likely there would be floods out from Lake Violet. Besides, Sally had lost confidence in Jane. Dinny was dubious even about risking the journey back to Kalgoorlie.

'Maybe she'll get bogged and break her axle,' Frisco said cheerfully. 'But it's a lark we started out on, man, don't forget. And we've had some fun for our money. Sally's enjoyed it, anyhow.'

'Have y'? Have y' really, ma'am?' Dinny asked.

'I wouldn't have missed it for anything,' Sally assured him. 'Being up here in the Laverton ranges, and seeing all the miles of gold-bearing country we've been through, Dinny! Miles more stretching away on the other side of the ranges.'

'I haven't been so far up as this, meself,' Dinny admitted. 'And cripes, I feel like stayin' and doin' a bit of prospectin'.'

'But you can't do that, Dinny,' Sally protested. 'Frisco and I couldn't wrestle with Jane by ourselves.'

When they started out on the return journey next morning Jane went like a bird. All through the mulga already tufts of wild spinach were sprouting. Now and then a flight of grey birds like swallows with black faces flopped across the track, or a flock of tiny green parrots flew with skirling cries through the silvery-grey and green of trees which had been washed clean by the rain. The pale blue of distant hills became red earth humped against the sky with purple mists in their deep folds.

Then, within a few miles of Leonora, Jane sank in the soft red mud of a depression on the track. Dinny was preparing to walk on into the township and get a truck to pull her out, but a string of camels hove in sight. He asked the 'Ghan in charge to hitch a couple of his most powerful beasts on to Jane, and give her a lift out of the mud. The 'Ghan refused. Camels, he grumbled, would carry loads, but could not haul. Dinny said he knew them better. They'd pull when an engine started behind them. His £1 note persuaded the 'Ghan, and with a ground sheet and blanket beneath her wheels the camels yanked Jane out of her bog at their first panic-stricken leap forward.

Coming into Leonora and Gwalia just after sunset the plains were blue as the sea: miners' white shacks on cliffs near the mine, rosy in the light filtering down from a sunset sky.

Everybody in Leonora was jubilant about the rains. At the pub where they slept Dinny and Frisco gave all the news of the back country. Sally was glad to be on the road again early next morning.

'Jane's racing for home like a two-year-old', Dinny cried, gleefully.

'Keep your fingers crossed,' Sally implored.

'I'll sing to keep her going,' Frisco laughed. 'It's a good way with horses when they're liable to crock up.'

But neither Frisco's singing nor Dinny's crossed fingers prevented Jane from having nine punctures that day and breaking her axle about five miles out of Kalgoorlie.

It was an ignominious return from the grand tour, to be towed behind a sandal-wooder's cart along Hannan Street, and hear the laughter and ribald exclamations of all who saw Jane teetering by, more jiggledy than ever and looking as if she had been dragged through red mud.

'Oh, well,' Dinny said, with a sigh of relief as he stepped out of her. 'She did about everything she could except break our necks.'

346

'You're a bit hard on the old girl, aren't you, Dinny?' Frisco queried with a gust of laughter. 'It was good to go bush for a while, anyhow, wasn't it?'

'Oh, yes,' Sally cried gaily, as Eily and Tom and the children came out to meet her, 'we've had a grand time! But the rains made the track too boggy to go to Wiluna! We'll do another trip up north in a couple of months.'

'Not if I know it,' Dinny muttered.

CHAPTER LVI

'SMATTERY was tellin' me the other day Detective Sergeant Pitman reckons he's goin' to clear up the gold racket,' Tassy Regan said, yarning with Dinny, Dally and Frisco on the verandah.

'He's not the first one to blow his bags like that,' Frisco said dryly. 'Kane was shifted when he got too energetic in the discharge of his duties.'

'But the men with a bit of stuff to get rid of are windy,' Dinny murmured. 'They reckon Walsh and Pitman've given the big boys some uneasy moments, lately.'

'Time was when I might've worried,' Frisco drawled. 'I'm not losing any sleep on what the dees are up to these days.'

Frisco knew more about that inner ring of the gold buyers than either of them, Tassy and Dinny were well aware; but although he was out of the game now his mind remained locked on the subject. It was safer that way, they understood. Frisco had struck too much bad luck to risk bringing the ill-will of the Big Four upon him by talking now.

'A couple of smart Alecs gave Paddy Cavan a nasty turn once,' Dally remembered. 'They tried to fix up things so as Paddy couldn't call in the dees. It was when Paddy used to drive out into the bush to collect a parcel now and then. Seems he was comin' back to town, well-loaded, when he got bailed up on the road and had his gold taken off of him. The bushrangers put a bullet in his tyres and left him marooned in the bush. But Paddy recognised them and tracked them into town. Before morning he'd stolen his gold back again.'

'Y' can't beat Paddy,' Tassy chuckled.

'A good many men'd like to,' Frisco said bitterly, 'but he's dug in too well.'

'Got a big house in London, they say, and lives like a lord. Has married again, and . . .'

Sally, watering the garden in the warm darkness, heard the scuffle of men's boots on the verandah, the sudden break in Dally's yarning: his muffled exclamation:

'Cripes, I forgot!'

She guessed that Dinny had put a stop to the gossip about Paddy and the new Lady Cavan. Sally herself could not forgive Amy for her last letter to Dick; or rid herself of the idea that it had something to do with his death. Her mind was still sore about it as she played a feeble trickle from the new hose, she was so pleased with, over some spindly geraniums and rose bushes beside the garden path. Dick was scarcely 'cold in his grave', as people said, before the news had been cabled that Sir Patrick Cavan and Mrs. Richard Fitz-Morris Gough had been married in London.

Dinny's voice turned the yarning back to its channel:

'Hear Sharpy Eyre had a narrow squeak on the Percy the other day,' he observed. "Sharpy'd brought up a bit in his crib bag. Not much—but enough to get him four months. He was under the shower, thinkin' the numbers were up and the dees outside waitin' for him, when his cross mate comes into the change room. He was goin' on shift and they did some quick thinkin'.

'His mate swapped crib bags with Sharpy and walked out of the change room, sneezin' and blowin' his nose. He'd got a cold and wasn't feelin' too good, it was easy seen: had second thoughts about goin' to work. Strolled over to the office, swingin' his crib bag, and put in his plod. Went off home afterwards, and Sharpy faced the dees as innercent as a lamb—with the prospect of gettin' four months' spendin' money out of the gold, instead of sittin' pretty at Fremantle short of smokes and drinks for all that time.'

'He done better than the old Ding was tellin' me his troubles the other day.' Tassy's great belly shook with the gurgle of his laughter.

'Be the Great Livin' Tinker, y' never see a Ding in such a stew, ma'am!' His smile flattered Sally as she sat down in her chair beside Frisco. 'He was spittin' fire and brimstone and the landscape was gory with his remarks when I come across him. Seems there's been a bunch of crooks turnin' out five-pound notes on the fields lately and they had a wad on their hands. Not good enough to pass in the open. So they hit on the idea of gettin' gold for the notes.

'Well, one of 'em heard this old Ding had a bit of gold he wanted to sell and worded him about it. They arranged to meet in a lonely spot on a dark night. The gold was all right. The blokes with the money flicked a light on it and showed the Ding their fivers. He was pleased as punch to get a good price for his gold and went off

348

with the fivers. The blokes who done a deal with him for the gold lost no time gettin' out of town, so I'm told.

'When the Ding trotted into the bank with his notes the teller didn't like the look of 'em.

' "Where did you get these?" ses he.

'The Ding ses he couldn't say.

' "That's a pity," the teller ses, "because they're wrong 'uns." '

Tassy's laughter was so rich and hearty Sally laughed with him and with Dinny and Frisco, though she couldn't help exclaiming: 'The poor old man! What a shame!'

'Spud Devine was tellin' me a close shave he and two other blokes had a while ago,' Dinny said. 'Young Buggins was up for handlin' a bit of gold. He'd got a plant out in the bush and they wanted to get him off the charge. Decided to try and get some telluride ore from Mulgabbie to counteract the suspicion he'd been smelting telluride from the Great Boulder. They say Mulgabbie's the only spot off the Golden Mile y' can get stuff the dead spit of Boulder ore.

'It's a long ride to Mulgabbie. Spud and his mates went out through Kanowna, takin' a short cut they thought nobody knew much about. A bad track; but they didn't want to arouse curiosity about what they were after.

'It was an awful night, wind and rain and freezin' cold. But they kept goin' to have a word with the boys at Mulgabbie before the dees caught up with them. Guessed they'd be watching young Bug's mates and start out after 'em as soon as they heard Spud was takin' a ride.

'Early in the morning who should they see but a cop ridin' out from Kurnalpi. Spud had a pair of field glasses on him, put 'em up and had a squiz. It was Maloney, who was in charge at Kurnalpi, sure enough.

'Spud and his mates reckoned they was pretty good pals with Maloney. He used to play cards and have a beer up with them when they had a show on Kurnalpi. So they thought they'd risk it and keep goin'.

' "What the hell are you devils doin' out here?" Maloney ses when he pulls up alongside of 'em.

' "Same as you," ses Spud. "Goin' where we want to git."

' "Nothin' doin' on Kurnalpi," Maloney ses. He was goin' into Kal, he ses. Got a message to go in the day before.

'Off he went, and the boys thinkin' the way was clear decided they might as well camp in an old shack they struck further along the road, and get a bit of shut eye. They lit a fire to make tea and had a drop of brandy. But before the billy was boilin' in

349

stalks the two dees who had trailed 'em out from Kal, and Maloney with 'em. They bailed up Spud and his mates and went over 'em.

' "Y're comin' back to Kal," they said.

' "By God, we're not," Spud told 'em. And after a bit made 'em believe it. Told 'em to get while the goin' was good. The dees did, leavin' Maloney.

'The dees'd cracked open the boys' guns to see if they was loaded and removed the cartridges.

'Maloney thought he could come the good sort over Spud and his mates agin.

' "You're gettin' too," they told him.

'He tried to argue the point.

' "Go,' ses Spud, and clipped a couple of cartridges into his gun.

'Maloney didn't lose any time then.

' "Here," ses Mick Thomas, "give me the gun, and I'll put a bullet into the swine just to learn him."

'Spud put a couple of shots into the air, and y' couldn't see Maloney for dust.

'But the men on Mulgabbie were too scared to hand over any telluride. Him and his mates didn't get a damned skerek, Spud said. Went back to Kal, and walkin' into the Reward bar for a drink who should they run into but one of the dees they'd sent out of the hut at Kurnalpi.

' "No recriminations," ses he, "come'n have a drink, boys!"

' "That's all right," ses Spud.

'Spud had a drink with the dee, and reckoned it was time to get one back on Maloney.

' "No hard feelin's," ses he. "Y'd've got something on us if Maloney hadn't've told us y' were comin', so as we could get rid of it before y' arrived."

'It didn't take that dee long to get out of the bar. Spud saw him skedaddle over to Walsh who was sort of admirin' the scenery on the Old Reward claim. The pair of 'em put their heads together over the news and walked off. Maloney got moved on before long.

' "Well," ses Jim Tully, "I don't know that we done the right thing by Maloney, Spud."

' "Hell!" ses Spud. "What did he do to us, the double-crossin' bastard? And what would the blasted dees've done if they'd got the telluride on us?" '

Dinny's yarn was chuckled and laughed over as a good joke put across the gold stealing detective staff. Then Frisco threw the item of news which created a sensation among his listeners.

'Was having a drink in the "Western Star" this afternoon,' he said, 'and Walsh and Pitman blew in. They've got Fred Cairns they told me. Suspected the white man who was killed by a native spear at Goongarrie a while ago was Fred. But seems it was his mate the natives got. Fred swears somebody bashed him over the head when he was fossicking around his old camp at Celebration the other day. It's too near the road for that sort of thing these days. When a car passed, Fred reckons, the blokes who meant to do for him cleared out. He managed to crawl to the road. A truck going in with ore for the battery picked him up and took him to the hospital. Fred's in a bad way, Pitman says, and he's whipping the cat because maybe Fred can't be made to talk before he pegs out.'

'Jesus, Mary and Joseph,' Tassy spluttered, 'if Fred opens his mouth—it'll be awkward for some blokes whose names I wouldn't like to mention.'

CHAPTER LVII

'HEAR Walsh and Pitman are missin'!'

Tassy trotted in, bursting with the news.

'Missin'?' Dinny queried. 'Got bushed or lit out with a bit of gold?'

'Not Walsh!' Frisco said. 'He's been in this country too long not to know his way about. And couldn't be bought. I happen to know.'

'That's right, Frisco.' Tassy's face was solemn as an owl's. 'Seems it's got the police worried. Pitman's been trackin' down a pretty hot mob on the gold stealin'. Maybe he got a clue from Fred Cairns before he died—though the dees didn't get much out of Fred, Detective Sergeant Gordon was tellin' me. 'T any rate, Walsh and Pitman rode out of town on their bikes several days ago, and not a sight or a sound of 'em has there been since. Dees of the Gold Stealin' Detection Staff don't have to report their movements to police headquarters, Gordon says. They report to the Chamber of Mines, which employs 'em, when they feel like it. So nobody knows where Walsh and Pitman were goin', or what job they were on. The police've been out tryin' to pick up their tracks and've drawn a blank. All they've got to go on is that Pitman and Walsh were makin' out Celebration way.'

'God A'mighty!' Frisco threw back his head as if a blast of bad air had struck him.

'Doesn't look too good,' Dinny muttered. 'What d'y' reckon's happened, Tassy?'

'Search me!' Tassy smoked as he cogitated. 'It's well known

some of the boys in the gold've been threatenin' to do for Pitman. He's been givin' them a rough spin: bullyin' their womenfolk and ransackin' their homes if he thought there was a bit of telluride stowed away on the premises. Turned one woman out of her bed when she'd just had a baby and was weak as a cat. Been askin' the kids: "Does y'r daddy bring home some of the yellow stuff?" But Walsh, everybody's got a good word for him: reckons he's a decent kindly bloke: straight as a die, does his job without any bluster and puts in a good word for a man when he can.'

For nearly three weeks the town was in a ferment with the gossip and rumours about the missing detectives. Police parties with black trackers scoured the country along the Celebration road and as far as Mount Robinson. Tracks and shafts between Kalgoorlie and Binduli were searched. A special squad of detectives came up from Perth to aid investigations. Seven car loads of trained men went out and combed the bush. The streets and bars were stiff with plain-clothes constables on the prowl for information. Foul play was suspected, the newspapers said, and the movements of any man attempting to leave the district were closely watched.

'They ought to send for Kalgoorla,' Sally said. 'She found Maritana.'

All the time an undercurrent of shrewd surmise and comment was going on among the miners and old timers who knew something of the ramifications of the illicit traffic in gold. It was generally understood there were men on the fields who could tell the police quite a lot if they chose. But their code forbade giving information about gold stealing to the police.

When the mutilated bodies of the detectives were found, however, horror and disgust swept everybody. The shame of the crime over-hung Kalgoorlie and Boulder.

It was some satisfaction to know that a couple of old miners did more than the whole detective force to discover the remains of Detective Inspector John Walsh and Detective Sergeant Alexander Pitman.

Driving into Boulder in a sulky the old miners worked out a theory as to what might have happened. The engine-driver of a woodline train had reported seeing the light of a car on the road, the night after the detectives had gone off to the bush. The car light was extinguished as the train passed over the crossing. 'Hullo, somebody got a snide job on,' the engine-driver thought to himself.

Supposing that car did have something to hide—wanted to keep out of sight—which way would it go, the miners asked themselves. They jogged off in the direction of the route they decided was the most likely. It took them along a track to Coolgardie, south of the

352

main road. They were just going to give up the wild-goose chase they had undertaken quite casually, when they noticed a loud buzzing of blowflies in the bush. A track led to a shaft near abandoned workings of the old Belle of Kalgoorlie, on Miller's Find. Big bronze and green-backed blowflies were swarming over it in a black cloud, and there was a terrible stench.

Next morning detectives took out a truckload of hauling gear and two experienced miners were lowered into the shaft. There they found the bodies of Walsh and Pitman, heads sawn off, legs and trunks cut into lumps of rotting flesh, which had been wrapped in bags and burnt, before they were thrown down the shaft. So sickening was the job of handling and sending this freight to the surface that the men could not work below for long. At the bottom of the shaft they found also a furnace for roasting ore, firebricks, gold scales and an old overcoat.

On the slope of the ridge, covered with the soft blue of saltbush and spindling trees, those hacked-off pieces of human bodies were laid out on filter-press cloth to await the arrival of the coroner and jury. On that quiet, sunshiny morning, in so peaceful a spot, with the top of the Golden Horseshoe dump showing up like a snow-covered hill in the distance, and the smoke from tall chimney-stacks of mines on the Golden Mile drifting across the blue sky, it was impossible to imagine how such a crime could have been committed.

The people of Kalgoorlie and Boulder were appalled by it: shocked to realise that men capable of such brutality were living in their midst. The murder of the detectives was almost the only topic of conversation for weeks. More than the murders, that ghastly butchering made even an old hard-doer like Tassy Regan 'sick in the stummick', he said.

A week passed, with the police hunting furiously for the guilty men: following every line of investigation, subjecting suspects to gruelling interrogations. Prominent citizens were questioned: a watch kept on the movements of gold buyers and hotel keepers; all the miscellaneous crooks and spielers who might be associated with any dirty work.

'The roots of the traffic in stolen gold are not in danger,' Frisco remarked cynically.

'I wonder if the same gang were responsible for Maritana's death,' Sally mused.

'For Christ's sake don't drag that up!' Frisco jumped up and walked away from her, angry and agitated.

Newspapers all over Australia were raising a great outcry about crime on the western goldfields. 'Make sentences for gold stealing heavier, and crime will be stamped out,' they said. Sentences for

353

gold stealing were levelled chiefly against working miners, everybody knew; and the report of a royal commission had stated that the pilfering of ore by miners was an infinitesimal fraction of the gold stealing which was depriving proprietary companies of their revenue. The big thieves, for the most part, contrived to evade detection. The people of Kalgoorlie and Boulder resented the imputation that working miners were chiefly responsible for crime on the goldfields. They were more stirred and shocked by the murders which had been committed in their midst than outsiders; but they did not believe that to increase the penalty for a miner who got away with a small quantity of gold occasionally would affect the operations of big men in the racket.

'The mining companies have boosted a get-rich-quick policy,' Dinny growled. 'If anybody wants to investigate the causes of crime in Kal and Boulder they'd better start with the mining industry.'

Bicycles which had belonged to the dead detectives were found in the bush off the track to Little Wongie. And five hundred yards further on, indications of a plant which had been used for the treatment of stolen gold. Here there were bloodstains and evidences of hastily dismantled gear. Miller's Find, where the bodies were discovered, was only a few miles away.

From then on the pace of the search for men connected with the crime quickened. A funnel and pipe from the Hidden Secret mine found at the treatment plant in the bush, it was discovered, had been delivered to Phil Treffene, barman of the Cornwall Hotel. A young miner confessed that he had handed a handbag of telluride ore to Treffene at the Cornwall. Treffene was arrested and also Evan Clarke, licensee of the hotel. Bloodstains on his six-cylinder car and the finding of gold-bearing ore on the premises incriminated Clarke as deeply as Treffene.

When Bill Coulter was arrested Tassy said: 'Now they're getting somewhere.'

A burly, bombastic go-getter, Coulter was a well-known bookmaker and money-lender in the town. He owned racehorses; but that he was well in on the gold racket most people suspected.

In his first interview Coulter thought he had cleared himself with the police. He played the bluff and hearty, honest rogue. At first denied having dealings in stolen gold, then admitted that he had handled a bit of stuff for Clarke at fifteen shillings an ounce under the assay value, and understood Treffene was in the business. But although he received gold, Coulter asserted that he would never have anything to do with the treatment of any gold-bearing material. Coulter swore he had never been on a treatment plant in his life.

He had been out in the bush shooting with Treffene on several occasions. They brought in a few rabbits, a turkey or plover usually. Dinny and Tassy guffawed when they heard that. Coulter going out into the bush to shoot plover with Phil Treffene! It was a good joke. The same rabbit had been used to decorate the car on three occasions, a girl working in the hotel testified.

Coulter's house was burnt down the day after the detectives had been murdered. In an attempt to establish an alibi Coulter explained that he lost everything in the fire. His wife had even to buy him fresh handkerchiefs.

The police did not tell him that there was a brand new handkerchief in the pocket of the bloodstained overcoat with the bodies of the detectives in the shaft on Miller's Find. It was that handkerchief as much as anything which put Coulter in the dock, though there were glaring holes in the statement he made to the police about his connection with Clarke and Treffene, and his activities on the day when it was supposed the detectives had been killed.

Dinny and Frisco knew all the men concerned. They had gone every morning to the inquest held by Warden Geary. A new sensation was added to the case when Evan Clarke turned informer and gave evidence for the police.

Clarke stated that Treffene and Coulter were concerned in the business of illicit gold dealing. They had a treatment plant in the bush, south of Boulder, and had told him Detective Inspector Walsh and Detective Sergeant Pitman came on them there when they were treating gold. Clarke said Treffene shot Pitman and Coulter shot Walsh, and they had cut up the bodies and tried unsuccessfully to burn them. They had then taken Clarke's car and thrown the bodies down the shaft on Miller's Find.

'Clarke's a fastidious little bloke,' Frisco said, 'an Englishman, dapper and shrewd—though he has done six months for receiving and selling! He's just the sort that would do any pimping to get out of trouble himself. But murder and cutting up bodies isn't his line.'

'Be the Great Livin' Tinker, I can't see Phil Treffene doin' it, either,' Tassy expostulated. 'He's a real likeable chap, Phil: good-natured and kindly, but a bit weak. About the last man, I'd say, could do a thing like that.'

'That's right,' Dinny agreed. 'A dusted miner pullin' beer. You can understand him doin' a bit on the side with gold: runnin' the treatment plant for Clarke and Coulter. But Phil was jest about cryin' in the witness box when Walsh was mentioned.'

'He wasn't shedding a tear for Pitman,' Frisco said.

'Phil didn't try to hide he'd no time for Pitman,' Tassy replied.

'That's why what he says sounds dinkum to me. It's easy to under-stand the shooting was done, accidental-like, in a hot moment when the dees came on him at the plant, but Phil wasn't responsible for what happened afterwards, I'll swear.'

'Coulter says he was on friendly terms with Pitman and spoke civilly to Walsh. He had nothing against the dees. They were only doin' their duty.' Dinny's grin flickered.

'Clarke and Coulter seem to have made up their minds Treffene's got to carry the baby,' Frisco said.

'And Phil's actin' as if he'd do it,' Tassy replied. 'Not fightin' like he ought. There's a rumour goin' round—because he's dusted—got one foot in the grave—he's agreed to take the blame for the other two, and Coulter's promised to provide for his children.'

'Coulter's got the money,' Frisco reminded them.

'And did y' ever know a big bully like Bill Coulter, got all the bluff and bluster in the world, and heaps of dough, take orders from weaklings like Clarke and Phil Treffene?' Tassy queried.

'That's right, Tassy,' Dinny said. 'In his statement to the police Clarke said Coulter and Treffene committed the murders. And Coulter says he was dumbfounded when he heard Clarke's state-ment. He just laughed when friends told him he was suspected. The only thing what worried him was bein' placed in a false position.'

'The only thing that worried him was plantin' the gold,' Tassy said. 'The prosecutin' lawyer pointed that out, and I reckon he was right.'

'Coulter admitted having lied to the police when they first inter-viewed him,' Frisco's voice lifted derisively. 'Out of "loyalty to Clarke and Treffene". He said he was very "sorry for Phil Treffene".'

Dinny and Tassy snorted and growled like surly old dogs.

All over the goldfields discussions like this were going on. Evidence was torn to pieces, analysed and weighed from the angle of local information and bits of gossip which never reached the courts. In the kitchens, over the back-yard fences, on the verandahs, at street corners, in the pubs, clubs and at crib time on the mines, the murder of the detectives and the trial of Coulter and Treffene for wilful murder at the criminal sessions in Perth were the chief topic of conversation for months. There was a lot of sympathy for Phil Treffene. Like a fly, it appeared, he had got himself tangled in a web of strangling circumstances.

Clarke aroused loathing and contempt because he had turned informer to save his skin, and pocket the reward of £1500, offered for information which would lead to arrest of the guilty man. But

Coulter was generally considered the man who had bossed the show. His, most people believed, as the prosecuting attorney put it, had been 'the master mind' in the whole affair.

When Treffene and Coulter were found guilty and sentenced to death, feeling for Treffene ran so high that the Miners' Union petitioned the Government to commute the death sentence to a term of imprisonment, arguing that 'it was better for a guilty person to escape the full penalty than for one innocent man to suffer by uncorroborated evidence'.

Appeals against the sentence were dismissed. Then just before the last act of this sordid drama Treffene's son told his story. It was a pitiful and tragic account of the boy's promise not to betray his father's confidence.

Tom knew young Treffene. He had been working underground on the Lake View and Star, and was a straightforward, likeable lad, Tom said. His promise to his father had put him in a terrible position; but after an appeal to the Executive Council failed Jack Treffene decided that he must tell what he knew.

He had expected Coulter to confess in the end. 'I never thought he would go to his death with a lie on his head,' Jack said. 'And dad always said: "Whatever happens I'm going to stand by Coulter."'

So Jack Treffene made a statement of what his father had told him.

'I didn't know what to do,' the boy explained. 'I'd never gone against dad. Father Melville said I must decide for myself.'

The newspapers reported that Treffene heard Coulter give instructions to Mr. Haynes, the lawyer, about leaving all his money to his wife and child. 'But I understand you promised Treffene some provision would be made for his children, too,' Mr. Haynes said. 'According to Treffene.' Coulter replied and told Mr. Haynes to carry out his instructions. Later Treffene had said to Mr. Haynes:

'Well, Mr. Haynes, I've been solid to Bill right through: but he's twisted on me at the finish.'

'Phil Treffene made his statement, finally, because Coulter had broken faith with him about providing for his children, most people believed. Treffene's statement bore out the main points of his son's story. It satisfied men and women on the goldfields that this was a true version of what had happened.

In black and white, there it was, like a crude drawing done by a trembling, unskilled hand: revealing all the weakness and misery of the man who had made it, and yet giving an impression of reality. Treffene's statement outlined the characters of both men, Dinny said, so that those who knew them recognised where responsibilty for the murders lay.

'Clarke and I were partners in the business,' Treffene told the police. 'He used to go out and leave me to put stuff in the fire, and then go back with him, and then perhaps go out again with Coulter next day, or Coulter and me would go out and put it in the fire and then go out the next day and dolly it up. Coulter nearly always went out with me to put stuff in the fire.

'We were sitting down dollying when Pitman and Walsh came on us. Coulter was always saying that if they came they would have to go. I saw them first and said to Coulter: "Here's Pitman." The gun was leaning on a bit of scrub. Coulter said: "Get the gun." I picked it up. Pitman sang out, "Don't shoot, Phil." Pitman put up his hand and I fired. I dropped the gun as Pitman was trying to get his revolver out of his pouch with his left hand. I did not mean to kill either man. If I had, I could have done so. The gun was loaded in both barrels.

'Pitman came towards me and I ran for the road. I had not gone far when I heard another shot, kept running till I got to the road. Coulter asked me where the cartridges were, and I said in the car. I saw Pitman walking about but did not see Walsh. I went further into the bush and heard another two or three shots. Then all was quiet. Coulter was up at the plant. I went up to him. He said Pitman was dead and Walsh was alive. He took a revolver out of his pocket and went away. Presently there was three more shots and he told me he had settled Walsh. He wanted me to help him burn the bodies, but I refused. He said we would have to come out and cut them up and burn them. I again refused, said I would have no part in it. He cleaned up the blood.

'We came home and he told Clarke and got Clarke to go out with him. Clarke went away, took my pants and shoes with him. Clarke said they tried to burn them, threw them down the shaft. Clarke said Coulter cut them up. Coulter was always urging me on. I would tell him Pitman was about a lot and he would say they would have to go. Two years ago he wanted me to get a knife, and saw and an axe, and have them ready so he could chop them up, but I took no notice. Coulter was always at me to take the blame. He said he had plenty of money and would look after my little children, and promised me anything, so I consented.'

In reply to Treffene's statement, Coulter said:

'I never killed either of these men. Treffene will find it hard for God to forgive him this terrible lie. God is the only one who knows the truth.'

No one was impressed by Bill Coulter bringing God into the argument.

Coulter and Treffene were hanged. Coulter, fighting to the last, and Treffene meeting his end with the resignation of a man who had nothing more to fear from death.

People of the goldfields did not recover from the impact of the tragedy for a long time. But there was an epilogue of macabre farce when Evan Clarke claimed his reward. That it was blood money, and that he had narrowly escaped the fate of his associates, did not deter him from bringing a law-suit against the Crown.

He lost his case on the grounds that he had given information to the police, not in order to further the cause of justice, but because he had been forced to do so to save his own neck. The verdict caused grim rejoicing.

Although Clarke returned to Boulder there was no place for him on the fields.

Sally hoped that the traffic in stolen gold would not survive the obloquy cast upon it by the murders, and the execution of Coulter and Treffene.

Frisco laughed at her optimism.

'They've strengthened the Gold Stealing Detection Staff,' he said, 'but the racket's still flourishing.'

CHAPTER LVIII

WHEN Mrs. Gough and Mme Robillard walked into town on a Saturday afternoon old timers followed their trim, energetic figures with ruminative eyes.

'Tare and ages, but they wear well,' Tassy Regan might remark to Yank Botteral; or Chassy McClaren and Speck Jones remember how slight and sprightly those figures had been thirty years ago. As likely as not there would be some gossip about both women: why Marie had never re-married, and what in the name of blazes had induced Missus Sally to take up with Frisco Jo Murphy after all.

The neighbours surmised all was well with the domestic affairs of both women when they could be seen, walking into Kalgoorlie on a Saturday afternoon, chattering and laughing light-heartedly. To be sure, Mme Robillard was stooping a good deal now. Her sallow skin had darkened and become more deeply lined than Mrs. Gough's, though her black hair showed not a thread of silver, and

359

Mrs. Gough's hair was grey. But Mrs. Gough was handsomer in her fifties than she had ever been, old friends liked to say.

For Sally these Saturday afternoons with Marie had become an occasion for the discussion of complications in her personal affairs. At home it was difficult to have any talk which might not be interrupted by Frisco or Dinny. So Sally was telling Marie about one of those absurd predicaments in which a quarrel between Dinny and Frisco so often placed her, and Marie was getting quite a lot of fun out of her story as they walked into town that hot afternoon towards the end of the year.

They were in good spirits and after their shopping, which consisted chiefly of window-gazing, buying some fruit and a few odds and ends of haberdashery, they went on to the Reward hotel for the glass of beer that was the highlight of this weekly excursion. Besides, God-Save-Us-Sarah was sure to be found in Adey's back parlour reserved for 'Ladies'; and to sit yarning with her over a schooner or two enlivened an otherwise uneventful jaunt. There was always something to laugh over, too, in the news of the town, filtered through the gossip of Rosy Ann Plush and Amelia Green.

They were all there, still happily discussing the murders, when Sally and Marie sat down at a table near the door.

'The husband's brother knows a miner went down the shaft to bring up the bodies,' Mrs. Green was saying. 'And he couldn't eat meat for a week. Got the spews every time he tried.'

'If I could spew as easy as that I'd never be sober,' Sarah grumbled.

'Many's the time I've seen Bill Coulter come in here for a drink,' Mrs. Plush cut in. 'Y'd never've thought, from the look of him, he could be a murderer. Always well-dressed and jolly, he was, takin' bets on the races and orderin' Adey round as if he owned the place. And there was a half-caste woman he used to get round with. . . .'

'But Bill Coulter wasn't the big man in the racket.'

Heads drew together and voices fell to hoarse whispers: a sly muttering about well-known citizens who might be the Big Four behind the illicit traffic in gold. Scared, sidelong glances to see no one overheard what was being said, discovered Marie and Sally.

They were hailed with convivial friendliness, and Adey bustled in to take their orders for drinks.

'Mum's a bit better to-day,' she replied in answer to Sally's inquiry about Theresa. 'She'd like you to go round and have a word with her presently.' Theresa had been ill for some time and a few minutes with her was always part of a visit to the Reward.

'We will, of course,' Sally promised. Adey's cheeriness had

become a little brassy and businesslike; but she was devoted to her mother and pleased when anybody showed concern for Theresa.

From where they sat Sally and Marie got a glimpse of the corridor opposite the bar, and could see men and women drinking at small tables in the parlour opposite.

When Adey went off to get their beer Sally noticed a group of men standing outside the bar, among them Mr. Dowsett and Mr. Malleson. They were talking to two other mine managers and a pompous, well-dressed stranger. Presently there was a gust of laughter and a rattle of high, shrill voices. Sally saw three women approach the men in the corridor. The men had looked curiously towards the women. One of the women half-stopped and smiled at Mr. Malleson; but he turned his back and the woman went on. She sat now in the parlour opposite, facing the group in the corridor.

Sally recognised her. It was Belle, and the women with her were Battleaxe Bertha and Lili. But all three looked shabby and down on their luck, rather like caricatures of the lively buxom girls she had first met on that indiscreet visit to Mme Marseilles, long ago, in Coolgardie; and later at Lili's party in the 'Western Star'. Lili had become fat and slack: her hair was dyed a bright gold, her cheeks carelessly rouged. Bertha slumped beside her, flabby and pallid in a shapeless black dress. Only Belle carried herself with assurance, tightly corseted under a shoddy tailor-made, a green felt hat set rakishly on coarse grey hair, the worse for henna, her china-blue eyes staring out from heavily blackened lashes, and her nose sticking up, bony and assertive in a hard, haggard face.

Marie and the other women had seen the incident in the corridor and watched Belle and Bertha and Lili settle down to their drinks, a little flustered by the way Mr. Malleson had turned his back on them. After all, everybody knew how it had been between Belle and Archie Malleson for a good many years; and although Mr. Malleson had become a prosperous and important man latterly, Belle and Bertha and Lili were accustomed to being treated with a certain amount of respect as old identities of early days on the fields.

Belle was furious at the affront Mr. Malleson had put upon her, it was obvious. She kept glancing at the man's back as if her blue eyes were daggers she could fling at it. Her angry exclamations reached the 'Ladies' Room'. She drank the glass of brandy Adey put before her at a gulp, and rose from her table.

There was a titter of excitement from Mrs. Plush and Mrs. Crabb as Belle stalked across the corridor. They scurried into the corridor to get a better view of what was happening.

'Mr. Malleson' Belle said, 'a word with you!'

'Oh, Belle,' Archie Malleson replied, a bit rattled, 'how are you? You look marvellous. Full of beans!'

'No, thanks to you,' Belle said. 'As a matter of fact I'm hard up, and I'll be obliged if you would repay some of the money you borrowed from me a while ago.'

Mr. Dowsett slunk away: and the men with Archie Malleson cocked their ears. Belle was not going to lower her voice to suit Mr. Malleson, after what he had done.

'For Chris' sake, shut up, Belle,' he begged.

'Shut up, is it?' Belle's voice could be heard all over the hotel. 'I've shut up long enough, Mr. Malleson. You're well in now and can afford to pay your debts. I've got some receipts that will come in handy if I'm forced to take legal action.'

The men who had been talking to Archie Malleson moved away to relieve him of some embarrassment in dealing with this irate female.

'You wouldn't do that, Belle,' Mr. Malleson said. His voice dropped to an urgent pleading.

Belle shook his hand off her arm.

'It's no good trying to soft soap me by talking of old times,' she said. 'You'll send me a fiver a week until the £ 400 I mortgaged the house for, and gave you, is paid off. And that's only half of what you owe me, you know darned well.'

Belle swung away and was going back to Bertha and Lili when Mrs. Plush and Mrs. Green grabbed her.

'Come'n'ave a drink, Belle,' Mrs. Plush begged. 'My, you told him off a treat!'

'Cold and haughty as a queen you was, Belle,' Mrs. Green exclaimed rapturously.

Belle turned into the 'Ladies' Room' with them and saw Sally and Marie.

'Why, if it isn't Mrs. Gough and Madame Robillard,'' she cried and sat down at their table. 'Did you hear me balling out that tripehound?'

'Of course,' Marie said laughingly. 'But he deserved it.'

'Too right he did.' Bertha and Lili had trailed over to join Belle, and Bertha spoke as if she were flatly contradicting any doubt on the subject.

Lili twittered delightedly to see Sally and Marie.

'It is so long time since we 'ave meet,' she cried. 'But you, you look so young and charrming as always. And me . . . I am become so fat—sans feu, sans everyt'ing.'

An old siren, a little drunk and disreputable, Lili might be, but

362

her blue-grey eyes held their fey, caressing glance. A malicious sprite still inhabited her corpulent body.

'Nonsense, Lili!' Belle sprang to her defence. 'Lili is a favourite with one of the old boys,' she boasted. 'He is chairman of half a dozen boards and supposed to be a real lady-killer.'

'Poof,' Lili giggled, *'qu'est-ce que c'est* the women see in 'im I do not know. 'E 'as nothing to blow about. Quite blue—and so big!' She waggled her little finger and set everybody laughing.

'Oh, Lili!' Mrs. Plush squealed.

'She's trick, isn't she?' Mrs. Green queried.

'Everybody knows I've always kept a respectable house, Mrs. Gough,' Belle continued. 'But business is bad. Not like it was in the old days when a prospector would come in with a few thousands in his pocket, and never mind how much he spent for a night out. Nowadays, the boys would rather get a poor girl into trouble than pay for their fun and be done with it. The abortionists make more money than we do. And the old men are all impotent, or they've got so prosperous and respectable they don't have anything to do with us.'

'Like Archie,' Lili murmured malicously.

'Damn him!' Belle flared.

'Between Archie and Belle it was a real love affair,' Bertha said in her slow, heavy way. 'He always said Belle was his wife really, the other just a housekeeper. And Belle kept the whole family when Archie was broke, didn't you, Belle? Paid his wife's doctor's bills and found the money for his daughter to stay at school in Perth.'

'More fool me,' Belle said harshly. 'In our game we can't afford to be sentimental. That's why I wasn't going to let Archie get away with cutting me dead to-day.'

She grabbed the schooner of beer Adey had brought and drank in thirsty gulps. Bertha blew off the froth and sucked her beer appreciatively.

'They're all the same, the men,' she said in her deep melancholy voice. 'Flies round a honey pot wasn't in it with Archie Malleson and his bunch round our place once. But it's off like a dirty shirt when they're done with you.'

'I'm not blaming a man for wanting to turn respectable and get on in the world,' Belle declared. 'But that's no reason to treat old friends like mud. When a woman's down on her luck, and he's well in, it's up to him to do the decent thing, I reckon. That's all. I could make things very awkward for Mr. Malleson if I talked now —not only about the money he owes me and all that. He knows it well enough, too.'

'Ah, ha-ha!' Lili's little laugh tinkled. 'We 'ave passed on ze gold

363

and made a good bargain for 'im many times. It would make ze sensation for Bobby Dowsett and Archie if we open ze mout' one leetle, leetle bit.'

'Shut up, Lili,' Belle growled.

'I must be gettin' a move on,' Bertha said reluctantly. 'Promised to let one of the boys have a clean shirt for to-morrow.' She trundled away like a lame duck in her rusty black dress.

'Poor Bertha,' Belle exclaimed, looking down her long nose. 'She's not working any more. Takes in washing out at the Boulder. Just comes in to have a drink with us Saturdays.'

'What's happened to Nina?' Sally asked.

'She's dead,' Belle said.

'Got a load, as ze boys say,' Lili explained. 'Ze 'eaviest load on ze Golden Mile.'

Sally wondered how Belle and Lili had escaped the same penalty: whether they had escaped as a matter of fact. Belle steered the conversation into safer channels.

'There's a lot of luck in our game, like in every other,' she said briskly. 'Lili and me, we've been lucky in some ways if we haven't in others. . . . They tell me there's a rush to the old alluvial diggings on Kurnalpi. Chook Dean struck six hundred ounces on a patch there!'

Belle was as jubilant as if she had found the gold herself. It's all very well to say the mining industry made and runs this town; but I reckon while there's alluvial in the back country we don't have to worry about another slump.'

'Me, I like mining shares,' Lili sighed.

'She's got quite a wad of scrip,' Belle laughed. 'Old Bunny gives her some good advice and a few shares now and then.'

'Oh yes,' Lili murmured. ' "You must give me some shares in zis mine, darrling, to bring you ze good luck." '

After Sally and Marie had shouted their round of drinks they made their excuses for breaking up the party and went to see Theresa. She had a shack across the back-yard: was more at home there than in the hotel bedroom Adey wanted her to use, she always explained. Sally almost wept to find her old friend so wasted by pain and yet joking about the cancer that was 'eating out her insides'.

'Having a baby is nothing to it, dearie,' Theresa croaked. 'Maybe I had my babies too easy, and that's why I've got to put up with a bit of hell now.'

'I don't believe it, Theresa,' Sally cried brokenly. 'You don't deserve to suffer like this.'

'There! There, honey,' Theresa whispered. 'Don't you take on so.

It'll soon be over—and I'm not goin' to grouse. I've had a grand life with my old man and the kids. Maybe I've been a terrible sinner and this is my punishment, as Father Flynn says. But I've had all the heaven I ever want, so what does it matter?'

'A priest thinks he's got to talk like that,' Marie said gently. 'But we know what a good woman you've been, Mrs. Molloy. Everybody on the fields loves and honours you.'

'Do they?' Theresa seemed to wonder whether it could be true that people thought well of her.

'They do! Oh, they do,' Sally assured her.

'Well I'm blest!' Theresa exclaimed, her pain-filled eyes smiling. 'I'll be getting swelled-headed with the pair of ye.'

They had kissed her and gone away, saddened that such cruel suffering should be the lot of a woman whose splendid vigour and warm-hearted kindliness had been spent so generously, helping other women through their pain and troubles.

This brief visit to Theresa made Sally feel guilty about having spent so much time drinking and gossiping with Belle and Bertha and Lili.

As she and Marie crossed the Boulder road on the way home, a black car dashed past, showering them with dust and gravel.

'*Mon Dieu*, did you see who it was?' Marie asked.

'No,' Sally replied indifferently.

'Paddy Cavan,' Marie gasped. 'And there was a woman with 'im. I think it was Amy.'

CHAPTER LIX

SALLY froze at the sight of the elegantly dressed young woman to whom she opened the door.

When the knocker clattered she had wondered who the stranger could be making such a noise. Goldfields folk usually rapped with their knuckles and called: 'Is anybody at home?' But there was Amy on her doorstep, all sweetness and appealing impetuosity.

Not waiting to be invited, she brushed past Sally into the sitting-room with a gust of delicate perfume, exclaiming:

'Oh, Missus Sally, you don't know how I've been dying for this! To see you again. You must listen to me. You must let me tell you. . . .'

Sally could not voice what her mind was crying: 'Go away, I don't want to see you! I don't want to speak to you!'

Amy seated herself and cocked her head so that a smart black hat sat perkily on the little golden sausages into which her hair was curled. Instinctively she was seeking Sally's admiration and approval of her appearance. She knew that she was still young and pretty, although her face had become flatter, thinner. A certain dissatisfaction and unhappiness lurked about her mouth and in her eyes. She wanted Sally to see that and commiserate with her when she had explained the cause of her loneliness and boredom.

Sally's silence and steady gaze were disconcerting. Amy tore off her gloves and her be-ringed fingers moved impatiently. For a moment she seemed no more than a girl nervous and ill at ease before a stern judge. But quickly again she was the charming Lady Cavan, sure of herself and playing for Sally's sympathy in order to get her own way in the battle of wits before her.

'I don't suppose you can forgive me, Mrs. Gough,' she said, something brittle and insincere in her voice, although she was striving to appear distressed. 'I can't forgive myself. It's hard to understand how I could have done such a thing—left Dick and Billy just to get away from the hard times we were going through then. I must have been crazy! Yes, that's what it was. I was just crazy.'

She paused, but no helpful word came from Sally.

'I loved Dick. Oh, you know I loved him. I've never loved anyone else, and I realise now what a fool I was to throw away our happiness. I've been eating my heart out about it for years—and longing to see Bill. I've had all the things I thought I wanted, but a gay social existence doesn't satisfy one, does it? I've been so restless and mopy, lately, Paddy hasn't known what to do with me. Oh, he worships me, of course. Has been wonderful. Would do anything for me. But nothing seems to give me the least pleasure.'

Amy was very sorry for herself. A tear shone on her eyelashes. Yet Sally could not believe in Amy's heartache and unhappiness; or rather that they were any more than a symptom of the overwhelming egotism which demanded a new diet, as well as absolution for its crimes. Amy hoped to use the old affectionate relationship which had existed between them for something, Sally divined. Was it to salve her conscience or to make some fresh demand?

Sally guessed the answer. But her mind remained cold and hard. She could not imagine herself doing anything which would enable Amy to recapture Bill. Dick had been sacrificed to her; but his son was not going to be if she could help it, Sally resolved.

As if deeply affected by a new vision of herself, and the pathos of her awakened maternal emotion, Amy was saying:

'For years I've been longing for Bill: to have him with me. You know how it is with a mother's heart, Mrs. Gough. Oh, I seem to have been remiss, I know. But now I want Bill more than anything else in the world. I can't be happy without him.'

Sally was conscious only of dumb rage and distrust of the motives behind Amy's babble. It was her own happiness she was talking about all the time, not Bill's or what was best for the boy.

'Paddy has been awfully good,' Amy went on, oblivious of any indecency in lauding Paddy Cavan to Dick's mother. 'He's willing for me to have Bill: will send him to one of the best English schools and the university: give him all the opportunities a son of his own would have. Of course, you know we've never had any children. Paddy's two step-daughters live with us, Pat and Pam. They're dear girls: I'm fond of them both. And they're thrilled at the idea of having a brother. That's what I've come back for. That's why I wanted you to understand. . . .'

'I see,' Sally said. She could see only that Amy was trying to appease a sense of guilt and frustration in seeking to regain possession of Bill.

'Where is he? Who is he like?' Amy asked eagerly. 'I'm dying to see him. Bill was a rather trying child, nervy and hot-tempered, I remember. More like me than Dick! But I don't mind what he's like now. We'll soon get used to each other, and I'd do anything in the world to make him love me. I'll give him a good time: the best of everything money can buy. . . . He's at school, I suppose. Will be coming home soon?'

'Bill doesn't live with me,' Sally said, forcing herself to speak. 'I was ill after Dick died. Tom took Bill home. He has lived with Tom and Eily and their children ever since.'

This information was not pleasing to Amy, apparently. She said: 'And Tom has told Billy about me, I suppose?'

'The boys at school told him his mother had run away with Paddy Cavan,' Sally replied.

Amy shrugged her shoulders as if no importance need be attached to what children said. 'I'll go over to Tom's and see Bill this afternoon, or do you think I'd better send a note to say I'm coming.'

'Don't ask me,' Sally said. 'I won't do anything to bring you and Bill together.'

'You don't approve of my wanting to have Bill,' Amy cried. 'You don't want me to take him away, I suppose, Mrs. Gough. But you must consider my feelings. After all, he is my child, and . . .'

'Bill is nearly thirteen and not such a child as you seem to imagine,' Sally replied. 'I dare say he'll decide what he wants to do. At any rate, I'm sure that's the way Tom will put it to him.'

'But I'm his mother!' Amy wailed. 'Surely, I've got some right to '

'Don't talk to me of any right you have in Dick's son,' Sally said. Amy's assurance and complacence crumpled. She had been prepared for an uncomfortable interview with Dick's mother: for recriminations and abuse perhaps. That she would be able to overcome Sally's hostility by talking of Dick, and appealing to her sympathy, Amy had not doubted. But Sally listened to her, unmoved, with a stony face. Amy was forced to realise that Missus Sally had seen through her expressions of regret, regarded her as an intruder. Inferentially, Sally had blamed her for Dick's death, and implied that she was not to be trusted with her own son.

Amy felt naked and ashamed. Such a situation was not to be endured. She moved restlessly, stimulated by a comfortable recollection of her wealth and security. It was no use Mrs. Gough trying to deprive her of Bill, Amy told herself. She was determined to regain possession of her son. As determined as she had been to marry Dick and to grasp everything in life she had desired.

She rose with a swirl of her stiff silk skirt.

'Good-bye, Mrs. Gough,' she said, an affectation of dignity. 'I had hoped you would not be so censorious.'

Quickly, angrily, she walked to the gate. The chauffeur in Paddy Cavan's shining car jumped to open the door for her with a white gloved hand, and presently the car glided away towards Boulder. Sally wished there were time to warn Eily of Amy's visit; but Tom and Eily would know how to cope with it, she was sure.

Amy remembered the street where Tom and Eily were living, although so many more small houses exactly alike and pressed close together lined the sides of it now. These long, wide streets of small, shabby dwellings ran out over the flat, red earth which had been familiar to her as a child. Amy gazed with distaste at them, the scraps of gardens achieved, now and then, ragged creepers on narrow verandahs, goats searching for refuse along the footpaths, reeking pans exposed in rows along the back lanes. She knew what these houses were like under a blazing summer sun, in the blistering heat and dust storms, with those poisonous fumes from the mines drifting over them.

'God, how glad I am to be out of it all,' Amy exclaimed to herself, reaffirming her intention to remove Bill from such surroundings.

But it would be futile to try and impress Tom with an account of maternal heartache or boredom, she decided. She must stress the practical benefits for Bill in going away with her: the importance of finishing his education abroad and going to Oxford or Cambridge. Tom could scarcely ignore the possibility of a distinguished career for the boy if he took advantage of the prospects opening up before him.

No, Amy assured herself, she had no regrets for what she had done. She was sorry, of course, that Dick had taken their separation so much to heart and that he had died. It was unreasonable for Mrs. Gough to suggest that she, Amy, was responsible for Dick's death. She had never been as indispensable to Dick as Sally seemed to think; and far from abandoning her infant she had done Dick a good turn by leaving Bill with him. He was wrapped up in the child; but that did not mean Amy herself was quite heartless, and had not fretted a good deal about losing Bill. It would have been ridiculous to drag him with her to London.

Now she must have someone to love and cherish: she must have someone who would be grateful to her for what she could do for him. There must be someone with whom she would have ties of sympathy and understanding to compensate for having to put up with Paddy, who got on her nerves and drove her almost distracted at times. His devotion could still be depended on, but he was exasperatingly mean now and then; and his jealousy always interfering with her slightest predilection for another man. Bill would fill a vacuum: give her a new interest and zest in life.

Bill's education, his sport, his career, plans for his future, would absorb and delight her. She would be the most indulgent of mothers. Bill would adore her: there would be an easy, go-as-you-please companionship between them. They would be pals, and she would be pals with his pals. Of course Pat and Pam might butt in and want to commandeer Bill. But always it would be understood that mother came first. Though she did not want Bill to call her mother. That might lead to unpleasant reminiscences.

She must think of some little, amusing name Bill could call her. Pat and Pam had called her Amy at their first meeting, though Paddy thought that was disrespectful. He had insisted on mamma. But Amy had taken the girls' part, and Amy she was to them, except when they spoke of her to their father. Aimée, perhaps, the loved one, that's what she would like Bill to call her, his mother reflected as she drove to Tom's house. It would be a thrilling experience to meet this schoolboy son of hers whom everybody thought she had forgotten, and whom she was determined to have and to hold —despite Mrs. Gough's disapproval and any objection Tom might raise.

Amy promised herself to woo and win the boy, as if he were a young man she were in love with. Surely she could do that? She had been able to captivate so many men. It wasn't likely her own son would fail to respond to her wiles. Unless he were too stupid and foolish for words. Amy could not imagine her little Bill being that. As a child he had had a certain wilful charm. With Dick's eyes, and built on the same lines, she expected that Bill would have grown into a slight, graceful lad. Not handsome, perhaps; but giving promise of becoming a rather personable young man.

Eily told Sally what happened when Lady Cavan called, late that afternoon.

Tom had just got home, and thrown himself down on a stretcher on the verandah for a few minutes' rest.

'He gets awfully knocked-up these days.' Eily could never talk of anything without referring to her concern about Tom's health. 'I'm so worried about him, mum. Since he got his dirty ticket he's not supposed to be doing heavy work, but it seems a man's got to work just as hard on the surface as he does underground.

'Well, Tom looked up to see a chauffeur, all dolled up in a uniform and white gloves, coming in the gate. "Does Mr. Tom Gough live here?" he asked. "He does," Tom said.

'The next minute Amy was rushing up the path and holding out her hand.

' "Oh Tom, I am glad to see you," she said.

'Tom didn't see her hand.

' "However can I thank you?" Amy went on, a bit flustered. "Your mother tells me you and Eily have looked after Bill. It was good of you—I *am* grateful. Don't look at me like that, Tom. You don't know what I've suffered. How miserable I've been. I don't blame you for feeling you can't forgive me. I can't forgive myself." '

'She said that to me,' Sally remarked.

'Of course, she wanted to see Bill. He was in the yard chopping wood. Tom called him, and Bill came into the sitting-room, just as he was, with his hair all over his face, and a bit dirty-looking, not having had his clean up for tea.

' "This is your mother, Bill," Tom said.

'Amy rushed at Bill and threw her arms round him.

' "Oh, my darling," she said, all wrought up, "my darling, darling boy." And kissed and hugged him.

'I wish Tom hadn't done it that way,' Eily went on. 'It was too much for Bill. The shock I mean. He went quite white. He looked dreadful, mum, he really did. I couldn't bear to see him so upset. And then his face went all funny and stiff as if he were years older. He seemed to have made up his mind what to say.

' "Are you Lady Cavan?" he asked.

' "Why, yes, Bill," Amy said. "That's my name now, but . . ."

370

' "My mother was Mrs. Richard Gough," Bill said. "I don't know you. I don't want to know you." And he walked out of the room.

'Amy burst into tears. "Oh, what have you done to my child? What have you told him," She turned on Tom.

'I went out to look after Bill and found him lying face down on his bed. But he was beside himself with rage, mum. "What's she come back for, Eily?" he said. "Why did she have to come back and remind everybody? The boys at school used to call me nobody's kid. They used to say . . ."

'It took me a long time to pacify him, and try to explain things.

' "You've never been nobody's kid, Bill," I said. "You know Tom and your father thought the world of each other. Tom feels about you as he did about Dick. I don't think he cares for Daphne or young Dick and La, more than he does for you. And gran— You're the very apple of her eye."

' "Cripes, Eily," the poor kid said. "You know how I feel about Tom. I reckon he's Christmas, and you've been more of a mother to me than she has."

' "Try not to be too hard on her, Bill," I said.

' "Hard on her?" Billy said. "I don't want to be anything to her. It doesn't hurt now, like it did when I first knew. Honest, Eily, I'd forgotten. But why has she butted in on us now? Why should I have to put up with her coming along and mugging me? 'Paddy Cavan's whore,' that's what the boys used to call her. Tom's got no time for Paddy Cavan, I know. I've heard Dinny and Sam Mullet talking about him. And that's the sort of lousy swine she takes up with. I hate her. If she thinks I'm going to have anything to do with her she's making a mistake." '

'I was hoping Bill would feel like that,' Sally said. 'But he's young. The chances are Amy'll get round him.'

'We've never talked about Amy,' Eily protested. 'We've never told Bill anything to make him feel so bitter about his mother. Bill was quite a little chap when he came to Tom and asked him if it was true his mother had cleared out with Paddy Cavan. Tom just said: "Yes, Bill, but that's got nothing to do with us. What other people do doesn't matter. It's what we do ourselves that matters. Your mother didn't like the goldfields, and wanted to live somewhere else. That's how it was." '

Bill seems to have known more than we realised and brooded over it,' Sally said.

'Tom says Amy wants to take Bill away with her: send him to an English public school and university,' Eily continued. 'He thinks it's only fair Bill should understand what she wants to do for him. They had a talk with Bill and made him promise to give Amy a chance to put her proposition to him. We don't want Bill ever to reproach us with having stood in his way, if he feels he can accept Amy's offer and go with her to London. But Bill has made his own terms about the interview. He won't go to the hotel where she's staying, and he refuses to meet Paddy Cavan, so she's taking him for a drive on Sunday morning.'

'Amy'll make the most of that,' Sally grumbled.

'Bill's promised me to be on his best behaviour,' Eily told her. 'As nice and polite as he is to Marie or Mrs. Potter. "Remember, Bill," I said to him, "if you're ill mannered Amy will think Tom and I are to blame. That we haven't brought you up properly."

' "Rats, Eily," he said, the dear kid. "If you haven't brought me up properly, who would?"

'I couldn't help feeling sorry for Amy when Bill gave me a kiss of his own accord, mum, and said:

' "Don't worry, I'll be a credit to you, Eily." '

'I wish I could be sure Bill will hold his own against Amy's blandishments,' Sally said crossly.

'I think he will.' Eily's confidence did not allay Sally's misgiving. 'We're as fond of Bill as if he was one of our own children. As if he was one of our own children he has learnt to hate wrong and injustice. He's got the workers' point of view. That's what Amy won't like. Tom says, young though he is, Bill is always asking him questions: eager to discuss things with him.'

'Maybe you're right,' Sally said. 'But it's a big temptation for a boy, and Amy will try her darndest to win Bill away from us. Talk about her loneliness and unhappiness: how young and foolish she was, and "we all make mistakes". They could have such wonderful times together, if only Bill will let her give him all the things she wants to. And "what's the good of all the money in the world if you can't share it with the person nearest and dearest to you?" '

'Yes, I know,' Eily said stubbornly. 'You couldn't blame Bill if he gave in to Amy. But I don't believe he will.'

CHAPTER LX

BILL himself came to tell Sally about that drive with his mother.

'She drove herself, gran,' he said. 'Let me take the wheel for a while—and gee, it was a beaut car. Went like a bird. A bit different from Dinny's old bone-shaker! We were doing seventy on that stretch into Coolgardie. Lady Cavan just laughed, but I got the wind up.'

Bill did not refer to Amy as his mother, Sally noted.

'She . . . she said she'd like to give me a little runabout of my own, and what model would I choose? Then she talked about going trips on school holidays, just the two of us, in a little car, driving through France and Italy and Spain. And I saw what she was getting at. I had to tell her then Tom had told me about her wanting me to go away with her. It wouldn't work, I told her, straight. I wanted to get a scholarship for the School of Mines and be a mining engineer.'

'I'm glad you did that, Bill,' Sally said.

'Then she went to market,' Bill explained, awkwardly, as if he were still puzzled by this part of Amy's performance. 'Started to explain about why she left dad, how broken up she was by his death, and how she'd always wanted to have me with her. But you and Tom wouldn't give me up. Gee, it was awful, gran, the way she went on, crying and begging me to forgive her, to have pity on her and let her make up for the past.'

'I can imagine it,' Sally said.

'You couldn't help feeling sorry for her,' Bill continued. 'I remembered what Eily said about not being hard on her, and that I had to make up my own mind about this, gran, so I said: "If you really want to be my mother again, you'll stop being Lady Cavan, and come and live with me here on the fields. Soon I'll be earning my own living and can look after you—even if we are hard up and can't have a motor car." '

'Oh, Bill, did you say that? Did you really say that?' Sally's smile flashed.

Bill nodded: 'But she was furious,' he said, still as if troubled by Amy's reaction to his suggestion. ' "Who put that idea into your head?" she said. "Tom, I'll be bound, or your grandmother! Don't be ridiculous, my darling boy. They've poisoned your mind about Sir Patrick. He's really the kindest, most generous of men. Of course, he's a rough diamond, self-made, and all that—and some of the people here can't forgive him for being a rich man, and having made such a name for himself in the financial world. But he's quite prepared to be a father to you, and give you everything a boy of your age should have!"

' "A father to me—the rotten old swine!" I let her have it then, gran. Forgot my manners and everything. Told her what I thought of Paddy Cavan and his sort, and that some day they'll be treated like the criminals they are. I didn't want him spending any of his money on me, and I wouldn't be seen dead in the same street with him.

' "Or, you're a little red-ragger, are you?" she said, with a sort

373

of laugh. "That's your uncle's doing, I suppose. I might have expected it. Tom Gough was always the fool of the family."

'I made her stop the car, gran, and got out. "You can't talk like that about Uncle Tom to me," I said. "Sam Mullet says: 'Tom Gough's one of the finest, whitest men ever drew breath. There's not two like him born in a century.' " And I walked home through the bush.'

Sally was proud of her grandson: glowing with pleasure that he could have come through this ordeal so well: that he had worked out his own course of action, by offering to provide for his mother if she would leave Paddy Cavan, and settled the matter in the most decisive way when he had come to a conclusion.

'Of course, she called after me,' Bill explained. 'But I didn't go back. Cripes, I was tired when I got home, though, gran. It must be thirty miles through the bush from that waterhole on the Coolgardie road where I left the car. Tom and Eily thought Lady Cavan must've kidnapped me. You should have seen their faces when I walked in on them. Gosh, it was as good as a play!'

Bill grinned happily and his schoolboyish laughter skirled.

'But I reckon I had to leave her and walk home to make her understand, don't you, gran?'

'I reckon you did, Bill,' Sally said. 'If other boys and girls stand up for what they believe is right, like that, all the things Tom has dreamed of and worked for, may come true.'

'Too right they will, gran!' Bill's voice broke to his eagerness. 'When the workers own and control the mines, profits will be devoted to big schemes for irrigation and new industries. We'll have boshter houses and sports grounds and a new swimming pool. Uncle Tom and I've worked it all out. What's the good of gold in the world to-day? Millions are spent digging it out of the earth and it goes back into vaults in America. We've got to find a better use for gold —if it is any use. Uncle Tom says Lenin said some day gold'll be used for making lavatories. Gee, how'd you like a golden lavatory, gran?'

'A decent sewerage system would do me,' Sally laughed.

Bill hopped on his bike, an urchinish grin lighting his face.

'Right-oh,' he cried. 'I'll see to it.'

He whizzed round the corner of the house and along the path to the gate. Sally heard him whistling as he rode off down the road. It was like a bird making a gusty little song of triumph and rejoicing, that whistling of Bill's. It stirred an echo of the same notes in her heart.

CHAPTER LXI

'WHAT'S this town comin' to, I don't know,' Dally muttered.

Many people had been saying that lately. Sally was thinking it herself even, but she could not endure to let Dally criticise her town and her people.

'What's the matter with you?' she asked. 'Got a touch of brewers' gloom?'

'That's about the strong of it, missus,' Dally admitted.

Frisco laughed. And Dinny chirped up:

'Y' don't want to let things get y' down, Dal.'

Dally was sitting on the edge of the verandah hugging his knees, his eyes watery, his thin face ghastly, his drooping moustache droopier than ever. It was New Year's Day, and he had been celebrating most of the night before. Frisco and Dinny in the armchairs which each of them had come to regard as his own, were waiting for the neighbours and old mates to drop in with their good wishes, as they usually did, during the afternoon of New Year's Day. Tassy was there already in Morris's chair, its springs sagging with his weight, his best trousers nearly bursting over his great belly, his ruddy face beaming with sweat and joviality.

Sally had put cakes and sandwiches on the sideboard in the sitting-room. A few bottles of beer and wine flanked them, and there was lemonade and raspberry vinegar for the children. She was in no mood to put up with Dally and his maundering. Dally had never done anything to improve the reputation of the town, and it was like his cheek to start moaning, she considered. Sally herself had been depressed by recent happenings, but Dally's grouch was not for the same reason, she was sure.

'That's right,' Dally was saying. 'But since they put me old mate, Shack, under the dog act I been kind of lonesome.'

'Shack's got over two hundred convictions for drunkenness, hasn't he?' Sally inquired crisply.

'Y' don't want to be hard on a bloke, missus.' Dally sounded aggrieved. "Wood-cartin's not the game it used to be, neither is collectin' dead marines. Shack's had a pretty crook spin, one way and another. If Shack gets on the beer a bit, and his old horse wants a feed, he makes his way to the police station because he's been in the habit of gettin' a good feed there. Shack reckons that old moke has turned informer on him. Sure as blazes, when the old so-and-so turns up, the police go round lookin' for Shack and run 'im in.'

'He was telling me his tale of woe the other day,' Frisco laughed. 'Seems the last time he was nabbed in a pub, Shack didn't have time to get a skinful.'

' "It was a hot day," Shack ses, "and I'd been workin' in the sun all day, Frisco. Had a terrible thirst on me: went over to the pub and was jest havin' a swig from me first pot when the constable grabs me. And there was me, cut off like a flower!'

'He put the hard word on the magistrate to let him off,' Dinny chuckled.

' "I got me faults, y'r worship," ses Shack, "but dirt's not one of 'em. Don't put me in. I know every fly in Kalgoorlie jail, and the place is crawlin' with 'em." Shack reckons the jailer's a good batsman: practises in the prison yard every afternoon and puts the prisoners on to fielding. Says they must have some exercise. But he likes Shack to bowl for him, and it's too much like hard work for Shack's liking.'

'Recollect the time the magistrate let him off with a caution?' Tassy gurgled. 'Shack'd been bendin' the elbow pretty willin' that night. Was up for "drunk and disorderly" and creatin' a disturbance in Hannan Street.'

'We was both in it,' Dally remembered. 'But I got a move on while the cops was busy with Shack. Went along to the court to put in a word for him—but didn't get a chance. The cops made it look pretty bad for Shack and the magistrate had a face on him like six months hard. Went on about it being a disgrace the way this man was continually bein' brought up before him.

' "What have you got to say for y'rself?" he ses to Shack.

' "Well, y'r worship," ses Shack, "if you put me in there'll be a terrible loss of life."

' "How do you make that out?"

' "Me old horse gets the gripes, and there's nobody but me can look after him," ses Shack.

' "Is that all?"

' "And there's me dog."

' "Your dog?"

' "She'll die if she's not fed. And she's just had pups. Four pups. That's six lives'll be lost."

' "Any more?"

' "And me cat, y'r worship. That's seven lives."

' "That all?"

' "She's just had kittens. Five kittens. That's twelve lives. It'll be a terrible loss of life if you put me in jail, y'r worship."

' "Oh well," ses the beak, "I'll let you off with a caution this time." '

The men's laughter eddied lazily. Tassy and Dinny and Frisco, mellow after a few drinks, were satisfied to smoke and brood over their yarns. But Dally had not got rid of his grouch.

'What with the cops stoppin' a man havin' a few pots,' he grumbled, 'raidin' the sway, and buzzin' round to scare the boys from gettin' away with a bit of gold, life won't be worth livin' on the fields soon.'

'About time something was done to clean things up,' Sally declared, her hands lying idle in her lap because it was a holiday. 'The two-up and boozing are ruining a lot of lads, and the stink there's been over the gold racket—the murder of Walsh and Pitman —have given Kalgoorlie a bad name. Decent people are beginning to be ashamed of saying they live here.'

'You've said it, ma'am,' Frisco declared. Not so much because he thought so, but because he liked to show he stood with Sally.

'Things usen't to be like this in the old days,' Dinny mourned. 'The old prospectors might've been a rough lot and played merry blazes now and then. But they had a moral code kept the camps fairly decent. I reckon there wasn't a working miner, or prospector, would've come at what these chaps done when they cut up the bodies of the dees and threw them down that shaft.'

'It wasn't until the mining industry got a grip of the fields there was any crimes of violence,' Tassy backed him up with that article of an old prospector's faith. 'The crooks came along with the mines, all right. When there was big money about, easy to get, things started to go wrong. And it wasn't only gettin' away with a bit of gold, or stickin'-up a mine manager for his wages bag, was to blame. Maybe share dealin's only a grill, gamblin' and brokerage only froth on the mining industry. But it's led to a lot of bribery and corruption: broken down many a good man. There was one of the wardens used to be a decent old stick, but he suffered from the concave restrictive carpus later on.'

'What on earth's that?' Sally asked.

Tassy's fat, jolly face split to a smile for her.

'Why,' he gurgled, waggling a cupped hand behind his back, 'the backhand dook, of course.'

Sally's laughter chimed with Frisco's.

'When George Brookman was in London in 1895,' Tassy spluttered, pleased to have amused Missus Sally, 'he said the Hannan's goldfield covered an area of sixteen miles and was four miles wide. It embraced three hundred different mines, and he could truly say there wasn't a duffer in the lot.'

'There were duffers all right,' Dinny said.

'But on the other hand the Great Boulder, Ivanhoe and Lake View turned out bigger gold producers than Brookman ever dreamed of,' Frisco warbled. 'When the Golden Mile was booming we didn't play up the golden miles underground enough, I reckon. The Mile only covered surface plant of the Boulder Group. But on the Great Boulder alone, in thirty years, they've carried out twenty-four miles of sinking, driving and winzing, and that's only one of a dozen mines that have miles of workings underground.'

'The area of the Western goldfields—that is gold-bearin' ground —not countin' the underground workings of the mines, runs into hundreds of miles,' Dinny said dryly. 'And they've produced millions in dividends during the last thirty years.'

'Mighty little of it has been spent in this country,' Sally said bitterly.

'That's a fact,' Dinny went on. 'The mining companies, the proprietary interests've grabbed the gold, and got a stranglehold of the economic life of the fields. They've been ruthless squeezin' wealth out of the mines, deprivin' men of decent living conditions, destroyin' their incentive to do anything but get rich quickly, and be as powerful in their way as some of the mine owners.

'The big bugs set the pace: gave the example, murdering men by thousands on the mines to keep up their profits. Is it any wonder the little bugs've killed off a couple of the bosses's dees in their gamble for money? That's what's at the bottom of all the rottenness on the fields to-day. The struggle for existence, the struggle for wealth and power's become fiercer, more desperate.

'Good on you, Dinny!'

Tom had come in by the back way. He kissed his mother and sat down beside her.

'Happy New Year, mum,' he said quietly. 'Eily and the kids'll be over presently. They called for Marie.'

'What I'm gettin' at, Tom,' Dinny explained, 'is, if the mining industry can't get along without assistance from the government— without taking money out of the pockets of the workers, that is— why shouldn't the government take over and run the mines for the benefit of the country and the people? Not let the profit be grabbed, all the time, by the mine owners.'

'A mine is a wasting asset,' Frisco butted in.

'So are lots of other things,' Tom replied, 'including the health of a people and the resources of a country. I reckon when the people own and work the mines, a great deal of the waste will be eliminated, and our assets, not only in the mines but in the development of the country, be improved.'

'Provided the value of gold keeps up,' Frisco argued.

378

'What's the good of it?' Sally blazed. 'All the gold dragged out of the ground. It's sent to America and put underground again!'

'The material basis of civilisation is metallic,' Frisco said.

'All the more reason,' Tom replied, 'to ensure the basis of a civilisation by the control of metals in the interests of the people.'

'Gold,' Dinny snorted. 'Time'll come when we won't need it. We won't dig gold out of the earth to dump it in vaults again. We won't give the boss class the stuff to boss the world. Could anything be crazier, as far as the workers are concerned, than to let gold be the measure of value. You can't eat it, it can't keep you warm in winter, or cool in summer. And yet under our present system it can be exchanged for the real values: food, clothing, shelter, the means of health and comfort.'

'That's right,' Tom pursued his line of thought with the tenacity and concentration he had put into his study of economics and industrial organisation. 'But we've got to face reality. While gold is the standard of value we must act accordingly.'

'Britain's going off the gold standard,' Frisco interrupted. 'And I'm betting most other countries will follow suit.'

'Australia's just shipped bullion and a million pounds' worth of sovereigns to the United States,' Tom told him. 'Gold's still a commodity, and Australia's a gold-producing country. While America wants to buy our gold we'll sell.'

'The mining companies are squealing now for Government assistance to install oil flotation plants and reduce their costs of production,' Dinny growled.

'And they're demanding a gold bonus to work low-grade ore,' Tassy chuckled. 'Why shouldn't the government take over the mines?'

'That's what I'd like to know, Tassy,' Tom said.

'Mean a new lease of life for the Golden Mile if we get the bonus,' Frisco declared jauntily.

'For the crooks who've run this town long enough,' Dinny growled.

Then Eily and the children appeared at the gate, and Marie and Bill came up the garden path after them. The children ran on to the verandah with shrill, sweet cries of:

'Happy New Year, gran!'

'Happy New Year, Dinny!'

'Happy New Year, Frisco!'

Eily's and Marie's voices joined the chorus and a clatter of greetings resounded. Bill went to Sally and she smiled at him as he squatted beside her. He understood well enough that her new year was going to be happier because he was there. Presently, neighbours and old mates of Dinny's called, making their round of New Year

379

visits. Sam and Mrs. Mullet, Eli Nancarrow, his wife and brood, arrived; Speck Jones and Tassy Regan, Danitzça and Toni with their two children, Perth Molloy with his wife and boys. Soon the house was full of the racket of children, the clatter of laughter and gay and friendly conversation. It was a pleasant, homely gathering of goldfields folk on good terms with each other and bound together by the same hopes and fears.

CHAPTER LXII

AFTER everybody had gone Sally went to the gate with Marie: and when Marie left her she stood there thinking of the tender friendship which had helped them both over so many rough places in their lives.

Sunset was fading out of the sky, leaving a burning glow along the horizon. Mellow light, bronze and golden, sprawled over the red earth and the mounds of rubble thrown up beside pot-holes on rising ground across the road. Dusk was gathering among the houses and shrouding the high, packed buildings of Kalgoorlie.

Sally thought the wide, dusty road stretching out from them and away towards Boulder was like the road of life she had plodded along.

She thought of Lal and Dick and Morris, grieving for them: wishing that Lal could have come in to yarn with old friends and neighbours to-night: that Dick could see the way Billy was growing. How proud he would be of the boy! And grateful to Eily and Tom for what they had done for Bill. And Morris—poor Morris, if only he had had more of the things he wanted from life! Such bad luck had dogged him always. How marvellous it would have been if his dream of going home and reinstating himself with his family could have come true. So pleased with himself and self-confident Morris would have been.

Curious how the loss of those shares in the Great Boulder had rankled in his mind! Sally remembered that just a day or two before his death Morris had referred to them again. He seemed to be convinced those shares would have made all the difference to his fortunes: that he would have been as wealthy as most of the original shareholders had he retained possession of those shares, though the chances were he would have sold when the market fell and the Great Boulder was supposed to have been worked out.

No doubt she had been careless, but still she could not feel guilty about the way Morris had lost his wallet, and the shares, that night when she had come to Hannan's. Sally had thought sometimes Paddy Cavan might have been the thief. He was a youngster then and light-fingered. There was no reason to suspect him at the time. And what did it matter now? After all Morris had beaten something out of his defeat. He was a finer man when he took over the undertaking business than he had ever been. Sally was sure that she had never respected him so much, or loved him more tenderly.

She could not regret all the days she had spent on the fields. Here her sons had come to her. And could any mother have had better sons?

She was worried about Tom's health. But soon they were all going to the coast for the summer holidays. Tom and Eily and the children, and she and Bill. That was something Den had planned, and his mother was longing to see him. They were going to the south coast: would camp on the shores of the bay where Sally and her sisters had learnt to swim and she had helped her father to haul in the net laden with fish for their evening meal. Sally could see the silky blue and green waters of the bay: smell the fragrance of brushwood burning on the camp fire. The youngsters would have the time of their lives splashing about in the shallow water all day; and Tom and Den go off to Cape Naturaliste if they wanted surf, or a day's sport with the groper and big fish which came round the rocks there.

Tom had been promising to arrange this holiday with Den for years; but now Den was threatening to drive up in his truck and remove the family by force, if they did not come to Warrinup before the end of the month.

Sally was sorry she couldn't take her old men. It would be hard on Dinny to be left. But she was afraid Tom would be displeased if Frisco were invited to join the party; and she would not go unless Dinny stayed at home to look after Frisco. Dinny understood that.

Of course, Frisco was an outsider; and Sally was aware that she had betrayed Tom's and Dinny's confidence in her by giving Frisco a place in her home and her heart. They could not forgive or forget what he had been. Sally herself did not approve of her passion for Frisco; but there it was, something imperious and irrational, putting a glory round her like the sunset. She was quite impenitent about it, and satisfied that she and Frisco could go on living together in their old age.

Dinny and Frisco observed a truce for her sake. As old timers they could be on quite good terms, although Dinny never treated Frisco as a mate and an equal.

'I hate the man's guts,' Sally had heard him telling Tom. 'But you've got to hand it to him for the way he takes his blindness, bluffin' and crackin' hardy all the time.'

The mines had not been working all day; but lights were winking now from the white sheds of treatment plants and offices. The spider legs of poppets and dingy sky shafts raked frail green of the evening sky. A tall chimney was belching out poisonous smoke, tainting the air with its familiar, foul, sour smell. A battery at work broke the silence: the hungry, hurrying tramp of its giant treads stirred Sally to a panic of fear and resentment as it had always done.

She was oppressed by a sense of power which seemed omnipotent behind all that complex, unwieldy mechanism of the mining industry entrenched on the ridge. Hatred of the mines which put a labyrinth of golden miles under the hills, and were responsible for the army of haggard and doomed men you could see pouring into them every morning, surged within her.

It was not true, she told herself, that 'booze and the illegal traffic in gold' were at the bottom of every crime in Kalgoorlie and Boulder, as the newspapers and strangers were saying. Behind the gold-stealing racket, as Dinny said, there was the struggle for wealth and power in which the mining proprietary companies had demonstrated the most unscrupulous efficiency, not only by extracting profits from production and sharemongering, but by sacrificing hundreds of lives to their greed for profits. There on the ridge was the basis of crime: a stronghold of the forces which ruled existence.

But Sally remembered the neighbours who had come in that afternoon with their good wishes: young and old friends forgathering to laugh and talk about the affairs of their families, and of innumerable other families bound to each other by the same kindliness and indomitable spirit.

Her depression lifted. It had been a typical goldfields gathering of ordinary working people in her home that day. And they did not show the moral degeneracy and criminal tendencies about which there had been so much talk. They were as fine men and women as you would meet anywhere: good-natured, generous and independent. Men and women who thought and talked about something more than booze and gambling: men and women who believed that they had to organise against the evils they saw generated by political and economic injustices.

This spirit was as strong to-day as when Dinny and his mates had defended their alluvial rights and when the miners put up their fight for union principles. It had brought about improvement of conditions in the mines, given victims of the industry some redress for injuries they suffered in its service.

There was more to be done: much more to be done before the mining industry would function in the interests of the men who worked in it; and for the benefit of dwellers on the goldfields who had borne the burden of making these cities and holding them together through crazy booms and devastating slumps.

It was all very well for Frisco to say that she clucked and fussed like an angry hen when anybody abused Kalgoorlie or Boulder and their people. Why shouldn't she? They were her cities and her people. Hadn't she seen them grow from the old rushes, weathering water shortages and dust storms, achieving success and almost crushed by economic disaster. And wasn't she a miner's mother? Weren't the interests of miners and their wives hers? How could she help having the workers' point of view and being enraged by the cruel exploitation of working men and women she had witnessed for so long?

Along the road from Kalgoorlie a horde of natives were drifting in a swirl of dust.

They moved slowly, dejectedly, three or four men out in front, several gins behind, with a youngster or two and slinking mongrels. A mounted constable followed at a little distance on a big grey horse.

The blacks, like a group of scarecrows in the odds and ends of old clothes people had given them, seemed to have decided to talk something over with the trooper. The men stood beside the road waiting until he came up with them.

'If I ketch you hangin' round the pubs again I'll run y' in— the whole lot of y',' the trooper shouted. 'I've told youse mob before, you can't come beggin' round the town any more. Clear out quick and lively now, or it'll be the worse for you.'

The men muttered among themselves and turned away. Sally saw their sullen faces as they passed. Their gins dragged along after them. But one bundle of rags remained squatted by the roadside.

The trooper rode over and shouted. It did not move. He dismounted and booted it.

'Shift y'r carcase,' he said roughly. 'No bloody good gammon sick feller.'

An old gin raised a morose and brooding face. She struggled to her feet and confronted the policeman with the aloof dignity Sally knew so well. Other old gins wore a man's felt hat and coat, their clothes were as dirty and bedraggled, but they did not hold themselves like that.

'Why, it's Kalgoorla,' Sally exclaimed to herself and hurried across the road. 'You can't chase her out of town, Constable,' she said. 'She belongs here. It's Kalgoorla. Besides, I'll take her over to my place and look after her.'

'I've got me instructions, ma'am,' the trooper said firmly. 'Reg'lations just issued lays it down abos is not to be permitted to approach within five miles of the city of Kalgoorlie without a permit. They've been makin' a damn nuisance of themselves, beggin' all over the place—and there's been a lot of complaints about petty thievin'.'

'Good Lord,' Sally exclaimed, 'and what haven't we thieved from them?'

'That's not my business.' The trooper was a young man recently come to the fields and anxious to prove his metal. 'My business is to run these niggers out of town if I find them disobeyin' the reg'lations. And that's what I'm doin' to the best of my ability.'

He jerked his head towards Kalgoorla.

'Get a move on, can't yer?'

Kalgoorla picked up a long stick and walked away, slowly, stiffly.

'It's a shame and a disgrace,' Sally stormed. 'We've taken everything they had. Expect them to live half-starved in the back country when we've ruined their waterholes and hunting grounds. A few years ago all the natives round about used to come in for the Reverend Collick's Christmas feast, but even that's a thing of the past. What do we do for them now? Give them a miserable ration at some government centre: a bit of flour, sugar and tea, sometimes a scrap of meat—not enough to feed a dog.'

'I don't know anything about that,' the trooper replied defensively. 'All I know is I've got to carry out me instructions, and me instructions is . . .'

'Blast your instructions,' Sally cried furiously and went after Kalgoorla.

She called to her, called several times, but Kalgoorla did not stop or turn round.

Sally knew that the new regulations to keep natives out of the town were intended, chiefly, to prevent them from hanging round the hotels and getting drunk. It was illegal nowadays to sell or give alcohol to an aborigine. But old prospectors celebrating their luck, and on a spree themselves, knowing the blacks' fondness for sweet, heady wine, would often smuggle out a bottle or two to a man hiding in the lavatory or behind the wood-heap in the pub yard.

There was a lot of sympathy for the blacks among men who remembered what they owed to an aboriginal guide in the early days. The native knowledge of tracks, wells and soaks, had saved many lives and often led prospectors on to the gold which started a flourishing township. Now that the natives were scraggy derelicts, wandering the countryside because their water holes had dried up and game was scarce, old hard-doers who knew what a few drinks did to cheer a man's soulcase could not refuse the black brother similar relief in his misery.

'If natives are put under the dog act,' Dinny said, 'something ought to be done for them by way of compensation.'

Some part of their old hunting grounds should be restored to them most people thought, so that the remnant of the local tribes could live out their days as they had been accustomed to. But in all the hundreds of miles of the gold-bearing areas there was no place where the aborigines might remain in undisputed possession. What wonder then that they sought the white man's drink to blot out for a few hours their degradation, and give them an illusion of jollity and vigour, although fighting and drunken brawls invariably resulted from indulgence in this alien magic?

There was that to be said for the regulations, and so far they had not been enforced very rigorously. But to see a pitiful remnant of the primitive people being ousted from their old camping ground near Maritana and condemned to extinction, moved Sally to a passion of shame and indignation.

The steady stride of her aboriginal gait had carried Kalgoorla some distance when she stood and, from a dump by the roadside, hurled her rage back at the trooper.

What she said Sally did not know. But Kalgoorla stood there pouring forth a torrent of native abuse and execration. She swung the long stick she was carrying towards the city, and back towards the darkening ridge littered with the poppet legs, chimney stacks and surface works of the Boulder mines.

It was as if she were driving away a narlu, an evil spirit, as Sally had seen her in a corroboree long ago, on the track to Lake Darlot.

Was she trying to do that now, Sally wondered? Was Kalgoorla attempting to thrust back all the forces of evil which had overwhelmed her people? Were her imprecations willing death and disaster to the white man and the mining industry, with the mysterious power the native tribes exercised?

Sally felt as if she could curse and wail with Kalgoorla about what the mines and the mine owners had done to the country she had come to regard as hers as well as Kalgoorla's. But there was a better way than Kalgoorla's to deal with the wrongs the natives had suffered, and the mining industry, she remembered.

Centuries of social organisation separated her from Kalgoorla.

What was it Tom said? 'Make the mining industry serve the interests of the people and we'd have nothing to grouse about.'

Fierce and mournful Kalgoorla's screeching ended on a high winding note of derision and defiance. 'Koo! Koo! Koo!' Like the cry of a bird it circled and flew in the twilight. A stark, wild figure, as if she were a dead tree, Kalgoorla stood against the sunset.